AMPYRIUM

Other Anthologies Edited by:

Patricia Bray & Joshua Palmatier

S.C. Butler & Joshua Palmatier

Laura Anne Gilman & Kat Richardson

Troy Carrol Bucher & Joshua Palmatier

Patricia Bray & S.C. Butler

David B. Coe & Joshua Palmatier

Steven H Silver & Joshua Palmatier

Crystal Sarakas & Joshua Palmatier

David B. Coe & John Zakour

Crystal Sarakas & Rhondi Salsitz

David B. Coe & Edmund R. Schubert

Stephen Kotowych & Tony Pi

Troy Bucher & Gerald Brandt

AMPYRIUM

Edited by

Joshua Palmatier

Zombies Need Brains LLC
www.zombiesneedbrains.com

COPYRIGHTS

Table of Contents

SIGNATURE PAGE

Joshua Palmatier, editor:

_____

Joshua Palmatier:

_____

Juliet E. McKenna:

_____

David B. Coe:

_____

Esther Friesner:

_____

Patricia Bray:

_____

S.C. Butler:

_____

Jason Palmatier:

_____

Justin Adams, artist:

_____

Yllaria

Joshua Palmatier

Yllaria scanned the myriad customers of the Crestfallen marketplace from behind the canvas flap of a spice merchant, searching for her target. Ruther was bulky, more of a brute than a thief, with ragged blond hair and a burn scar that twisted the left side of his face; he should be easy to pick out in a crowd. Cinnamon, mint, and cardamom assaulted her nostrils and she tried not to breathe in too deeply, her eyes already watering. The vendor's attention was caught by an Ampyrian woman, his voice smooth as he let her sniff a pinch of this and that, expounding on the individual spice's uses, but Yllaria let it fade into the background.

"Where are you?" she muttered to herself. Her hand clenched reflexively on the knife held tucked against her thigh. Her back muscles ached with tension, an itch that crawled from the nape of her neck down her spine, fanning out to either side as it descended. She resisted the urge to scratch it.

She still hadn't located Ruther—perhaps he hadn't been assigned to this task—but her eyes locked on the next best thing: a wheeled wagon, the bed covered with a squat wooden house, the roof peaked, the sides studded with windows, shutters closed and latched from the inside. It was being pulled by two horses handled by two drivers in the seat up front and was surrounded by half a dozen mercenary guardsmen.

Yllaria grinned. "Gotcha."

The spice merchant latched onto her arm and growled, "What in Batchul's Hell do you think you're doing?"

Her back-of-the-throat hiss and baring of teeth was instinctive; the slice of the blade across his throat was not.

He gasped and lurched back, releasing her as his hand shot to his neck and he stumbled into one of his stands of spices. Yllaria heard the splintering of wood as it collapsed beneath his weight, and the sudden clamor as pedestrians and customers reacted to the disturbance, but she witnessed nothing, already behind the spice merchant's tent, darting in the direction of the wagon she'd spotted. A woman screamed and she rolled her eyes, muttering, "It was barely a flesh wound," beneath her breath.

She neared one of the walls of the marketplace, scaling the stone briefly, fingers pinched into the creases in the mortar between the masonry so she could see above the myriad tents and into the pathways between. A crowd had formed near the spice merchant, but she saw no white-fire Eye and no white-robed Magnum…yet. Her altercation with the spice merchant shouldn't have attracted their attention, but one never knew what the Magnum would find of interest. They'd been known to arrive on scene and in person for much less. But the appearance of a Magnum right now would crimp her plans.

She swung her attention to the wagon and the red and silver Ampyrian banners flapping from the front of its carriage. It had forged its way deeper into the marketplace, headed for the eastern gate. She marked its position and rate of progress through the crowds, then dropped to the ground and took off.

Weaving through the stakes and wires and stacks of supplies behind the tents near the wall, she burst out onto the main thoroughfare at the western gate, then hustled forward, slipping through the throng of people like silk through fingers. Her slight form—nearly five feet high and lithe—gave her an advantage, but her nimble movements meant she merely brushed an arm or hand in passing, a touch so light most barely registered it. Fresh scents drifted past as she moved—rank sweat, pungent incense, horse dung, and the char of grilled meat. Conversations flowed over her—a sharp bite of laughter, feverish haggling, a strident argument between a Daruvian man and a Theran woman. All of it prickled against Yllaria's skin, made her back itch all the more.

Then she caught sight of the wagon at a dead stop ahead, two guards at the back, another two along the right side. She couldn't see the two on the left or the drivers. More importantly, she didn't see Ruther or any of the other Wands.

She slid her knife into the sheath in her boot, then charged up to one of the mercenaries, faking a heavy pant—she didn't have to fake the sweat—and gasped, "You have to turn back! It's a trap!"

The mercenary's hand fell to his sword but he hesitated and she leaned forward, one hand against the wagon, as if to catch her breath.

"What's that you say?" the mercenary asked, searching the nearby market for signs of trouble. His partner did the same, keeping one eye on Yllaria. She caught him signaling the guardsmen on the left side of the wagon.

"The Wands," she heaved. "The Wands are here."

Fear tightened his grip and his stance grew rigid, even as suspicion creased his forehead. "How would you know that?"

She looked him dead in the eye. "Because I'm one of them."

She yanked back the sleeve of her grungy shirt and exposed the mark nestled in the crook of her elbow—an open circle with a narrow black line extending toward her wrist, no more than an inch long.

His eyes widened and he barked an order to the second guard—a code word, because it made no sense—then shouted to the guards on the right. All four of those she could see reacted instantly, drawing blades and positioning themselves defensively around the wagon. One of the drivers called down a question and a guard snapped back, the wagon lurching forward a moment later. Yllaria let the hand against it fall and stepped back into the crowd, the people nearby already reacting to the sudden tension from the guardsmen.

She was ready to turn and run when she spotted Ruther.

Rage stilled her, her hands balling into fists, but she didn't dare approach him. He'd already noticed the wagon, the mercenaries, their readiness. Confusion slowly etched itself onto his face—well, half his face; the scarred side didn't move, the burned flesh immobile. He flicked a signal to a fellow Wand, a woman, and then the Wandspeak was flying, half a dozen members conversing in a sign language Yllaria only knew a portion of from observation. The members she could see were spread out around the far side of the wagon, but there must be more on her side, for some of the questions were flung in her direction. She craned her neck, trying to identify them all, but then she caught the question as to whether to proceed or not and her breath caught.

No matter the answer, she'd done what she'd intended. She should leave.

But if there was a chance to kill Ruther...

The response was *Go.*

She turned and fled to the nearest stall, ducking behind its minimal shelter a moment before an explosion rocked the street behind her. Spinning, she caught sight of stone and wood debris arching into the air, punctuated with screams from the pedestrians and ragged commands from both the mercenaries and Ruther and the Wands. Men and women were scattering from the remains of the wagon, one of its wheels crumpled, the axle broken, a chunk the size of a shield ripped from its side. One of the mercenaries—the one she'd spoken to—lay motionless on the ground, two bystanders' bodies nearby, blood on the cobbles. The mercenary's partner had levered himself to one knee. Unsteady, he shook himself and shoved to his feet a breath before one of the Wands emerged from the tattered smoke and stabbed him through the neck. The Wand lowered his twitching body to the ground and motioned another Wand forward. From either side of the wagon, the clash of blades rang out. The wagon rocked, wood groaning. The second Wand, a thin man in drab clothes too loose for his body, stepped over the still-spasming guard, raised both hands, knuckles to knuckles, and pulled them apart.

The back of the wagon split open like wet paper, traveling trunks and sealed barrels spilling onto the street. Wands appeared as if summoned from the air, snatching up whatever was readily available and dispersing at a run in all directions. Some paired up to grab the heavier trunks. Others tipped barrels and rolled them away by hand. Yllaria quelled a modicum of respect for the efficiency, if not the subtlety, of the thefts.

Ruther rounded the side of the wagon, bloodied sword in one hand, a spray of blood across his chest. He wiped at a dribble on his cheek, smearing it, then focused on the mercenary Yllaria had warned. Kneeling down, he cleaned his blade on the man's shirt, then rolled him over and slapped his face.

The man jerked and coughed, one hand rising, but Ruther moved faster. Grasping his throat, Ruther hauled him upright so they were nose to nose. The mercenary's hands scrabbled at Ruther's wrist.

"Who warned you we were coming?" Ruther asked.

The mercenary struggled a moment, until Ruther shook him, grip tightening. The mercenary gasped, although one hand dropped toward his back, where Yllaria could see a thin knife tucked into his belt.

"It was a girl," he wheezed. His face was turning red. He sucked in a ragged breath and managed, "A child…one of your own."

Yllaria sniffed. "I'm not a child."

"What do you mean one of our own?" Ruther asked.

"A Wand!" the mercenary croaked. "She was…a Wand! She had…the mark!"

Ruther's grip relaxed in shock and the mercenary struck, pulling the knife and digging it deep into Ruther's side. Ruther grunted and punched his sword through the mercenary's chest. He held it a moment, blood bubbling on the mercenary's lips, then shoved the guard to the ground and rose. With a wince, he yanked the knife in his side free, stared at the blood on it, then let it clatter to the stone road.

He scanned the stalls and tents nearby, his fellow Wardsmen still ransacking the wagon around him.

Yllaria tensed a breath before he caught sight of her.

She spat a curse and bolted behind the stall.

At the next tent, she dodged left, away from the street, then right, leaping over a cloth merchant's brightly-colored bolts. Thirty feet beyond, she thought maybe she'd slipped away when Ruther stepped out from behind another stall and she slammed into his chest.

His bulky arms surrounded her, his musk—a combination of sweat and smoke and, oddly, oranges—penetrated her sinuses as he held her. She struggled, managing to twist enough she could suck in a breath spiced with fresh air, then stilled. Her arms were trapped against her sides. Her heart thundered against her ribcage. The itch across her shoulders felt enflamed.

"Let me go," she spat. "I've done nothing."

Ruther's chest rumbled, the vibrations shivering against Yllaria's skin. It took her a moment to realize he was chuckling.

"Nothing?" he said. "You interfered with the Wands."

Without warning, he shoved her back, turned her, and pulled her in close again, holding her with only one arm, above her elbows and across her chest. Her arms rose and she tried to scratch, to bite, but he'd positioned her so his body was out of reach.

"Ah ah ah, none of that now," he said. "You'll hurt yourself."

She huffed and settled back down. "I was ordered to interfere. By Tellus himself."

Ruther grunted in disbelief. "Why would Tellus order us to seize the wagon and then send you to betray us?"

"I wouldn't know. You'd have to ask him."

Ruther didn't respond, the pause long enough she thought the ruse might work, but then he grabbed her arm with his free hand, grip so tight she nearly buckled at the knees in pain, and rucked up her sleeve to expose the Wand's symbol with the other. He was forced to release his hold across her chest, but the hand on her arm kept her in check.

She felt his body relax as soon as he saw the mark. "How——?" he began.

"I told you," Yllaria said through gritted teeth. "Tellus ordered me here." She began to struggle again.

"I don't understand."

"That's not my problem."

She'd almost broken free when he stiffened in sudden suspicion and swiped his meaty thumb across the mark.

The ink she'd used to draw it smeared.

"You bitch," he said.

She elbowed him in the side where he'd been stabbed by the mercenary and smirked as he gasped and dropped to one knee, his hand releasing reflexively. Spinning, she faced him, her knife drawn from its boot sheath in the same motion. One hand clutching his wounded side, blood trickling between his fingers, he raised his head, eyes narrowed in anger.

"Why?" he asked.

"Because you killed my mother."

The look of confusion that crossed his face twisted in her gut and she gave an involuntary cry of grief. He didn't know! He'd taken her mother's life and he didn't even remember!

Tears pricked her eyes and her fingers tightened on the knife. She heaved in a ragged breath. "And now I have to kill you."

"Ruther!" someone shouted. One of the Wands from earlier appeared from around a tent twenty paces away and stumbled to a halt. "Ruther, we have an Eye!"

"Two of them!" someone else added from the street.

Ruther swore and faced her. "Two Eyes means the Magnum will be here any second. Will you kill me with one of them as witness?"

She wanted to scream in frustration. He knew she wouldn't, knew she *couldn't*, not with Eyes in the area. The Magnum would be on her before she could pull the knife free. Yet still she wavered, body rocking forward and back, muscles tensed to lunge, to sink the blade into his eye, so that his blood flowed warm and slick between her fingers...

With a tortured growl, she sprang for the nearest break between the tents, glancing back once to see if Ruther were following her. But she could see one of the Eyes above the street behind, its white light so intense it hurt to look directly at it. Its fellow was farther away but approaching fast. She ducked behind stalls and wagons as she fled, to stay out of its line of sight, merging with the crowds of the market as soon as she was far enough away from the altercation to run into people again. Most were staring at the Eyes in concern, mumbling to themselves about what was happening, but most merely ducked their heads and ignored them.

Until there was a clap of sound, like thunder, heralding the arrival of a Magnum. Then suddenly everyone had somewhere else to be.

* * *

Yllaria kept her head down and pace swift but not fast until she was certain neither the Magnum nor either of the two Eyes were following her. When she reached the southern gate, she hopped up onto the back of a cart loaded with turnips and looked back.

The white-robed Magnum was easy to pick out in the empty area surrounding the destroyed wagon. The smoke had dissipated and she counted seven bodies. One Eye hovered above the wreckage; the other had spun away, circling in a widening spiral. The Magnum knelt next to the mercenary she'd spoken to, hand poised over the man's face. Yllaria thought she saw tendrils of light emerge from the mercenary's eyes and nose and mouth, like smoke, coalescing into an image in the Magnum's palm, but when she blinked the image was gone. She shuddered and muttered a warding beneath her breath—no one understood the Magnum's powers, not completely—but then the Magnum stood and turned, looking directly at her.

Her muscles locked and her heart stuttered in her chest, even though she couldn't see the Magnum's eyes, his face covered by a cowl. She would have sworn their gazes had met. The Magnum's pale citadel, situated directly behind him, its ramparts towering over the city, appeared to pulse in her vision.

"What do you think you're doing?" an elderly man shouted, slapping a hand on the bed of the cart and tearing her attention free from the Magnum. "Get down from there!"

A smile exploded across her face. "So sorry! Just taking in the view." She jumped down to the flat cobbles and darted through the gate, headed east, the farmer grumbling behind her. Half a block away, she had to catch herself against a building, her legs uncharacteristically weak, her hands trembling. She tried to shake it off, but felt a disturbance behind her.

One of the Eyes had emerged from the gate and now hung over the street intersection, unmoving.

Yllaria shoved away from the wall beside her, eyes locked forward, gait purposeful, as if she knew exactly where she was going and needed to get there soon. Many of those around her had reacted the same way, studiously ignoring the Eye behind. A few were attempting to go about business as usual with varied success.

At the next intersection, she crossed the street behind a merchant's carriage and headed south. She didn't begin to relax until she'd made two more turns and one switchback without sign of the Eye. Satisfied, a smirk stealing across her face, she skirted south again, toward the Fifth Gate, also called the Sealed Gate or the Black Gate, because it had been closed for nearly three hundred years and appeared as a black void into nothing. Those who had come from the world beyond the gate—the ethereal but deadly Tikmadrell, the stone-skinned Gosdrell, the winged Pikturell, others—had been hunted down and slaughtered by the hundreds, if not thousands, at the time of the Sealing. It's said the walls surrounding the gate were stained red by the blood spilled from those the citizens of Ampyrium had hung from the heights, that if you touched the stone, you could hear the screams of the dying, hear them pleading for mercy, for sanctuary.

Yllaria snorted. "Death screams. Mercy. There is no mercy in Ampyrium."

It was all superstition and myth anyway. No one had seen any of the races from Imadria, the world beyond the Fifth Gate, in two hundred years, let alone spilled their blood on Ampyrium's streets…or walls. Not that she'd been close enough to see the walls herself. She hadn't even stepped inside the Fifth Gate's inner district. Once the sole domain of the Imadrians, it had been taken over and subsumed into Ampyrium proper. The wall that had separated the two had crumbled and collapsed in some places.

"Yllaria!"

She focused on the Ampyrium merchant who'd called her name. "Umboldt, what are you doing here?"

Umboldt huffed his way to her side, his face red with exertion. He wore common clothing, not the fancy embroidered splendor of merchant finery, although she noticed he hadn't removed his gold rings. Yllaria glanced behind him to scan the street as he dabbed the sweat away from his face and leaned in close. "I'm afraid I need your help."

"I see." She took his elbow and guided him down the street, searching ahead of them. They were near the inner district wall, a few blocks away from Farrew's place.

"There's been a bit of a mistake, you see—" Umboldt began.

"Not here," she said sharply, and winced when she felt Umboldt flinch. He was trembling, which was unlike him. "There's a place nearby where we can speak."

"Of course."

By the time they reached Farrew's Yarrow & Yew apothecary, Umboldt's color had lightened and he'd caught his breath. A tinkling of bells sounded as they entered and Farrew glanced up from the counter toward the back of the open front room. Tall, lean, and narrow of face, his eyebrow rose when he caught sight of Yllaria. He set the pestle he held in one hand aside. Yllaria picked up the scent of crushed thyme, stronger than the amalgam of other herbs and medicines kept in jars and hanging in dried bundles about the room. The shop was empty.

"Can I help you?" Farrew asked, as if they were random customers.

"We need the back room."

"Of course."

He stood, stool scraping on the wood floor, and ushered them behind the counter and through the opening behind him, holding the curtain aside. Stairs led up to the second floor, where Farrew lived, but to one side there was a door that led into a musty storage room filled with burlap sacks, crates with straw sticking out between the wood planks, and shelves upon shelves of jars and urns of every size and shape imaginable. Most weren't labeled. Farrew shifted a couple crates and shoved a barrel half his size aside, some kind of liquid sloshing around inside, then pulled on a hidden latch.

With a soft click, the entire shelf swung outward a couple of inches. Umboldt grunted in surprise. Farrew caught it and pulled it open farther, then all three of them stilled as they heard a tinkling of bells from the outer room.

Yllaria started when Farrew said loudly, "Be there in a minute! Just gathering some wares from the storeroom!"

He motioned Umboldt through the door, handed Yllaria a small oil lantern, and then began to close the door behind them. But he paused, brow furrowed in concern. "Is that still itching?"

Yllaria jerked her hand away from her shoulder where she'd been scratching behind her neck. "A little."

"Let me see." His tone suggested she shouldn't argue.

She pulled her collar back, exposing the upper part of her shoulder. He leaned close, the scent of thyme increasing, touched her skin in a couple places, his fingers cold.He was silent for a long, uncomfortable moment. Then: "The rash has gotten worse. And spread. Have you been using the poultice I gave you?"

She shrugged her shirt back into place. "Of course I have." At his look of disbelief, she repeated, "I have! Now don't you have a customer to tend to?"

At a thump from the outer room, Farrew said, "I'll mix up something stronger, but for now…" He closed the hidden door in her face.

Darkness settled like a comforting blanket. Yllaria could hear Umboldt's breath quickening, heard him suck in air to speak, but halted him with a soft, "Hush," as she placed her fingers on the lantern's wick and snapped them.

An ember sparked and caught and a moment later the tiny back room was lit with warm light. It contained a table with a deep bowl and pitcher, a plate, cup, knife and fork, two low stools, and a cot in one corner.

Yllaria motioned toward one of the stools as she set the lantern on the table. Through the door, she could hear Farrew's muffled voice speaking to the customer. When no one burst into the room, she settled into the stool opposite Umboldt.

"Tell me what's going on, Umboldt."

"They took it," the Ampyrian merchant said, his voice quiet with despair. He glanced down at his hands, resting on the table, fingers twisted together, then sighed, the tension draining from his shoulders. "They took it all."

"Who took what? Start at the beginning."

He didn't look at her, couldn't look at her. "You know I've been struggling lately—the business, I mean. Trade has been light. Not profitable. Our clients have been disappearing. We're down to a few dozen now, and most of those left haven't been in contact for a few weeks, some a few months. I've had to cut workers, consolidate. I don't know how much longer I can—" The words caught in his throat, but he shook his head.

"I was forced to eliminate all but one warehouse, near the Brush. I moved everything there, slashed security to the bare minimum. I was dealing with a potential new client from the Mercador Province in Calamunda, someone who could potentially save the mercantile, but when we reached the warehouse— where I was going to show her the wares—we found the guards dead inside, throats slashed. All of the merchandise was gone."

For the first time since he'd started, he looked up, met Yllaria's gaze. "Everything is gone. The potential client left me there. I didn't know what to do, didn't know who to report to." His breath hitched. "I fled without thought, found myself here, near the Fifth Gate, then I saw you and—"

Yllaria placed a hand over Umboldt's. "Did you contact the Magnum? Was there an Eye present?"

"N—no. No, I don't think so. I don't remember much beyond seeing the… the bodies of the guards and then seeing you."

Yllaria patted his hand. "Good." She'd helped Umboldt acquire some of his wares and not everything that came through her network could be said to be legal by the letter of the Magnum's laws. "Do you know who did it?"

"I didn't see anything at the warehouse. Everyone was already dead and I didn't stay—"

"What about this client? What was his name?"

"Her. Geaenja, But she couldn't possibly be involved. She hadn't even seen the warehouse yet!"

Yllaria didn't respond, considering what he'd said, what she'd heard recently about the state of trade in Ampyrium, especially near the Fifth Gate. Merchants had been grumbling. Clients were disappearing, and not simply moving their business on to other districts or gates. Some had vanished completely, shops and warehouses and houses abandoned. She hadn't paid it much attention. But now, with Umboldt involved, it was infringing on her own operations.

"I'll need to see the warehouse," she said abruptly, standing.

"Of course. I can take you there now, if you'd like."

*　*　*

The first thing Yllaria noted when they reached the warehouse was that Umboldt had left the door open. The second was that no one had paid any attention to it.

Umboldt halted five paces from the entrance, Yllaria taking three more steps before noticing. When she turned, his eyes were wide, his mouth open, and his hands were fluttering before him.

She swallowed her snort of disgust. "Stay here. Warn me if any Eyes or Magnum appear."

He nodded and spun to face the street.

The interior was dark, but she smelled the bodies the moment she stepped through the door. Raising her hand, she snapped her fingers and a spark appeared, hovering beside her shoulder. It gave her enough light she could see the slashed throats of the guards—three ragged rents, the middle deeper than the others—when she knelt to inspect them. "That wasn't made by a blade."

She stood and strode deeper into the warehouse. Umboldt hadn't lied. The building had been stripped bare. Her footsteps echoed, scraping through scattered remnants of straw and a few crumpled pieces of paper. She created a few more sparks and sent them out toward the side walls, their light fading the farther from her they got, but there wasn't a barrel, crate, or clay urn left.

She halted when she reached the opposite side. The back wall had been rent wide open, wood planks splintered and jagged, thrust in all directions.

"Like wet paper," she muttered to herself, eyes narrowing.

Back outside, she descended on Umboldt. "Tell me you know how to get ahold of this Geaenja woman. I want to speak with her now."

*　*　*

Umboldt led her toward the center of the city, toward the citadel of the Magnum, where those with power well beyond what Yllaria and Umboldt wielded lived. The streets here were clean, the shops and buildings pulled back, some of them enclosed by gated walls, the interior privy only to those who could get past the gatekeepers. Carriages abounded, with escorts and guards, and even those on the walkways beside the roads had guardians or trailed a servant or two. Yllaria felt conspicuous, fingering the coarse fabric of her clothing as Umboldt drew up outside a wrought-iron gate near the center of a block of brownstone buildings. Through the bars, a tiny courtyard with a splashing fountain fronted a large wooden door painted a forest green and studded with iron. Narrow windows stood to either side and a stunted balcony only a few feet in depth hung above the door along the length of the second floor. Curtains blocked the view inside the paneled glass doors above. All of it reeked of wealth and power and Yllaria's unease grew.

A Valleri manservant appeared before Umboldt could reach for the gate.

"May I help you?" he asked, voice soft and servile. Thin to the point of emaciation, dressed in understated livery, his eyes drifted over Umboldt and latched onto Yllaria. A frown touched his lips for the space of a breath and Yllaria fought the urge to reach for her knife.

"I wish to speak with the esteemed Geaenja Malefalli. We were discussing a business proposal. Tell her Umboldt Egeria is here to see her." Umboldt's shock over the death of his guards at the warehouse and the theft appeared to have worn off. He spoke with confidence, more like the Umboldt she knew.

The manservant's gaze had not left Yllaria's. "And who is this?"

"My associate, Yllaria. She helps me procure some of my wares. I can vouch for her."

The manservant hesitated, then said, "Wait here," turning toward the green door without looking again at Umboldt. He moved swiftly, with a fluid grace Yllaria had never seen in any of the servants she'd dealt with in the past.

As soon as he slipped inside the manse, she edged forward and said in a low murmur, "That man is not a manservant."

"I'd be surprised if he was even human," Umboldt said, fingering a sleeve. "The Mercadori rarely use servants. Or rather, their body guards often assume the role of servants. He's likely one of the *avati*."

Yllaria shuddered. The *avati* were rarely seen in Ampyrium, although even that was in question. Known for their shapeshifting ability, there could be hundreds of them on the streets and no one would know. Vicious, ruthless, and brutal, they were excellent bodyguards and came at a hefty cost.

The manservant reappeared, sliding up to the gate, unlatching it with a mocking flourish. "Mistress Geaenja will see you now."

As soon as they stepped into the courtyard, he latched the gate again and led them to the green door, holding it open and ushering them inside. "Mistress Geaenja is waiting for you in the audience chamber to your left."

Yllaria followed Umboldt to the left, but paused before entering and glanced back to the door. The *avati*—if that's what he was—glowered at her a moment before closing them inside.

The audience chamber held a lounge and two comfortable chairs surrounding a low table. The walls were adorned with hundreds of small items, hung individually or positioned on various shelves. Statues, stone carvings, wooden instruments, woven tapestries—every imaginable form of portable art was present. Yet the central table was empty except for a single cobalt blue vase and a tiny tray full of ash. Wispy smoke filled the room, cloying, with a sweet scent.

Geaenja Malefalli sat cross-legged on the lounge, a long-stemmed pipe in one hand. Dressed in pale green silks trimmed with gold, she regarded them both with cold eyes as she drew on the end of the pipe and blew a plume of smoke into the air. Then she focused on Umboldt.

"I thought our business ended," she said. "You have no wares. And after what I saw at the warehouse, I don't trust you to hold any of my own wares securely."

"That's my fault," Yllaria said, stepping forward before Umboldt could say anything.

Geaenja's eyes narrowed. "And who are you?"

"Yllaria. I provide Umboldt certain…services. He hadn't informed me that he'd been forced to consolidate his goods to one warehouse, which would obviously require heightened protection. If I'd known, I would have been prepared."

Umboldt appeared about to protest, so she seized his wrist and squeezed in warning until he subsided.

"What about you, Mistress Geaenja? I find it interesting that the moment you propose a business deal with Merchant Egeria here, he ends up robbed. By the Wands, no less."

Geaenja stilled. "The Wands? How do you know it was the Wands?"

"I know their signature. I've dealt with them before. You haven't answered my question."

She regarded Yllaria a long moment without moving, not even a blink, then tapped the ash from her pipe into the tray and said, "There is nothing of interest here. I sought a merchant near the Fifth Gate and approached Umboldt. We agreed to meet, to discuss his wares, at his warehouse. That is all."

"Bullshit."

She began to refill her pipe, not glancing up. "Why do you say that?"

"You're affecting nonchalance over what happened at the warehouse, but you're clearly interested, especially with regard to my mention of the Wands. You're looking for something."

She tapped the leaves down in the pipe, then reached for a burning incense taper from a shelf to one side. When she turned back, one corner of her mouth was quirked in a smile. "You're perceptive. I like that." She relit the pipe, puffing hard and exhaling long as she considered, then sat back in the lounge. "Very well. I *am* looking for something—the Wands themselves."

A hitch appeared at the back of Yllaria's throat, but she swallowed it down. "Why is that?"

Geaenja hardened. "Because they're encroaching on my territory. At first, their little thefts were mere nuisances—a missing crate here, a pallet there—annoying but negligible. But they've escalated. In the past two weeks, entire shipments have been taken, including one this afternoon, taken in broad daylight in the middle of a crowded market, while I was meeting with Merchant Egeria in fact. The losses have become significant and can no longer be ignored."

"Why seek a merchant near the Fifth Gate then? Why not go to the Magnum? You clearly have wealth enough to gain their attention."

"The Magnum do not seek wealth, only justice…their *own* justice," Geaenja said bitterly. "Regardless, the Mercadori do not seek help from others. We handle our own affairs. I do not wish to bring the Magnum's attention to these matters."

Yllaria wondered how much that had to do with what Geaenja was actually trading and how legal those transactions were, but kept quiet. "So why seek out Umboldt?"

She glanced toward Umboldt, now standing a few paces behind Yllaria. "I needed someone established in the district, someone the Wands would take notice of, with the right trade goods in play."

Yllaria considered her words for a moment, then gave a bark of irreverent laughter. "You needed bait for a trap. Umboldt's lack of security was actually an asset!"

Geaenja looked disgruntled, taking another drag on the pipe. "Too much of an asset, apparently. The Wands struck before the trap could be set."

Yllaria began to pace, thinking furiously. She'd been trying to figure out a way to hurt the Wands since she'd run across Ruther four months ago and recognized him as the one who'd killed her mother. Once she'd realized he was part of the Wands, all of the pieces fell into place. For some unknown reason, her mother had been taken out by the Wands; Ruther had simply been the weapon. Killing him would give her immense satisfaction, but it would only be a flesh wound to the Wands. She wanted to inflict mortal damage. Her warning to the wagon in the marketplace—Geaenja's wagon, apparently—had only been a petty first strike while she considered what else she could do. But here, she was being presented with something more significant. Geaenja had more power, more resources. If she could lead her to the Wands, or guide them into her grasp...

She halted and faced Geaenja, who'd remained quiet, brow furrowed. "We could still set a trap, using Umboldt, just as you planned. You'd have to provide the wares, but you were planning on doing that anyway."

"And what about you? What are you bringing to the table?"

"Cover. You can't provide security for the shipment yourself. The Wands will find out and back off. I know that wasn't your own security force on the wagon in the marketplace this afternoon. Those were mercenaries. I can provide the men who guard the shipment, locals the Wands will know, enough to make them interested, but not enough to scare them off."

"How do you know about the security on that wagon?"

"Because I was there. I tried to warn them the Wands were coming."

Geaenja grunted, the pipe flicking with the movement, ash floating down from the tip to the floor. Geaenja didn't seem to notice. "And what is your stake in this, Yllaria?"

"You don't need to know."

Yllaria held her breath as Geaenja considered, only releasing it when the wealthy merchant said, "Very well. I will have Laes, my manservant, coordinate with you and Umboldt. But we should lay this trap soon. The Wands have taken enough from me already."

* * *

"Are you certain about this?" Umboldt asked for the hundredth time.

They stood beneath an awning on the edge of the Fifth Gate's district in a section called the Neck because for a hundred yards one of the main thoroughfares leading to the inner city was hemmed in on both sides by stone walls. No cross streets, no alleys, not even a walkway between buildings. Only a few doorways, niches, and loading bays. Carts and carriages were trundling up and down the Neck at their usual pace, along with pedestrians, but Yllaria didn't see any signs of an Eye or any Magnum. She and Umboldt had been scoping out the street for at least half an hour.

"I'm certain, Umboldt." She turned to face him. "Now remember, you're to stay here. Don't get involved, no matter what happens. You're going to be the eyes. If something goes wrong, you're to report to Farrew and Laes."

As Umboldt nodded, Yllaria fingered the packets Farrew had prepared in her pocket. She'd prefer they be in a satchel, but that would only be a hindrance in whatever happened next. She hid her own apprehension in a grim smile as she caught sight of their wagon a block away.

"Here they come. Let's hope the Wands take the bait."

Without waiting for Umboldt's response, she headed away from the Neck, toward the approaching wagon. Two of Umboldt's men sat on the driver's bench, nudging the horses along, while some would-be mercenaries who were actually men Yllaria used for grunt work on occasion walked beside the wagon on either side. It was a similar formation as the wagon she'd warned earlier in the marketplace. One of her men gave her a terse nod as she stalked past and slid into position twenty paces behind, mingling with the ebb and flow of the street. Additional men were scattered up and down the Neck, acting as lookouts and backup.

Inside the wagon were chests full of silks from Mercador that Geaenja had provided, initiating a formal contract with Umboldt a few days earlier. The partnership had been duly registered and stamped by the traders guild, so as to make it official and solidify the ruse, while hopefully drawing the attention of the Wands. Yllaria had had her network spread rumors about the shipment and its course over the past few days. Everything was set.

She drew in a steadying breath as she passed an Ampyrium vendor of pottery, who gave her an all clear and ready signal. She let the breath out slowly as she scanned the last of the shops and stalls along the street.

And then the wagon passed into the Neck.

The sounds from the street behind grew muted while the clop of the horses' hooves and the jangle of the reins bounced back from the three-story walls to either side. Yllaria glanced up with a shudder as the road narrowed to a width that barely fit two carts side by side, a pedestrian walk of a few feet on either edge. A carriage sidled past on their left, the two guards on that side stepping up onto the edge of the wagon, hands wrapped in rope so they could hang on, in order to get out of the way. Even then, the side of the carriage nearly knocked one of them off. The citizens on the street thinned, only a few men and women hurrying down the lane ahead. Her presence became more conspicuous the deeper into the Neck they went.

The lane crooked slightly to the left, enough she couldn't see the end of the Neck, and she tensed as the wagon rounded the turn, expecting the ambush to occur here. But there was no one waiting on the far side and, when she glanced back, no one behind either.

One of her guards shot a glance back toward her, but she signaled for them to keep going. Had the Wands found out this was a trap? Or were the silks inside the wagon not something they were interested in?

Before she could decide, a startled shout from ahead drew her attention to the wagon. Her guards on either side were stumbling away with cries of alarm as the wagon lifted off the ground, directly into the air. The two drivers were panicking, one of them leaning out over the side to look down. Yllaria gasped, wondering about the horses, but as the wagon rose high enough, she saw both of them barreling down the street away from them. They'd been cut free somehow.

Then her attention returned to the wagon, still rising. Glancing up, she caught movement on the rooftop on one side of the Neck. The thin Wand in drab clothes from the marketplace—the one who'd split the wagon apart without touching it—hung over the edge of one of the buildings, grasping the air and hauling upwards, as if he were pulling on a rope. His face was red with exertion. Two others stood on either side, watching.

Yllaria snapped into motion. "Up there! On top of the building!"

Before any of her guards could move, she'd bolted for the side wall beneath the Wands. Her guards shouted orders, one of them drawing a crossbow. She streaked past them, then leapt for the wall, grabbing onto the stone crevices and pulling herself upwards. She heard scrambling behind and beneath her as she climbed. A bolt snapped past her and she looked up.

The Wand mage had stopped hauling at the invisible rope and now caught her gaze. She'd made it ten feet up the wall, but the wagon had been lifted at least twenty. The two drivers were crouched low, hanging on to handrails, terrified. Yllaria spared them barely a glance, her attention focused on the mage.

The Wand tensed and Yllaria said, "Don't."

With a smirk, he let go.

The wagon fell, the two drivers screaming. Yllaria swore, released her grip, and dropped to street level, although she didn't know what she could do. Her guards were scattering. The pedestrians in the Neck had already fled. There was nothing—

She landed with a thud, pain twisting up one leg.

The wagon hit with a thunderous crunch that Yllaria felt in her chest and through the street beneath her knees. The wheels collapsed and the base spit stone chips from the cobbles. The sides burst with a crack and splinters of wood flecked the air. The drivers slammed into the forward bench, their screams cut short. Their bodies bounced out onto the road. Neither one of them moved.

Yllaria drew in a ragged breath, coughed on the stone dust that hung on the air, then stood and brushed wood shards from her clothing. A few chests of silk had spilled out of the destroyed wagon, some of them broken open, but her focus was on the drivers.

She took a step toward them, but staggered and gasped in pain when her left leg barely held her weight.

Twenty feet farther down the Neck, a pair of loading dock doors slammed open and seven Wands flowed out onto the street. One of her guards cried out a warning, but another set of doors were flung open behind them, five more Wands streaming into the lane.

A dozen Wands, ready and waiting. More than she'd expected. But fewer than she'd planned for.

She reached into her pocket and grabbed one of Farrew's tied paper bundles. Before she could draw it, a couple of the Wands in front of the wagon stepped aside and Ruther jumped down from the loading dock. Her hand clenched into a fist, crushing the spell. She felt herbs and other particles trickling between her fingers, smelled the biting scent of cinnamon and mint. The fingers of her other hand twitched toward her knife, but she didn't dare draw it. Not yet. She needed to stall.

Ruther stepped toward the body of one of the drivers, keeping clear of the pool of blood. He nudged the man with his toe. When there was no reaction, he rolled him over with his foot, exposing the sickening dent in the man's forehead where it had slammed into the bench in the fall.

Ruther glanced around, eyes landing on Yllaria as he said, "Surrender and no one else has to die."

"What makes you think we'd believe you?" Yllaria asked.

"Oh, I wasn't speaking to you," Ruther said.

Behind him, the ragged mage appeared at the loading dock. "Time to clean this up."

Ruther nodded and gestured with one hand.

The Wands attacked, charging forward from both directions. The six guards Yllaria had placed on the wagon converged on her position as she drew her knife and groped for more of Farrew's packets. Snatching one up between her fingers, she created a spark and flung it toward the seven Wands with Ruther, the woman in the lead flinching back as it landed on the cobbles.

It smoked for a second, then exploded into a purple plume.

Within seconds the entire section of the Neck they were in was encased in colored fog. Shouts of confusion pierced the narrow, the sounds oddly distorted, but as Yllaria lurched toward where she'd last seen Ruther, hissing at each jolting movement of her leg, the clash of blades cut the confusion short. She grabbed a few more of the packets, setting them alight and tossing them to either side as she moved. One of them began spitting sparks in random directions, spiraling out and away in sizzling swirls of color. The second gave out a piercing whistle and made Yllaria flinch even as she thanked the spirits that the signaling packet hadn't been the one she'd crushed; the whistle was meant to summon their reinforcements.

She'd begun to think the fog had disoriented her as well as the others when she stumbled over the body of the driver. Cursing, her hand landing in the pool of blood, she spun into a crouch and scanned the smoke. It had begun to thin and she could see vague shapes now, ten paces distant, locked in a fight. The shadow of the crushed wagon loomed to her left. But she didn't see Ruther.

An arm snaked around her throat and squeezed, a knee jutting into her back, making her arch backwards. She flailed and choked on another curse.

Tightening his grip, Ruther leaned close to her ear and said, "Someone wants to see you."

Spots began to form in her vision and she cocked her head forward, then hammered it back, hearing a satisfying crunch and yelp. The arm slackened enough for her to grab it with her free hand and slice down its length with her knife. The muscles flexed beneath her throat and then she was flung to the side, twisting in midair.

She slammed into the side of the wagon, splinters of wood digging into her back and side. A sweet agonizing pain flared up from the rash as she hit the ground and rolled, as if her entire upper back and shoulders had caught fire. She gasped where she'd landed, leg throbbing, then gritted her teeth and heaved back into a crouch, foot slipping in some of the spilled cloth from one of the chests. Ruther was hunched over five paces away, hand over his face, a dribble of blood splattering to the ground. He stood upright, head tilted back, gave a snort, then spat to one side.

"I'm going to kill you for that, bitch." He wiped a hand carefully across his broken nose and split upper lip, while the other drew his own knife.

"You can try," she said.

He lumbered forward, Yllaria ducking his first swing, countering with a strike at his leg, but he shifted out of the way with a grunt. He was faster than he looked. She seized the opportunity to step away from the wagon, give herself some room. Her left leg rippled with pain when she put weight on it, but it held.

Ruther closed in again, coming in with a lunge. Yllaria realized too late it was a feint and stepped into range of his other hand. He tried to catch her and pull her close, as he'd done at the market, but she dropped back to the ground and kicked up, catching him in the side. He pulled back as she scrambled back to her feet, facing off against him again, both of them huffing.

Around them, the sounds of the fighting had died down and the smoke had nearly cleared. Bodies lay on the cobbles, not all of them her guardsmen. Two of her men were surrounded, back-to-back, holding off seven of the Wands.

"It's over," Ruther said.

A shout came from down the Neck, followed by a ragged, "Get them!" A dozen men and women Yllaria had had stationed around the shops as eyes and ears before the Neck emerged from the last of the smoke, Farrew leading the charge.

Yllaria stabbed forward when Ruther glanced toward the new fighters, but Ruther let the knife graze his side, bringing his arm down to capture hers and wrapping it up behind her back. With a wrench, a twinge of pain forced her palm open and her knife clattered to the cobbles. She ducked and curled around his side, until she was behind him, her arm slipping free, then clambered up his back and clamped both arms around his neck, squeezing for all she was worth.

He grunted, his free hand clutching at one of her arms, trying to pull her free. She could feel the muscles straining in his neck, skin slick with his sweat. She squeezed harder, buried her head at his nape, sucked in the rank odor of cured leather and five-day-old Ruther—

And then he leaned back.

She had a split second to realize his intent before his body weight crushed her between him and the cobbles. If her upper back and shoulders had been enflamed before, they erupted into a firestorm of pain now. She couldn't contain a howl, her arms releasing Ruther as he heaved up off her and turned. Tears blinded her, the pain so intense she couldn't move. Ruther hauled her up by a limp arm and tucked her against his side.

Through a haze, she heard someone step close, realized it was the Wand's mage as he spoke. "Play time is over. We got what we came for."

"The others—"

"I've already ordered the retreat. Now come."

Yllaria managed to raise her head and glance back, blinking away the tears. Farrew and the others had put the Wands on the defensive, driven them back nearly to the wagon. Wisps of purple smoke lingered, but Farrew caught her eye as Ruther and the mage leaped up onto the loading dock and fled with her through the doors.

It was only as the mage threw the latch that she realized not one of the Wands had touched the cargo they'd been transporting.

Then the mage said, "No need to reveal the location of our lair now is there," and he struck her on the back of the head.

* * *

Yllaria woke with a start, pain instantly radiating from her back and shoulders into her neck and arms, overriding even the ache from her head. She was hunched over, tied to a chair, hands behind its back, her hair hanging limp, obscuring her vision. She gave an involuntary moan and heard movement, the scrape of feet against stone.

"She's awake, Tellus."

"I can hear that, Ruther. Make her more comfortable."

Yllaria tried to sit up, but couldn't lift her weight, her muscles numbed. Someone grabbed her hair and jerked her backwards until she was upright. She cried out as her muscles protested and began to tingle, blood beginning to flow again. She blew her hair out of her eyes and surveyed the room.

It was dank, made of stone, water dripping from the domed ceiling in places, lit by a half dozen torches in sconces placed around the sides. She could see four arched doorways from where she sat, three in the far wall across from her, one to the left. An Ampyrian stood before her, tall, slender, dressed in clothes best suited for someone who lived closer to the citadel rather than someone from the Fifth Gate district. He watched her closely, hands on hips, expression grim but determined. He was surrounded by a motley crew of Wands—the mage, a hybrid beast from Calamunda, and two women on his right, three others on his left. She recognized a few of them from the marketplace raid on the wagon. The hybrid as a blend of human and hawk, feathers ruffling up from under the shirt along the head, ending at the beak. She couldn't tell how intelligent it was from the hawk-like eyes.

Her gaze fell to the beast's hands, but each arm ended in a three-fingered talon. This was who had killed Umboldt's guards, then.

She could feel Ruther's presence beside and slightly behind her, like a weighted stone. She twisted her hands, testing the bindings—rope—but Ruther's hand fell onto her shoulder in warning. She swallowed back the whimper at the touch, the fire she'd felt during the fight in the Neck returning.

Tellus stepped forward. "You have become somewhat of a nuisance. Ruther tells me you warned the mercenaries guarding the Ampyrian merchant transporting goods through Crestfallen market of our presence. That you impersonated a Wand in order to do it." He'd reached Yllaria's chair, knelt down in front of her so they were eye-to-eye. "The mark of a Wand has to be earned, little one. We don't care for those who attempt to steal its power."

He stood again, Ruther pulling her head back so she was forced to look up at him. "I might have let that little slight go, since it didn't hinder our operation much at all, but now…now you've taken it a step too far. That wagon in the Neck—it was bait. You wanted us to try and take it. You were waiting for us."

Tellus paused, to let Yllaria speak, but she ground her teeth together instead.

He smiled. "Silent, I see. Too bad. We need some answers. Ruther, show her the pit."

Ruther grabbed the back of her chair—his other hand still tangled in her hair—tilted it back and spun it around, slamming it back down with enough force to rock Yllaria forward. She found herself staring down into a circular pit, the legs of her chair mere inches from its edge. It gaped before her, black in its depths, about twenty feet in diameter. A faint odor of shit and rot and decay gusted up from below. Before she could gag on it, Ruther pulled her back. Tellus came up on her other side, leaning in, his breath tickling her ear.

"We don't know exactly how deep it is, but it's sufficient for our purposes. A handy place to dispose of…nuisances. A few of the Wands even think something lives down there. They've heard sounds. It wouldn't surprise me. Unless you want to experience it personally, I suggest you answer our questions.

"Who are you and why have you decided to irritate the Wands?"

She hesitated and Ruther shoved her forward again, so she had a full view of the pit, his hand on her upper back excruciating. The skin there felt hard, almost brittle, yet pliable beneath. Her breath accelerated. She had to give him something.

She'd always said the best lie was to tell the truth.

"It wasn't the Wands! It was *him*. I was after Ruther."

Movement to the side and behind her. "Ruther?"

Not holding her anger back, she snarled, "He killed my mother. That was bad enough. But back at the market, I learned he didn't even remember, which only makes it worse."

A silence. Then Ruther said, "She said the same thing at the marketplace. I don't know who she's talking about."

"It was years ago," Yllaria said. "I was a kid. Barely eight years old."

"And you've been harboring this resentment since then?" Tellus asked. "Why didn't you come after him sooner?"

"Because I was busy surviving. And because I didn't know how to find him. But then, suddenly, four months ago, there he was on Bleeker Street. He nearly tripped over me, didn't even apologize, and all of that hate that had been simmering since the fire came rushing back."

Her chair thunked back to the floor and Ruther grabbed her chin, twisted her head around so she faced him, so she could see the tortured and bubbled flesh on one side of his face. "Fire?" He searched her features, stared hard into her eyes, then snorted, releasing her. "The Hickman Job. This is Warthol and Sillium's kid."

"Is that so?" She could hear Tellus approaching, and the sudden interest in his voice unnerved her. "We assumed you'd died in the fire. But if you truly are Sillium's daughter, then perhaps you're more useful to me alive than dead."

The Wands' leader thrust her head forward, so her chin was against her chest, then grappled with the neck of her shirt. She didn't understand what he was trying to do until the shirt tore and exposed the rash on her upper back. A rash that now throbbed with the pulse of her blood.

The chamber was dead silent except for the drip of water, until Ruther asked, "What in all bloody hells is that?"

"That is the sign of a half-breed, at least, on the verge of molting. Those are wings. This little shit is a Pikturell."

Yllaria's blood ran cold, a frisson of fear that coursed down through her from head to toe. It couldn't be true. The Pikturell were all dead, along with all of the other creatures from Imadria on the far side of the Fifth Gate. They'd been exterminated hundreds of years ago. And a death sentence had been placed on any Imadrian found alive since. She couldn't be Pikturell.

Everyone in Ampyrium would want to hunt her down.

Her back spasmed and she groaned, leaning farther forward, the hardened skin on her back straining as something pushed forward from underneath, seeking to break free. When the spasm ended, she realized Ruther and Tellus were arguing about what to do with her.

And then a little packet of folded paper landed under her chair.

She sucked in a sharp breath, mind blanking. Had it fallen out of her pocket? Had she had any of Farrew's trinkets left?

Except this one was already lit.

She closed her eyes and tensed.

At the same time, Ruther yelled, "Tellus!" in warning.

Someone shoved her chair forward, hard.

And the next moment she was falling.

Her eyes flared open to darkness. Without thought, she sparked fire into the ropes that bound her, hissing as the heat seared her wrists.

In that brief burst of light, she saw the pit's bottom rushing toward her.

She landed right shoulder first and would have screamed had her breath not been knocked out of her. The wooden chair cracked beneath her weight. She rolled onto her stomach, feeling wooden shards and splinters beneath her, along with the squishy muck that coated the bottom of the pit. Her lungs refused to function and she struggled to inhale or to cough, anything. Then something clicked painfully deep inside and she heaved in a thin gasp. The stench made her gag, but she drew in another breath, and another, whimpering with each movement. Placing her hands beneath her, she tried to push herself upright.

Her back spasmed again and she moaned, the sound degenerating into sobs. When her muscles spasmed again, something split and she screamed.

The pain was exquisite, white hot and icy at the same time. A tacky fluid soaked into the tatters of the shirt hanging from her shoulders. Something tugged and pulled and she sobbed again, but an intense sense of relief flooded through her. The pressure that had been building in her back and shoulders—first an incessant itch, then a rash, then a dull throbbing pain—released. She felt loose and free, no longer trapped and constrained.

She lay in the sickening muck, gasping, trembling, until she heard a bellow and the clamor of fighting overhead.

Farrew. It had to be him. And whoever he could pull together to come get her.

She shoved upwards out of the muck and sloughed her way toward the pit's stone wall on hands and knees. Her back and shoulders flexed and strained with an unfamiliar weight, dragging at her in odd ways. She knew what must have happened, knew what Tellus had said must be true, but she couldn't believe it.

When she reached the wall, she pulled herself upright on her knees and looked over her shoulder.

And saw nothing. The only light came from above, where purple smoke roiled, internally lit by the torches. The bottom of the pit was nearly pitch black.

Smothering an irrational irritation, she snapped a tiny ball of flame into existence—

And gasped. She had wings. Four of them, two on top and two others—larger—beneath. Nearly transparent, the veins of the main wings shimmered in the light of her spark, flexing and fluttering without her consciously thinking about it. The top two wings were less flexible and were the color of her flesh.

"I'm a Pikturell," she breathed to herself in wonder.

Someone screamed, close, the sound cut short with a nauseating crunch of bone and squelch when the body hit the muck at the bottom of the pit. Yllaria directed the spark toward the body, relieved when she recognized one of Tellus' Wands, body contorted unnaturally by the bad landing. She also noted six rounded holes, each six feet in diameter, set an equal distance apart around the bottom of the pit. Any one of them could lead her out. But how long would that take?

She glanced up toward the smoke, then pulled herself to her feet. She flapped the wings a few times, the sensations coursing through her back and shoulders unnerving, then said, "Nope. Nope, nope, nope. I have no clue how to use them."

She reached for the wall, scaling the stone like she'd scaled the wall at the market and the Neck. Her new wings shivered as if in affront, as if her body were trying to use them, but she didn't trust them. Her right shoulder ached from the hard landing earlier, and her left leg sent shooting pain up into her hip, but she climbed, aware the smoke above was thinning, that Farrew's moment of surprise and confusion was fading.

Halfway up, her right arm threatened to give out. Three-quarters of the way, her right toe slid from its toehold and her weight wrenched both of her arms as caught herself. Her wings began flapping in a frenzy and she would have sworn they provided some lift as she found a new toehold and hauled herself upwards again. The rest of the climb felt easier.

She reached the edge of the pit and glanced around.

The purple smoke had almost cleared. Five bodies were scattered around the room. The two closest still had weapons in their hands—one a dagger, the other a short sword. The hybrid hawk faced off against three ruffians, two of whom she recognized as eyes and ears she'd used at the Neck. The hawk kept them at arm's length with swipes of its talons. Tellus and the Wand mage were retreating toward the entrance to the left, the Wand's leader limping, the mage holding him upright.

Ruther and one other Wand held off Farrew, Umboldt, and two others, each feint and parry edging all four of them closer to the pit even as theyr tried to outflank the Wands.

Yllaria pulled her upper body up over the edge, paused to regain her strength, then heaved herself out completely and scrambled for the sword and dagger.

The hawk shrieked a warning, the cry piercing in the enclosed space, but Yllaria didn't hesitate. She snatched up the short sword with her right hand, dodged left for the dagger, took two running steps toward Farrew and Umboldt, just beginning to turn in surprise, then leapt upwards.

Her wings fluttered madly, strong enough that she hovered for a brief moment over Farrew's and Umboldt's heads, long enough for her to meet Ruther's shocked gaze and say, "For my mother."

Then they gave out and she dropped.

She crashed into Ruther. The short sword cleaved into his side; the dagger found his neck, sinking deep. He grunted as her weight drove him to the floor and then she was thrown free, dagger ripped from her hand. She kept the short sword. She hit the flagstone floor with her hip and rolled, her wings tucking in without her volition, then flaring wide again once she'd regained her feet. She spun to face Tellus, found him at the cusp of the left entrance with the mage, the woman who'd been at Ruther's side racing toward him. He gave her a subtle nod, mouth turned in a disturbing smile, then shouted, "Arturus! Retreat!"

The hawk gave another ear-shattering shriek, then swiped at its attackers with both sets of talons and fled toward the entrance. Tellus, the mage, and the woman were already gone.

Those holding off the hawk began to give chase, but Farrew called out, "Wait!" When they halted, he turned to Yllaria. "Should we follow them?"

Yllaria shook her head and gestured with her sword, then collapsed to her knees.

Farrew barked an order and concerned cries rose as everyone converged on her position. She tried to wave them off, but it was no use. Her entire body was exhausted, her right shoulder and left leg still throbbing. Every part of her ached, inside and out. She wanted to sob, to sleep, to scream, but settled for clutching at Farrew, the only one who ignored her new wings and the reeking muck and came close enough to touch her. Without his support, she would have slumped to the floor.

"What—? How—?" he asked as he held her.

"I'm a Pikturell."

Shocked silence as he helped her stand up. "Did you—?"

"No, I didn't know." She hesitated, then thought about their conversation in the hidden room at Yarrow & Yew. "But you did, didn't you?"

"I had my suspicions."

Before she could respond, Umboldt shouted, "He's still alive!" He'd knelt down next to Ruther's body and now waved them over. "Still breathing at least."

With Farrew's help, Yllaria staggered over to Ruther's side. Blood had pooled beneath him, still seeped from around the dagger in his neck. Every breath gurgled and, as they watched, he coughed, blood splattering around his mouth.

His eyes flickered open, focused on her, on Farrew, on her wings.

He grinned, his teeth bloody.

"What's so funny?" Yllaria asked.

"You're dead, Pik." The words were barely audible, blurred by fluid in his lungs. He coughed again, a fresh gout of blood dribbling from the corner of his mouth. "Dead. And you don't even know it."

"Tellus has already fled. And you're dying."

His grin widened. "It isn't Tellus you have to worry about."

His next breath set off a cough and then spasm deep in his chest. He hunched forward in pain, one bloody hand clutching at Umboldt, then fell back and didn't breathe in again. His hand dropped from Umboldt's shirt, leaving a glistening hand-shaped stain.

Yllaria stared down at his slack features, feeling oddly empty, until Farrew tugged her away, toward the same opening Tellus had used.

"We need to get out of here," he said, then waved at Yllaria's wings. "Can you...I don't know...put those away?"

Yllaria chuckled, then winced at the pain. "No. I don't know how to use them. They're...irritating."

Farrew frowned. "We'll think of something."

* * *

Yllaria found herself in the back of a wagon, lying on her stomach to protect her wings, covered in tarps, trundling through the streets in the dark. Every jolt of the wagon on the cobbles or sudden halt or lurch forward hurt. She tried to relax, to jostle with the movements, but her mind wouldn't remain still.

She was Pikturell. They existed. They still existed. Were there others? Were they hidden? How had they remained hidden for so long? Or was she the only one? And what about her mother? Had she been Pikturell? Had she been hiding her wings, even from her own daughter? Or her father, apparently named Warthol, who she'd never known? He could have been Pikturell. He could have been Tikmadrell or Gosdrell or any of the races from Imadria for that matter. Her only memory of him was of a vague shadow that had come to visit one night when she was five, after she'd been put to bed. She'd heard voices, had slid from her blankets and trundled to the outer room to see her mother speaking to a shadow outside the door.

As soon as her mother saw her, she shoved the shadow away, closed the door, and ushered Yllaria back to sleep.

The wagon jerked to halt and she hissed at the twinge in her shoulder. Urgent whispering, followed by someone saying, "All clear," and then the tarps were being pulled away.

Farrew lifted her up carefully, but she couldn't stifle the moan. Umboldt and the others gathered around her, shielding her from the entrance to the

alley. She recognized the delivery door at the Yarrow & Yew as Farrew and
Umboldt steadied her through the opening, past the storage rooms, and into
the hidden room at the back. They eased her down into a stool at the table, and
she leaned forward for the support. She certainly couldn't lean back against the
wall, not with the wings unfolded. Umboldt lit a lantern while Farrew muttered
something about getting some poultices and ingredients from the front. As he
left, Yllaria noted two of the others stood guard at the door. That had never
happened before.

"Why are they guarding the door?"

"Because you are Pikturell," Umboldt said as he hung the lantern and settled
into the chair opposite her.

"I don't know what that means."

"None of us do. But we do know that the Magnum never rescinded the
mandate to kill all Imadrians within the city. If anyone sees you…"

Yllaria hid her face in her hands, shook her head. Her wings shivered. "I
can't live like this."

Umboldt gave a sharp laugh. "Everything about your life is going to change
now. But you won't have to stay hidden forever. You'll figure out how to…
sheath your wings eventually. Then you can walk the streets again. But not like
before."

"What do you mean?"

Farrew arrived, setting down a slew of bottles, clay pots, a mortar and pestle,
a bowl of water, and a handful of rags. "He means, too many people have seen
you. Tellus and his Wands, Umboldt, myself, the others outside taking care of
the wagon. Too many for us to quash the rumors that there's a Pikturell living
in the city. Even if we swore our crew to secrecy, there's nothing we can do
about Tellus and the Wands. And even then, I can't imagine our own crew
can keep a secret like this. One of them will get drunk and talk when they
don't mean to." He began mixing an unguent in the mortar, crushing various
ingredients together with the pestle. The scent prickled Yllaria's nose.

"So…what? I'm supposed to go into hiding?"

"For now. Nowhere near any of the places you usually associate with. This
will be the last night we use the Yarrow & Yew." Farrew dipped a rag in the
water and washed off a portion of the muck that had dried to Yllaria's skin,
then took a swab of the paste he'd made and dabbed it onto the clean spot.

She yelped. "It burns!" He ignored her, spreading it around, and within
moments the burn died down to a tingling sensation, then a soothing coolness
that numbed the pain. She sighed. "That's better."

He began washing and applying the unguent liberally.

"About the Wands…" Yllaria said.

"They're going to be a problem, I know," Umboldt answered.

"Perhaps a bigger problem than you realize. They knew the wagon at the Neck was a trap."

"Then why attack the wagon at all?" Farrew asked.

Yllaria considered, grimacing under Farrew's ministrations. "They weren't after the wagon at all," she said, talking more to herself than to the others. "They were after me."

"That would explain this." Umboldt dug into a pocket and removed a piece of cloth, tossing it onto the table. "The chests in the wagon were supposed to contain silk, but they were all filled with coarse muslin. Worth one-tenth what the silk would have been. Geaenja duped us."

Yllaria picked up the fabric, feeling the texture between her fingers. "Of course she did. Why risk actual silk when you can rely on a rumor of silk?"

But she was recalling the fight at the Neck, the attack, the mage, Ruther, what he'd said, what the rest of the Wands had done. None of them had even approached the wagon, had even attempted to steal any of the trunks…

She looked up at Umboldt as it hit her. "Geaenja and the Wands are working together."

Umboldt considered with a frown, then leaned forward. "We've stumbled into the beginning of a Merchant War. And now, with this," he nodded toward her wings, "I don't think there's any way we can step out of it."

Unseen Hands

Juliet E. McKenna

"Your first time waiting at the gate?" A thin-faced old man in a faded blue doublet offered Kitri a friendly grin.

"That's right." She didn't want to start a conversation, but she didn't want to cause offense by rudely ignoring him. Casually turning away, she looked past her brothers to assess the knots of other people standing well apart on this cobbled expanse.

Riesel shifted impatient feet. "So much for no one knowing in advance when passage between the worlds will be possible."

Kitri gave him a quelling look as she smoothed the skirts of her plainest gown. Both her brothers wore the same dun cloth. Neat, respectable, and unmemorable.

"Perhaps these folk were passing by, the same as us. Why wouldn't they be curious when they saw the Commissioner's men lining up?" She hoped her expression reminded him they had better stick to that story.

No one strayed within fifty paces of the massive barbican's locked and barred black gate. Jutting forward from the city wall, the fortification guarded the magical portal that would soon bring travelers from another world. Size apart though, Kitri thought it looked much the same as the entrance to any sensibly secured warehouse. Though there was no smaller wicket gate, so people could slip in and out without having to open both heavy doors. She guessed there was some other entrance to the barbican that she couldn't see.

Distant noon bells chimed. Kitri snatched a glance at the well-armored guards holding gleaming halberds, drawn up ten paces in front of the barbican. More guards in the Commissioner's scarlet livery lined the battlements directly above the gate. With crossbows at the ready, they watched the waiting people intently. Presumably, so did the Magnum, the sorcerers whose magic made this marvel possible. One of their Eyes hovered high above the Daruvian guards. Though since that featureless glowing orb was too bright to look at for more than a moment, there was no way to know where its focus might be. No one could ever understand what interested the faceless wizards hidden in their white-walled citadel in the center of Ampyrium.

Kitri didn't want to draw the Magnum's attention by looking at the Eye, so she studied the barbican. The fortification had been built in the same imposing style and using the same golden stone as the Daruvian Commissioner's hall and his guards' barracks, both on the far side of the cobbles and facing the gate. Though the doors and windows of the hall and the barracks were framed by ornately carved trees and branches. No pleasing details softened the portal.

When Kitri and her brothers and sisters were little, Father told them how the first bold travelers from a handful of worlds had ventured through the mysterious gates that appeared in those realms. When they found the untouched stone and wilderness that would become Ampyrium, the Magnum invited them to stay. They offered every group a stretch of land to be their own, inviolate, protected by the immense city walls. Each contingent soon learned they weren't the only folk to accept the wizards' invitation.

Mother wondered who among the strangers had shown those first Daruvians what to do with stones and mortar. Back home, Daruvians lived safe and secure among the great trees that cloaked all but the highest, driest, and coldest terrain. Living branches framed dwellings walled with wood and bark, insulated and roofed with moss and foliage. Mother insisted she had never seen masonry before she had come through the gate as a child, after a Kind Elder decreed Grandpa's poetry was insultingly subversive.

To Kitri's irritation, the old man moved closer. "Sometimes a bare handful of folk come through. Not like the old days. Whole families could be dragged from their homes in the night and sent into exile."

He stood close enough for Kitri to sense painful memories beneath his words. He had been banished to Ampyrium decades ago. The Kind Elders who ruled the province where he lived had decreed merely being seen near a notorious troublemaker warranted exile.

She saw herself in his thoughts. Like Reisel and Anchin a few paces away, Kitri had inherited Father's sharp features, warm brown skin, and silky dark hair. At first glance, no one would suspect the gift Mother's Daruvian blood had given her. She must never give anyone cause for the least suspicion.

She forced the old man's despair out of her mind. Most folk in his situation got on with life on this side of the gate as best they could. Before the path to Ampyrium had opened, exiles had been driven out of Daruvia's forests into the barren lands, to take their chances with the giant birds and murderous lizards prowling beyond those terrifying horizons. At least now they were sent to a place somewhat civilized.

Kitri focused her attention on the other folk waiting for the gate to open. The closest handful of men and women would offer reassurance and practical support to innocents driven through the gate. Exiled Daruvians arrived with only the clothes on their backs, maybe clutching a small bag of possessions if their province's Kind Elders wished to be seen as generous. The merchants waiting wanted first pick of the goods the licensed traders brought over. Fragments and echoes of their thoughts hinted at well-established ties in Vedrana, the province immediately on the other side of the gate.

Somewhere inside the barbican, heavy wood scraped along iron brackets. The gate swung open behind the guards.

"Here they come." The skinny graybeard caught her unawares with a nudge of his elbow.

Old and feeble, he came here every day. Soon, he swore to himself, he would rush past those guards and run back through the portal. If he died skewered by halberds or crossbow bolts, his spirit would make it home.

Kitri gasped and her vision blurred. She felt Reisel grab her arm. "Trying to steal my sister's purse, are you?"

"Leave him!" Anchin's curt words to his brother cut through the graybeard's stammering protests.

As the old man fled Reisel's fury, Kitri's vision cleared. She saw the guards were drawn up on either side of the gate, facing each other across the paving there. Every second warrior held their halberd horizontal to make an unbroken barrier. The rest were ready to scythe down anyone trying to breach their line. The guards on the battlements had their crossbows cranked and loaded.

The first three travelers driven out of the gate had red dye smeared across their faces. That told everyone they were guilty of murder, arson, or rape. The stain couldn't be washed off and took years to wear away. So folk said. No criminal sent to Ampyrium lived long enough to find out. Meantime, the Kind Elders who ruled Daruvia's provinces could say with perfect truth that even the vilest offenders were spared execution and offered the chance of redemption elsewhere.

Bounty hunters wearing creased leathers, and with swords in hand, pushed past the traders. The bounty the Commissioner paid for any one of these criminal's heads was more money than most folk could earn in a year.

The first man with a red-stained face was a brute taller than Reisel with scarred, muscular arms. He had torn the sleeves from his filthy shirt to wind the cloth around his fists and forearms and he bared his teeth in a snarl.

A sly-faced, shaven-headed man in a brown doublet and breeches followed, slow and reluctant. No one would give him a second glance on Ampyrium's streets. The gaunt woman who came last was obviously Daruvian, with a pale complexion and matted blonde curls. Her yellow tunic was spattered with the red stain that condemned her, and she wore black silk trews and soft leather shoes. No one living in the great trees wore skirts. Mother had never seen such garments before she came here.

"Kitri," Anchin prompted.

"Right." She focused on the other people being driven out of the gate's shadows. A plump bemused man in forest floor herder's garb squinted in the bright sunlight. Three defiant young women in ochre Daruvian jerkins and creamy breeches walked side by side with their curly heads held high. The last two were a clean-shaven man about Reisel's age and a woman a little older. Both were Daruvian, but in Ampyrium, their plain gray clothes and neatly laced boots would be suited to a merchant's clerks, or tutors in a prosperous household.

"That's them," Kitri said quietly.

Linane had seen these two arrive. He could read the future, just as Kitri could read people's thoughts. Since he favored their mother, he looked a lot more Daruvian, so he had to be even more careful to hide his talent. But he had seen these two arrive from Vedrana today. He knew whatever they were going to do here would be of vital importance for their family. Kitri had seen the strangers' faces clearly in her brother's mind's eye.

The clean-shaven man collapsed as if he had been poleaxed. The girl dropped to her knees, too startled to scream. She started shaking her companion, frantic.

"Shit. Come on!" Reisel was already hurrying towards them.

Anchin and Kitri followed, keeping a wary eye on the bounty hunters. The murderous brute charged forward with a roar of defiance and the bounty hunters attacked. The stolid guards looked on, unmoved. They stopped anyone from Ampyrium stepping into the paving in front of the gate and that was all.

"Mirvat!" The girl pleaded, hysterical. Seeing three strangers running towards her, she froze. Her consternation overrode the chaos of the fight battering Kitri's thoughts.

"We're here to help, I swear it," Reisel called out to her.

Kitri couldn't tell if the girl had heard. If so, she wouldn't believe it. No one here was her friend. Panic-stricken, she scrambled to her feet.

Two more paces and all Kitri could sense was the fallen man's mental agony. He was a people reader, vastly more sensitive than her. Within moments of reaching Ampyrium, he had sensed the countless thousands who called this city home. The relentless clamor overwhelmed him. He was sinking deeper beneath the onslaught. He wasn't even breathing.

Kitri wished Linane had foreseen this, but that couldn't be helped. She pulled a silver vial out of her pocket. She never went anywhere without it. The stranger needed the dose more than she did. "Hold him still."

The stranger was in the throes of a seizure. Anchin knelt on the cobbles to grip the man's head with his thighs. He pressed down hard on the traveler's chest, using all his weight. "Quickly!"

The man's jaw was clamped tight, with his lips drawn back in a gruesome mockery of a grin. Kitri hooked a finger in the corner of his mouth and poured the contents of the vial between his teeth and his cheek. His thrashing boot kicked her so hard that she staggered. At least the physical pain helped ward off the stranger's anguish.

"Where's she gone?" Reisel was looking around. "I can't see her."

Kitri grabbed his hand. "We have to go."

"Help me with him, Reis." Anchin got to his feet. "Kit?"

She nodded mute reassurance now that the stranger lay limp and unconscious. As her brothers wrestled with the stranger's dead weight, Kitri realized the bounty hunters had gone. The only trace left of the red-stained criminals was blood smeared across the cobbles. She hadn't felt anyone die. The turmoil overwhelming the stranger had been too intense. Even so, more than the usual random assortment of minds brushed against her thoughts.

She felt a stab of sudden distress. She looked past the Commissioner's hall to see the stranger's companion and the three girls who had arrived hand in hand. Four muscular men forced them into a fancy carriage. A fashionably dressed woman got in quickly afterwards. A wagon blocked Kitri's view. When it had passed by, the carriage was gone.

"Kit!" Anchin had the limp stranger secure on his shoulder. "Let's go!"

Incredulous, she felt the traveler's wits stirring. That shouldn't be possible after the dose she had given him. The vial she still clutched was empty. But there was no mistaking that sensation. They had to get the stranger somewhere safe before he woke up.

"Right." She stayed as close as she could to Anchin. Reisel cut a path for them through the crowded streets.

* * *

"So that didn't go as expected." Father looked at the senseless stranger sprawled across the narrow bed.

"Forgive me," Linane began stiffly.

Affectionate, Father clapped him on the shoulder. "How were you to know he would be a sensitive?"

"What are we going to do?" Reisel looked from Father to Linane to Kitri to Anchin. Daylight filtered through the slats of the window high in the eaves of the small room.

"I had better stay," Kitri said before anyone else could speak. "I can tell him what's happened when he wakes."

"Not on your own," Father said firmly. "There's no telling what he might do when he learns we've lost his—wife? Sister?"

Father looked at Linane who could only shake his head and shrug.

"The fewer minds he feels, the more rational he will be." Kitri gestured at the bare wooden walls of this warehouse guard's lodging. A stool, a washstand, a small table, and the bed where the stranger lay were the only furnishings. "That's why we brought him here instead of going to the benevolents."

Anchin spoke up, absently rubbing his shoulder. "He'll want to know what's happened to the girl. The sooner we find out, the better for everyone."

"Does she—you know—matter?" Reisel raised a hand to ward off the looks everyone gave him. "I'm not saying we shouldn't try to find her, if she doesn't."

He wouldn't meet Kitri's eye though. As if he could stop her seeing that was exactly what he had thought.

"They both matter," Linane said firmly. Despite their different coloring, he looked strikingly like Father as he scowled. "I only wish I knew why."

"It may come to you," Father said, bracing. "Let's not waste any more time. Reisel, you stay in case Kit needs you, but at the bottom of the stairs." He glanced at her. "That's far enough away?"

Satisfied as she nodded, he snapped his fingers at Linane. "Fetch more of those doses from Mistress Symena so Kit has what she needs ready to hand. We'll make some discreet enquiries at the Merchants Exchange."

The brothers nodded and followed Father towards the door. Linane glanced over his shoulder. "I'll be back as fast as I can."

"Shout if you need me." Reisel was sulking, however much he tried not to show it.

"I will." Kitri knew he wouldn't let her down.

As the footsteps on the wooden stair faded, she sat down on the stool, beside the unshuttered window that looked out across the warehouse's empty interior. There was nothing for Ampyrium's enterprising thieves to steal here, though that wouldn't be the case for long. Father was one of the city's busiest traders, thanks to Linane advising him on the best deals to pursue, and Kitri meekly taking notes as he negotiated, so she could tell him later what his business partners were really thinking.

Even before he had their help, Father had proved he was more astute than any merchant in ten. Maybe any one in a hundred. He had come from a world the Ampyrians called Calamunda. The only world whose gate stood open night and day. Most days anyway. Occasionally the Magnum would close it, for their own mysterious reasons, but Kitri couldn't remember the last time that had happened. People from Calamundan towns and cities came and went, buying and selling, and Ampyrians did the same.

Father had walked across half a continent to reach that gate with only the clothes on his back and a purse of meager coin. That had been his share after the family farm was sold, when the heartlands had been stricken by drought and disease. Where stories of the gate and the worlds beyond it were scorned as make-believe. But Father had believed he could find a better life on the other side. Arriving in Ampyrium, and spending every penny on pins, buttons, ribbons, thread, and a street peddler's tray, he soon doubled his money. He doubled that twice as fast. By the time he had met Mother, he owned a warehouse and was negotiating to buy another.

Once he met Mother, he learned how profitable trade with Daruvia could be. Brightly-colored and extravagantly-shaped feathers molted by tropical forest birds were highly sought after by Ampyrium's wealthy, and many others beyond the different gates. Daruvian gossamers were lightweight yet so strong they reputedly never tore. Dyed every color of the rainbow, the fabrics were never known to fade. Consequently they were prized and priced above any other silk.

Most valuable of all, the traders brought remedies and nostrums, tinctures and poultices concocted by Daruvia's herbalists. No apothecaries in Ampyrium could match their efficacy. People queued for days outside the Commissioner's Hall to pay for His Kindliness's stamp of approval on a letter detailing some ailment. There was no fee for sending those appeals through the portal. No payment was sought for the medicines sent in reply until a cure was found. As His Kindliness's representatives told anyone who would listen, Daruvia's apothecaries worked for the betterment of everyone, whatever their world might be.

Father said the people sending those apothecaries the details of their spots and itches were the ones who should charge a fee. Once the herbalists devised an effective salve for some ailment, the Kind Elders would profit handsomely by selling it to everyone else ever after.

Time passed. Kitri heard the bells announce the next hour. Distant voices passed by in the street below, too far away for her to sense the thoughts behind them. She wondered when Linane would come back.

All the while, she felt the stranger's wits stirring. Kitri expected the sensation to strengthen and she was puzzled when he didn't wake up. But what did she know? She had never met a sensitive from Daruvia. She knew of vanishingly few others in Ampyrium, and they took care never to meet in person. If they didn't know what each other looked like, no one could be betrayed and forced to sign punitive indentures to serve His Kindliness, the Commissioner.

The stranger's eyes opened the merest slit. She felt his thoughts try to reach into hers. Startled, she rebuffed him. Even with Mistress Symena's dose still dulling his wits, that wasn't easy. She pushed back harder. He yelped and pressed a hand to his forehead.

"I'm sorry," Kitri said guiltily. "It's just—we don't do that." She floundered. She had no notion of customs and courtesies among Daruvian sensitives.

He moved his hand to look at her. "Who are you?"

"Kitri." That was all he needed to know for the moment.

He struggled to sit up, leaning against the wall. He was pale and breathing heavily. "Where's my—my sister?"

"Tigaze?" Kitri heard the name as clearly as if he had spoken aloud. "Ow!"

She yelped as he lashed out, even though she hadn't tried to look into his thoughts.

"Forgive me!" He buried his face in his hands. "I don't know what's wrong."

"You were overwhelmed when you came through the gate," Kitri said warily. "The pressure of so many minds—"

"How do you stand it?" He looked at her and grimaced as he ran his tongue around his teeth. "What *is* this foul taste?"

Kitri smiled, rueful. "A physic that reduces our sensitivity when we need to protect ourselves."

"Really?" He looked startled.

"How—?" Kitri broke off. She shouldn't interrogate him while he was still recovering.

"How do people like me cope in Daruvia?" He heard the question in her thoughts. He looked around as if he could see through the warehouse's wooden walls. "For a start, we don't live piled on top of everyone else like forest floor ants in a heap. When a child shows the first signs of sensitivity, their family moves as far from other folk as they must, until they—we—" His crooked smile was charming. "—learn to ward off other minds sufficiently well to mix with other people."

He sat up straighter. "Please, may I have something to drink? Your potion is very effective, but forgive me, it does taste vile."

Personally, Kitri didn't mind the physic's sharp flavor, but that was beside the point. She stood and looked, but the washstand's ewer was bone dry. "I'm sorry, I have nothing to give you. We weren't planning to bring you here."

"What did you have planned?" He stiffened, alarmed. "How did you know—?"

"We didn't know," she said hastily. "That's to say, we didn't know you could read people. We only knew you and your sister were coming and that we needed to meet you."

He frowned, uneasy. "Someone sent you word from Vedrana? We were betrayed?"

"What? No," Kitri assured him. Then she realized she had to give him some answer and he would know if she lied. "We were warned by a future seer here in Ampyrium."

She kept her thoughts locked tight shut. This stranger didn't need to know about Linane. He might be charming and handsome, but they still didn't know the first thing about him.

He stared at her, half-disbelieving. "I've never heard of sensitives born outside Daruvia. You're not even pure Daruvian blood."

Kitri drew a sharp, shocked breath. He saw her as a mongrel? A crossbreed? "Ampyrians don't talk about people as if they're animals because their parents came from different places," she said angrily.

She wished there was water in that jug, and soap to hand as well. She'd wash his mouth out for thinking such filthy insults.

"I'm so sorry." The stranger raised his hands in surrender. "My head is still ringing like a bell hit with a hammer. Please, I beg you, where is Tigaze?"

Kitri bit her lip. "We're trying to find out."

Someone knocked quietly on the door from the stairs. To her relief, she sensed Reisel's thoughts on the other side. "Come in."

He opened the door. "I heard voices…"

Kitri held out her hand as Reisel offered her a small box of woven straw. Cheap pottery clinked inside. She looked at the stranger. "If you need another dose, ask me."

She saw the faint crease between his brows and sensed his dissatisfaction. He opened his mouth and she expected him to ask for a vial right now. Instead, he stood up as Reisel offered his hand. Kitri felt the stranger do his best to wall off his own thoughts before he forced himself to return the gesture.

"Please, call me Mirvat."

"I'm Reisel." He shook the stranger's hand briefly before looking at Kitri. "Lin brought a message from Father with those doses. He says our unexpected guest is welcome to join us for dinner."

Kitri nodded, hiding her surprise. A lifetime of hearing unintended revelations made her very good at that. "Let's go home."

"I cannot intrude," Mirvat protested.

"You won't," Reisel assured him. "Besides, with luck, someone will have news of your companion."

Mirvat nodded abruptly. "Then thank you, I will come."

"This way." Kitri went down the stairs to the floor of the warehouse. Reisel locked the door behind them. When they stepped out through the wicket in the main door, he locked that, too. the warehouse might be empty, but Father wasn't going to risk finding a beggar gang making themselves at home.

Outside Reisel took the lead. There was no one in the back lane between the tall storehouses, but Kitri saw Mirvat swallow hard when they reached a broader street with workshops and traders supplying artisans. A handful of men and women were going about their business. The Daruvian sensitive winced each time someone glanced in their direction. His face was the color of spoiled milk and his lips were bloodless.

"Mirvat." Kitri opened the box and offered him a crudely glazed vial. "Take little sips until the pressure eases."

"Thank you," he said tightly. He worked the stopper free and raised the vial to his lips. His color improved after a few paces. Kitri sensed Reisel's relief that he wouldn't have to carry the stranger over his shoulder. Mirvat's blush betrayed his humiliation as he read her brother's thoughts.

It wasn't a long walk home. The plain and practical buildings of the commercial district gave way to houses of two or three stories on plots of varying size with walled yards to the front and gardens behind. Kitri had never thought about that before talking to Mirvat. Now she realized the first Daruvian exiles who had built these homes sought as much distance from their neighbors as they could get within the crowded city. Colored tiles brightened roofs, and gate posts were decorated with carved garlands of leaves and flowers.

Father could have afforded a house in a far more exclusive neighborhood these days, but he preferred to be within quick reach of his business interests. Mother was content to stay within half a morning's walk of the official Daruvian enclave. This district was close enough for her to stay in touch with her friends, and far enough away that no one could claim she was subject to His Kindliness the Commissioner's edicts or decrees.

"Here we are." Reisel pushed open the gate to the paved courtyard that separated their house from the street. Fragrant selberry trees planted in halved wooden barrels offered shade, blossom, and fruit according to the season.

Kitri felt Mirvat's relief. That's all she could feel. As the streets had grown busier with Ampyrians heading home from their day's labors, he had lifted the vial to his lips more often. By her reckoning, it must be nearly empty. But the dose had done its work, for the stranger and for her family.

Anchin lounged on the bench in the entrance hall, reading a broadsheet folded down to a manageable size. He grinned at Mirvat. "You look better than you did."

"You are—" Mirvat closed his eyes momentarily.

Kitri saw he was disconcerted to realize the dose that protected him also restricted the reach of his thoughts.

"Follow me." Anchin opened the double doors to the dining room where the polished table was set for dinner.

Kitri saw half the chairs had been moved back against the plaster walls painted with murals to resemble an arbor in a garden. Her younger brothers and sisters had been sent elsewhere after school then. Anchin's thoughts told her this evening's conversation wouldn't be suitable for young ears and careless lips. She could also sense Linane was nowhere in the house.

Was that merely a precaution, to make sure the sensitive stranger had no chance to identify him as the future seer she had mentioned? Or had Lin seen some misfortune to come, if he joined them for this meal? But if Father had invited Mirvat here, Lin must have told him that all would be well. Not for the first time, Kitri was grateful she had been spared the endless questions and frustrations that came with future sight.

"You're here. Good." Father came out of his office on the other side of the hall. Sisky was with him.

"Please, sit." At the other end of the dining room, Mother came through from the kitchen, carrying a basket of spiced bread rolls. She smiled at Mirvat. "You are very welcome."

Father took his place at the head of the table as Cook and Dila, the household's maid of all work, set down a platter of greens wilted in fragrant oil and a hefty tureen of goat stew.

On Father's left, Reisel and Sisky left the chair between them for Mirvat.

"Thank you." He forced a smile as he sat.

Kitri took her usual seat opposite between Anchin and Mother. Father poured wine from the silver jug and passed it to Reisel, who passed it to Mirvat.

The Daruvian looked at Kitri. "May I?"

It took her a moment to realize he was asking if he could drink it safely after taking the physic. "Oh. Yes, of course." She accepted a glass of wine from Father as well.

Mother ladled stew into her own shallow bowl and topped it with greens. "Help yourself," she invited Mirvat.

"After you, please." Mirvat looked around the table, saluting everyone with his wine glass.

Father was already dipping a torn roll into his filled bowl. "First things first. No one will ask what you did on the other side of the gate to get sent here. No one will thank you for telling them either, so keep it to yourself. What's done is done."

"Don't ask anyone else with a raw Daruvian accent about their past," Reisel interjected. "At best, you'll get a smack in the mouth. At worst?" He shook his head as he helped himself to food.

"Put whatever you did behind you," Father went on, "with whatever life you used to lead. And whatever you may have been told about earning the right to go home, that's a fool's daydream."

He swallowed a mouthful of bread before he calmly stated the brutal facts of exile. "Before His Kindliness will even consider granting an exile passage home, the appellant must lodge a substantial surety with the Commissioner's Secretary. How much that might be is decided case by case. You must also prove you've been employed for a year and a day by a trusted Daruvian on this side of the gate. Anyone the Secretary calls to vouch for you must appear before the Commissioner and swear to your good character. You will be expected to compensate them for their time and trust. Their affidavits will be weighed against any evidence that might be found by the Secretary's agents. If they find the least indication that an appellant has so much as set foot where they're not welcome, that surety is forfeit. If there is the slightest evidence that a Daruvian has knowingly sworn to a false affidavit, they will be fined into beggary."

"Oh." Mirvat sipped his wine, dumbfounded.

Mother looked across the table, sympathetic. "It's all moot anyway. Few exiles can ever earn the sum that the Commissioner demands up front."

Father nodded as he picked up his spoon. "That warehouse where we took you? I could fill it with the finest trade goods Ampyrium has to offer for the price of a modest surety."

"Exiles with the talents to amass such funds generally decide they'd rather stay," Sisky said with a grin. "Why go back to a place that doesn't want you where you'll only get into more trouble? Eat something. You'll feel better." She ladled a modest serving of stew into Mirvat's bowl.

"Thank you." Mirvat's lips tightened as he contemplated the food.

Kitri could tell he was offended. He had been on the verge of a curt rebuke.

"Do you know about the other gates?" Reisel didn't wait for an answer. "They're—"

"Get your bearings here in Ampyrium first," Father advised. "Before you get curious about going anywhere else. Oh, and if anyone tells you there's a secret passageway leading out through the city walls, which they can let you use for a price, they're lying through their teeth and out to steal your coin. Though you'll read that in them, won't you?" He grinned at Mirvat.

When Kitri had learned about that deceitful trick, she had been astonished that anyone would fall for it. Like all of Ampyrium's gates, the city wall had been built—if "built" was even the right word—by the Magnum hundreds of years ago. Every rugged black stone in the monumental barrier was taller and wider than a grown man. Each one was a different, irregular shape, fitted together so tightly that a dagger tip couldn't get into the cracks. Every youngster born in Ampyrium verified that as soon as they got hold of a blade.

Then she realized Mirvat already knew there were other gates. He wasn't in the least interested in where they might lead, or whatever might be outside the great walls. That struck her as odd. For a fleeting moment, she thought he was going to say as much to Father. Then he forced himself to ask something else.

"Please, what has happened my sister Tigaze? Do you know where I can find her?"

Kitri wasn't sure who he was asking, but Anchin answered.

"We have some news, and please, hear me out. Did you see the people waiting to welcome the exiles from Vedrana? No?" He grimaced as Mirvat shook his head. "Well, the hunters were out to collect the Commissioner's bounty on the condemned. The benevolent societies were there to offer shelter and introductions, so innocent exiles can find work and start a new life. Others dangle the lure of an easier life, with promises that turn out to be lies. Those charlatans are interested in women and girls, the prettier the better."

Mirvat stared at Anchin in horror.

He nodded, unemotional. "She was grabbed by a brothel keeper. Don't fret. We've found out where she is and we plan to rescue her."

Kitri felt the surge of Mirvat's relief as well as something else. Before she could grasp what that might be, his resolve overrode everything else.

"Let's go." He pushed his bowl away, ready to get to his feet.

"First thing tomorrow," Father said firmly. "At the moment, the brutes who guard the women will be on their guard. If any of the benevolents saw what happened, they can expect a deputation to challenge them. By tomorrow, they'll think they've got away with it. If we kick in their door at dawn, everyone will be half-asleep. That'll do half the work for us."

"I'm coming, too," Mirvat insisted.

"Of course." Father was surprised he might think different. "Your sister needs to see someone she recognizes. Otherwise she'll think she's being stolen by a rival gang."

"As soon as you show me the building she's in, I can find her and tell her what will happen," Mirvat assured him. "Come to that, if I don't sense her presence, you'll know to look elsewhere."

"You can do that?" Kitri stared at him, astonished.

"You can't?" He was equally taken aback.

Kitri felt some reaction she couldn't quite decipher. Pity for her lack of talent? Contempt for her inadequate skills? Before she could decide, Mirvat shook his head and the sensation faded.

He picked up his spoon and looked across the table. "Please, who are these benevolents you keep mentioning?"

Mother explained as the stranger began eating. Father commented that households with the slightest Daruvian connections, in the enclave and across Ampyrium, received regular visitors soliciting charitable donations to support their work.

Kitri concentrated on her own meal, keeping her thoughts to herself. The societies of Daruvians across Ampyrium were certainly benevolent, but they weren't stupid. Not everyone the Kind Elders exiled was merely guilty of challenging their tyranny. Banishment was the penalty for a host of other crimes besides murder, rape, or arson. No benevolent would cause offense by asking what a newcomer had done to get sent through the gate, but finding that person a place to stay, and helping them get a job, made keeping watch on them a great deal easier, until they revealed their true character. Not that Mother mentioned any of that.

Kitri set her spoon down in her empty bowl as Mother warned Mirvat: "Don't ever tell anyone that you can read people. Not anyone. Not ever. If the Commissioner in the enclave hears even a rumor, his brutes will snatch you off the streets. Once he's certain, your life won't be your own, not ever again. Oh, you'll be promised generous rewards for using your skills to help maintain good order. They'll say you can earn passage back through the gate. That's a lie. You'll never get away. The doses they give you will make sure of that. If you ever stop taking their physic, your wits will unravel completely."

He looked at her, aghast. For one dreadful moment, Kitri thought he was going to bring his meal back up. Instead, he fumbled in his pocket for the pottery vial she had given him.

She answered his unspoken question. "No, that's different. It won't enslave you."

"The price for further supplies is your oath that you won't betray Kitri," Anchin said bluntly. "We'll keep your secret as long as you keep hers."

"Don't imagine you can find the herbalist who makes that physic on your own," Reisel warned, amiable. "As soon as an apothecary realizes what you want, they'll betray you to the Commissioner so fast, you might as well go and knock on his door."

Kitri sensed the utter confusion that the others saw on Mirvat's face.

Sisky explained. "Daruvian apothecaries who've made their home in Ampyrium have the closest ties to Vedrana. They swap notes with the herbalists on the other side of the gate, detailing beneficial interactions of native Ampyrian plants with blends of leaves and barks and berries from Daruvia's forests. A few even have permission to go to and fro through the gate as and when they wish. That comes at a price. They pay with information about particular exiles, where they go and who they meet."

"The Kind Elders of the tree-cities are quick to get rid of those who might question their rule," Mother said quietly, "but gadflies are never forgotten or forgiven."

Mirvat buried his face in his hands. All Kitri could sense was his desperation to find the woman who had come through the gate at his side.

"You must wonder if you're on your head or your heels," Mother said, sympathetic. "You should rest."

"Get some sleep," Reisel agreed, "and you'll be bright-eyed when we rescue your sister."

Anchin drained his wine glass. "I'll take you to the benevolents at—"

"Can I go back to the warehouse, just for tonight?" Mirvat begged. "Even with this physic's help, I can't bear the touch of any more strange minds, not today."

Father looked at Kitri. She nodded. Mirvat was telling the truth about that. Mother rose to her feet. "We'd better find you a few necessities."

* * *

The Daruvian looked better in the dawn twilight. Kitri was glad to see it. He was surprised to see her, but beyond that, he was guarding his thoughts tightly.

Anchin locked the warehouse door and everyone followed Father. Mirvat walked beside Kitri. She expected him to ask who these strangers were. Reisel was the only other face he would recognize. Instead he gave her a tight smile.

"Do you need a dose?" she asked him quietly.

"I still have the vial Anchin gave me last night," he replied under his breath. "With so few folk around, I could manage without it. Tell me, what's the plan?"

"Did you see the condemned criminals who were sent through first, when you were on the other side of the gate?"

He nodded.

"One got away." Kitri still found that hard to believe, but she had seen events unfold in Anchin's recollection.

The brute with the cloth-wrapped fists had put up a mighty fight. The sly-faced man in brown had been quicksilver-fast at dodging slashing steel and fists alike. Somehow he stole a hunter's sword and killed the man with his own blade. The brute seized his chance to snatch a weapon for himself, breaking a distracted hunter's jaw with a punch. That didn't save them, outnumbered as they were. Once they had been cut down, and the bickering started over who claimed their heads by right of the killing blow, a vile oath had silenced them all. Someone had realized the woman in the stained yellow tunic was nowhere to be seen, dead or alive.

"We sent word to a crew of bounty hunters, saying she's hiding in this brothel," Kitri explained. "No one will be surprised when they break down the door. The Daruvian Commissioner will never know anyone else had a hand in it."

"Won't that start a bloody fight with the brutes who guard the whores?" Mirvat glanced at her.

"I'll stay far enough away to be safe," Kitri assured him, "but we're not only going to rescue your sister. She'll recognize you, but the other girls will need to see a friendly face. As soon as I know what they're thinking, I'll be able to reassure them."

"I can tell Tigaze—" He shook his head. "No, I can't. She'd have to explain how she knew what was coming."

Kitri was pleased to see he was learning the rules of his new life. "We can't say those girls would betray you, but there's no way to know they wouldn't simply let your secret slip by accident."

"This place is nothing like home," he muttered savagely.

Kitri felt the heat of sudden fury behind the steely resolve shielding his thoughts. Before she could ask about that, Mirvat had another question.

"What happens when these bounty hunters realize the woman they're hunting isn't there?"

Father glanced over his shoulder. "That's not our concern."

They walked on in silence. The daylight strengthened. Truth be told, Kitri had no idea where they were. The style of the houses and shops that they passed was wholly unfamiliar. Most of the buildings were run-down and some were derelict, plundered for tile, timber, and stone. She never ventured into these perilous districts, and not only for fear of being knocked on the head and waking to find herself captive in a brothel or worse. If people around here had been awake, sensing their thoughts would have felt like wading through sewage. Even with the reassuring weight of her silver vial in her pocket, she fervently hoped they would be well away soon.

A gang of men emerged from an alley, wearing studded leathers and sword belts. Several carried long bundles on their shoulders, wrapped in sacking and secured with ropes. Seeing their shaved heads, dead eyes, and expressionless faces, Kitri dismissed any notion of trying to learn more and locked her thoughts down tighter still.

Father and the gang leader exchanged a nod. As the bounty hunters led the way, Kitri looked at the back of Father's head. It was one thing to know his network of contacts across Ampyrium included men from discreditable ventures undertaken many years ago. It was something else entirely to see these stone-cold killers greet him with respect.

Finally, they turned into a short, wide street of what had once been spacious, desirable homes. Some shift in taste had made another district more fashionable years ago. Nowadays, all these houses had to offer was their size. Their generous rooms must house entire families, Kitri guessed, judging by the quantities of threadbare laundry hanging from balconies on their second, third, and fourth stories, out of the reach of passing thieves. Only the grand mansion towards the far end was spared such indignity.

The bounty hunters could have strolled into most of the other houses unchallenged. As they walked up the street, Kitri saw some doors were standing ajar, presumably for fear of fire. Missing doors had presumably gone for firewood. Few windows were shuttered, giving those sleeping inside at least the chance of fresher air to breathe. Once again the grand mansion was different. Its front door was solidly shut. Every shutter was closed from the ground floor to the attic.

Feral dogs lounged in the gutters. They watched, incurious, as the bounty hunters huddled around their leader. Everyone else gathered in a circle around Father. He indicated who should go in, once the brothel was breached. He pointed to a narrow gap between two nearby houses. "Anchin, you wait over there with Kitri and Mirvat."

She thought the Daruvian was going to protest, but his impulse faded fast. He followed her and her brother into the dubious shelter of an alley that reeked of piss and worse.

Mirvat's attention was fixed on the brothel. He didn't even blink as he stood stock still. Kitri guessed he was searching for his sister's thoughts. She tried not to envy his ability to do that over such a distance. What would he do if Tigaze was asleep? Could he wake her by speaking to her, mind to mind?

The Daruvian drew a sudden breath. "Yes!"

A crash shattered the peace and quiet. Kitri saw one of those bundles the bounty hunters carried was a battering ram to smash their way inside. The dogs sprang up, barking. Bounty hunters bellowed threats as they surged up the brothel's steps. Others swung grapnels and hurled them upwards to snag on balcony rails. They yelled, triumphant, as they tested their ropes and began climbing.

The cacophony echoed down the street. No one appeared at any other windows to see what might be amiss. Father's friends followed the bounty hunters through the shattered front door. Father and Reisel stayed at the bottom of the front steps with two others. Swords drawn, they were ready to repel anyone arriving to lend a hand to the brothels' guards. Reisel warned off a snarling dog with a growl of his own.

Shrieks of outrage inside the house were muted at first. They grew louder as the brothel's shutters flew open. Threatening voices answered defiant yells. Women in various states of undress began appearing on balconies.

"I hope none of them try to climb down," Anchin said uneasily.

"There she is!" Mirvat darted forward.

Cursing under his breath, Anchin followed the stranger. Kitri hurried half a pace behind her brother.

One of Father's friends came out of the brothel with an arm around Tigaze's shoulders. His bloodied blade warned off anyone hoping to seize her. The three girls who'd been grabbed at the gate followed close behind, flanked by two burly protectors. Tigaze was fully dressed, though dishevelled. The other girls had managed to don their shirts and breeches, but they were all barefoot. Only one carried her boots and none had their jerkin.

The stern-faced men at the foot of the steps looked in every direction for any sign of a threat. As soon as the men and the girls reached the street, Father led them away from the mayhem inside the house. They met and Mirvat wrapped his arms around Tigaze. He buried his face in her untamed gold curls.

Father looked at Kitri, concerned. "Are you alright?"

She nodded, wide-eyed.

* * *

"Lock the door behind me." Reisel handed Mirvat the keys. He put a basket of bread, meat, and fruit on the table beside a leather bottle and a lidded bowl with a spoon.

"I'm not sure if I'll be back later with more food or if Father will send Anchin, but sit tight and stay out of sight, for today at least." His glance included Tigaze in this warning.

She was sitting on the bed. "Of course," she said meekly.

"If we can't find you another lodging, we'll bring a pallet and another blanket for tonight." Reisel wrinkled his nose. "Use the drain downstairs to empty the chamber pot. We can fetch a couple of buckets from the nearest well to sluice it after dark."

"We'll be fine." Mirvat ushered him to the door. "I cannot thank you—*we* cannot thank you enough."

As he followed Reisel down the stairs, their voices grew fainter. Tigaze stripped off her high-necked, long-sleeved bodice and dropped it on the bed. Crossing the room, she took a bread roll from the basket. Stuffing it into her mouth, she worked the leather bottle's stopper free. As she sniffed at the bottle's contents, she looked agreeably surprised. She washed the bread down with a long drink.

"Leave some for me." As he came back into the room Mirvat didn't seem surprised to see her wearing only her thin chemise and gray skirt. He tossed the keys onto the table.

"Sod off," Tigaze said without rancor. "You didn't spend the night in a room with three wailing halfwits."

"I got you rescued, didn't I?" Mirvat took the bottle from her and slid his other hand around her waist as he drank.

"I could have got myself out of that whorehouse any time I chose," Tigaze scoffed.

"Why didn't you?"

"I thought I'd see what I could find out." She took the bottle and put it on the table. Wrapping her arms around his neck, she kissed him long and deep.

Mirvat murmured wordless appreciation. His hand slid up from her waist to cup her soft, full breast. His thumb teased her nipple, pert and dark beneath her chemise. A moment later, he pulled away.

Tigaze scowled. "You have something better to do while we're shut in here all day?"

Mirvat picked up Tigaze's bodice and handed it to her. "We only need to wait in here until that halfwit's out of sight. Let's finish the job and get back to Vedrana."

"Finish the job?" Tigaze dressed and fastened her buttons. "What have you learned?" Her voice was sharp with jealousy.

"Watch what you're thinking." Mirvat winced, and took the cheap pottery vial out of his breeches' pocket.

"What's that?" Tigaze held out her hand.

Mirvat took a sip. "The only way people readers here can stay sane."

Tigaze frowned. "I don't understand. What are you talking about?"

"The Kind Elder who told us there are no sensitives in Ampyrium, beyond the few Daruvians who live in the enclave, was as ignorant as dirt or lying through her teeth," Mirvat said savagely. "Did you see that girl with a face like a caramel-glazed bun? She's a people reader, and there's a future seer lurking somewhere around. That's how they knew we would come through the gate."

Tigaze was horrified. "Then they know—?"

"They don't know shit. All their pathetic future seer could say was significant events would follow our arrival." Mirvat smiled with cruel satisfaction. "The bun-faced girl could barely read me if I went to the next room. But stay away from her. We do not want her to learn what you can do with your unseen hands."

Tigaze sniffed. "That's unexpected, but it shouldn't be a problem. They must be so feeble because their Daruvian blood has been thinned. She's clearly a—"

"Don't say it," Mirvat warned her. "Don't even think it."

Tigaze ignored that. "Are they working with the Seditionists? What other talents can they call on? Readers of the past? People seers? Do *they* have anyone with unseen hands?"

"I don't know," Mirvat admitted. "But we had better stay as chaste as the brother and sister I told them we were, in case anyone is watching from afar." He laughed suddenly. "You think I want to bed the bun-faced girl? Trust me, when we get home, I'll leave you walking bow-legged for a week."

"You think you'll get the chance?" Tigaze gestured and the leather bottle flew through the air to smack him hard on the back of the head.

"Pack that in." Mirvat wasn't smiling. "If they do have a people seer, you'd better hope they were looking elsewhere just now. From what that girl said, you really don't want His Kindliness the Commissioner to learn what you can do."

Tigaze smoothed back her long blonde curls. "So what's your plan? Tell them to spill whatever they know about the Seditionists or we'll send the Commissioner's brutes after the girl?"

"Only if we have to," Mirvat said with distaste. "I'd rather keep that secret safe in case we need to trade it later on. Let's start by watching their house and seeing who comes and goes."

Tigaze took a ribbon from her skirt pocket and tied back her hair. "We can try that until noon. After that—" She broke off, pressing a hand to her head.

"After that, we will discuss our next steps. You don't do anything we haven't agreed on," Mirvat said curtly. He stared until Tigaze nodded. "Right, let's go."

He headed down the stairs. As Tigaze followed, she glanced over her shoulder at the door to the upper room. The lock secured itself with no need for a key. Mirvat opened the wicket in the outer door cautiously. He peered out. A moment later, he stepped over the raised sill.

Tigaze followed with her eyes downcast and her expression demure. Mirvat led the way to the house where he had dined last night, unerring at every turn. Neither one spoke until Mirvat's brisk pace slowed.

"Don't get too close," Tigaze began.

Mirvat rounded on her with a scowl. She recoiled, pressing a hand to her head.

"Very well," she said curtly. "But what's our excuse for idling on the street like beggars?"

Mirvat pointed to a closed gate beneath an archway of carved branches. "There's no one in there. We can stay out of sight while you keep watch and I focus on who comes and goes at that seditionist lair. Now, open it up!"

As Tigaze focused on the empty house's gate and the bolts on the inside slid back, Mirvat pushed it open.

Tigaze slipped through after him. "What do I do if someone turns up?"

But Mirvat was leaning against the wall, staring straight ahead, blank-faced. Tigaze glowered at him and stooped to hitch up her skirt's hem. She slid a thin, needle-pointed dagger from its hiding place in her boot. She peered in through the house's front windows. Moving to the porch, she stirred windblown dust and leaves in the corners with the toe of her boot. The trees that had shed them had been taken elsewhere. Only stains on the paving showed where their pots or half-barrels had stood. She laid a finger on the door knob and the lock clicked obediently open. Tigaze went inside.

"This place has been empty for a while," she remarked when she reappeared. "Let's hope the owners don't come back today."

Motionless, Mirvat showed no sign he had heard her. Tigaze pursed her lips and studied her dagger. She didn't put the blade back in her boot, but sat on the stone bench for visitors inside the intricately carved porch. Every few moments, she glanced from Mirvat to the house and back again.

Time passed. People wandered by on the other side of the gate. Wagons trundled down the street. Voices floated over the wall, speaking different tongues. Some were cheerful. Others challenged or threatened an unseen companion. Across the yard, Mirvat hadn't moved a muscle. Tigaze's eyes slowly closed. She was soon soundly asleep.

"Shit." Mirvat doubled over. "Shit."

Tigaze was instantly awake, on her feet with her dagger ready. "What?"

"She's—" Mirvat coughed and worked his jaw, trying to summon spit to moisten his parched mouth. "She's just gone in there."

"The seditionist?" Tigaze winced and jabbed her dagger in his direction. "Don't do that. I know what she looks like."

"I'm making certain you don't miss," Mirvat growled and took a sip from his pottery vial. "Be ready. We don't know how long she'll be inside."

"I imagine they'll offer her a drink at least," Tigaze murmured. "Lucky bitch."

She waited by the unbolted gate, watching Mirvat intently. He stood facing the wall with his hands flat on the masonry as he stared straight ahead. Somewhere, chimes sounded. Neither Daruvian paid any attention as the resonant sound died away.

Mirvat stiffened. "She's leaving. No, let me go first. I'll recognize anyone I met last night."

"You could always show me their faces."

But he slipped through the gate without answering her. Tigaze followed, sliding her dagger's blade inside her sleeve and cupping the hilt in her hand. They walked along the street, unhurried and staying close to the walls of the houses' front courtyards. Enough folk were headed in the same direction for them to mingle unremarked with the Ampyrians.

Tigaze lengthened her stride to walk at Mirvat's side. "Where should I—?"

He silently told her to do the job as soon as an opportunity presented itself. They followed the oblivious seditionist to a crossroads where their target headed left. The exiled Daruvian passed the first side street and turned into the next.

As soon as the seditionist was out of sight, Mirvat broke into a jogtrot. Tigaze had to run to keep up. They turned the corner. The silver-haired seditionist was nowhere to be seen. Ahead, the street widened to accommodate a small local market where the older Daruvian neighborhood met a medley of newer buildings. This late in the day, few stallholders were still trading. Most were folding up their trestles and brightly-striped canvas awnings, ready to head home.

"There." Mirvat pointed, hoarse with relief.

"I see her." Tigaze weighed the dagger in her hand as she watched the woman walking away.

She tossed the blade into the air. Instantly, it swooped upwards, well above any casual observer's eyeline. Invisible against the backdrop of mismatched tenements, the slender dagger moved as fast as an arrow loosed from a bow.

The seditionist drew close to an alley some way beyond the market. She stumbled and fell to her knees. In the next instant, the woman collapsed onto her face. Tigaze's unseen hands shoved her victim into the alley. As the woman's feet disappeared, she glanced at Mirvat. "Well?"

A moment later, he nodded. "Yes. Let's get out of here."

He turned around and strolled away. Once again, he took care not to walk too fast. They still had to get back to the Daruvian enclave, and into the Commissioner's office, unchallenged. He took another sip from the pottery vial and shook it, trying to assess how much of the potion was left. Could he risk calling at the bun-faced girl's house to beg another dose? It would be some while before the seditionists heard of their fellow-conspirator's death.

"Where are we going?" Tigaze demanded.

Mirvat blinked and saw unfamiliar streets with no hint of Daruvian architecture. He slowed to a halt as he realized he had no idea where they were. How had they got here? "I—I don't know."

His head was pounding. He screwed his eyes tightly closed. Tigaze grabbed his hand. At least she knew enough to wall off all but her surface thoughts when she touched him. That didn't stop the countless Ampyrian minds crowding him. Mirvat's vision blurred and he retreated as far as he could inside his own head.

"Move!" Tigaze kept walking. She held his hand painfully tight.

Mirvat picked a few thoughts out of her irritation. Standing still wouldn't make them any less lost. At least she had studied the maps of this city. She just had to get her bearings. Mirvat kept tight hold of her hand. If she abandoned him, he would be utterly lost in this awful place.

He had no idea how far they had walked when her relief washed over him. "There's the Silk Exchange."

Mirvat recognized the trading hall with its ornate pillared arcades mimicking a forest grove below its cobalt-tiled roof. That had been one of the pictures they had been shown before they came here. He tried to remember how far the landmark was from the Daruvian enclave. Doing that threatened the concentration he needed to keep the clamor of Ampyrian thoughts at bay. He settled for keeping pace with Tigaze and shaking off her hand. He wasn't going to arrive in front of the Commissioner being dragged along like a naughty child.

Tigaze's determination reassured him. She didn't have the slightest doubt they were going to see the Commissioner, collect their fee, and go home. As they passed under the lofty arch of the Daruvian enclave's main gate with its intricate fan-vaulting overhead, Mirvat swallowed the last of the potion in the pottery vial. Squaring his shoulders as they approached the Commissioner's hall, he strode ahead of her up the steps.

A bored soldier stood guard at the door. He reached for his halberd propped against the post carved like a tinas tree. "No entry without a token."

"His Kindliness will see me," Mirvat assured him.

The guard was unmoved. "No one gets in without a token from the Secretary's office."

Mirvat knew Tigaze was ready to kill the fool with his own halberd. He slapped down that thought and ignored her gasp of outrage. They must not draw attention to themselves, he silently reminded her.

He smiled at the halfwit with the halberd. "Where is the Secretary's office?"

The man jerked his head. "Other side of the building."

"Thank you." Mirvat wordlessly promised Tigaze she could shove this fool down the stairs as soon as the door to the Commissioner's hall closed behind them.

They retreated and circled the building. The tinas tree door they wanted was easy to identify from the queue of Ampyrians, Daruvians, and more outside it. Mirvat walled off his thoughts as he and Tigaze walked to the head of the line. They went inside without asking permission.

The petty functionary in charge of a tapestry-hung anteroom gaped, outraged. Several men and women waiting on chairs stood up to protest. Mirvat looked at the inner doors and swiftly found the room with the mind he sought. He went in without knocking. Tigaze followed close behind.

She glared at the couple, who had just been admitted to the Secretary's presence. "Get out."

Even without a blade in her hand, Tigaze could be surprisingly scary. The couple chose caution over confrontation and scurried away. The door slammed shut behind them, untouched by any hand.

Mirvat didn't give the expensively dressed Secretary a chance to speak. He forced a recollection into the balding man's mind. He showed the Secretary his conversation with the Kind Elder who governed Entasek. He showed him the face of the seditionist they had been sent here to kill. The silver-haired woman with resolute eyes whose letters had been found in discreet pouches stuffed deep in barrels of Ampyrium leaves, barks, and berries. Her name had been plucked from the minds of the unsuspecting Daruvian merchants trading with her. Finally, Mirvat showed the Secretary the woman falling to lie dead in that alley. Doing that took the blink of an eye.

The Secretary tried to stand up. Tigaze's unseen hands shoved him back into his chair. Ashen-faced, the man stared at them both.

"You know who we are," Mirvat said calmly. "I saw you on the far side of the gate, while we waited to pass through. You know why we were sent here and I've shown you what we've done. Pay up and open the gate so we can go home."

The Secretary fumbled in a pocket for a handkerchief. Bloodstains bloomed on the white cloth as he held it to his nose. "It's not that simple, you fool," he said thickly.

Mirvat barely had to brush against the man's thoughts to understand they had been betrayed. Despite his wrath, he did his best to keep his voice level as he explained to Tigaze.

"He was told not to let us go back. This was a one-way trip. The Kind Elders of Entasek think we have become more of a threat than an asset."

"I can persuade him to open the gate." Tigaze reached down to take the dagger from her other boot and smiled coldly at the Secretary. "I'll use this if I have to, or we can agree on a different price. Do you want to fuck one or both of us or have us suck you? We know secrets you can turn into coin in this city, or into influence beyond the gate in Daruvia. We know—"

"No." Mirvat stopped her before she could betray the bun-faced girl and her family. "He'll take everything we offer, but whatever he promises will be a lie. He has no authority to open the gate."

"Then I'll open his throat." Tigaze stepped forward. "That'll persuade the Commissioner to send us home before we kill him, too."

Mirvat heard voices in the anteroom. He looked at the Secretary, alarmed. The man smiled at Tigaze, spitefully triumphant.

"My guards have arrived. They've been watching and waiting for you to come here. Credit where credit is due. We had no idea you would work so fast." He spat blood into his handkerchief. "Kill me and you'll be thrown onto the streets with your faces stained red in accordance with Daruvian law. My guards will take bets on how long you'll survive. No more than a few days, most likely."

"You'll still be dead." Tigaze was desperately trying to deny the trap closing around them.

The Secretary ignored her and turned to Mirvat. "You can start a new life in Ampyrium with the considerable benefits of working for me."

"No." Mirvat didn't wait for the treacherous swine to make the offer Kitri had predicted. He turned and walked to the anteroom door.

"Mir?" Fear made Tigaze shrill.

He opened the door to the anteroom hung with silken tapestries depicting Darvuvia's forests. Four armored guards with halberds faced him. Everyone else had been sent away.

"Let them pass," the Secretary ordered.

Mirvat knew the man was confident they would come crawling back within a few days. If he refused to bow his head? The Secretary's guards would find him, collapsed and drooling in a gutter, unable to withstand the pressure of so many Ampyrian minds. If Tigaze had already abandoned him, the Secretary was sure she would be found, chastised and brought to heel, or simply killed. Everyone had to sleep sooner or later, even murderers with unseen hands.

He pushed past the guards in the anteroom. Nobody tried to stop him. Tigaze followed close behind. Mirvat sensed her rising fury. She still had that naked blade in her hand.

"Where are we going?" she demanded as they went through the outer door.

"Outside the enclave," he said through gritted teeth. "Put that knife away."

Tigaze slid the blade up her sleeve. Neither of them spoke until they had gone out through the great arch and walked some distance into Ampyrium's haphazard streets. Kitri had said sensitives worked for the Commissioner. Mirvat must get beyond their reach first of all. If he was forced to come to some arrangement with the Secretary, he didn't want anyone to know what he was thinking. If he was going to trade the identity of that people reader working with the seditionists—

"Don't bank on that." Kitri was strolling beside him along the busy sidewalk.

"You?" Mirvat halted, astonished. "Where did you come from?"

Why hadn't Tigaze seen her approaching. Why wasn't her blade already at the girl's throat? She was usually as swift as a striking snake. But Tigaze stood still as a marble statue. Mirvat could feel her rising panic. He shared her astonishment as he realized none of the passers-by seemed to notice anything was amiss. No one even glanced at them.

Kitri took the dagger from Tigaze's unresisting fingers. "You're not the only one with unseen hands in this city," she said coldly. "And now we have this valued possession of yours, our people seer will always be able to find you. We'll be watching."

She turned to Mirvat. "I might not be able to send silent word to a person I can't see, but at least I don't leave my mind wide open when I'm searching for someone. Anyone sensitive could have read your thoughts. Your lies. Your foul plans."

The lash of his own contempt for the girl seared Mirvat as she flung it back at him. The sting as he realized his own arrogant carelessness was equally painful.

Tigaze forced a defiant laugh. "I still killed the bitch. If you knew what we planned to do, why didn't you stop us?"

"We mongrels may not be as powerful as sensitives in Daruvia, but some of us have talents you don't." Kitri held Mirvat's gaze.

As he looked into her brown eyes, he felt his memory of the seditionist's death dissolve. He saw the woman go on her way unharmed. Someone tall and slender with a hood hiding their face stood in the alley where he thought she had fallen. Whoever that was, they were somewhere close at this very moment. He felt them inside his head. They were unmasking his true memories.

Mirvat's skin crawled. The seditionist's death had been an illusion. An illusion he had just forced into the Secretary's mind as the unquestioned truth. Shocked, his defenses faltered and countless minds oppressed him.

"Get me more of those doses," he said tightly, "or I'll tell the Secretary where to find you."

"He won't believe a word you say when he learns that you lied about killing your prey." Kitri was unconcerned. "He'll hear she's alive soon enough, and thanks to you we know to keep her hidden."

"I still know your face. I know where you live," Mirvat said desperately.

"Do you?" Kitri glanced at Tigaze. "Do either of you?"

Mirvat felt his memory of the route to the girl's home dissolving, along with every recollection of the house and her family. Tigaze sniffed. He saw blood oozing from her nose to drip from her chin and stain her tight-buttoned bodice. Her terror stabbed him like a knife in his eye.

"What are we going to do?" As he asked Kitri, Tigaze's thoughts battered him with the same questions. "Where are we going to go?"

"If I were you, I'd leave this city as fast as you can, before Their Kindlinesses send hunters after you. As it happens, you're in luck. Ampyrium has one gate that anyone can pass through. Oh, you didn't know about that? Well, it has a bronze griffin on top. You won't be able to miss it."

She pointed away over the sprawling, uneven rooftops. "You can picture a compass, can't you? If you think of the Daruvian Gate at the north-west point, the Calamunda Gate is due east."

Mirvat gaped at her. "I'd have to cross pretty much this entire cursed city…"

"That's no concern of mine." Kitri shrugged. Then she offered him a cheap glazed pottery vial. "Sip this slowly and you should reach the gate before your wits dribble out of your ears. If you hurry."

He snatched that salvation from her. "Why?"

"Because we're not murderers, even if you are." Kitri walked away.

Before she had gone ten paces, Mirvat knew he would never recognize the girl again. He couldn't even remember her name.

"Mir!" Tigaze collapsed, sobbing.

Mirvat left her sprawled on the cobbles. If the seditionists' people seer could find her by means of that dagger, she was a threat to him now. Which street looked likely to offer the most direct path to this gate that no treacherous bastard in Vedrana had thought to mention? He studied his options and shaded his eyes with a hand as something small and painfully bright floated in the air overhead, catching his eye. He recalled hearing rumors of this Ampyrian magic, but it was nothing of any significance. The Kind Elders had assured him of that.

Mirvat ignored the ball of radiance and chose a route. He walked quickly. Once he passed through this gate to wherever it led to, he would get far enough from anyone else to be truly alone with his thoughts. Then he could decide what to do next.

Grub

David B. Coe

By day, he sought out the Shattered Gate, walking by it even if this meant going out of his way. After dark, he kept his distance, fearing that the fractured stone, twisted iron, and piles of rubble harbored shadows and wraiths, a haunting of thwarted magic and the restless souls of those trapped on this side.

He never spoke of this—not of his daylight pilgrimages, nor his nighttime terror. He endured enough ridicule in the normal course of his existence. Why invite more?

Today, he'd ventured to the gate later than usual. He stood in the gloaming, on the cusp of eventide, afraid to linger, unable to walk away.

"A'lo, Grub!"

He cringed, cursed. The street-name rankled. He was closer to thirteen than not, old enough at this point to have earned a new one. Most others his age had already shed their childhood tags.

Grub turned, cursed again, under his breath.

Ember and his gang stalked toward him in a loose pack, like wild dogs on the prowl. Grub raised a hand in greeting, fixing a smile on his lips. Not that any of them would be fooled.

You have nothing to be afraid of, said a voice within his mind. *This is commerce. There are rules.*

To which a second voice, this one sounding more frightened, replied, *That only holds if we get as far as commerce. They might just beat us bloody and take the sack.*

Grub had heard the voices before; they were growing more assertive, more distinctive. He wondered if he was going mad. Did that happen to kids his age?

"What got, little Grub?" Ember asked, halting before him.

The others surrounded Grub, silent and menacing. Grub chanced another glance at the darkening sky. He needed to make this quick.

"Norms," he said, slipping into the street patois. "Qual, though, eh?"

"See." A command, not a request.

Grub swung his worn rucksack off his back, set it on the cracked stones, and opened the top. As Ember and the others watched, he pulled out piece after piece, setting them in a precise row on the street. Chipped pitchers and plates; a worn leather purse—empty of course—with a small hole in one corner; a knife with a stone hilt and a notched, dulled blade; a crude wooden doll that was missing a piece of one hand; and a small glass bottle of deep blue, which Grub thought was the pick of the lot. It had a small crack at the lip and was badly scratched, but otherwise it was in good shape; when it was new it would have been worth a lot. He hoped no one would notice it next to the blade and purse.

He should have known better. Ember had an eye for quality.

"How much the bottle?"

Cobble, a boy about Ember's age and size, scowled. "Bottle? What do with that?" He scooped up the blade. "How much this?"

The others watched Ember the way seamen would a cloudy sky. The two closest to Cobble edged away from him.

"How much?" Ember asked again, ignoring the other boy.

Grub stared at the items he'd taken from the sack. He had set prices in his head for every piece except this one. He really didn't want to sell it, but he'd put it out, which meant it was fair game. As the first voice in his mind had said, there were rules to street commerce. One was: no going back once a piece was offered.

He met Ember's gaze. "Twelve."

Cobble laughed. No one else made a sound. Ember stared back at Grub. His eyes were dark brown—almost black—and his hair hung in ebony rings to his shoulders. He had high cheek bones, a white scar on his chin and, Grub knew, another on his forehead, though his hair had grown long enough to hide it. He was lanky, graceful. On those rare occasions when he smiled, he showed straight white teeth. Grub had heard girls in the lanes talk about how beautiful Ember was. He didn't know how to judge such things, but he guessed Ember had heard some of them say this. The boy moved like a person who believed in his own beauty.

Grub wouldn't have dared be so bold with him in any other situation. Ember could have crushed him like a bug, or simply made his life a nightmare by declaring him outcast from this part of the Kaeza district. But this was trade, and they were negotiating, and Ember wasn't allowed to hurt or threaten him in order to get the price he wanted. Another rule of the streets.

These streets at least. Ampyrium rules—not that there were many of those—held sway in trade with beings from other districts. Here, among those descended from the Stranded, things were done differently. Some of the old Kaezan rules lingered from a time when the gate still worked and their old world still awaited them on the other side. Other laws had been lost to the years. Eventually this one might be, too. But not yet, not today.

Ember picked up the bottle and scrutinized it. "Twelve too high. Nine."

They would settle at ten, but Grub wasn't ready to concede that yet.

"I think on it. Meantime..." He gestured at the rest of his wares. Ember hiked a shoulder, accepting this for now. The rest of his crew crowded around the goods. Another boy, Salt, who was only a couple of years older the Grub, picked up the doll, drawing smirks from his companions.

"Ma-sis's birthday," he said, sounding defensive. "Need present."

Cobble laughed again, too loudly. "Yah, sure."

Ember eyed him, his mouth twisting. Grub didn't think he liked the other boy.

Cobble refused to pay six for the blade, but claimed the leather purse, which cost seven. Fly, who wore her hair long on one side and shaved on the other, bought the knife. No one else wanted anything, but if Grub could finish the sale with Ember, he would consider this a good day. So long as he got to his shelter before dark.

Still, he didn't want to rush the sale. A thought had come to him as he waited for Ember's companions to make their choices.

"So, nine." Ember canted his head, eyeing him again.

"Should say ten, but nine, if you give something else."

Ember narrowed his eyes, appearing intrigued.

"New name."

He shook his head. "Grub too perfect."

Grub looked away, pressing his lips thin. He'd heard this before. They called him Grub because he was small and he had a knack for finding stuff. Like the bottle and the purse and the blade. He wasn't afraid to crawl into spaces that scared smaller, younger kids, and even some older ones.

"You young still. Names come when they come. Asking..." Ember shook his head. "Don't work that way."

Grub faced him again. "Then ten."

Ember dipped his chin. "Ten."

They paid him. Coins of copper and tin, some square with rounded corners, others elongated, and still others circular with holes in the middle. Twenty-three amps in all. Enough to keep him fed for days.

Ember paid him last and, as he dropped coins into Grub's palm, he took hold of his wrist, forcing Grub to look up at him.

"Not long for a name," he said in a low voice. "Promise."

Grub couldn't help but grin.

The older boy clicked his tongue, drawing the attention of his gang. "North."

They set out that way, none of them sparing Grub another glance. He returned to his rucksack the items that hadn't sold, regarded the broken gate one last time, and hurried away. A single star shone above the city, pale still in the deepening indigo.

Grub passed others heading for their shelters, including several kids his age. He waved to a few, pointedly ignored a couple, and hid from one, a tall girl who had threatened the previous moonround to beat him bloody after he found and took a well-made cloth cap on territory she claimed as her own. He paused a few paces short of the hidden entrance to his place, scanning the street, trying to appear unconcerned. Everyone knew he lived around here. But only he knew how to access his shelter. He hoped.

If anyone else could get in, they might steal his goods, his clothes, his food. Everything. Just as he could steal from someone if he figured out the way into their place.

He didn't mistrust everyone, and he knew a few people who didn't seem to care if he knew the way inside their shelters. But most among the Stranded lived meal-to-meal, barter-to-barter, theft-to-theft. Trust, Grub had learned, was for fools.

Convinced that no one was watching, he eased closer to the entry, still alert, the straps of his sack gripped tightly in one hand, the other hand in his pocket, fingers wrapped around the hilt of a knife he'd found two years before.

"Do you live around here?"

He whirled at the sound of the voice, stumbling backward and yanking the knife from his pocket. His heart pounded at his ribs, like a trapped rat desperate to be free.

A girl stood a short distance from him. Yellow hair hung loose and lank to her shoulders. Large, pale eyes stared at him from a tapered, dark face that shone with sweat. Damp strands of hair clung to her brow and her neck. She was breathing hard, and she clutched one arm around her middle.

"Where did you come from?"

She bared her teeth in what could have been intended as a smile. It looked more like a grimace. Her teeth were as straight and white as Ember's. "Been following. You look around a lot, but you never bother to check behind you. That's not smart." Her gaze dipped to the blade, met his again. "I'm not going to hurt you. I need your help."

He frowned and lowered the knife, but he wasn't ready to put it away. "You scared me."

"Not my intention. Please, I need to get inside. Quickly."

Grub eyed her more closely. She wore a simple shift, much like those worn by others in the streets. But aside from where sweat had darkened the cloth, around her neck and under her arms, hers was clean, whole. It wasn't even frayed at the edges. She was clean, too. There was no dirt on her face or arms or knees. She didn't look well, but neither did she belong here, on his street, among the Stranded. He guessed that if she weren't sick or hurt, or whatever she was, she would be beautiful.

He realized he was staring and forced himself to look away.

"Where's your home?"

Grub shook his head, gaze fixed on the crumbling stone wall beside him. "No tell." Easier to speak to her in the street patois.

"I don't have time for games. People are after me, and right now you're the only one who can help me."

She took an uncertain step toward him, then a second, and she laid a hand on his shoulder. She was a full head taller than he; Grub thought she must be closer to Ember's age than his own. *Ember would know what to do in this situation.* "I won't stay long. I just...I can help myself, if you just allow me to hide in your place for a short while."

When he didn't answer, she stepped past him. "It's this way, isn't it?" She staggered on, heading unerringly toward the entrance to his shelter. She took a few more steps, until he could no longer contain himself.

"Stop!"

She turned to face him, the motion seeming to take great effort. "Was I getting too close?"

He approached her, anger overmastering shyness. "Who are you? What are you doing here?"

"I live here."

Grub shook his head. "No, you don't. I've lived here all my life, and I've never seen you before."

She stared off to the side. "That means nothing."

"You're too...perfect. Nobody in these streets looks like you do."

Her smile transformed her face, proving his point. "That was a very sweet thing to say."

His cheeks flamed. "I didn't mean it that way."

"You didn't mean to be nice?"

"I meant that you don't live in the streets. I can tell. I'm not stupid."

She shook her head in apparent frustration. "I never said you were. But not everyone who lives—"

The girl broke off, eyes widening, riveted on something behind Grub.

He started to turn.

"Don't." She spoke with her teeth clenched, her lips barely open. "Two Magnum just turned the corner from the Shattered Gate. There's at least one Eye with them."

Grub held himself still, as if a hornet had landed on his neck. "We're not doing anything wrong."

"As if that matters." She stared down at the cobblestones, gave another small shake of her head, making her hair fall like a curtain around her face. "I need to get off the street. Please."

"Why?"

"I'll explain." Her eyes flicked in the direction of the Magnum. "But after we're out of sight. *Please!*"

Grub slanted a glance at the two figures near the end of the street. Tall, shrouded in white, hooded robes, their faces obscured in shadow. A brilliant orb hovered at the shoulder of one—the Eye. They had halted and were surveying the lane. He turned away before they spotted him, though who could tell what the Eye saw?

He had avoided entanglements with the Magnum, had managed not to make himself a target of their interest. The last thing he wanted was to draw their attention now. Best to leave the girl here, allow her to fend for herself. What did he owe her? *She* had followed *him*, after all. Why should he care whether the Magnum took her to wherever they dealt with those who ran afoul of their laws?

The shudder that wracked his form with the thought was answer enough.

"Follow me," he whispered, starting forward, the back of his neck tingling as he imagined the Eye staring after him.

The girl fell in step beside him. "Thank you." She spoke in a whisper as well.

Sweat ran down his back, making him twitch. *I'm not doing anything wrong. I'm just walking home.* But what might the girl have done? Already he had decided this was a bad idea. He very nearly halted, intending to send her away. He regarded her sidelong, noting her delicate features, the taut set of her jaw, her slender hands, which were as clean as her face and clothes. Not a creature of the streets. Certainly not one of the Stranded. She wouldn't survive the night without his help.

They walked on.

At the mouth of the narrow corridor leading to his shelter, Grub halted and gestured her inside. She ducked into the passage, tucking a strand of golden hair behind one ear and eyeing the walls and ceiling with uncertainty.

Grub peered back at the Magnum again. They hadn't moved, but they seemed to be watching him. Them.

"Turds!"

"What?"

He motioned her to keep going and followed close behind her. "They were watching us."

"Are they coming this way?"

"They weren't. I'm not going back to check if they are now."

She stopped before his closed door and leaned against a wall, perhaps to let him pass, perhaps to stay on her feet. It was dark here, but he was aware of her breathing, and a faint scent that surrounded her—floral, sweet, light. As out of place in this part of the city as…he couldn't even imagine what. But it didn't belong. Again the words echoed: *This is a mistake.*

His key hung on a lanyard around his neck and he drew it forth to open the padlock he used to guard his shelter. The lock and key might well have been the most valuable things he possessed; he was smart enough to grasp the irony. But the lock kept out raiders from elsewhere in his district, and any who might encroach on Stranded territory from the other gates. That was happening more and more.

He opened the door, hinges creaking. "Wait here."

Grub entered the shelter, found his flint and a candle, and lit the wick. The candle had less than a finger of wax left. He needed to find a new one soon.

"All right," he said, crossing back to the door. "You can come in now."

She moved past him with an effort that made her gasp and wrinkled her nose at something. Too late it occurred to him how his place would look—and smell—to an outsider. What few clothes he possessed were strewn across the floor. The air smelled of stale sweat, old food, must, even faintly of piss. He wanted to tell her that last was the mice, not him, but he was too embarrassed to admit he smelled it at all.

"You live here by yourself?"

He nodded. "Yes," he added, when he realized she wasn't looking at him.

"It's…nice."

"It a shithole." He retreated into the patois again. "Shitholes everywhere in Stranded terr. I help you. Now, you answer who you are, where you from."

She continued to orbit the small space. "Why do you talk like that?"

"You dress for streets, but you other."

The girl finished her small circle, stopped in front of him, a scowl hardening her features. "Speak normally and I'll answer your questions. First though…" She winced. "I need a moment of privacy."

"What?"

"I know it sounds strange. You'll understand soon, I swear. But I need you to face away from me until I tell you it's all right."

Grub forced a harsh laugh. "You must really think I'm an idiot."

She closed her eyes and shook her head, swaying slightly. "I don't. Not at all. But…I need to get out of this shift, into something else. Something of yours. And I don't want you watching. That's all." She paused, then removed a necklace he hadn't noticed before. The chain was fine, the pendant small but elegantly carved in the shape of a flying dove. Both appeared to be made of gold. She held it out to him, the pendant dangling between them. "You can hold this for me. If I try to take anything of yours, you can keep the necklace."

If it was gold, it was the most valuable thing he'd ever seen much less held. He took it from her and, thinking himself a fool, turned away from her.

"Thank you," she said.

Moments ticked by. He heard clothes rustling. More than made sense. But she didn't attack him, and he didn't think she was stealing anything. As if he had stuff worth stealing.

"All right." Her voice sounded stronger.

Grub faced her once more and froze, his world shifting as if from a ground tremor.

There were three of her.

A Trin. He had heard of them. As far as he knew, he'd never known one until now. Her kind were feared and hated throughout this sector of Ampyrium, and, he'd heard, back in Kaeza as well. In the Kaezan home world, they had been seen as strange, abominations against the gods, dangerous to those who viewed themselves as normal. As a result, they had been hunted down. That practice persisted here, except it was the Magnum who hunted them, who took them…to wherever the Magnum took people they didn't approve of. Most of those taken, it was said, were never seen again. People in the streets feared the girl's kind as well. Many Trins who were discovered by street gangs or random mobs were burned alive or hanged, or simply murdered with a blade in dark corners of the city.

Grub agreed that seeing the girl divided into three versions of herself was odd. But was she a threat? An abomination? Who was he to say? She didn't look any more dangerous now than she had before, except there were more of her.

One of the three still wore the shift. Her arms were down, exposing a blood-stained slit in the cloth over her belly. She had claimed for herself his lone chair. The other two wore items of clothing that had been on his floor. The shirts and pants didn't fit them well, but at least they were covered. In every other respect, the three girls in his shelter appeared identical. They also seemed to be in less discomfort than the single girl had been moments before.

"You know what we are," said the one in the shift. A statement, not a question.

"You're a Trin."

"That's right. By revealing ourselves in this way, we've put ourselves at risk. You can go back outside, find those Magnum, and report us. Me. You literally hold our life in your hands."

"Why did you do it, then? If the danger to you is so great—"

"I was hurt. By splitting into my individual parts, the physical me can heal faster."

Grub tried to react as if he understood what she meant. Clearly, he failed.

"Trins can split into our three component parts—the physical, the emotional, and the logical. We do that sometimes, even when we're not hurt, because there are advantages to giving one element or another dominance. When we are hurt, or sick, removing distractions and allowing our physical to concentrate on healing can speed up the process."

He eyed the other two before looking at her again. "So, you feel no emotion?"

"That's a stupid question," said one of the others. "You just heard her speak. Did she seem to lack all sense of the logical? Have Emotion and I fallen over in lifeless heaps on the floor?"

The third girl frowned at this one. "There's no need to be rude. He's still figuring this out."

"That doesn't mean it wasn't a stupid question."

"The split is never complete," said the one in the shift, drawing Grub's gaze. "I retain some emotion. Pragmatic retains physical control over herself, and some small shred of emotional decency. Emotion has physical control and the ability to think logically."

The one who'd called his question stupid slanted a glance at the third girl. "Questionable, that."

"Obviously, though, there are advantages to giving ourselves over to our emotional selves, or our logical selves, or our physical selves, at different times. Trins can do that."

"That's it?" Grub asked of all of them.

"You think there ought to be more?" Pragmatic asked.

"No. I mean, that's really interesting and everything. It's just…I don't get it. That's why people are so afraid of Trins?"

Pragmatic smiled at him. "That is a far less stupid question."

He grinned back.

"There are advantages to being a Trin," Physical said. "In a place like Ampyrium, where commerce is all, being able to minimize emotional and sensory distractions makes Pragmatic a formidable negotiator. An army of Trins, all of them physicals separated from their emotional and pragmatic selves, would be formidable in a different way."

That made sense, although it didn't explain the viciousness of the assaults on Trins.

"Clerics don't like us," Pragmatic told him. "We're unnatural. There's nothing about us in the teachings of the Ancients, which they see as proof that we're evil."

Grub knew he should respond to this in some way, but in that moment, he couldn't. A memory from just a short while before—a debate within his own mind. That's what he thought it was. That or madness. But what if...

"How do you know if you're a Trin?"

The three of them exchanged glances.

"You're young yet to figure this out," Pragmatic said. "A Trin first gains the ability to split as they pass through puberty."

"Are there hints before then?"

She eyed the others again. "Maybe you should tell us what you've experienced."

Grub shook his head. "I don't think I want to do that."

For several minutes, none of them spoke. Eventually, Pragmatic said to Emotion, "You're uncharacteristically quiet."

"I thought you'd welcome that."

"Most times I would. Under the circumstances, though, you might be best equipped to reassure our young friend here."

"I have no reassurances to give. If he's a Trin, he has a hard road ahead of him. Maybe meeting us will help him prepare, at least teach him to keep quiet about what he feels and does."

Pragmatic dipped her chin. "A surprisingly logical response."

"Can I have some food?" Physical asked.

Grub ignored this for now. He still had too many questions.

"What's your name?"

Physical eyed him from where she sat, leery even of such a simple question.

"Tace," Pragmatic said. "Tacey." She gave an icy smile. "That works for all of us."

It didn't sound like a street name.

"Where do you live?"

"Near the center of the district."

"Our district? With the Stranded?"

"Yes."

"I don't believe you."

"I don't care. It's the truth."

"Then why haven't I ever seen you before?"

Her laugh was sharp, cruel. "Aren't you an arrogant one?"

That stung. He'd been thinking the same of her. Them. "Fine, let's say you are one of us—"

"We are."

"Why are the Magnum looking for you? They are looking for you, aren't they?"

The haughtiness leached from Pragmatic's expression.

"Is it that they know you're a Trin? Did you let them find that out in some way? Or is it something else, something bigger than being a Trin?"

Emotion stared at him, looking young, uncertain. "We're not ready to tell you that."

"You should be. You've put me at risk by coming here."

She narrowed her eyes, and he thought she would deny this. After a moment, though, she conceded the point with a twitch of her shoulder. "Yes, we have. We're sorry for that."

Unexpected.

"Please can I have something to eat," Physical broke in again. "Accelerated healing is hard enough. Without some food in me, it's too draining."

Maybe he should have refused, but he couldn't. It didn't help that all of them were prettier than anyone he'd ever met, or that their scent was filling his shelter, replacing the other smells. He slipped by Pragmatic—why hadn't he noticed before now how small his place was?

"Bread and cheese?"

"You have cheese?" Physical asked, sounding truly surprised.

"And smoked meat. Deruvian sour fruit, too."

"Can I have some of everything?"

"I suppose." He started to pull food from his small larder, regretting having offered so much. "Do all of you need to eat?"

"Sadly, no," Pragmatic said. "We all enjoy eating, but when we're split, Physical gets to do all the fun stuff."

As he gathered the food, Emotion joined him.

"You haven't told us your name."

Grub didn't look back. "None of you asked."

"I'm asking now."

There were two possible answers; he didn't really want to give either, but refusing to tell her anything struck him as rude.

"It's Grub."

"Grub?" Her voice carried a thread of laughter. "As in the little worms you find in garbage?"

"It's my street name, all right?"

"It's not a very good one."

He rounded on her and she backed away a step. "You don't even have one, so you shouldn't talk!"

"How do you know we don't?"

"Because if you did, that's the name you would have given."

None of them argued and he allowed himself a moment of satisfaction. Obviously, they were beyond their depth talking about the streets. Who was this girl?

"Why do they call you that?" Emotion asked, uncertain, her voice low.

Grub turned back to the food. "I'm a scrounger—most of us are—and I'm small. But I'm also fearless when it comes to finding stuff, and I get in places other kids won't go. So that's what they call me." He cast a glance at her. "It's not forever. They'll give me a new name before long. For now, that's the one I've got."

"Who are 'they?'"

"Other kids. Bigger kids. People I know who live and work in the streets." He stared at each of them in turn. "How is it possible that you live in this district but know so little about life here? Who are you?"

Pragmatic wouldn't meet his gaze, and Physical had her eyes closed. Emotion glared. After several seconds, she looked past him at the bread. "Is the food ready?"

He glowered back at her, then piled the bread, meat, cheese, and fruit on an old wooden platter, placed a knife next to the food, and set the platter on the table in front of Physical.

She opened her eyes, sat forward, and wasted no time carving into his cheese and the half-loaf of bread. She did seem to be famished.

"Do you have water?" she asked around a mouthful of food.

With some reluctance, he pulled his skin of water from the rucksack. "There isn't much here. Don't finish it."

She reached for it, but he held it away, eyeing her, awaiting some response.

"I won't. I promise." Mockery tinged the words. "Bala take me if I finish your precious water."

Grub hadn't expected her to invoke the Kaezan goddess. It seemed Tace really was one of the Stranded.

"Why are you looking at me like that?"

"I'm...I'm trying to make sense of all this."

None of them responded, and after some time Grub reached for the knife and bread. He and Physical ate without speaking. Grub stole glances at her. Her color had improved, and she gave no more indications of being in pain. She had a small scar on her forehead, over her left eye, and a pale circle on the fourth finger of her right hand, where she might have normally worn a ring. Had someone taken it from her? Or had she removed it for some reason? Could a ring reveal something of who she was?

Maybe, if she's rich enough and important enough.

He heard this in Ember's voice, and he studied her again, looking for more clues, his gaze dropping repeatedly to her hands. No dirt, no scars, no sores or cuts or scrapes. Even her fingernails were flawless. This wasn't someone who scrounged for food or money, who went to bed at night worrying about her next meal or the lock on her door. The hints were all there, waiting for him to do the math. He'd always been good with numbers, with riddles.

"I know who you are," he told her, them. "Who your father is."

Physical paused in her chewing and stared at him. The other two regarded Grub as well, but he kept his attention on the girl sitting before him. So pretty. So dangerous.

"Perhaps we should leave now," she said. "Thank you for the food."

"I didn't say that to make you leave. But I would like some answers to my questions."

"Sounds like you've answered them yourself."

"Why would the Magnum be after you? That makes no sense."

"Think, Grub. Consider who we are—who you believe us to be. And then consider *what* we are—what you *know* us to be. Do you really have to ask why the Magnum would be interested in us?"

Put that way, he realized she was right. But other questions remained.

"What happened to you? Who cut you?"

"We can't tell you that."

"Can't?"

"Can't. Won't," Pragmatic said. "It amounts to the same thing. We could tell you that by refusing to answer, we're keeping you safe, and in a way it might be true. But the truth is, we're keeping things from you to protect ourself. We're in danger and we need to find our way out of it on our own."

"Will you be able to?"

Emotion's smile made his chest hurt. "We don't know. But thank you for asking."

Physical jammed one last hunk of bread into her mouth and stood.

"How are you feeling?" Pragmatic asked her.

Physical nodded. "We're better. Not fully healed, but close enough." To Grub, she said, "We need you to look away again, to let us become one."

He didn't hesitate this time. Their transition took mere moments. When she said, "It's all right," he turned to find himself alone once more with the girl in the shift. The clothes the other two had used sat folded on his chair. Tace's eyes looked clearer, her features less pinched. Her hair had long since dried. It was as light and fine as spun gold. He supposed. He'd never seen any such thing, of course.

"Do you want me to walk with you to your house?" As much as Grub didn't like to be out in the streets after dark, he would have done it for her.

"You're kind to offer. But I'll be fine." She drew herself up, seeming very much the daughter of important parents. "Thank you for the food and the water, and for giving us—me—time to rest and heal. That was helpful."

She stepped past him toward the door.

"What does it feel like?" he asked before she could leave. "When you split and you join, does it...does it hurt?"

"No. Not at all. It takes some concentration at first. Eventually, it becomes as easy and natural as speaking or walking." She reached for the door handle.

"Oh, it's locked." Grub hurried to her side, fumbling for the key. He unlocked the door and stepped back out of her way. Before she could let herself out, though, he remembered her necklace. "Wait!" He strode to the table, retrieved it, and brought it to her.

"Anything else?" she asked, appearing amused.

"Y-yes. My real name is Marsin."

She canted her head. "Thank you for telling me that."

She regarded him for another moment before walking out. She shut the door behind her almost silently. Grub listened as her footsteps retreated. When he could no longer hear her, he locked the door again and put the food away. He hadn't eaten much, but he wasn't hungry. He wondered if the Magnum and Eye were still waiting outside. A part of him wanted to check, but even if they were, what could he do? She was older than he was, smarter, probably stronger, and she was daughter to the regent of the Stranded. She'd be all right.

But he wanted to know more about being a Trin. And he wanted another chance to speak with her, without all the questions and evasions, without worrying about who might be after her. He didn't imagine he'd ever have that chance again.

* * *

The shelter still smelled of her when Grub woke. Hungry now, he ate most of his remaining food, dressed, shouldered his sack, and left the shelter. The sky over Ampyrium was clear, and a cold wind whipped through the lanes, carrying the smells of fish and tar, cooking fires and roasting meat. A Magnum stood at one end of his street, still as a statue, robed in white. An Eye hovered at the other end, gleaming balefully in the shadows of old buildings.

Grub tried to ignore them, but as he set out northward, the Magnum started in his direction. Glancing back, he saw that the Eye was following, and was gaining on him.

Turds! What had Tace done to him?

He turned off the street before either of them caught up with him, and, once out of sight, sprinted for the next corner. Before reaching it, he turned again and veered into a narrow, covered alleyway that accessed the catacombs, ancient tunnels beneath the streets. The older kids claimed these had once been tombs, but Grub had dismissed these tales as attempts to scare him and the other younger ones. That said, he rarely used the tunnels, even when it would be convenient or helpful. Why risk an encounter with a wraith or revenant if he didn't have to? Only the pursuit of an Eye and Magnum could have driven him underground.

Torches burned at intervals in the tunnels, maintained, he understood, by merchants of the shadow market, who used the catacombs regularly. He'd never heard of Magnum entering the tunnels. Not because they were afraid— the Magnum feared nothing and no one—but rather because they took a percentage of all that happened under the city, and were happy to let the shadow trade flourish so long as they received their cut.

It took Grub several moments to orient himself to the dark passages, but eventually he figured out which way was which and set out for the heart of Stranded territory. He wasn't sure why he chose the destination he did. He didn't like visiting her, and she gave little indication that she cared about him. But she knew things, had spent enough time on the streets to understand its rhythms and mysteries, and he needed information, preferably from someone who wouldn't make him pay. At least not a lot.

When Grub thought he had covered enough distance underground, he found a stairway back to the street and climbed cautiously. At the mouth of this spur of tunnel, he paused to scan the lanes and the sky. Seeing no Magnum and no Eyes, he stepped into the street and navigated the remaining distance past ramshackle shelters and worn-down peddlers' carts. Fires burned in the open on cobblestones, some offering warmth, others crackling beneath spits that held fowl, rodents, and the occasional feral pig. Men, women, and children in threadbare clothing and half-finger gloves marked him as he passed, appraisal and suspicion in their glances. No one here knew him—not as they did in the streets around his home. He tried to keep his gaze on the lane ahead of him. He certainly didn't stare or say anything. The last thing he wanted was more attention.

Her shelter was much as he remembered it—a bit nicer than those around it, and vastly better than his own. She had wooden walls and overlaid scraps of metal for her roof. A sailor had built it for her—him and his friends. That was what she told Grub a few years before. A favor she said. Only as Grub grew older did he come to understand what that meant, and what sort of favor she had granted in return for the comfort and security she enjoyed.

He approached her door, halted, glanced around. No one seemed to be watching or listening.

"A'lo, Jikenna!" he called. She had made it clear to him years ago that she preferred to be called by her name. Not by "Mama" or "Mother." It wasn't just him; she was this way with all her sons and daughters.

At first, he heard no response, and he wondered if she might be in the market or somewhere else in the city. He should have known better.

"Who that?" she called from within. Her voice sounded raspy, the words slightly slurred.

Grub shifted his feet, uncomfortable already. "It Marsin. Talk a bit?"

Footsteps echoed, uneven. A piece of furniture shifted and she muttered a curse. Finally, the door opened. She wore a robe that was almost sheer, and beneath it a shift that was much tighter and far less clean than the one Tace had worn. She was barefoot, and her hair, auburn still, and as thick as a lion's mane, fell to her shoulders. She had a sharp nose and full lips, large dark eyes and rounded cheeks. She was said to be beautiful. He'd heard this on his own streets, from men who didn't know he was one of her sons. He supposed she was, if a boy could judge such a thing about his own mother.

She smiled at the sight of him, lines crinkling around her eyes and mouth.

"You look good. A little thin. Come in. I feed you."

"Ate already."

Her expression hardened. "That supposed to impress me? That you can feed yourself? That you don't need me? You came here, to me, eh?"

He dropped his gaze. "I'm sorry. I didn't mean anything by it. I was just saying I don't need food. But I do need help. Information. I would like to come in, if I may."

She started back into the house, but not before making a vague gesture that Grub took as an invitation, or at least acquiescence. He followed her inside.

Jikenna's shelter was the nicest Grub had ever seen, though, honestly, he hadn't been in many, other than his own. She had a good deal of space, enough to have separate rooms, as people were said to in some of the wealthy parts of Ampyrium. There was an outer room where she had chairs, a low table, and a sofa. She had a separate kitchen, with a makeshift chimney that vented through the metal roof, and a separate sleeping room as well. The place was a mess—clothes and other belongings were scattered across her stone floor and on the furniture—but this was normal for her.

The shelter smelled of smoke and her perfume—a heavy, sweet scent he had never liked. But it was warm, comfortable. Someday he would figure out how to rig a chimney for his shelter. He dreaded the cold of the coming winter.

She put a pot on her cooking grate. "I'm having tea. Kaezan mint. You want?"

In recent moonrounds, he had seen Kaezan mint being sold in one marketplace or another and he wondered how this was possible. The gate to Kaeza had been broken for decades. Surely, any stash of tea had long since been discovered and consumed. Maybe someone was growing it somewhere nearby, but he doubted this. More likely, some peddlers realized that if they labeled common mint as "Kaezan," it would seem exotic and would fetch a better price. They would have found a willing buyer in Jikenna, who, despite being too young to have ever set foot in the world beyond their gate, worshipped all things Kaezan.

Of course, he couldn't say any of this to her. Nor could he refuse the tea, having already turned down her offer of food.

"Yes, please. With honey, if you have it."

A faint smile greeted this. "Of course."

He started to wander around the shelter, only to realize he was doing precisely what Tace had done the evening before. He stopped and made himself sit on the sofa.

"They still calling you by that awful name?"

"It's not so bad."

She had been bent over the kettle in her kitchen, but she straightened now. "I'll take that as a yes."

"I'll be old enough for a better name soon. In the meantime—"

He'd intended to say something about the string of sales he'd made recently, but that would lead to requests for money, and he didn't want to give her the opportunity. As it was, her gaze had sharpened at his hesitation.

Grub covered his reticence with a small lift of his shoulder. "—it's not so bad. It's just a name, right?"

"I suppose." She turned her attention back to the tea.

Silence settled over them, until at last Jikenna brought him a steaming cup. "I have sweet rolls. You sure you don't want nothing?"

He was sure, but he needed her help and didn't want to incur her ire a second time. "A sweet roll would be great. Thanks."

Another smile, warmer than the last. She brought out the rolls and her tea and settled into a plush, stained chair next to his end of the sofa.

"Now, what do you need from me?"

"I met someone yesterday. It was…strange, and you know more about the district and its politics than I do."

Flattery and a mystery; she couldn't resist. She straightened, watching him, avid for more.

He recounted his encounter with Tace and shared just a bit of his conversation with her, making no mention of anything having to do with Trins. Jikenna listened closely, frowning at times, at others, motioning for him to hurry the tale along. When he mentioned giving the girl food, she interrupted to ask, "How much you get for it?"

"What?"

"How much did you make her pay for the food?"

Grub shook his head. "I didn't…I…I just gave it to her."

She sagged, appearing disgusted. "You saw she was clean. You said so. And you guessed that she wasn't from the streets. And still you ask for nothing. Bala help me. I thought I taught you better."

A dozen responses leapt to mind, none of them likely to take their exchange in a helpful direction. She *had* taught him better, but only by showing him how miserable a person could be if they turned every conversation into a transaction.

"Do you know who she was?" he asked, trying to move Jikenna past her disapproval.

"She was pretty, yes?"

Grub's cheeks warmed, drawing a bark of laughter from his mother.

"I thought as much. You want to find her again."

"I live in the streets. I don't think she does. I'd be crazy to care about her."

"True. But love makes us do crazy things."

His face grew hotter, and she laughed again, though with more kindness.

"I don't love her, and she wouldn't be interested in a kid like me. I'm just… curious."

"I see."

He knew another denial would do him no good. And he wasn't completely certain she was wrong. "So?" he asked instead. "Do you know who she was?"

"Who do *you* think she was?"

He faltered, not wishing to give her another reason to ridicule him. But eventually he said, "My best guess is that she's the regent's daughter."

"Did you ask if she was?"

"No. But it would explain a lot—her clothes, the way she looked, the Magnums' interest in her."

"I think you're right. She has the name right, too. The regent has a daughter named Tacey. She could lie about that, of course. But given the rest…" Her turn to hike a shoulder. "You have to remember, though: she's his only daughter. Regents and such aren't like the rest of us. No ma-brothers and da-sisters. He has one mate, and they have three kids. That's all. Tacey is the oldest, and the only girl."

This much, Grub knew. He had heard stories of the lavish wedding the regent and his consort had when Grub was still in diapers. No one in the street married, not since the destruction of the gate. The Stranded were doomed to extinction if they lived under the old customs. The only way to grow their population was to mate and breed freely. That, at least, was the thinking of his people. Given how many of them lived in shelters that barely kept out rain and snow, cold and wind, he wasn't entirely convinced.

But even this served only to perplex him more. If she actually was *the* Tacey, why would she leave the comfort of the Regent House and the security of her normal family? Who would attack her and why?

"What would the regent's daughter be doing in the streets?"

"That I don't know." Jikenna grinned. "Good mystery, that. You find out, you tell me."

"I will. Do you like the regent?"

She sipped her tea, eyeing him coyly over the rim of her cup. "I don't know the regent."

"That's not what I meant, and you know it."

"He's no worse than the last, or the one before that. Then again, he's no better, either. Since he took power, the gate has gotten no closer to being repaired or replaced. And other districts are encroaching on our territory as never before. So, maybe he *is* worse."

"There was a Magnum outside my shelter this morning. I lost him and the Eye, but they're interested in me now."

"They were already interested in you. You my boy. That makes them interested. If you don't have a few Magnum and a couple of Eyes watching you now and then, you wasting your time."

Grub grinned. He ate his sweet roll and drank his tea, enjoying this moment of approval. When he finished, he carried his cup and plate back to her kitchen.

"You always had manners. I like that about you. Your father had manners."

He turned, surprised. She rarely spoke of his father or, as far as he knew, the fathers of her other children.

"One of your ma-sisters works in the Regent House. Her name is Dasia. If you decide you want to know more about the girl."

"Really? What does she do there?"

Jikenna opened her hands. "I don't know. She told me once. I don't remember. Runs errands for people more powerful than she is, most likely. Her father got her the job." She walked to him, ruffled his hair, then cupped his cheek with a hand. A rare display of affection in a visit filled with surprises. "Go now. I have things to do." The warmth in her eyes softened her words. "I'm sorry for what I said about the food. You're kind is all. That's not a bad thing."

"Thank you, Jikenna."

He exited her shelter and paused a moment to stare off in the direction of the Regent House. What would it be like to work there, to spend his time among important, powerful people, rather than in the streets, scrounging like the other children of the Stranded? He laughed at himself, knowing he wouldn't find out any time soon, if ever. He started back toward his home.

Before he'd taken five steps, he saw an Eye swoop into view ahead of him, gleaming like a small moon. Grub halted, took a step back.

"Do not."

The words came at him from several directions at once. He spun. Magnum had him surrounded. One behind him, two more emerging from buildings on either side of the street. A fourth followed the Eye from its hiding spot.

There were people in the lane. None of them looked at him, or at the Magnum. They went about their business, gazes lowered, mouths pressed in taut, thin lines. No one wanted to draw the attention of the Magnum; none would risk themselves to help a dirt-covered nobody in ill-fitting clothes. Grub couldn't blame them.

The robed figures converged on him, appearing to float along the street. Grub stared at the one ahead of him, the one with the Eye at their shoulder, trying to see what lurked within the hood of that white robe. It was a bright day. Something should have been visible—the contour of the Magnum's features, the reflection of a person's eye. Anything.

But no. He saw only darkness. A shiver passed through him, making him jerk.

"You will walk with us," the Magnum said, speaking alone this time. The voice sounded low, but female.

"Where are you taking me?"

"You will walk with us."

So much for getting information.

The other Magnum surrounded him, almost as if they were guarding him from some external threat, though he knew better. They herded him along the street away from the regent's residence and then onto a narrow alleyway.

Grub's pulse raced and his hands shook. He wanted to protest his innocence, but he didn't even know what they thought he had done.

You spoke to the regent's daughter. You fed her.

Could that be considered a crime?

Maybe, if she's a Trin.

"Your given name?" the Magnum demanded.

"Don't you know that?"

No reply.

"Marsin, son of Jikenna and...and..." Jikenna had told him his father's name long ago, but he'd never met the man, and now he couldn't remember.

"That is sufficient. You met a girl yesterday at undece, on Kevari Street. Do you recall the encounter?"

Was that really the name of his street? "Yeah, of course I do."

"Two Magnum tried to engage with you at that time. You fled from them. Why?"

Turds. He swallowed. Despite the cold, sweat tickled his spine, his temples. "She asked me to. She was...she was frightened. Or she said she was."

"And so you broke the law."

Grub thought it best to say nothing.

"Had you met this girl before?"

"No! Never!"

"Then what made her choose you?"

Grub went still as death. What *had* made her choose him? He'd assumed random chance led her to his street and to him. But what if it was something more? What if she sensed that he would someday be a Trin and *that* was why she chose him? He didn't even know if Trins could sense others of their kind, much less a person who might someday become one. But he had no other explanation for her being on his street just as he returned home.

"I don't know," he said. "It was just...chance."

"We deem this unlikely."

"Then you should ask her, because I don't know."

Too late, he realized that people usually didn't speak to the Magnum in that way, at least not if they wanted to remain free and alive. And definitely not if the Magnum had reason to believe they were Trins.

"We would ask her, but she has vanished. As far as we know, you are the last to have seen her, which makes you the most likely suspect if it turns out she has come to harm."

Bala's tits! What had she gotten him into? "I didn't do anything to her! I gave her food. That's all. She was fine when she left my shelter!"

"And where did she go from there?"

"I don't know! She didn't say where she was going!"

"Your responses strike us as evasive."

"That's because I don't know anything!"

The Magnum turned its head so the dark, empty hood was directed at its companions. For long moments, none of them spoke, at least not that Grub could hear. He had the distinct sense that the Magnum were communicating in some way among themselves. Through it all, the Eye floated before him, brilliant and unblinking. Grub held himself motionless and tried not to stare back at the orb.

At last, the Magnum turned back to him. "We will speak with you again."

That was all. The robed figures pivoted as one and walked away. The Eye lingered briefly, still watching him. Then it swooped after its masters.

Once alone, Grub sagged. By now his entire body was trembling and he struggled to draw breath. After taking a centcount or two to regain his composure and slow his pulse, he glanced around. Others on the street continued to ignore him. A short time before, he'd understood, had even guessed, he would do the same in their position. Now, their indifference angered him.

Perhaps that was why he didn't head back to his shelter. Nor did he commence his usual hunt for discarded items that he might sell. Instead, he strode toward the Regent House, following the instinct that had nearly driven him eastward immediately after his conversation with Jikenna.

Yes, the Magnum or one of their Eyes might follow him. So what? He wasn't doing anything wrong. There were no laws against walking in this direction. People passed by the Regent House every day. Why shouldn't he? This is what he told himself as he walked, fighting the impulse to peer back over his shoulder every few ticks.

As he put more distance between himself and the Shattered Gate he noticed subtle changes in the streets and buildings. All of the Kaezan District had suffered since the destruction of the portal. Even he could see that. He refused to believe their part of Ampyrium had always been so dilapidated and sad. But the decay was worst near the gate. The farther from it he walked—the closer he drew to the Regent House—the more the lanes came to resemble those he had glimpsed in other districts.

Shelters like his—pieced together with junk—gave way to more traditional homes, in buildings fronted by clean walkways. The structures weren't fancy, at least not anymore. They might have been once, but they looked tired now, the stonework stained and chipped, the windows clouded, the wooden doors worn gray by wind and rain and sun. But they appeared solid and far more comfortable than his home.

Grub spotted the Regent House several city blocks before he reached it. The street he was on ended at the low stone wall of the residence. Beyond it, a vivid green lawn sloped up to the house, a startling expanse of color amid the stone and ancient brick.

The house itself had as much in common with the neighboring homes as its garden did with the cobblestone streets and byways. The gray stone façade was immaculate and the windows glittered with sunlight. White columns defined a half-moon portico, and two guards in clean white uniforms stood on either side of the double-doored entrance.

Coming here had seemed like a fine idea, but now that he had arrived, Grub was at a loss as to what to do next. According to the Magnum, Tacey was missing. And while he might have had a sister in the regent's office, his sister didn't know him and was probably as reluctant as he to place much faith in anyone Jikenna claimed was her sibling. He couldn't imagine those forbidding guards allowing him into the building and, even if they did, who would he speak to and what might he say?

He'd allowed gossamer hair, stunning gray eyes, and an elusive scent to draw him from the safety of his familiar streets.

"Turd for brains," he muttered to himself, starting back toward home.

He'd take a different route, use the opportunity to scrounge for new goods. Maybe he'd get a sale or two out of this waste of time.

Grub continued to berate himself as he walked, and so was barely aware of passing a shadowed alleyway. As he did, though, someone grabbed him by his collar, clamped a hand over his mouth, and dragged him into the filthy byway. He flailed and twisted, trying to break free, but his captor held him fast. At last, some distance from the mouth of the alley, he was thrown to the ground. He landed in a rank puddle that smelled of rotting food and other things he didn't care to name. He scrambled up and whirled, grabbing for his knife, only to stop and glare.

Tacey stood a few steps away, glowering back at him. "What are you doing here? Who sent you after me?"

"No one! I—"

"The Magnum got to you, didn't they?"

"No! I mean, yes, they stopped me, questioned me. But I didn't tell them a thing! I swear!"

"Then why would you come to my house?"

"I wanted to see you again!" He snapped his mouth shut, feeling his face heat.

She stared, her expression softening. "You wanted… What did you think would happen when you did?"

Grub shook his head and said nothing, refusing to look at her. He wished he were anywhere else.

"Grub—"

"Don't say it, all right? You're way older than I am, not to mention important and rich and…and there's no reason why you would want to have anything to do with a runty street rat like me."

"I'm not sure any of that is true, except the part about me being older. But right now, I'm a dangerous person to be around."

At that, he looked up. "I know. That's the other reason I'm here. I'm a Trin, too. I'm sure of it."

She glanced around them, stepped closer. "Have you split?"

"Not yet. But…but there are voices. I hear them all the time, arguing in my head the way your different parts did. They're my Emotion and Pragmatic. I can tell."

Tace chewed her lip. In time, she nodded. "I remember experiencing the same thing."

Cold washed through him. A part of him had hoped she would dismiss what he'd told her, deny that the voices he heard meant anything. Another part had known she wouldn't. Frightened as he was, he preferred to know. He recalled what Tace's Emotion had said the day before: *Maybe meeting us will help him prepare…* He knew already that it would.

"I'm not sure I can help you with this," she said, filling a growing silence. "Both of us have to keep this secret, like all Trins do."

"Seems like your secret's already out."

She frowned, and he feared he'd angered her. A heartbeat later, she raked a hand through her hair and blew out a breath. "You're right. All the more reason for you to stay away from me."

"Or, all the more reason for us to be friends. It'll help me talking to someone who knows and understands. And maybe that'll be helpful for you, too. And we can watch each other's backs, keep an eye out for people who might want to hurt us."

"Maybe." She didn't sound convinced.

"Did you know the person who attacked you?"

She eyed him for several moments, as if weighing whether or not to answer. "No. I'd never seen him before."

"All right. Then, who knows you're a Trin?"

"I didn't think anyone did." She shrugged. "I guess my parents might. Or someone who works in the house. I tried to be careful, but—"

"Your parents wouldn't try to hurt you, would they?"

She considered this. "I don't think so."

"Would someone else in the house?"

"I don't know. Possibly, if they were devoted enough to the old faith, or had ties to the Magnum." She shook her head. "That last is unlikely—they're as afraid of the Magnum as anyone. But almost all of them go to the shrine every other day."

"And what would the clerics do if they thought a Trin was next in line to be regent of the district?"

Tacey's eyes widened. "Turds," she whispered, sounding more like one of the Stranded than she had at any point since they met. "They'd try to kill me." She stared past him toward the mouth of the alley. "That's not the real question, though. What I need to figure out is, who would my parents side with: me or the clerics?"

Grub thought the answer should have been clear. Then again, he didn't think Jikenna would have hesitated to choose the old faith over him.

"Shouldn't we find out first if it was the clerics who sent the killer after you?"

"How?"

The idea that came to him then was, he believed, rather brilliant, except for one obvious flaw. Obvious to him; she would have no idea. And he could live with that if it meant helping her. First, though, he needed to try something new.

* * *

Later that day, perhaps a clockround before dusk, Grub walked with Tacey to Rénu's Shrine, which was not far from the Regent House. Like Tace's home, the god's sanctuary looked out of place in the drab squalor of the Strandeds' district. It was an ancient building, one of the few still standing along these streets, and its spires and carved gables were delicate and beautiful, even to Grub, who knew nothing about old buildings.

A huge oval window above the front portal and its twin oaken doors held colored glass that created an image of the god inside the shrine. Tacey told him it was quite stunning. This wasn't a day to risk seeing it for himself.

The first part of his plan was simple, and risky. Tacey had been missing for almost two days now. Her parents had to be frantic; she assumed they had guards scouring the district for her, and others making inquiries with the Magnum and with the leaders of other districts. The clerics had to know of her disappearance as well, and so their response to her arrival in the temple would be telling. So, too, would what they chose to do with her.

Worshippers had begun to fill the shrine for the sunset devotions, making it unlikely that she would be abducted or hurt while inside. More likely, if the clerics were behind the previous day's attack, they would make another attempt on her life between the shrine and the Regent House. Grub and Tacey were counting on that.

Tacey wore one of Grub's shirts over her shift, hiding the slit in the fabric and the bloodstain from her injury. She had tied back her hair, but otherwise looked much as she had the day before. She wanted to be recognized.

Grub walked with her to the gate in the fence surrounding the sanctuary grounds. From there, she was on her own. He retreated to a stretch of lane from which he could see the shrine entrance and began to scrounge the walkway, all the while monitoring the arched doorway. He actually found a small nickel brooch and a child's bracelet, both of which would bring him some coin. Mostly, though, he waited for Tace, his apprehension building steadily. He felt strange, oddly detached, but also strong, confident. His fears should have overmastered his courage by now. They hadn't.

The sky had started to cloud over, and a steady wind blew in off the Tragian Sea, heavy with brine and the promise of rain. Already, shadows engulfed the narrower lanes. Windows and shelters began to glow with candlelight and the blaze of oil lamps. Grub hadn't been by the Shattered Gate all day. It seemed he wouldn't be back in his shelter before nightfall. An odd day, to say the least.

And it wasn't getting any better. Centcounts crawled by without any sign of Tace. Supplicants continued to file into the shrine, but no one emerged. At least not through the main entrance. It occurred to Grub that there had to be other exits and entrances. Someone could have dragged Tace out through a doorway on the far side of the sanctuary and he would be completely unaware. Panic threatened to flood his chest, yet his thinking remained clear. Neither of them had considered this, though now he realized that they should have, that any fool would have taken precautions against such a possibility.

Turds!

He couldn't leave to check for other entryways. What if she came out while he was gone? He also wasn't ready yet to risk going inside. He could only remain where he was and wait.

The sky darkened. Grub muttered to himself under his breath, drawing stares from passers-by. There were other components to this plan, other factors to consider—constraints on his time, on his ability to help her. The longer he waited, the more uncertain everything grew.

The flow of worshippers had slowed to a trickle. No doubt the evening devotions were about to begin. Grub had made up his mind to enter the shrine and search for Tace when one of the double doors opened a bit, so that a shaft of light carved across the front courtyard and pooled on the stone. Two figures slipped out of the building: Tace, trailed by someone in a dark robe, fringed in lighter piping. A cleric? To accompany a girl to her home?

Not just a girl. The regent's daughter, and a Trin.

As Tace and the cleric exited the sanctuary grounds, Grub emerged from his hiding place and approached them. Tace shifted directions slightly to meet him in the middle of the street.

The cleric slowed, then halted, regarding them both with unconcealed suspicion. "Who is this?"

She was young, probably only a few years older than Tace, with dark, short-cropped hair, and angular features that gave her a severe appearance. She stood two hands taller than Tace, with broad shoulders. Grub thought she looked more fit than any cleric he had ever seen.

"This is my friend," Tace said with an innocent smile. "He gave me some food and water, and he wanted to be sure I had a place to stay tonight."

"Well, now that you're going home, I don't believe he needs to accompany us." She barely glanced his way. "You can go to…wherever it is you live. You're not needed anymore."

Grub hoped his grin conveyed the same naïve, trusting simplicity Tace's had. "That's all right. I don't mind!"

He thought the cleric might argue, but instead she stepped past them and gestured sharply for the two of them to follow. Without a word passing between them, Tace and Grub fell in behind her and followed her up the lane. As they did, Grub glimpsed another form, lithe and quick, dressed in ill-fitting clothes, darting into a parallel byway.

He said nothing.

At first, they walked in the direction of the Regent House, but before long the cleric turned off the street they were on and entered a poorly lit, foul-smelling alley. One could have argued that they were still on course for Tace's home, but Tace and Grub shared a grim glance before following the cleric. Upon entering, they halted, seeing no sign of the woman. Another look passed between them. The cleric expected them to call for her, to walk farther into the gloom, to trust. And for the moment, that was what they chose to do.

"Sister Gesel?" Tace called, venturing deeper into the alley. Grub walked behind her, his knife in hand. He swept the byway with his glance, but he could see little. His heartbeat echoed in his ears like a drum.

Tace eased forward another couple of steps. A refuse can fell over with an echoing metallic clang. Tace cried out. Grub charged forward with his knife raised, only to be struck hard in the gut. He grunted, folded in on himself. A second blow, this one to the back of his neck, drove him to the paving stones and left him addled.

"Let her go, cleric!" A boy's voice, deeper by far than Grub's.

Firelight brightened the alley, from ahead of them and behind. Ember's gang, as they had arranged.

"Get out of here," the cleric said, sounding self-assured and dismissive, "before one of you gets hurt."

"Release her, and maybe you walk out of here alive."

The woman laughed. "The girl is not your concern. Now leave!"

Grub looked up at her, his vision swimming, the scene around him spinning to sickening effect. The cleric stood with her back to one of the stone walls defining the byway. She held Tace in front of her like a shield, an arm crooked around the girl's neck, a long, lethal-looking blade pressed to Tace's throat. When the pitch and roll proved too much for him, Grub squeezed his eyes shut against his dizziness.

"We'll leave with her. And if you kill her, you're a dead woman."

"Do you know who you're defending?" The woman's voice dripped with contempt. "She's a filthy Trin. An abomination. She is foul, not worthy of the air she breathes. Bala and Rénu agree on that much. The Two, who exist in opposition to one another, whose differences define our universe—even they are as one in this single respect. And you defend her? You defy them?"

Grub held his breath. He and Tace had told Ember and the others nearly everything. The gang knew the Magnum were after her, that the clerics wanted to hurt her or worse, that even the regent and consort might wish her harm. They had been as honest as they felt they could be. But this—the fact that Tace was a Trin, that both of them were—they had kept to themselves as best they could. That was how much Trins were despised, even in the streets.

Grub opened his eyes again and watched Ember, trying to anticipate his response. The older boy glared a moment longer at the cleric before glancing back at the gang members behind him. Grub couldn't tell what passed among them, but a moment later, he faced forward again.

And he gave the most uncaring of shrugs. "I can't say I give a turd. Let her go and you can live. Harm her and you will die."

"Have you ever killed before, boy?"

At that, Ember's expression wavered, like a candle flame guttering in a sudden draft.

Sister Gesel laughed. "I thought not. I have, and I will again if it serves the God and Goddess. Gladly. And I will kill this one right before your eyes if you don't leave us now."

Grub eyed the cleric. His vision was clearing, and he still held his blade. He didn't know if he could do anything with it without endangering Tace. And he didn't dare move and draw attention to himself. All of them appeared to have forgotten him. Hardly surprising.

Well, all of them except Tace. She dropped her gaze to meet his. Grub shifted his blade ever so slightly. Her eyes widened. Then she winked.

He would have only one chance to get this right, and not a lot of time. The cleric was close enough to lash out at him with a kick, if she didn't simply jam her blade into Tace's neck.

Grub tightened his grip on the knife. Ember said something about this being as good a night as any for his first kill, but Grub wasn't listening. He took a breath, readied himself. It was helpful, he realized, not having his emotional and pragmatic selves around to talk him out of what he had to do.

Even he hadn't known he could move so fast. He levered himself up and in the same motion hammered his knife into the back of the cleric's knee. It went in hilt-deep. Blood spurted and the blade scraped on bone. Gesel howled, jerked, collapsed. Tace cried out, fell away from the woman. The cleric swept at Grub with her knife. He rolled beyond her reach.

Before she could do more, Ember and his gang fell upon her with fists and feet, knives and bottles and torches and anything else at hand. She fought back but not successfully and not for long. Grub crawled to Tace. She bled from a gash on her neck, but it didn't look serious, certainly not bad enough to kill.

"All right?" Grub asked.

She nodded. "You?"

"Never better."

He stood, and after steadying himself, helped her to her feet. The cleric no longer moved. She might have been unconscious; Grub assumed she was dead. She looked a mess—bruised and bloodied and burned. Ember sauntered toward them, eyeing Tace. She stared back at him, grim and wary.

"Thank you," she said. "I'm in your debt."

"To the tune of twenty silvers. Each!"

"You'll get your money. I promise."

He dipped his chin, turned to Grub, and extended his hand. He held Grub's knife. Grub took it from him. The blade had already been cleaned, so he returned it to his pocket.

"That was impressive," Ember said. "You struck hard and fast and true. A lot of older kids would have done far worse. I'm thinking 'Adder,' like the snake. What you think?"

Grub nodded, grinned. "Like it."

Tace had joined the others in Ember's gang. Since coming up with his plan, Grub had assumed he would lose her to Ember himself, with his curls and dark eyes. But she was talking to Fly, both of them acting nervous. Tace played with her hair; Fly toyed with the knife Grub had sold her the day before.

"She really a Trin?" Ember asked.

Grub wasn't sure it was his place to say. Then again, Ember and his gang had saved their lives. "She is."

"And you knew all along." Ember didn't offer this as a question.

He had to know. He had seen the other Grubs, or at least one of them. They had delivered messages to him and his gang as Grub and Tace walked with the cleric. Surely a boy as smart as Ember had figured out all of this by now.

"Yeah. I knew. I chose to help her anyway, just like you did."

"And she's really the regent's daughter?"

"Yeah." Grub looked him in the eye. "Guess Trins can show up anywhere."

Ember nodded slowly, clearly thinking this through. "I guess they can. That's fine with me, as long as they follow the laws of the street. And as long as they handle a knife like you do."

A groan from the cleric silenced them all. It seemed she had survived the beating. Ember gestured, and he and his gang melted in the gloaming. Within seconds, Tace and Grub were alone with the woman. They didn't linger, but crept to the far end of the alley and, upon checking to make sure no one was watching the broader street, continued toward the Regent House. In the next alley, Pragmatic Grub and Emotional Grub met them. Tace turned her back, and all three Grubs stripped down, then blended, becoming one, himself, whole again.

The first time, earlier in the day, when he had forced himself to split and then rejoin, the transitions had been disorienting and unpleasant. Not painful, but uncomfortable. This second time, they proved far more simple. They didn't feel effortless or natural. Not yet. But if what Tace had told him was true, this new element of his life would only get easier.

As he dressed, he felt an odd mixture of embarrassment and pride, of wonder and foreboding. He was a Trin. No wondering about it anymore. He just was. His life would never be the same.

Grub told Tace she could turn around, but after that, neither of them spoke. Grub sensed Tace's apprehension. The gash on her neck had stopped bleeding, but it was stark and angry against her bronze skin, evidence of how close she'd come to dying tonight.

"You did well," she said, after they had walked some distance. "How do you feel?"

"I'm not sure yet. I don't think I will be for a little while."

She gave a faint smile. "Pragmatic me approves of that answer." Her smile faded and they lapsed back into uneasy silence.

He watched her. "Your mother and father will be glad to have you home."

"I'm not so sure."

"Is being a Trin hereditary?"

She faltered in mid-stride. "I don't know. I suppose it might be."

"Something like that, it would almost have to be. Which means, you might be about to learn something amazing about one or both of them."

She eyed him. "You, too, right?"

He stared straight ahead. "It'll be my father. I'm sure of it. And I haven't seen him in years."

They fell silent again, though not for long.

"You really deserve a better name. I don't like calling you…by that one."

He couldn't keep from smiling. "Ember gave me a new one."

"Ember did? He has that power, does he?"

"Well…yeah. He's a big deal around here. And he happens to have saved our lives."

She sent a sly glance his way. "The way I see it, you did that. But fine, what's your new name?"

Her first remark had made his head spin, but he pushed past his delight and discomfort. "Adder." She stared blankly, and he added, "You know, like the snake. Because I struck at the cleric so…so fast."

If he had to explain it, maybe it wasn't such a great name after all.

"Well, it's better than Grub," she said. "But if it's all right with you, I'd like to use Marsin."

"I can live with that."

As they neared the Regent House, he slowed, forcing her to do the same.

"What are you doing? I want you to meet my parents. They'll want to thank you."

He gazed at the house and gave a small shake of his head. "I don't think so. Not yet. Not tonight."

"Are you sure?"

He nodded, eyes still on the house. "I have a sister who works there. My mother told me."

"Really? What's her name? Maybe I know her."

With all that had happened this day, it took him a few moments to remember. "Dasia."

"Oh, I know her. Not well. She works for my mother. But she seems nice. You should come and meet her. And visit me."

He found it hard to imagine doing so, but he said, "I will."

"I'm serious. No one will bother you. I'll make sure of it. I owe you that."

"All right, I'll come visit."

She stared, canting her head.

"I will, I promise."

Tace graced him with one more smile, stooped to kiss his cheek, and set off for her home. Grub watched her until she climbed the steps to her door. Then he started away.

He surprised himself by heading for the Shattered Gate rather than his shelter. It was fully dark by now. Usually, he wouldn't have gone near the gate after sundown.

That was Grub. I'm Adder now.

He didn't feel afraid as he walked. He didn't bother glancing over his shoulder or hurrying past the entrances to shadowed alleyways. He simply walked, only slowing as he neared the gate. In the dark of night, it sat like some hulking, slumbering beast, misshapen but quiescent. He sensed no magic, no wraiths, no haunted souls. And he laughed. He laughed at all the foolish tales he had believed. He laughed at his younger self, who, up until the day before, had cowered in his shelter at night. He laughed at the joy of being unafraid.

A light touched him from behind, pearly and faint, though strong enough to cast his elongated shadow toward the gate. He knew before turning what it was from.

An Eye hung in the air perhaps twenty paces away. As far as Adder could tell, it was alone, bright and alert and intent on him.

He stared back at it, still unafraid. He wasn't doing anything wrong, and it hadn't been in the alley earlier, when he did. He glanced once more at the gate before walking toward the Eye. It drifted higher, swooped past him to the gate, as if to see what he might have been doing there.

Adder didn't slow, and he didn't peer back to check on the Eye. If he was going to spend more nights abroad in the streets, if he was going to run with Ember and his gang, if he was going to claim the regent's daughter as a friend, if he was destined to be a Trin, the Magnum and their Eyes would be ever more a part of his life. It was time he got used to them.

Pick of the Litter

Esther Friesner

Niss twitched when his queen flung the first pot against the wall, turning a costly piece of merchandise into polychrome shards and dust.

He cringed when a second heavy pot went flying, this time sailing clear through the unglazed window that fronted on the fountain square below. The crash was followed by a chorus of outraged howls from the plaza two stories down, accented by a hail of stones thrown in response to the queen's display of temper. Clearly, the blind fury of the Beast Gate citizens caused them to forget that not a single soul among them had enough physical strength to send a rock arcing high enough to reach the royal window. Their impotent missiles all fell back, spent, and caused more damage to those who had launched them than the queen's tossed pot ever did.

Praise the great goddess B'stah for the breadth and depth of stupidity she has seen fit to bestow upon those chaff-heads, Niss thought. *If more of them were actually capable of simple common sense, Her Imperially Unassailable Majesty would be dethroned in an instant and I'd be out of a job!*

He stuck his head out of the window frame. "Anyone dead down there?"

There was a brief pause, eventually followed by a number of muttered variations on the theme of "No," plus one reedy, piping voice eagerly inquiring, "Why? Who'd'ja have in mind? Cadmin and me, we can give ya a discount—"

Niss made a wearied sound. "Go home, Keel, and stop trying to break into the assassination game. You and your chunk-head brother couldn't even kill time."

The crowd's massed voices surged back in protest. Keel and Cadmin were extremely popular in the Beast Gate neighborhood. Niss simply could not fathom why this should be so. The brothers were two of the scruffiest, kink-tailed ratlings ever to have scrambled through the shabbiest of shabby streets, foraging, filching, and filthying up everything they touched. As for their attempts at setting themselves up in business—well, this murder-for-hire endeavor was merely the latest in a string of self-employment idiocies. The only positive thing about it that Niss could see was the distinct possibility that someone would actually hire them to kill a target who'd prove to be bigger, stronger, and smarter than the ratling brothers.

And yet...

Why does everyone like *those little puke-stains so much?* Niss wondered, his tail slashing back and forth the way it always did when something irked him. *Hmph. Probably because they're a living reminder that no matter how low your own life is, there's someone lower.* He felt his fur beginning to puff out. *No,* he thought. *Pull back, Niss, pull back. Let it go. Let. It. Go. You've got worse on your plate right—*

Another crash of crockery sounded in the chamber behind him, followed by a tiny, terrified mew.

—now.

He took a deep, centering breath. *First things first.*

"Good kindred, am I hearing you right?" he called down from the window. His beautifully pointed dark brown ears twitched forward to accentuate the question. "You almost sound...*disappointed* to have dodged death by, mmm, I think it was a tureen?"

The multitude below broke into smaller groups to wrangle over the original function of the terra cotta projectile now in fragments on the cobblestones.

"Look, friends," Niss went on, raising his voice to recapture their attention. "If you'd *really* rather die, I'll see what I can do to get Her Serenity to aim better next time. Now get the fitz out of the royal courtyard!" He paused for effect. Then, in dungeon-deep tones worthy of one of Ampyrium's more cruelly zealous bringers of doom disguised as justice, he thundered: "She's in a *mood.*"

The reaction to this announcement was gratifying: the courtyard emptied of *Moora* Meeya's loyal subjects as quickly as though one of the Magnum had made a sudden appearance in their midst asking for a good price on pelts. Even sucklings knew the freight of dire dread attendant on one of their sovereign's *moods.*

Niss strode away from the window, well-pleased with how he'd handled matters down below. His smug attitude was abruptly cut short, for he had made the tyro's mistake of forgetting that when his sovereign lady was in a *mood,* she did not abandon it before blood was drawn or serious property damage was effected. (Sometimes not even then. The lore describing the ungovernable and unpredictable temperament of tortoiseshell-furred royalty was laden with tales about how an improperly fileted breakfast sardine sometimes ended in the complete destruction of the *moora*'s palace and most neighboring streets.)

Pot number three came within a claw's length of Niss' head, wiping the smirk from his whiskers, and taking a sizeable chunk out of the priceless, irreplaceable mural behind him.

A low growl kindled in Niss' throat. If his nerves had not been taut to the snapping point already, he might have chalked up this latest assault to the business-as-usual dung-load of his days in *Moora* Meeya's service. But the mural—! That was his tipping point. It had been lovingly created by the great artist P'rra, famed for her use of brushes created solely from the long hairs of her own pure white coat. Art historians attested to the fact that in creating this mural, P'rra rendered herself so dreadfully denuded that her condition was noticeable even when she wore layer upon layer of garments. But even the deepest hood of the most voluminous cape could not conceal the sacrifice of her facial fur. Thus it was recorded that she was frequently mistaken for one of the Holy Hairless, the sacred keepers of B'stah's mysteries.

"Look at that! *Look at it!*" Niss shouted, pointing one claw at the despoiled mural. "Was it worth it, to devastate something so precious, so matchless, the glorious immortalization of the greatest moment in our history?"

As he grew more heated in his denunciation, Niss heard his voice skirling up and up into the higher reaches of its range. He knew it was just a few notes away from becoming the same impassioned yodeling yowl of the Moonlit Rites, a vocalization that the Holy Hairless decreed must remain devoted solely to that sacred time.

What are you doing, *you ninny?* The desperate cry came from the lone sliver of Niss' brain not blazing with outrage over the ravaged mural. *Control your voice even if you can't control your words! A Moonlit yowl now, out of season? Any punishment Moora Meeya would give you for scolding her like this is nothing next to what she's entitled to do if you commit sacrilege. She'll throw you to the wolvenkind guards without a second thought. And that's only if you're* lucky!

And if I'm not *lucky?* he asked himself. It was a formality; he knew the answer, and he shuddered from ear-tips to tail to toes.

If you're not lucky, she won't report you. She'll just get the wrong idea about that glorious yowl of yours. It's quite seductive, you know. Very distinctive. A caterwaul to be reckoned with. Something guaranteed to get a lady's attention, let alone a queen's!

He stole a glance at his sovereign lady. She was no longer standing, no longer on the lookout for additional treasures to destroy in order to satisfy the demands of her *mood*. His diatribe had hit her like a physical blow and she had reeled backward under the impact, tumbling gracefully into a landslide of jewel-toned silk pillows that occupied one entire quarter of the royal presence-chamber. Every other room in her palace held a similar nest, for such were the queen's preferred seat, bed, and royal throne. Ordinary chairs were for ordinary subjects and visitors.

Niss felt his stomach tighten. She was eyeing him in a most disconcerting way. Had his voice hit a note too high, too suggestive? His whiskers began to flick faster than a bee's wings as he uttered soundless prayers to Orgl'orr, imploring the great Lord of the Dead to intercede for him. Orgl'orr would understand his plight. The Holy Hairless taught that in the shadowed days before the Great Crossing, the mortal Orgl'orr had coupled with the divine lady B'stah. (There was some scriptural debate as to whether or not Orgl'orr had *wanted* to experience B'stah's embrace, but all sources agreed on the foolishness of saying *Not tonight, O radiant one* to a goddess.) Their mating resulted in the birth of stars, moons, galaxies, rivers of celestial milk, and deluges of descendants. Orgl'orr was very proud of himself.

Or he would have been, if the transcendent copulation hadn't killed him.

"Nissssss?" A low, melodious voice slinked its way into his ears. *Moora Meeya's* unnerving gaze had turned into a simple look of puzzlement. "Are you through trying to give me a reason to end you?"

Ah! Death threats! All praise and laud be given to his savior, Lord Orgl'orr! Niss was much relieved to find his relationship with the queen back on familiar if perilous ground.

"Splendid one, I don't ask for your forgiveness," he said suavely, executing a flawless bow. "I stand by every harsh word I spoke. You have wrecked a work of art as matchless as it is—was—hallowed. I might pardon your action if you could somehow justify it. Mother of a Hundred Princesses, when your handmaiden raced to fetch me and I heard the racket you were making in here, I feared your life was in danger. I implored all the gods that no accursed assassin had managed to elude your palace paladins and do you a mischief. My poor heart! I scarcely had the strength to lay my paw to your closed door."

His eyes narrowed. "But what did I find? A *mood.* Furniture in fragments. Costly embroidered wall-hangings clawed into mere threads and tatters. And when I asked you what was wrong, you started flinging pots."

"I had good reason!" the queen shouted, claws gutting a purple pillow. White feathers rose up to dance on the air. "I have been *given a gift!*"

Niss' mouth dropped open. He closed it, but could not keep it from falling open once more. "You were given…a gift," he repeated dully.

"More like an insult. An affront! A paw to the face intended to strike not only me, but all our kind!"

For the second time since his intrusion on the queen's tantrum, Niss heard another nigh imperceptible mew come from the corner where most of a chair had been demolished. He had dismissed the sound as an illusion when it first reached his ears, despite his pride in having an extremely keen sense of hearing, even for a *nyaari* of his breed. There had been too many distractions then, thanks to the queen's rampage, but now he was certain he heard it.

Moora Meeya snickered bitterly. "As my old nursemaid taught me, to speak of an abomination is to summon it. That's the loathsome thing now."

Niss moved slowly and silently to the corner and with great care began to move aside the remains of the chair. His blue eyes grew wide when they confirmed what he had been expecting to discover. He crouched before the remaining debris, extended one slender, dark brown paw in a non-threatening manner, and mimicked the gentle, trilling call he still remembered fondly from his infancy.

A black and white head the size of a plum emerged tentatively from the pile of wooden rubble. Minute forepaws stepped into the light. Bit by bit the trembling object of *Moora* Meeya's fury left its place of shelter and dared to sniff Niss' proffered paw. Suddenly reassured that here was nothing to fear, the creature rubbed its chin against its newfound savior and began purring madly.

Niss picked up the little thing and cradled it against his velvet robe of office. The costly azure cloth was immediately marked with splotches of silky fur, but he didn't care. He had more pressing concerns than matters of haberdashery.

"*This* is an insult?" he demanded of his queen. "This—this *gattin*? Who sent it—" He made a quick, expert inspection of the small one's hindquarters. "—*her* to you? One of our nobles?"

"Don't be a fool, Niss. I appointed you my chief counselor for your brains, not your looks, fetching though they be. If a noble family wants to place one of their offspring in my service, there are established applications and procedures that must be followed. You ought to know; you wrote half of them."

"Then how—?"

"A messenger left *that* with Lady H'rr'p, our esteemed house steward. She reported he was not someone of our own royal realm, but a *Hyrkitti*." She spoke the *nyaari* term for the ordinary humans of Ampyrium as if it tasted foul. Her whiskers curled forward in revulsion at the very thought of such a vile creature sullying the doorstep of her palace. "He told her it was a gift that his masters, merchants from the central marketplace, bestowed in hopes that it would improve trade relations between us and—" Her lip lifted in supreme scorn, revealing one gold-inlaid fang. "—*them*."

B'stah bless and sustain our moora, and keep her out of card games, Niss thought. *She'd be plucked hairless quickly. That lovely face of hers is never shy about showing her every feeling. Well, I suppose deception, er, diplomacy is why she hired me.*

"Lady H'rr'p—" Niss struggled to find a kindly way to say what was on his mind. "Lady H'rr'p has...seen much in her lifetime. Her long, *long* lifetime. I believe it has made her readier to take others at their word. Being the vessel of so many accumulated thoughts must often be quite wearing on her."

"Niss, if you want to say that Lady H'rr'p is so old that her mind is like a newborn *gattin*'s, just come out with it." *Moora* Meeya snorted. "Half of Ampyrium knows that her thoughts bounce here and there among the clouds. Surely the *Hyrkitti* merchants knew this when they dispatched their messenger. A simple matter to have him gauge his arrival to coincide with her time on duty at the palace gate!" A furtive glimmer of tenderness lit the queen's golden eyes. "These days she can be as much of a trial as a help to me. Even so, I will not banish her from my service. I hold her dear."

Niss bowed. "Revered *moora*, your compassion is the stuff of legend." *Mostly because precious few folk believe it exists*, he thought. "But tell me, how is this *gattin* an insult? You have raised hundreds like her—your own, your fosters, even some that caught your eye by chance. She is not the first *gattin* offered into your care. It is always done to honor you, as heartfelt praise of your motherly virtues!"

"Tell me this, Counselor," *Moora* Meeya rumbled. "How much of that praise has ever come to me from the *Hyrkitti?*" She practically spat the last word.

Niss shrugged. "Maybe they just heard of the custom recently and want to see if it brings them your royal favor in matters of the marketplace." He couldn't resist giving the purring bundle in his paws a fond look. "She is an exceptionally pretty one, worthy of your attention and favor for that alone."

"If they wanted my favor, their lackey would not have thrust that scrap of skin and meat into Lady H'rr'p's paws and fled."

"They might have been too nervous to dare come into your august presence," Niss suggested. He hugged the wee furball tighter, feeling a relentlessly snowballing anxiety over her ultimate fate. Suddenly, it became vitally important for him to shield this innocent from the queen's wrath, even if it meant deflecting some of that wrath onto himself. He decided to drop his courtly speech and go back to the no-holds-barred way he'd addressed her when her thrice-cursed *mood* obliterated P'rra's masterpiece.

"None of that justifies behaving as you did! Look, you've terrified her." He held out his black-and-white ward for the queen's inspection. "No matter how she came to be here, you've still failed to explain *why* she's an insult, *why* that insult gives you permission to pitch a fit, and *why* you can't just accept her and place her with your other *gattins*."

"Because she is no *gattin*!" *Moora* Meeya roared, claws fully extended. "And because the misbegotten sons of muck who thrust her upon Lady H'rr'p expected me to be too stupid to notice!"

"Not a *gattin?*" Niss gave the beastlet in his paws a careful inspection. Baffled, he added, "I see no difference between her and your other—"

"You wouldn't." *Moora* Meeya snapped. "You're male."

Before Niss could take a step back, the queen lunged at him and snatched the not-a-*gattin* from his paws. "Look!" she cried, holding her shivering captive by the scruff of the neck. "See how her tail curls tightly to shield her secret gateway? No true *gattin* old enough to be taken from their mother's teats ever shows such blatant cowardice! And study her hind legs. They are *primitive,* like those of the lowly felines who dwell among the *Hyrkitti.*"

"Er, well, I admit that whenever I've left our quarter to do business in the marketplace I've never had occasion to look closely at the—the—"

"*Cats,*" *Moora* Meeya said a trifle smugly. It was not every day she caught her chief counselor in a moment of ignorance. He was usually the one correcting her. "They are called cats, and they are as far below us as a lump of dung is from a maiden's-blood ruby. If you had given any of them the most casual inspection, you would now know what sets even our newborn *gattins* apart from them."

"Yes, but—" Niss' eyes turned cautiously in the direction of P'rra's masterpiece. There were certain obscure figures among the shadows in the lower left corner of the mural that had intrigued him for a long time, but he had never been granted permission to remain in the queen's chamber long enough to satisfy his curiosity.

Moora Meeya ignored Niss' attempted interruption. "That is no *gattin* but a kitten, a miserable *kitten*! Her legs will never straighten and grow strong enough for her to walk upright as we do. She will never be able to speak intelligently or do more than mew. Ugh, what a wretched, benighted existence. Poor little thing."

*Is that…*kindness *I hear in her voice?* Niss marveled. *Blessed B'stah, am I dreaming?*

Full proof that he was wide awake came swiftly with the queen's next words: "Such a shoddy life. It would be generous of me to end it for her now."

With that, *Moora* Meeya strode toward the window, the kitten dangling from her paw.

Niss never could remember why he next acted as he most certainly and quite irrevocably did. One moment he was staring in horror at his queen's monstrous intention to extinguish an innocent life, the next he had tackled her from behind with such force that her chin made an audible *whap!* when it hit the floor. The kitten sailed from her grasp, landed gracefully on all four paws, and fled back to the haven of the broken chair, leaving her savior to face his doom alone.

Moora Meeya arched her back violently, easily throwing Niss to one side. She was on top of him before he could catch another breath and slashed his pointed muzzle with first one set of her claws, then the other. Terrible curses poured from her mouth, broken by bursts of hissing and spitting. She was much larger and heavier than he, but Niss was supple and strong enough to wriggle his way out from under and scramble back onto his feet. Desperate for a means to protect himself, he cast his eyes around the room and snatched up the last substantial piece of ornamental pottery left whole.

"Don't make me do something stupid, O Exalted One!" he cried in a voice that didn't quaver *too* much.

The enraged queen froze in place at his words. She stared. She blinked. She tilted her head and asked, "Did you just say—?" Then she exploded with laughter.

Three handmaidens, two janitors, a third-rank healer, and seven royal chefs later, Niss was seated on a pile of cushions second in luxury only to the queen's. The royal chamber was cleared down to the last shard and splinter, and a low table had been brought in, already laden with all manner of delicacies. *Moora Meeya* herself had piled choice morsels on a large silver platter for Niss and a smaller one for the kitten.

"Eat up, my dears," she said with a graceful wave of one forepaw. "Have no fear. After all, my good Niss, it was you who taught me the wisdom of taking all of my own meals from silver vessels."

Niss nodded dumbly, still unable to comprehend the change in his sovereign lady's disposition. *I suppose what I blurted out was funny, but that funny? Funny enough for this? I have seen* Moora *Meeya laugh just as much over some other poor soul's quip while simultaneously beckoning the royal executioner to take them away. Yet here we sit, the kitten and I, not merely served by the queen's own paws but fed from plates that can detect poison!*

He glanced at the kitten, who was stuffing her diminutive body with gravy-drenched tidbits. She seemed healthy enough, with no evidence of any fatal effects in the offing. He stiffened his spine, seized a goblet brimming with the herbal wine usually reserved for nobility of the highest rank, and drained it.

He was quietly delighted when he did not die in agony, although it did give him an attack of burps.

He regained command of his digestive system, then bowed deeply to the queen. Most *nyaari* wouldn't have been able to do so while tucked into a pile of pillows on the floor, but those of Niss' breed were as famed for their flexibility as for the distinctive marks of darker fur on ears, paws, face, and tail. He made the obeisance beautifully.

"Gracious daughter of *B'stah*," he purred. "How can I thank you enough for your kindness and mercy? I promise that I will repay your benevolence by redoubling my efforts in loyal service to you. As for the *gat*—the kitten—I will bear her out of your sight at once. I will then make it my sacred mission to discover the identities of the knaves fool enough to underestimate your unbounded intelligence. I will bring them to justice in our own court of law! I will see to it that they are so thoroughly punished for their disrespect that none else will dare affront your eminence in future! I will—"

"You won't," said the queen.

"What?"

"You're fired."

"*What?*"

"What me no whats. After what you did to me, what did you expect? Indeed, what would become of my reputation—to say nothing of my personal security—if anyone were to learn I allowed you to get away with that atrocious assault?"

"Wha—?" Niss began, then thought better of it and let his luminous blue eyes plead his case silently to his sovereign.

It didn't work.

"Tsk. Don't give me that look. You may remain here until after dessert. But once the servants begin clearing away the dishes, I expect you to clear out your apartments, return all the records, ceremonial robes, symbols, trappings, and—um—thingamajigs pertaining to your *former* position, and leave. Taking *that* with you, of course." She smiled pleasantly as she indicated the kitten, who was still happily eating her way into either a trance or a belly ache.

"But—but my queen—!" The protest perished on Niss' tongue. *Moora* Meeya's smile had vanished. He knew that look of hers too well. He recognized how perilously close he was to having the floor beneath him crack open and send him plunging to the doom he had only just managed to avoid.

He sighed and surrendered. "What's for dessert?"

* * *

The only rooming house that Niss could find with a proprietor willing to lodge someone in *Moora* Meeya's disfavor was called the Sunflower Inn. The modest two-story building was sturdy enough, with brick walls clearly visible in places where the pumpkin-colored stucco had flaked away. The name of this somewhat run-down establishment was painted over the door, part of a frieze of sunflowers so superbly rendered that Niss gasped.

"Mrrew?" said the kitten he carried tenderly in the crook of one arm.

Niss looked at her fondly. "I was just admiring the sign," he told her. "I wonder who did it. Do *you* know, my pretty one?" His playful question earned him one of those *Who is this idiot and why is he bothering me?* expressions so popular among cats.

"Even if we can't stay here, I ought to ask the owner about that," he went on. "Anyone with this much talent would be perfect to restore P'rra's painting. Too bad I can't hire them myself, but I could send them to the palace with a recommendation. My old friend Eril—" His face fell. "If I still *have* any friends, old or new, under *Moora* Meeya's roof."

He pulled his shoulders back smartly and struck a determined pose. "Bah. Never mind thinking over what we *haven't* got. My sole duty now is to get us a place to stay." He rang the little iron bell that dangled from a frame beside the door.

The door opened and the lower half of the entryway was blocked entirely by an elderly creature in a workaday linen smock and woolen skirt, both partly covered by a once-white apron. The peak of her housework headcloth only came up to Niss' hip. Her face was even rounder than her cobby body, and her swollen cheeks seemed to say that the poor thing was suffering from toothache. Niss immediately recognized what she was.

A chomiki*!* he thought, using the term such creatures called themselves. What others chose to call them wasn't always kind. The *chomiki* looked harmless, vulnerable, the perfect target for those who couldn't feel big unless they made others feel small. But any bully fool enough to harass one of them soon learned better. They were fierce, with the formidable teeth of their ratling kinfolk, usually backed up by an unknown number of weapons stashed in their clothing. Some of the larger *chomiki* were warriors able to win a fair fight even against a *nyaari*, definitely able to win an unfair one against anybody.

Niss became uneasy. He'd never had to interact with one of these beasts before. He knew that ages and ages of being discounted and belittled had made the *chomiki* highly sensitive about protecting their honor. Having spent so many years in a position where success often depended on diplomacy, he feared accidentally saying or doing something that might offend this one and cost him any chance of finding a new home.

While he fretted, beady black eyes sized him up shrewdly. "Y'want s'thing, fine sir?" she asked, her words hampered by those distended cheeks.

"Have—have you a room to let?" Niss asked.

"Hmph. Wouldn't think this old place'd be one y'd fancy."

"I'm sure you're just being modest, ma'am," he replied. "I don't need much to be comfortable."

"An' what d'*that*'un need?" The *chomiki* pointed one of her tiny paws at the kitten. "We m't *do* meals here, b' we don't *be* meals."

Niss ventured a laugh. "What a delightful sense of humor you have, ma'am. I promise, she will never pose any sort of danger to you or our fellow lodgers. That is—" He put on his best cajoling look, blue eyes wide and pleading. It had worked wonders when negotiating with representatives of the other Gate-realms of Ampyrium. "—if we might have your gracious consent to *make* them our fellows?"

The landlady laughed. "Listen to that load o' poop pellets! Y'r palace-kind, ain't'ch? Ohhh! More'n that, I wager." She nodded knowingly. "Y'r him as fell afoul o' that dagger-tongue queen o' y'rs. Say truth now!"

Niss' ingratiating smile froze. *She* knows. *She's heard about my banishment already. Curse it all, words travel too damned fast here. Blessed B'stah, please don't let her be like those who turned me away because they feared losing the queen's favor! No, nor like those who took one look at the kitten and slammed their doors. This place is our last hope. If we can't get a room here, we'll have to leave the Beast Quarter, and who knows how badly those people in other parts of the city will try skinning me for rent? One look at a* nyaari

who's forced to dwell among 'Pyr and they recognize desperation. Profitable *desperation.*
They'll bleed me down to the bone.

"M-Ma'am—" he began. "How did you—?"

The *chomiki* managed to shrug even though she appeared to lack shoulders.
"Y'fetch water, y' meet friends at the fountain, y' find out. So y'are him? Well,
then! Let's give y' a look at th'room t'see if y'like it." She turned her back and
started into the house, then looked back when she was a few steps over the
threshold. Niss hadn't moved. She tsk'd.

"Whut. Din'ch' hear wh'I said? Ah. Wait. I'll mend it." She put both paws
in her mouth and began pulling out a crumpled cloth, a small coin purse, one
chomiki-sized slipper, and an assortment of sweetmeats and raw vegetables.
The landlady's swollen cheeks deflated bit by bit as each item emerged and was
laid at her feet. When the last one was out, she grinned.

"Whoosh! There, that's better. Now we can talk more easily." She saw Niss'
gawping at what he'd just witnessed and added: "Pull in your eye-stalks, my
fine sir. I was in the middle of tidying the lodgers' rooms when you rang. Most
of us tote our this-and-thats in bags and baskets, but I say the old ways are the
best." She gave him a mischievous look. "Besides, it lets me keep my paws free.
Now, are you coming?"

All Niss could do was nod.

* * *

The first three weeks Niss and the kitten spent as residents of the Sunflower
Inn were like a dance atop a floor covered with perfectly round polished
pebbles. Each step felt as though any moment would send the unwilling dancer
crashing to the ground.

It was a dance performed by both sides—the other tenants scrambling and
scuttling away in a nigh-farcical manner any time they crossed paths with the
banished *nyaari* councilor—with their landlady Lillumi seated comfortably on
the sidelines, enjoying the show.

Niss finally cornered her in the kitchen and asked what he was doing wrong.
"I greet them courteously, hold the front door open for them, try to introduce
myself, but all they do is run away. Maybe they'll mutter some excuse for their
haste, but the ultimate result's the same: I'm shunned!"

"You must understand, fine sir," Lillumi replied. "Y'may recollect what
I said t'you when you first wanted lodgings here? About not wanting to be
meals?"

"Since you did take me—us—in, I thought you were joking."

"Er, somewhat, true, but…not entirely. The Sunflower Inn's traditionally
been lodging for creatures like—well, like me, for one. You know*, chomiki,*
ratlings, the *musmusi,* sometimes even *konjin,* though most of them soon move
out, saying that my ceiling's too low to accommodate those long ears of theirs.
Once, though, I made the sad mistake of admitting a young *fretka*—one of

those long-bodied sorts that look so attentive and innocent you forget their reputation." She shook her head. "We *chomiki* aren't as keen on preserving lore as other creatures. We looked back over the Prism Pass, then across the First Bridge, and saw a life of eternal scuttling through narrow conduits and frantic scampering inside circular treadmills, always going nowhere. Do you blame us for wanting to forget such a humiliating existence?"

"But—" Niss ventured. "But wasn't there something good to recall from the time before?"

A faraway look came into Lillumi's eyes. "There was the love," she said. "Yes, and so much of it, or we wouldn't be here today. Still, I wish we—I—had recalled what sort of beasts some *fretka* are by nature and so remain, even when they seem to be as civilized as you or me. It isn't *evil*, but it isn't good for other folk. It took me losing three *musmusi*, two ratlings and a lop-eared *konjin*—all good tenants who paid their rent on time, too!—before I called in one of the wolvenkind guards to investigate. The scent-trails took them straight to the truth *and* to the *fretka*'s room. Stupid thing put up a fight." She made a face. "I hope I never have to do that much floor-scrubbing and laundry again."

"Then you're saying that we're being treated to nothing but side-eyes and frost because the other lodgers don't trust us not to *eat* them?"

"Or kill them for sport. Don't forget that."

Niss' sleek fur puffed out as far as possible with indignation. "When have the *nyaari* ever done something like—?"

"Not *nyaari*, fine sir," Lillumi cut in. "Her." She pointed to the kitchen corner where the kitten was diligently trying to kick the guts out of a parsnip.

"They fear *that* little thing?"

"'That little thing' won't stay little long. And when she grows, she won't be one of your kind, all civil and too polite to gobble down your neighbors. Unless you didn't mean it when you said she was no *gattin*?"

"If she were a *gattin*, I wouldn't be here," Niss said dully.

"There it is, then!" Lillumi clapped her paws together. "She's an ordinary kitten, such as live with nigh all the other sorts who share our Ampyrium. I hear tell that even the Magnum don't deny these fluffballs a place by the fire."

"The Magnum *keep cats*?"

The landlady shrugged. "Could be so, could be just a tall tale made for better gossip. Who knows with them?"

Niss felt a twisty sensation in his stomach. The *nyaari* had entered Ampyrium so long ago that most of his kin had forgotten how they'd come to this world. Instead they spun scraps and splinters of truth into a host of outlandish tales. Many of those who had been born here in Ampyrium seldom even heard tell of their ancestors' home.

But there were some, like Niss, who loved to immerse themselves in the old legends and winnow precious grains of history from the chaff of grandmother stories. Among the tidbits he gathered was the tradition of the Prism Pass, which was the name the *nyaari* gave to the Gate that appeared on their world ages ago. The multicolored archway itself glittered like a fire opal, twinkling with a host of hues that fascinated all who beheld it.

The *nyaari* were not the only beings who stood witness to the Gate. Their world teemed with many other creatures, even beyond the fur-clad. Niss had seen many a palace *gattin* grow old enough to speak and be told about a homeworld called Hearth where slick-skinned green farmers with mouths as wide as their faces kept insects from harming the crops by having all their relatives use their whip-like, sticky tongues to pluck them from the plants. It was both family reunion and banquet.

Then there were the Airy, singers of sweet songs and gifted by *B'stah* (so the *nyaari* taught) with wings as well as slender forelimbs. They lived in colonies high on the cliffs of Hearth, with a fine view of that world's emerald sea. Most were beautiful, but some of them were both beautiful and quite annoying, having song *and* their own speech *and* the ability to mimic the languages of other creatures. They could and did out-swear the worst wolvenkind ever whelped.

Of course no *gattin* believed such rubbish, so every year *Moora* Meeya sponsored an educational group trip back to Hearth through the Prism Pass. They returned to Ampyrium with their skepticism banished. Some kissed the ground in gratitude for living in a world where all was familiar to them and the only birds were small and speechless and tasty.

But some remained behind. Some went so far as to declare their intention was to explore the unsettled regions of Hearth and find the Prism Pass' legendary precursor, the First Bridge.

Niss spared a sorrowful thought for P'rra's mutilated mural. Possessed by a visionary urge only another artist might understand, she had chosen to paint an epic image of that glorious span as it brought the ancestors of all beasts now in Ampyrium first to Hearth from the world before.

"Hoy!" Lillumi's voice snapped Niss out of his reverie. "Where did you fly off to when I was talking to you? I thought palace folk had manners."

"I—I'm sorry, very sorry. I hope you can forgive me. If you have any ideas about how I can reassure my fellow lodgers that the kitten is no more of a threat to them than I am—? I will vouch for her." His words were as humble as his otherwise housingless situation demanded.

The landlady gave a snuffly snicker. "Vouch away, fine sir! Swear on your mother's grave or gravy boat, for what good it'll do you. But it'll take more than words to convince some of my lodgers that *you're* safe as a bowl of oatmeal, let alone the kitten."

Her words made Niss forget to play the humble petitioner. Indignant, he exclaimed, "Are you serious? Are all of your lodgers so milk-blooded that they believe something *that* size—" He jabbed a claw in the kitten's direction. "—could take more than a nibble out of the smallest and weakest of them before they could kick her away?"

"Fair enough, fine sir," Lillumi replied calmly. "Let's set aside their fears of yon kit and turn the troublesome part back where it belongs: on *you*."

"I would never—!"

"Peace, fine sir. I know that, else I never would've taken you under my roof." She thought a while, then said, "I suppose the rest of us do believe you're no danger, you and all your kind. We've never heard of a *nyaari* killing any of us smaller ones for sport or supper; only for sophisticated reasons, like robbery gone wrong, or getting in a drunken tavern brawl, or revenge." She cocked her head. "I keep watch on my lodgers, and it seems to me that some of them are beginning to trust you, but as for the kitten—" She spread her paws in a helpless gesture. "Some fears outlast our ancestors' journey from the world before Hearth, and there's little we can do to reason away such fears."

"Isn't there *anything* to be done?"

"Wellllll…" Lillumi's black eyes suddenly sparked. "How about giving her a name, for a start? You know, something to separate her from the general notion of *kitten*, and what kittens grow up to be, which is cats, and what cats can do? Make her different. Make her *special*."

"A name…" Niss chewed one claw in thought. "A name."

* * *

Lady Moonglow made her naming debut five days later. Niss gave the landlady a share of his dwindling resources and asked her to prepare a modest but festive meal for all the tenants of the Sunflower Inn. Lillumi offered to deliver the invitations herself, lest the actual presence of a *nyaari* at their bedroom door be too much for some of her more susceptible lodgers. She not only invited everyone, she made it a point to secure their promise to attend.

"Don't you look at this as me favoring you," she told Niss with mock severity. "I'm only doing it because parties don't happen often enough 'round here. At my age, I don't have time to wait long for the next one! Anyway—" she added with an impish look. "—I'm perishing to see how all this goes over."

If the landlady was hoping for something dramatically dreadful to occur, she was disappointed. She'd given Niss leave to have the event in the Sunflower Inn's gathering room with the big fireplace and the tables where the lodgers who'd paid for board as well as room took their meals. He had used his years of attending palace fêtes to decorate the space and the table to the height of sumptuous poverty. He scrounged up a broken basket from the marketplace, covered the pillow from his bed with one of his older velvet tunics, and set it at one end of a table generously covered with food and drink.

The basket was for the kitten, of course. Any guest who wanted to indulge in all of the good things on the table would have to come near her.

Niss stood within paw's-reach behind her, ready to grab the kitten if she got scared and decided to make a break for it. If that happened, she might by chance pounce on one of the guests, and *that* would be disastrous. Blessed *B'stah* was on his side, for the kitten sat primly, too fascinated by everything going on around her to be frightened.

When all of the lodgers had taken food and drink, but before they could go back for second helpings, Lillumi banged a wooden spoon on a skillet and declared, "All right, everyone, hush your chatter and let's give our attention to the one who's treated us like royalty tonight. And he ought to know royalty! If you'd ever had the manners to trade a word or two with him, you'd know that Niss here held high office in the *nyaari* palace until that queen there got a flea up her nose over some minor thing and showed him the door."

A wave of muttering surged across the room as the guests reacted to this revelation. There were more than a few hard words said about *Moora* Meeya, whose *moods* had often done ill to those who deserved better.

"Dunno why we put up w'her ridin' high over us," one ratling grumbled. "'Tain't like she's our sort o' critter."

"Yeah, whyn't you tell that to her wolvenkind guards, smarty?" a somewhat drunken *musmusi* squeaked. "I'm sure they'd be happy t'give you a lesson is poli- poli- *urp!*- politics."

"Look here, fellas," a young male *chomiki* cut in on the conversation. "If the *nyaari* themselves couldn't stand her holding the reins, they'd've got rid of her long since. And face it: she may be twelve kinds of petty tyrant but she's gotten our part 'n' portion of Ampyrium some pretty sweet trade deals."

"Hmph. That's what *would* impress you, y'seed-grubbin' little shopkeep," the drunk *musmusi* sneered. "Who cares if we live or die at her whim, so long as the profits roll in, eh?"

Insulted, the *chomiki* pointedly turned his back on the *musmusi* and gave his attention to Niss, who had just finished thanking Lillumi for her kind introduction.

"My friends—if I may be bold enough to call you that?" He cast a hopeful look about the room and saw an encouraging number of full-fed smiles. "My *good* friends, I know that my presence under this roof came as rather a shock to many of you. Nevertheless, you have tolerated me and this little one." He indicated the kitten with a graceful sweep of one dark brown paw. She purred and tilted her head in a most fetching manner, causing several of the guests to utter variations on that eloquent syllable, *Awwwwwwww!*

Niss went on: "We *nyaari* have a saying: Memory is a treasure house whose doors are always open to us all. *All*, not just my kind! I know this is so, at least as far as one most precious memory is concerned. For tell me now, isn't it true that many of us here in this room, in this house, in this Gate, know the tale of the First Bridge? Haven't we heard how our mothers and fathers crossed over that shining span and came to Hearth from yet another, former world? In some stories that was a world where our ancestors led hard lives, but in others it was a world of warmth, full bellies, every kindness given to us by mysterious beings who always looked upon us with love.

"We *nyaari* were different then." He deftly plucked his wine glass from the table before him and raised it high for all to see. "In that world, before the First Bridge, I could not do this any more than she can now." He nodded to the kitten, who seemed to acknowledge this with a sweet, small *"Mew?"* that further captivated the increasingly tipsy guests. "No, in that world, the best I could hope to accomplish was to knock this glass off the table."

His sapphire gaze swept the room. "Look to the lore that your own kind have preserved, my friends. Surely you are not ignorant of how different things were for your ancestors before they crossed the *First* Bridge?" He paused to permit the guests to trade murmured assertions of knowledge that they might or might not actually possess. Some did seem to have a legacy of legends that stretched back into the past, crossing both the Prism Pass that led to Ampyrium and the First Bridge that brought them to Hearth.

"You're gonna laugh, but grand-dad said we crossed the First Bridge *naked!*"

"My pa said the same, but I think he did it just to make ma mad."

"Well, my great-aunt told me we used to live in a world that looked wide and free, except if you went too far in one direction you bashed your nose against *solid air!* Couldn't go no further after that."

"And you swallowed that? My gramma's brother-in-law knew your great-aunt and told me she *drinks.*"

"Yah, my mam usedta say we was so small, back then, we could squeeze through a hole no bigger'n a grape."

"How big a grape?"

Niss allowed himself a carefully moderated chuckle. It wouldn't do to have the others think he was laughing *at* them. "Ah, so all of us *do* have our own memory tales! I am glad, though there are some I wish were well forgotten. For here in Ampyrium we face the shadows of the past we never had to deal with back on Hearth. Here the *nyaari,* the *wolvenkind,* and the *musmusi* can be rivals in business, neighbors, or even—" He raised his wine glass. "—friends. But on this world we see both *musmusi* and mice, *wolvenkind* and dogs, *nyaari* and—" He nodded to the kitten. "—cats. We see, and the memories return, and we cannot separate what we dimly recall from what we know. The *wolvenkind* see the dogs of Ampyrium chasing cats, and sometimes when they see a *nyaari* their eyes glow with irrational longing to do the same. The *musmusi* see the marketplace cats ki—er, regulating the mice that rummage through the merchants' stock of grains and they give the most peaceful, friendly *nyaari* a look of undeserved revulsion and fear!"

He slammed the wine glass down, but took care to do so in a way that emphasized his words without damaging the fragile vessel. "My dear fellow lodgers, we have become captives of the past! We surrender mastery of our own lives to ancient tales when we would be infinitely better off trusting the evidence of our eyes! And that, my friends—" He took a deep breath he didn't really need, except for the perfect dramatic pause it afforded him. "—that is why I am especially grateful to you for showing yourselves to be better than the ordinary run of your kind. You respect the past, you recall the past, but you do not *submit* to the past! You see this sweet, innocent, harmless kitten, and you realize that however large she may grow, she will never pose a threat to any of you. Come, come, have you not encountered other cats in the markets of Ampyrium?"

"Welllll, not if I can help it," one of the smaller *musmusi* shyly volunteered.

His comment was greeted by snickers and jibes at his cowardice by the other guests. Niss heard and approved: *That's what you get for being honest, you poor fool! At least your straightforward fright will discourage anyone else from admitting to their own fear of felines and that is just what I want!*

He made it a point to step forward and give the cringing *musmusi* a comforting pat on the shoulder. "Do not feel shame at feelings you can *change*, my good fellow. Whatever the roles of your ancestors were before the crossing of the First Bridge, you *know* all of that is long behind us! You are and will always be *bigger* than she, *stronger* than she, and above all, *smarter* than both this kitten and any of your kin fools enough to tremble and mistrust the very sight of her! Behold, I bow to you all, for I must do proper reverence when I recognize that I stand in the presence of *wisdom*."

So saying, he executed a graceful obeisance that had been honed to perfection by his years in underappreciated service to *Moora* Meeya. He straightened up again as a murmur among the guests rose around him like the rush of the incoming waves.

"—says we're smart? Uh, I dunno—"

"Pfft! Knock off that fake modesty, chum. He says that, you'd best believe it. He knows smart when he sees it."

"Yeah, he's seen *palace* smarts!"

"We ain't *ord'nary* smart; we got *wisdom*. Any idjit knows how wisdom's better'n smart. Wisdom's like what the Magnum themselves hasssss, errrrr… that is, I mean we got it in our own way and no disrespect intended to the Magnum, perish forbid."

"Nah, nah, we can be our own sort of wise."

"'Course we can!"

"Yah, 'cause we *are*. That's what my mam used to say about me, anyway."

The murmur grew in volume into delighted chatter as the Sunflower Inn's lodgers reveled in their newly discovered intelligence. Some of them decided to show off by striding right up to the kitten and daring to stroke her silky head. Others saw this and clamored for a turn.

Niss allowed this to go on for as long as he thought the kitten would tolerate it. *It won't do if she gets fed up and takes a swipe at someone*, he thought. *Or worse yet, if she bites! Then all my good work will be undone in one snap of those teensy teeth.* He put on a smile heretofore reserved for buttering up his former employer and scooped the kitten out of her basket, to the protests of her adorers.

"Forgive me, good souls," he said suavely. "Surely you are aware that for as long as we may dwell in your midst you will enjoy ample time to play with and spoil this sweet, gentle darling? But now—now it is time for the purpose of this feast, to wit—" He lifted the kitten high. "—to officially bestow upon her a name."

There was a brief pause to allow for strident, drunken cheers.

"What'cha gon' call her, then?" a *musmusi* demanded, waving his cup wildly and spattering all nearby.

"I?" Niss echoed. He lowered his eyes. "Oh, she will not receive any name of *my* devising. You see, this wee darling has been blessed to have a *mysterious benefactor*."

The former counselor's melodramatic revelation immediately captured the imagination of his audience. Their chorused "*Oooooooh!*" was quite gratifying.

(Unlike so many of his peers, Niss had not limited his life to the royal palace. He often prowled the byways where the *other* classes lived. He observed their taste for scare-your-fur-off story-tellers and blood-and-thunder acting troupes, remembered what he'd seen, and thought it might come in useful one day.)

Holding his audience in the pad of his paw, Niss went on: "As you know, I was exiled from the palace for a lackwit's act: I defended this little one in the teeth of my sovereign's displeasure. I saved her tiny life but lost my position. It was a high price, but one I was glad to pay!" His voice dropped to one best used for confiding juicy secrets. "Many would think me a fool for that, yet when I arrived here, at the Sunflower Inn, imagine my astonishment one day to find a note in my room, praising my actions, offering to help me shoulder a modest part of the kitten's sustenance, and accompanying it with a gift of tidbits for her."

Fresh muttering ran through the crowd. Niss heard words of speculation, saw glances darting left and right. It was plain that his fellow lodgers were wondering which one among them had done such a thing.

Perfect, he thought.

"I cannot know how this *mysterious benefactor* heard of our reduced circumstances," he said softly. "I can only feel deep gratitude for their help and admire their modesty, for their initial message made it plain that they would never reveal their name. Truly the highest form of charity is anonymity." He allowed a few moments for some of the guests to translate his words into less high-flown language, for the benefit of the others. "Nonetheless, I vow that when my fortunes are restored I *will* make it my life's work to discover their identity and reward them beyond their dreams!"

He allowed this information to settle with his audience before concluding: "Even now they continue to watch over us, for somehow they heard of my plans to name the kitten. Thus it was that I found another note in my room, politely inquiring if I might consider giving her a name that once belonged to someone very dear to them. How could I refuse?"

He lifted the kitten as high as the ceiling of the common-room would allow and declared, "Hear me, O our revered-if-still-completely-mysterious benefactor! As you no doubt stand in our midst at the very moment, know that from this day forth, according to your request, this little one shall be known by all as *Lady Moonglow!*"

A chorus of toasts arose, wishing the kitten good health, good fortune, and long life.

Lady Moonglow received the adulation of the crowd and peed on Niss' tunic.

* * *

Back in his dimly lit room, Niss stripped off his affronted tunic and frowned at Lady Moonglow. The kitten repaid his expression with yet another charming head-tilt and eyes luminous with innocence.

"Well, I hope you're satisfied, you imp," he said, trying and failing to sound stern. "This is velvet. It's beyond my poor capabilities to clean properly." He clicked his tongue. "It's not as though I've got the funds to squander on taking this to an *elite* laundry. I'll have to make do with giving it a scrub myself."

The kitten merely tilted her head to the other side and mewed once, which her besotted guardian chose to interpret as approval of his plan. Even though the dismissed Chief Counselor had a reputation for good judgment and logical thinking, something about Lady Moonglow's very presence persuaded him that it made perfect sense to converse with a creature who didn't understand a word he said.

Niss flung himself into his narrow bed. "I suppose I could ask one of the other lodgers for a small loan. I'm fairly sure I primed them to be generous to us. Sweet *B'stah*, did you see their expressions when I spoke of how richly I'd reward our mysterious benefactor some day? You could almost hear them calculating how to claim that title!"

He grinned. "I can hardly wait. They'll come to me singly and secretly, speak in self-effacing tones of their benevolence, and then—" His grin grew wider. "—and then I'll express my heartfelt gratitude as I presume upon their generosity once more! What can they do but say yes, trapped in a lie they wove from the little threads of other lies I first spun? And the beauty of it is that I'll swear each of our callers to secrecy and end up with a crowd of mysterious benefactors who'll support us, hoping for their own future reward."

Lady Moonglow leaped onto his chest and began to knead, purring happily. A wistful sigh stirred Niss' whiskers as he stroked her head. "I'm not proud of myself for plotting such a thing, my Lady, but I had to come up with something. My funds are running low and I've still got no idea how I'll manage to earn more. I've left you here every day, seeking some sort of work, and found nothing. I'm afraid too many folk have heard I'm in our *moora*'s bad graces and fear that hiring me will draw her wrath on them as well. And I— we—must eat!"

The kitten froze in place. She gave Niss a stare so intense, so unlike her usually guileless expression that for a moment he doubted his eyes. Then she jumped from the bed to the floor to the unshuttered window and out into the moonlit courtyard. Niss was puzzled at her sudden departure but wasn't worried. The modest courtyard of the Sunflower Inn held several flowerpots and a failed herb garden where Lady Moonglow was in the habit of doing… her business. She always came back.

Niss threw one arm across his eyes and sighed yet again. *I envy you your carefree life, little one,* he thought. *If only I—*

A sudden scrabbling sound made him sit up and turn toward the window. Lady Moonglow sat perched on the sill for a moment before landing lightly on the floor. Niss peered at her by the glow of the lone candle he could afford for a night's illumination. There was a strange shadow just beneath her chin, a small, dark object he could not quite distinguish.

"What have you got there, my Lady?" he asked with a smile.

The kitten came closer and dropped the body of a dead mouse at his feet.

"Well, what are you waiting for?" she asked. "Eat up."

It took the deposed Chief Counselor every scrap of self-control he had, but somehow he managed to strangle the startled scream that leaped halfway up his throat. The effort cost him much, and "much" included consciousness. He collapsed back onto his bed, insensible.

* * *

The candle lighting Niss' room was burned down to a stub by the time he opened his eyes again. He blinked rapidly as memory returned.

Did I dream—?

A cautious peek over the side of his bed revealed the dead mouse, still there.

All right, yes, so the kitten caught a mouse. Fine. Good. That's what cats do. The only thing this proves is that she's small but precocious, nothing more. My mind was just a tad fuddled. Of course. Yes. That's what happened. I must've had a drop too much to drink tonight. When I served Moora Meeya *I had the sense to stay sober at parties. No wonder I imagined the kitten spoke to me!*

Niss relaxed, once more secure in his sanity. *I'll have to get rid of that sad little corpse without the landlady seeing it. Or worse, one of the* musmusi *tenants! They might claim not to fear cats, but you never know when a long-buried instinct will leap out and throttle common sense.* He sat up slowly and surveyed the room by the inadequate, flickering candlelight.

"I wonder where my mighty hunter's gone?" he said with an indulgent smile.

"Hey! You up, Pa?" The kitten wiggled out from under Niss' bed and stretched her tiny body. "Took you long enough. I almost ate that tidbit myself, but that would've been rude. I caught it for *you*." She sat with her fluffy forepaws together and stared at the *nyaari*. "Well? Go on. You were the one said we must eat!"

"Ah…uh…um…" Niss was dumbfounded and his usual eloquence suffered for it. "I—I thank you, my dear, but if it's all the same to you, please eat it with my blessing. And then tell me—I beg of you, *tell* me that you are no kitten, but a *gattin* after all!" The last sentence spilled from his mouth with the force and speed of a river's whitewater rapids.

"First things first, Pa," Lady Moonglow said coolly, and devoured the dead mouse until nothing remained but a nauseating array of anatomical bits-and-bobs. "Ahhh, that was good! I bet it was a granary mouse. Nice and fat and stupid, easy catching and good eating." Satisfied, she began to wash her paws and muzzle, immune to Niss' horrified stare.

When she was quite done, she looked up at him and said, "I owe you a lot, Pa, and that includes owing you the truth. I'm no *gattin*."

"Well, you're no kitten, either. Kittens can't talk! What *are* you?"

"I don't know." Even though she lacked the shoulders for the task, Lady Moonglow still managed to communicate the essence of a shrug. "No one ever bothered to tell me. I suppose the bastard who took me from my ma and tinkered with me couldn't be bothered to say."

"Tinkered…?"

"Pff! If you've got a better word for it, feel free to make an offer. I guess it'd be simplest to say it was—" She assumed a portentous tone worthy of a streetcorner seer. "—*maaaaagic!*"

"Magic," Niss repeated dully. "You—you mean you were transformed by one of the Magnum?" A chill pierced him to the bone.

"I guess so." The kitten did not appear to share Niss' sense of awe at the mention of Ampyrium's masters. "All I know is that one day my life is centered on my ma and her milk, the next I'm being held face to face with one unbelievably ugly human. Ugh. He had a nose like a peeled beet, yellow, bloodshot eyes, a beard stuck full of enough crumbs and meat scraps to fill my food dish twice, and garlic breath that ought to be declared a danger to public safety!" She paused for a moment, then added: "I think his name was Ralph.

No, wait, *Raffeler*. Raffeler the Redolent, and as meddling a Mag*numbskull* as you'll ever meet!"

Niss pounced on the kitten and clapped one paw over her tiny mouth. "Shh! *Shhhh!* Lower your voice, or better yet, don't say anything more! Do you know the penalty for failing to show the Magnum proper respect?"

Lady Moonglow jabbed all her claws into Niss' paw, forcing him to drop her. She landed neatly at his feet and gave her rumpled fur a few quick licks before saying: "Oh, come on, Pa, you're no coward, so stop acting like one. You weren't afraid of what's-her-name, the hairball who fired you and pitched us out of the palace!"

"I assure you, Lady Moonglow, there are worlds of difference between the power of *Moora* Meeya and that of the Magnum," Niss said sternly.

"Not really." The kitten spoke with an annoying level of self-confidence. "Both of them can kill you. What does it matter if they do it with an executioner's ax or a flashy fireworks show?"

"The difference, you saucy snip, is that the Magnum have more ways of *finding out* when they're being spoken of without the proper courtesy," Niss snapped.

"Oooh, 'saucy snip'? I like that, Pa! Is it too late to make that my name?" The kitten's whiskers swept up in a huge grin. "We both know you pulled our *mysterious benefactor* out from under your tail, so my name's all your choice. Why did you burden me with a deadweight like 'Lady Moonglow'?"

"You should feel *honored* to carry such a name," Niss snarled. "Lady Moonglow was a legendary heroine, first of our kind to make the crossing to Hearth from the First World in the days when we were worshipped there as gods!"

"Gods, huh? Hmph. Sounds like she traded down, Pa."

"I'm going to ignore that blasphemy because you are too young and uneducated to know any better," Niss said stiffly. "And while we are on the subject of names, will you *stop* calling me 'Pa'?"

"Nope." The kitten's grin grew wider. "Regular cats, we don't have more than a ma and a memory of whoever took her fancy. Well, I'm no regular cat anymore and I like the idea of having a pa, especially since you've been taking care of me like a good parent ever since we met. You gave up a lot of good things to do it, too! Tell the truth: you *like* me, don't you?" She repeated her devastating head-tilt and with perfect calculation added: "*Mew?*"

Niss could only laugh.

* * *

A bargain was made.

Niss would be Pa because the kitten made it clear she was determined this be so. The kitten would remain Lady Moonglow for similar reasons.

The kitten would let no other inhabitant of the Sunflower Inn learn of her gift for speech nor—most important—that its source was an eccentric member of the Magnum…possibly.

That seemed to cover everything, at least as far as Niss saw the situation. As for the kitten…

* * *

"Where have you been?" Niss demanded.

"Out," said the kitten.

"Clearly. But where?"

"Does it matter, dearest, darling Pa?"

"Don't you try to soften me up with *that* look! I want an answer."

"Whyyyyy?" The kitten almost purred the word.

"Because you are my responsibility. I am accountable for your welfare!"

"Oh." Lady Moonglow seemed to be giving this news serious consideration before saying: "Accountable to who? Seriously, if I were to slip away from this place tomorrow, never to return, who would come calling on you, wanting to know what had become of me?"

Niss uttered a terse cry of frustration. "All right, all right, *I* would care. You have become—dear to me. And don't bother asking 'why' again because even I don't know the answer to that!"

The kitten smiled. "Maybe it's part of the spells Magus Raffeler slopped all over me. Or maybe I was simply born with it. Consider it my most dangerous gift." She leaped onto Niss' shoulder, stuck her nose in his velvety brown ear, and whispered: "*Fear* the endearing cuteness!"

Niss tried and failed not to laugh. "And now that you know I care about you, no doubt you'll be turning that knowledge into a weapon to use against me, you wretched kitten," he said, giving her fluffy chin a gentle *skritch-skritch-skritch*.

"Of course! I use it against any susceptible target. Once they are in my power, I exploit them to my advantage until they are no longer useful, and then—" She flashed the miniscule claws of both forepaws. "Grr. Gone."

"My, my," said Niss vastly amused. "It seems I'm harboring an assassin in my bosom."

"Wow, Pa, you're smart." The kitten spoke with a level of irony-free sincerity found only in the very, very young. "How did you figure *that* out? Assassination is part of—well, pretty much the whole reason Magus Raffeler crafted me in the first place."

"Is that so?" Niss scooped Lady Moonglow from his shoulder and set her down on the bed beside him. "Well, as your beloved custodian and, er, Pa, I'm ordering you to forget all about following such a dangerous career path. I don't know what that Mag—*person* was thinking, but you are far too dainty a creature to do a hired killer's work."

"Even with the right tools?" There was that accursed, enchanting head-tilt again. "Raffeler gave me the means to be very good with tools."

"Ha. I can just see you trying to heft a dagger or wrestle the stopper out of a vial of poison!"

"Spoilsport." The kitten pouted. "Can't you let me have my *dream*, Pa?"

"Killing others is *not* a respectable dream to have, especially for someone who has decided that I am her Pa. It reflects badly on how I'm trying to raise you and I disapprove."

"Not even for the money I could bring home?" A wheedling tone crept into Lady Moonglow's voice. "Maybe a lot of money? You do keep saying we're hard up, and if we don't forage some funds soon, we'll be homeless."

"Our finances are my concern, little one, not yours. Even if I went broke tomorrow, I'm sure Lillumi would give a grace period before she threw us out." *And I'm also sure I can play the* Mysterious Benefactor *ruse with some of our fellow lodgers long before it comes to that*, he thought. "Tsk. I don't know why I'm even having such a discussion with you. I *will* find employment."

"Doing what? You were trained for palace work. Good luck getting any of *that*, with *Moora* Meeya still on the throne."

Niss' whiskers drooped. "If it comes down to the grit and grime of things, I will seek work in one of the *other* quarters of Ampyrium. I am certain that there would be at least one employer happy to have one of our kind drudging for him."

"Drudging? What kind of job is that, Pa? What will you have to do?" There was a rising note of concern in the kitten's voice.

"Anything." Niss sighed. "It won't matter what, as long as I'm there to be scorned and insulted, abused and browbeaten by an employer who only hired me so that he'd have someone from the Beast Gate to lord it over." He saw the horrified look in Lady Moonglow's eyes and stroked her head. "I'm sorry to teach you this so soon, dear one, but we are perhaps the least welcome of all Ampyrium's dwellers. We have sinned by being at once too different, and yet, too like, other folk. Worse, too many of us have prospered here. How dare we?"

"Yes," Lady Moonglow said softly. "How dare we."

* * *

Keel the ratling stared at the fish set out at his feet. It was small but plump and quite fresh, its one visible eye still clear and glittering. It was, in fact, too great a bounty to be true.

"What's the catch?" he demanded.

"Mmmfno ca'ch," his brother Cadmin said around a slobbery mouthful of his own half-eaten fish. He swallowed it and repeated, "There's no catch, stupid. Why'ncha give it a big sniff fer poison like I done? Nothing wrong with it, 'less ya got a problem with food that's this tasty and free besides. But if you won't eat it—" His paw darted out to seize his brother's share.

"*Yowch!*" Cadmin jerked back his trespassing paw, which was now bleeding from four short, slim, but effective slashes.

"Mind your manners, Cadmin," Lady Moonglow said as sweetly as if she had not just sliced the ratling's flesh. "We are trying to make this the start of a profitable business venture, but if you can't be trusted to respect your own brother's property, why should I put any faith in you respecting mine?"

Cadmin's eyes narrowed. "What prop'ty *you* got? 'Sides the fish, I mean, and that's mine now." He patted his shaggy belly with a self-satisfied air. "Y'ain't even dressed civilized, so not even an apron pocket on you t' stow any coin!"

"When I managed to carry *two* fish to your doorstep without an apron pocket to my name, you didn't seem to care how I did it." the kitten replied smoothly. "You just stuffed your face."

"She's right, Cad," Keel said. The scrawnier ratling plucked a morsel from his fish, gave it a dubious sniff, then popped it into his mouth and swallowed. When he didn't die, he smiled and added: "Could be she's got, like, magic?"

"Then why di'n't she magic herself up an apron, hey? Or even a cloak? An' mostly, why'd she want to come here, to us, and treat us to a meal?" He gave her a narrow look. "This some sort o' whatchacallit, *gattin* prank? Something you highborn beasts think's fun? What d'you got in store for the two poor, dumb ratlings after the feed?" He glanced up and down the narrow, slop-strewn street where derelict houses shouldered tightly against one another. "Maybe a bunch of your kin are waiting in the shadows with a *wolvenkind* you paid off to play along? When are you gonna do—whatever you've got in store? 'Ooooh, help, help! I'm just a poor, helpless *gattin* an' these nasty ratlings stole the lovely fishies I was bringing home!' And there comes the wolvenkind whelp and the rest of your pals to give us a beating, and if it stops at that, I call us lucky." He spat out the last words, then snapped, "Get back in the house, Keel. Door won't stop 'em for long, but at least we can—"

The kitten swarmed up Cadmin's body, wreathed herself around his neck, and laid a slim, glittering blade against his throat.

"Shut up before you say something really stupid," she purred. "Let a lady get a word in edgewise."

Cadmin froze, eyes goggling in terror. A telltale dark stain spread across the front of his pants.

"P-please, lady," Keel whimpered. "Please don't hurt my brother. He can't help saying dumb stuff on account of he's got a lot of imagination."

"Does he now?" Lady Moonglow maintained her hold on the tiny knife. "So I heard when I was prowling. You might be surprised to know how many folk talk about the two of you around here. You're surprisingly well-liked, though perhaps it's simply because your antics are so amusing. Think of my surprise when I overheard your neighbors laughing about your latest scheme! It's rare to hear *assassins-for-hire* used as the punchline to a joke." She smirked. "Well? How's that career choice working out for you?"

Cadmin scowled despite his highly vulnerable position and uttered a low grumble. "*B'st'ds.*"

Lady Moonglow's ears twitched. "Don't like being laughingstocks, then? Well, that's the very reason I've sought you out." She released Cadmin and jumped to the ground where she sat twirling her blade in a manner that should not have been possible to do with an ordinary kitten's paws. "Gentles, it would be my pleasure to show you how to turn being underestimated into wealth beyond your dreams."

"Huh?"

"What?"

"I'll be happy to explain—" Lady Moonglow flashed her tiny teeth in a grin at once adorable and vaguely disquieting. "—but not out here. We wouldn't want any of the neighbors muscling in on your good fortune, would we?"

The ratling brothers exchanged a look. Cadmin rubbed his neck cautiously.

"Well, c'mon inside, then," he said, opening the door to their house.

"You are too kind," said Lady Moonglow as she stepped gracefully over the threshold.

Keel gobbled up the last of his fish before hastening to follow. "Don't mention it, ma'am. 'Snot like we got much t' offer a guest."

"That's not what I meant. You are too *kind*." The unnerving smile was back. "Don't worry, lads; I'll fix that."

* * *

Niss paced the floor of the smaller room where he and Lady Moonglow lived on Lillumi's charity. He'd run out of both hope and money a fortnight ago and had been pawning his finer garments since then so that he might offer his landlady a token payment. "On account, and I swear you'll have the balance of my debt soon!"

"'Course I will, dearie. I trust you," the *chomiki* had replied in a voice so filled with poorly concealed pity that Niss wanted to weep. When she asked him if he'd mind the move to far smaller quarters at much lower rent, due far less frequently, his humiliation was complete.

His scheme to entice help from his fellow lodgers was not going as well as he'd imagined. Though many were willing to pretend to be that Mysterious Benefactor of his, in anticipation of future reward, they could not give what they did not have.

The Beast Gate quarter had come into hard times. The most successful traders were still comfortable enough, but their wealth remained in circulation among their own class, with little to none of it trickling down to less fortunate creatures.

"This is *her* fault," Niss grumbled. "Our *moora*'s been piling one tax atop another, like a child playing with blocks. No need to wonder why she does it: I've caught sight of her when she parades through the streets and her gowns and jewels keep on growing more and more lavish. Lavish *and* extravagant! Why in *B'stah*'s blessed name doesn't my successor rein her in, even a little? When I was Chief Counselor, we had none of this spendthrift nonsense! There are ways of making *Moora* Meeya see reason. Why doesn't he *try*?"

But he knew the answer to that. Most royal counselors were males and either feared a fate like Niss' or hoarded hopes of ingratiating themselves with their queen to the point where she might finally choose a consort, namely one of them.

Niss shook his head violently in an attempt to banish his dark thoughts. He glanced at the rickety table where his humble, scanty breakfast lay untouched.

Fish again, and again, it was a gift from the kitten. Though his belly rumbled with hunger, he couldn't bring himself to touch the food. *I should be the one providing for her, not her for me,* he thought. *I've got to find work, if only to stop her from all this theft! What if she gets caught? What if she's brought before the Magnum and she encounters that Raffeler fellow who created her? What might he do to——?* Niss groaned aloud and sat down hard on his narrow bed. *I've sought any job anywhere, but there's none to be had. Moora Meeya's endless self-indulgence has swamped Ampyrium with idle workers whose masters couldn't afford to keep them on the payroll any longer.* He covered his face with his paws.

"Pa? Pa, are you all right?" The kitten was suddenly in his lap, her dainty pink nose working its way under his paws.

"I——I'm all right, my dear." He stroked her silky head. "I'm glad you're back. You've been staying out longer and longer. Sometimes I fear you'll never return."

"Pff! Don't be silly, Pa. How could I leave you? We're family. I love you." She began to purr earnestly.

Niss blinked in surprise. "That's the first time you've said that to me. If it's true—and even if it's not, I want it to be. I love you as well."

"Aw, I'd never lie to you!"

"Really? In that case would you mind telling me where you go to so frequently and for so long?"

"Oh, just here and there. But don't worry; I'm with friends."

"I'd like to meet them. You know, just to make sure my little Lady Moonglow isn't hanging out with disreputable types." Niss' heart felt lighter, being able to talk so playfully with his small ward.

"They're nothing *but* disreputable types, Pa," the kitten replied merrily. "And *I'm* their leader! We get along very well from the moment they accept that I'm the smartest and that I have the *best* plans for us to prosper!"

"Plans for your prosperity?"

"*Ours*, Pa." Now the kitten was quite serious. "Yours and mine."

Niss was no yet ready to return things to a more sober mood. "Very well, I shall allow you to continue doing—doing whatever it is you and your friends are up to—as long as you don't steal too much at a time and don't get caught." He wagged a claw in the manner of a scolding schoolteacher. It was so easy to trade jokes with Lady Moonglow, and such a relief to his spirit!

"Oh, we don't *steal*," she said, all seriousness. "If we did, I'd have some clothes already."

"Clothes?"

"I'd look more like my friends. Dress like them, I mean. None of them are kittens."

So she's made friends with gattins? *And they don't care that she's different from them?* Niss didn't know whether to be pleased or worried. *Hmm. Suppose it's all part of being young and curious, and she does have the power to fascinate and charm.*

"I'll tell you what, little one," he said. "I can't afford to buy you clothes, but I have an old tunic too shabby to sell and too threadbare to wear. I'll ask our landlady if she can scavenge a scrap of usable cloth from that and make it into a bit of garb for you. Nothing fancy, of course. And in exchange, I'll offer to clean and scour her kitchen for ten days!"

Lady Moonglow gave a happy cry. "You won't regret this, Pa, I promise!"

Niss scratched her under the chin. "I'd like to believe that," came his wry reply.

* * *

Seven days later, Niss was in the kitchen of the Sunflower Inn, elbow-deep in dishwater that was part suds, part grease. Lillumi sat at her worktable, peeling vegetables, and singing an old song. She paused in her tune and said, "Y'know, fine sir, it's true you promised me ten days' labor, but I'm willing to end it today, a bargain made and met."

Niss looked up from the sink. "Why? I don't think I've broken *too* many dishes."

"Ha! You've not even broke one. I'm glad of your work, but you made a poor bargain, overvaluing the worth of my part in it."

"You made Lady Moonglow a wonderful tunic that fits her well, *and* a belt to go with it, *and* you even embroidered it, cuffs, neck, and hem! What's more, she loves it."

"Don't you mean *you* love it?" Lillumi gave Niss a quizzical look. "Truth, I was surprised when you made the request to clothe a kitten, but I don't know nigh anything about the fancies of palace folk."

"Er, yes. Just so, a fancy of mine. But you must still be properly repaid for your labor in the only coin I've got." He waved his dripping paws.

Lillumi's pink nose flushed crimson and she wrapped her own paws in her apron. "Well, the truth is, fine sir—" She turned her face from Niss. "—I just this morning received some actual coin on your account."

"What?" A terrible suspicion darkened the *nyaari*'s mind. "From whom?"

"Er, from her, fine sir. The little one. When I opened my door, there she sat with a wee pile of coins at her feet and one in her mouth. She dropped it and gave me one of her darling looks, then scampered. I counted her gift and she'd left more than aplenty to settle what you owe. I figured you'd found work and wouldn't be back in my kitchen this day, yet—" She made a vague gesture. "—here you are. So now I'm wondering, well, wondering where she—how she—who she—"

Niss' guts turned cold, but he put on his long-disused dignity. "My dear *chomiki*, pray excuse me. I shall obtain the answers you desire straightaway." He wiped his paws on a dishtowel, removed and hung his apron, and added: "The answers we *both* desire. Meanwhile, might I beg you to keep this matter between us?"

Lillumi nodded, but Niss was already gone.

* * *

Moora Meeya's sleek tortoiseshell body sprawled motionless across the mound of pillows that now claimed a full half the floor space in her royal presence-chamber. They were among the many indulgences she'd claimed for herself with the new taxation revenues, but they could bring her precious little pleasure now. An eerie stillness pervaded the room, broken only by the muted sound of servants' and courtiers' paws passing back and forth in the corridor beyond the closed door. A single oil lamp burned low in a niche beside P'rra's desecrated mural. The atmosphere of the room felt more proper to a tomb than a palace.

"How much longer, boss?" Cadmin whined from a spot at the queen's feet. "I'm gettin' a cramp!"

A few of the other pillows moved as the voices of Keel, a trio of *musmusi*, and a pair of hidden *chomiki* also made their own discomfort known.

"Indeed." Lady Moonglow shifted her small body slightly, but the miniature dagger in her grip never wavered from its place against *Moora* Meeya's throat. "Well?" she purred into the royal ear. "You heard my esteemed colleagues: how much longer will we wait? I wouldn't advise testing my patience too much. My friends and I could decide that you are not the only possible answer to our prayers. Your successor might be more open to cooperating with us."

The queen's body trembled. "You heard me. I sent for him. He will come."

"In time? You'd better hope so. I want this business settled."

Moora Meeya sobbed softly. "Why are you doing this to me? I said I was sorry for trying to kill you!"

"And—?" Lady Moonglow prompted.

"And for dismissing Niss. As soon as Brother N'jel gets here I will swear to him by *B'stah* and *Orgl'orr* and any other gods you name that I will bring him back into my service."

"*And*—?"

"I don't know any more *ands*! What more do you want from me, you dreadful little monst—Oh! Oh, I'm sorry, I didn't mean that, please don't hurt me. If my stupid cousin Lady Nekayuri gets to be *moora*, I'll just *die*!"

The kitten sighed. "I'd never hurt anyone for telling the truth. You're right: I *am* a dreadful little monster. I was made so."

"You can't blame me for that! *I* didn't make you anything. I have no magic."

"Yet you had the power over me of life or death."

"It's not like I ever wanted it. I am the *moora*! Power over life or death comes with the job!"

"As it does with mine."

Moora Meeya could have sworn that the blade at her neck grew perceptibly colder, although that was most likely an illusion springing from the mortal terror engulfing her.

"Did you ever think *you* were to blame for how I treated you?" she said in desperation. "You let me believe you were an ordinary kitten that a loathsome *Hyrkitti* merchant had dropped on me as an insulting prank. You should have spoken when you first came into my presence. If you'd done that, I would have kept you to entertain our palace *gattin*s. You could have lived in luxury instead of consorting with a gang of wretched street-sweepings!" (This declaration was greeted with assorted cries of umbrage from several spots under the pillows.) "You know, I could still give you a wonderful life within these walls if you would only—"

A faint tapping sounded at the door to the royal presence-chamber, interrupting the queen's frantic attempts at sidestepping all culpability.

"My Supreme One?" The aged Lady H'rr'p's feeble voice quavered. "Brother N'jel has come. May I admit him?"

"Not yet," the kitten hissed.

"Not yet," *Moora* Meeya called out. "I—I must make myself presentable to receive one of the Holy Hairless. Take him to the second smallest dining room and entertain him well until I am ready to join him."

"As you wish, Most Excellent."

The kitten heard the retreating footsteps with satisfaction. "So he came. Good for him, lucky for you. With just a little more luck, you will soon be in his presence making your desires known."

"Desires?" *Moora* Meerya echoed. "What desires do I—?"

"Lady, do you love your *gattins?*" Lady Moonglow broke in.

The queen blinked. "What a question! Certainly I do. None of them are mine by birth, but they were entrusted to my care by their noble parents and I adore them all."

"Want to keep them safe, do you?"

"Of course!"

"Safe from things like *this*?" Lady Moonglow moved her blade just enough to emphasize its position and her own. *Moora* Meeya gave a small, sharp gasp.

"You see?" the kitten went on. "*This* was what I was created for: to find my way into your palace as a marvelous, unique plaything, a kitten who could *talk*. To endear myself to you and all your household. To be given a place as a cherished companion for the *gattins* you foster here, and then—" She gritted her fangs. "—to kill them."

"To—to—to kill our—?" The queen could barely speak. "How could you—? Why—?"

"Because that was the purpose for which I was made: to be the perfect assassin. When death visits a household, highborn or low, nobody ever suspects the kitten. I was imbued with speech, dexterity that I could use or conceal at will, a thorough knowledge of weaponry, including poisons, and the cunning to create…accidents. My creator was so pleased when he finished with me, only the first player in his wicked game, that he brought me to your door with his own hands and returned to his lair to await news of—" The kitten took a deep breath. "—a tragic and sinister series of mysterious deaths claiming the lives of the *gattins* left in *Moora* Meeya's care, with inexplicable clusters of fatalities occurring suspiciously close to times when the *nyaari* queen herself visited the soon-to-be victims." Her sing-song recitation dripped irony.

"Then the blame for their deaths would fall on me." The queen was so stunned by what she had just heard that she didn't notice that Lady Moonglow had subtly withdrawn her dagger from the royal neck. "Why didn't you fulfill your purpose?"

"You mean *his* purpose. I was his first attempt at sowing terror, mistrust, and ultimate chaos among the *nyaari*. Even if you fell from power, the deaths would continue no matter who sat on the throne, er, pillow pile. Fear breeds suspicion, grief breeds the hunger for revenge. The peaceful governing of the Beast Gate quarter would be wrecked and the chaos would spread throughout the rest of this sector of Ampyrium."

"Why?" *Moora* Meeya no longer spoke like a proud ruler, but in the soft, wounded voice of a sheltered soul suddenly confronting the world's brutality. "Why would anyone wish such a terror upon us?"

"Because the *nyaari* have had the gall to be different and yet successful," the kitten said. "You are envied. Many view you as abominations, but abominations can be tolerated if they know their place. My creator will find ample backing from merchants beyond the Beast Gate who would like nothing better than to see your portion of Ampyrium collapse." Lady Moonglow purred. "Count yourself lucky that *I* don't want that. I have friends here, you see. Family. Love."

"You have the power to defy your creator?"

"Well, I *am* a cat." The kitten gave the queen an uncharacteristically serious look. "He intends to begin work on more like me as soon as he hears the first rumors of *gattins* dying in significant numbers under questionable circumstances. I will not serve his aims and I will not let him work his painful spells to turn any other helpless kittens into his tools."

Moora Meeya fell silent for a while. At last she said: "When you and your team of assassins slipped into this room, captured me, and ordered me to summon Brother N'jel—"

"Or suffer a hidjus *death*!" one voice from beneath the cushions declared with relish. Lady Moonglow thumped the offending pillow hard. "Ow."

"—it was part of your plan to thwart your creator?"

"Even so. You see, O queen—"

"Never mind all that. I'll do it. Whatever it is, I will do as you say. If it will protect our *gattins*, your will is mine. I swear this by blessed *B'stah*, on forfeit of my life! No task you will set will be too difficult, no obstacle too hard to overcome, no pain too great!"

"Oh good," said Lady Moonglow. "You are going to make a lovely bride."

* * *

When the royal wolvenkind guards pounded on the door of the Sunflower Inn and demanded that former Chief Counselor Niss be produced to accompany them. Lillumi leaned out of an upstairs window, did a fine imitation of a helpless old *chomiki* who trembled in fear, and "accidentally" lost control of the mop bucket that had somehow made its way onto the windowsill. She bustled downstairs to make amends, managing to smear slop-water onto those guards who hadn't been caught in the initial deluge while dabbing at their drenched companions with a flailing washrag.

She was in the middle of this when Niss returned from his search for the kitten.

"Ohhhh, my goodness, fine sirs, I have *no idea* where your friend can be!" she fairly shouted, doing her best to give Niss the unspoken signal that he might want to be anywhere but there, and damned soon.

Niss shook his head over his valiant landlady. It was the first time he had witnessed the *chomiki* reputation for courage despite their small size. *Those wolvenkind wear the royal livery,* he thought. *I don't know what I've done to draw* Moora Meeya's *fresh wrath, but I can't let Lillumi risk her life for mine.*

"Noble guards," he said with all of his dignity. "I am at your service."

As the wolvenkind closed ranks around him and began to stride away, he called out what he fancied were his last words to his weeping landlady: "When my girl comes home again, tell her she was loved!"

* * *

Three days later, after the briefest of royal weddings was followed by the somewhat more extended royal honeymoon, Niss sat swathed in a satin robe across the breakfast table staring mystified at Lady Moonglow.

The kitten did not stare back. She was too preoccupied with consuming a roasted salmon three times her size. Like most heroic labors, it would be futile but glorious in the attempt. When she reached a good stopping point, she finally looked up.

"Yes, Pa?"

"She told me everything," Niss said.

"Good. Saves me the bother." The kitten dipped her head back to the salmon, then paused. "Did she treat you well? I mean as far as—"

"Yes, yes, don't ask, you're too young and innocent to—well, maybe not *innocent*, but you are definitely too young to know. It was actually pleasurable and I'm still alive, praise Lord *Orgl'orr*'s eternal mercy." He reconsidered. "Mostly. She's bathing now, while I…refuel."

"Also good. I let her know that if she harms you, she will regret it."

"Mmhm. She likewise told me that you and your *associates* have the ability to get into places you have no right being, undetected."

"And any time we like! Don't forget that. She'd best remember it, too, because if she ever goes back on her promise—" Lady Moonglow smiled. "We *are* the best corps of assassins in Ampyrium." Her grin widened. "Maybe the only one, eventually, depending on how I feel about it."

"So that's where those coins you brought came from." Niss hung his head. "I never expected you to go down such a dark path."

"Pa, be reasonable. This world has so many dark paths that you'd best make them your own if you want to survive. And I do. I have unfinished business with…someone."

"Fine, fine." Niss poked at his own breakfast. "What I don't understand is why you coerced the queen to marry me. I do appreciate that her morning-after gift was a vow to restore P'rra's mural, but you could have just ordered her to heap us with wealth and left it at that."

"Pfft! Don't you see? *Moora* Meeya is willing to be part of my plan to put an end to any fresh schemes against the Beast Gate quarter, but she's all enthusiasm and no wisdom. That is your role. You are not just her partner in the Moonlit Rites, but her co-ruler, the king regnant, the—the—whatchamacallit?"

"The *manyaara*." Niss pronounced the elevated title gloomily. "I didn't want this."

"And I didn't want to be a magically created perfect assassin, but what can you do? Never mind, I'll tell you: You can become the *shrewdness* that guides her on a better path, just as you were before she kicked you out. Except now, she can't! You're here to stay!"

"Until someone outside the palace wants me removed."

"Good luck to them, with my *associates* on the job, protecting you." Lady Moonglow managed to elevate ordinary feline smugness to a previously unthinkable degree. "I'm kind of proud at how good they all are, especially Keel and Cadmin."

"The ratlings? *Those* ratlings?" To Niss' horror, Lady Moonglow nodded. "Those inept little—? Oh, *fitz*, I'm dead."

The kitten sighed. "No, Pa; I've trained them. Now they only *look* inept. You don't know what a plus that is for an assassin. It's like having a cloak of invisibility. It worked really well for us when we were hired to—"

"I do *not* want to know!"

"Suit yourself, but just accept that you're safe now. And so is Lillumi and all the Sunflower Inn folk. Call it my way of saying thanks."

"Thanks," Niss repeated. He fell silent, mulling over the word. "I should thank you, my dear. You've done so much for the *nyaari* and maybe for the entire Beast Gate quarter, too. But how can I do that? Is there anything you lack? Anything you desire or fancy?"

"Welllllll." The kitten ate another bite of salmon. "I'd love a pair of boots."

Half-Life

Patricia Bray

Valeria paused at the top of the ramp, looking down toward the gate pool below. The torchlight cast strange shadows on the water, providing the illusion of life and movement beneath the surface. But it was just that, an illusion. For all but a few hours a month, the gate pool was a lifeless imitation of the world she had left behind.

At the base of the ramp, a series of shallow steps led up from the gate pool to a broad platform that ran the length of the chamber. The scant dozen cargo nets took up only a fraction of that space. Operarios passed by, carrying wooden chests, sealed amphoras, and oilskin-wrapped packages that were placed in the nets. As each net was filled, it was carefully tied off and a coiled tow rope attached.

Not wanting to risk being jostled, she waited until the last of the cargo bearers had returned to the waiting chamber before making her own way down.

The remaining operarios took their places, each standing beside a net, tow rope in hand. Their eager chatter subsided as she approached, but there was no mistaking their excitement.

Anselmo completed his inspection, then met her at the foot of the ramp. He nodded to indicate all was well and she was reminded of how much she would miss his quiet competence. After spending a term here as a youth, he had returned as an elder, spending a season in the gate world before returning home, then repeating the cycle. He'd been invaluable to her, both in his ability to manage the young operarios and his willingness to work with the Ampyrians.

But the last season had worn on him and he'd confessed that his bones ached and his skin felt stretched and worn.

Seasickness. He'd lasted longer than most, but so many moons spent away from home waters took a toll on even the strongest of them. And while no words were said, she doubted very much that he would volunteer to return.

"Open the gate," she called.

At her command, the watcher on duty began to turn the great wheel. The waters came rushing through the protective screen, frothing and splashing as the gate pool filled. Warm humid air rushed by, bringing the briny scents of home.

One operario cast off his robe and started forward, but Anselmo caught him before he could transform. "Step out of line again and you'll stay here for another season," Anselmo threatened as he dragged the young one back to his net.

The waters rose, higher and higher, until they lapped the edge of the top step. Valeria knew that it had not always been this way. Once the gate had opened at will and traders had walked freely between the two worlds. But things were different now. In many ways.

When the waters stilled, she gave the order for the bronze screen to be lowered. Then she turned and bowed to Anselmo. "Warm seas and easy passage, my friend. Please convey my respects to the Rainha. And to the Princeps," she added, conscious of their audience. She handed him the sealed document cylinder that held this month's reports.

Anselmo gave a much deeper bow. "I will assure them of your esteem, and devotion to their service." He was kind enough not to utter the traditional farewell, and for that she was grateful.

Anselmo slung the cylinder's overlong strap over his chest, then dove, already transformed before he hit the waters. There was a flash of fins, then he was through the gate.

One by one the operarios followed him, some more gracefully than others. A young speckled-belly became entangled in his cargo ropes and had to be freed by his companions. She suspected it was the same young one who'd lost control earlier, but having only known him on two-legs she couldn't be certain.

There was a brief pause after the last of the operarios passed through the gate. Then a tall black fin appeared, followed by a mixed school of lesser blacks and grays. At the foot of the stairs he transformed into a Fomorian of mid-years, dark hair contrasting with his moon-pale skin. Tall for his kind, he towered over her even before he reached the top step.

Reaching into the basket, she handed him a robe, which barely came down to his calves. He grimaced. Instead of greeting her, he turned his attention to the waters below. He gave a short nod as the last of the swimmers approached the stairs.

"Close the gate," he ordered.

The watchers hesitated.

"Raise the screen and close the gate." Then she turned to the newcomer, "I am Senior Envoy Valeria and I bid you welcome to the gateworld."

"I know who you are. I am Archon Marius of Fomor. The Princeps is displeased with your performance and sent me to investigate."

She was too old a player at this game to respond directly to his remarks. And in truth, there was much to displease the Princeps, though little of that was her doing.

"I would be happy to speak with you, once the trade goods are secure."

She waited until the gate was sealed shut and the pool started to drain before signaling to the bearers to return. While it was her custom to supervise the unloading, it wasn't necessary, and it was better to have the first conversation with the archon away from curious ears.

Beatriz, who was now senior, seemed pleased to be entrusted with the responsibility for inventorying the goods and assigning quarters to the new operarios.

Valeria made no attempt to disguise her limp as she led the way up the ramp, through the stone halls, to the records chamber that served as her office. Marius's disgust was apparent as she lowered herself into her seat. Disdaining the guest chairs, he began to pace, perhaps hoping to intimidate her, but he merely looked foolish as his topknot brushed the low ceiling with each step.

Others in her position might have offered explanations or apologies. Valeria knew her worth, and the value of silence.

"The Princeps is displeased," he repeated, when it became clear she would not be the first to speak.

"As you have said."

"And is it no wonder? I saw the tradenets as they passed through the gate. Less than half of what we expect and deserve."

"True, the shipment was smaller than some, but I selected the most valuable items from the markets. Rare oils, jewels, and I was able to source the silks requested for the weavers."

"Your weavers, not ours. And what of our demands? Where are the weapons? Where are the star-steel ingots for our forges?"

Valeria spread her hands wide. "What did you bring me to trade for them? The Magnum allow only a handful of weapons traders, and their craft is in high demand."

It was a partial truth. While the Magnum did not officially control what was traded through the gates or by the various merchants of Ampyrium, those who dealt in weapons were under constant scrutiny by the orbs and were more likely than most to disappear without warning. Still, with skillful bargaining, she could have traded for a shipment of daggers or a handful of short swords, but she had no guarantee that any such weapons would not be immediately used against her people.

"I oversaw this shipment and know its worth. I will direct the trade and ensure that the Princeps is pleased by the results."

"As you wish."

After casting aspersions on her character, her management of the gate trade, and a lecture on why the Fomorians were superior in every way to the Therans, Marius finally allowed her to summon an operario to show him to his quarters.

Valeria sighed as he left. Marius was a problem, and one she would have to endure for at least a moon-cycle until the next opening of the gate. He was not the first sent to inspect her work, but the others had been of lower rank. As an archon, he had the potential to make real trouble for her, both here and at home.

And there was some truth to his accusations. Once, the Therans had controlled a vibrant gate trade, with caravans passing through the gate in both directions. Mastery of the gate had made the Theran kingdom the pre-eminent power in the Great Basin. But the cataclysm that had crippled her had also crippled the kingdom. As the earth shook and the island tore itself in two, the gate sank into the ocean. The capital lay in ruins, and by the time Valeria had been found under the rubble, the damage had been done. Unable to transform and barely able to drag herself along on two-legs, she'd cursed her saviors.

The Fomorians had arrived with desperately needed aid, but the price of that aid was agreeing to joint control of the gate. Though with trade limited by the lunar tides, and trade goods limited to those that could traverse the sea gate undamaged, neither side was satisfied with the arrangement.

According to the treaty, the gateworld outpost was to be staffed by an equal mix of Therans and Fomorians, who would serve for a season before being sent back home. Some, like Anselmo, returned again and again, gaining rank and prestige for their knowledge of the markets and trade speech. And some did not survive even one season, driven mad by the constraints of a life lived solely on dry land.

Command of the outpost was to alternate between the Therans and Fomorians. But since Valeria had taken control of the outpost, no Fomorian had lasted long enough to replace her. And she would do whatever it took to make sure that Marius was not the first to break that chain.

* * *

"Master Ola is here, and wishes to speak with you," Beatriz announced, as she stepped into the office.

"Of course," Valeria put aside her ledger and wiped the pen before returning it to the base. "Did he say what it was about?"

Beatriz shook her head.

Valeria turned the matter over in her mind as they left the inner gate rooms, walked past the workshops where hired crafters turned raw materials into trade goods, then into the outer chambers that led to the marketplace. They weren't scheduled for a shipment from him until Fifth Day and, even then, it would be his factotum who supervised the exchange, not Master Ola himself.

"Master Ola, you honor us with your presence," she bowed low.

"The honor is mine," he replied. "I thank you for taking time out of your day to meet with this humble trader."

Master Ola was many things, but a humble trader he was not. From his estate near Plague Gate he ruled over a network of lesser traders. His warehouses held goods from all the living trade worlds, and she knew that, for every merchant who publicly wore his colors, there were an equal number who served him in secret, allowing him a near-monopoly on certain goods. It was even said that he had once visited the citadel of the Magnum and emerged unscathed, a rumor that he took care to neither confirm nor deny.

They traded pleasantries as a servant poured fragrant tea from Daruvia, then offered a tray of nut-filled sweets.

Master Ola sipped his tea and ate a single bite, showing his trust in her hospitality, before getting to the reason for his visit.

"Word has come to my ears that you are seeking to renegotiate your trade agreements. I thought it wise to confirm your intentions for myself. Our partnership has served us well over the years, and I would not want there to be any...misunderstandings."

Anger rose as she realized the extent of her miscalculation. While she'd been willing to let Marius play at being a trader with the Fomorian goods he'd brought, she could not afford to have him jeopardize the arrangements she'd already made...especially not the ones that weren't recorded in any of the trade scrolls that made their way back to the home world.

Valeria sipped her tea as she considered her response, knowing that the servants would likely report every word of this conversation to the Archon.

"You may rest assured of our friendship. We have no intention of trading our perfumes with any other. As for the rest, our new Mercator is to be commended for his diligence in exploring the opportunities Ampyrium provides. No doubt any confusion is due to the inadequacies of the translator that accompanies him. I will ensure that is corrected."

Master Ola seemed to accept her explanation, and their conversation turned to the recent violence near Black Gate and their mutual hopes that it was not the start of a new trade war. Both had their own reasons to wish to avoid such chaos—Ola because such trade wars held the potential to disrupt the balance of power among the merchants. And since Black Gate bordered her own, it was likely that any disturbances would spill over to her own quarter before the Magnum deigned to intervene.

After the trader left, Valeria was surprised to find Beatriz lingering in the outer corridor, rather than the customary runner. "Good, I was about to send for you," she said.

Beatriz fell into step beside her as they headed toward the workshops. "What brought Master Ola to our halls today? Is there something amiss?"

"Merely a courtesy to let us know that the Archon's efforts to find new trade goods were creating uncertainty in the marketplace." Valeria chose her words deliberately—Beatriz's loyalty was certain but the same could not be said for the operarios who passed by on their various tasks. Any one of them could be lining their pockets with Marius's silver. "Santiago is clearly not worthy of the honor of serving the Archon, and I blame myself for not insisting that the Archon be accompanied by a senior operario."

"Santiago was the Archon's choice and he would accept no other. Though after returning empty-handed, he may be reconsidering. Perhaps I should approach Santiago and suggest that he invite a senior to join them? If the suggestion comes from him the Archon may be more inclined to agree."

"Please do so. And let him know he can request any of the seniors, including yourself."

It was worth a try. If the Archon refused, as she fully expected, he could not later blame her for failing to offer her full support. And if Santiago somehow convinced him that they needed a senior trader to accompany them, odds were it would be a Theran who was loyal to her

They reached the workshops where hired crafters turned leviathan essence into perfumes and unguents that were prized by wealthy Ampyrians. After consulting with Beatriz and the supervisor, she selected a half-dozen vials of their newest scent and directed a runner to deliver them to Master Ola. The trader would recognize the gesture for what it was, a recognition of their mutually profitable partnership and thanks for his promptness in reaching out to her.

When he returned, the runner brought news of fresh riots near Black Gate, and when the evening repast arrived with no sign of the Archon, Valeria allowed herself the brief hope that he and his companions had fallen victim to the violence. She went to bed that night wondering how she would explain such a circumstance to the Princeps, but her musings were for naught as she woke to the news that Marius and his companions had just returned after spending the night in the city. According to his watcher, the Archon had spent the afternoon in an inn near the so-called Death Gate, and then elected to spend the night there. The watcher had been unable to determine who Marius was meeting with, and she dared not test the loyalties of those that had accompanied him. While the Archon did not have the authority to remove her from her position, half of the gate staff were Fomorian and likely to choose his side in any conflict that arose.

The key, of course, was not to let Marius know that they were in conflict. Present the façade of cooperation, all the while keeping him unaware of her true mission in Ampyrium.

After a light breakfast of bread and fruit, she returned to her inner chamber to dress for the day, selecting a linen stola and a silk shawl. Rather than immediately donning the shawl she carried it with her to her outer office.

The Archon entered moments later, not even bothering with a customary knock. His features twisted with disgust as his gaze lingered on her withered left arm and she congratulated herself for throwing him off balance even as she took her time donning the shawl.

"With the recent unrest, I was concerned when you did not return last evening. Perhaps in future you could send word of your plans, or allow me to provide an escort? The dangers of Ampyrium are not always obvious and I would not want anyone to think I was careless of your safety."

Since his arrival a fortnight past, the Archon had made several trips into the city, accompanied by two of the newly arrived operarios who had been tasked as his servants. She'd offered to assign one of the outpost's traders to translate for him, but instead he'd chosen Santiago—a Fomorian operario on his third assignment in the gateworld—apparently valuing loyalty over proficiency.

"I heard you met with a master trader yesterday. I should have been informed so I could be present."

"Master Ola's visit was a surprise." No doubt his own spies had told him as much, but it seemed he was in the mood for a quarrel. "Though we do need to discuss his visit. The master was concerned that we wished to break our long-standing agreements. I assured him he was mistaken, as we have no desire to lose such a valuable partner."

"What use is this master to us, if he cannot deliver star-steel?"

"And have you found any other who can? At a price we can afford?"

She knew he hadn't. Her watchers had reported his frustration at discovering the goods he'd personally selected and brought through the gate were barely enough to afford a single star-steel blade. With gates connecting to a variety of worlds, items that were luxuries at home were commonplace in the city markets. It took skill and patience to get the most out of what they had to trade, something that the Fomorian clearly lacked.

"While not a trader yourself, you must realize the importance of honoring our agreements. Master Ola is well-respected in the city markets. If we break faith with him, few others will be willing to trade with us. It has taken years to rebuild our relationships after the great flood destroyed our warehouses and angered those whose goods we could no longer deliver."

The cataclysm had sent a giant wave of water rushing through the open gate, flooding the gate complex. Some of the staff had transformed only to be crushed as the outer chambers collapsed. Dozens of Ampyrans browsing the market stalls drowned. It was only when the flood waters reached the outer gatewall that the Magnum intervened, closing the gate.

The sparse accounts of those days gave only hints of the terror the surviving Therans must have felt, their anxious speculation over what might have caused the flood warring with their fear over being trapped in Ampyrium. Each day they tried and failed to open the gate, until the night of the first spring moon, when the gate finally allowed itself to be opened.

Her family dead, her former life in ruins, Valeria had answered the Rainha's pleas for volunteers to serve in the gateworld. There had been much to do—chambers had to be cleared of debris, rotting goods sold for a fraction of their value or destroyed outright. With the flow of goods restricted to a single day a month—and not at all during the winter moons—they had to find new trading partners and new goods to trade. She'd spent over a decade in exile transforming the devastated tradepost into a bustling market once more, all the while ensuring that her people received the lion's share of the wealth that flowed through the gate, even as the Fomorians believed that they held the upper hand. She had dealt with challengers before, but they had been traders who found themselves out of their depth, or minor functionaries easily distracted by the gate city. The Archon was a different kind of threat, and would have to be managed carefully.

Marius followed as she left her office for her customary morning inspection. They passed by the counting house, then the inner warehouse where operarios packed this month's goods for transport. A quick glance showed spindles of silver thread being packed in oilskin pouches before being placed in chests for transport, with bolts of silk on the shelves ready to be packed next. Fortunately, Marius showed no interest in the packing room; instead he continued to harangue her.

"You talk of trade, but half the outpost is workshops and living quarters for foreign laborers."

"Those rooms were sitting idle with the reduced trade schedule. I saw an opportunity for profit—exiles from Forest Gate welcome the work, and they cost us a fraction of what we would pay our own people. Assuming we could find enough volunteers willing to serve."

She glanced over at him. "You've inspected the account books so you must realize those workshops make up half of our profits."

He was not the first to question the value of the workshops, or the presence of outsiders within the gate complex. She was fortunate that Fomor had sent traders and bureaucrats to oversee her work. A master crafter—one accustomed to running such workshops—would soon realize the official account books reflected only a fraction of their worth. Such deception would prove deadly for her, and might well result in her people losing control of the gate.

It was a risky game she played. But it would be worth it, in the end.

* * *

A brass bell tinkled overhead as Marius and Santiago stepped into the dingy storefront. Inside were tables piled high with jumbled goods—mismatched crockery next to worn leather bags, dented brasses next to porcelain votives. There was no attempt at organization and a thin layer of dust covered most goods. Unmarked urns filled the shelves behind the counter, and he breathed in the scent of spices underlaid by a hint of rot. A weedy young clerk stood behind the counter, polishing a chipped vase with a dirty rag.

"The Lord Mercator is here sees Master Ullmark," Santiago announced.

Marius hid a wince. Santiago's grasp of the trade tongue was abysmal, hardly better than his own. But he could not risk using any of the outpost's translators—those loyal to Valeria would report back to her, and if he requested one of those he'd managed to suborn, that would only serve to call them to Valeria's attention.

"I will see if she is available." The clerk stood, then disappeared behind the curtain that separated the front room from the back. A few moments later he returned and beckoned them on through.

The backroom was smaller and much cleaner than the front. Mistress Ullmark appeared to be a native Ampyrian, with dark eyes and white hair braided in a crown. Her brown robes showed signs of wear and there were inkstains on her right hand.

At their approach, she set her quill down but did not rise from her desk.

"Was there something that caught your eye out front? I don't often see those from Water Gate," she said.

Marius withdrew the battered star-steel dagger from his messenger bag and laid it on her desk. "I understand this came from your shop," he said.

The trader eyed the dagger but did not pick it up.

"What of it?" she asked with a shrug. "I don't recall this item, but it may have been part of a death lot. White brass used to be fashionable but today most prefer iron or bronze."

"It's star-steel."

"Truly?" She leaned forward to poke the dagger with one finger, doing her best to appear shocked. "Then I was cheated, or whoever sold it to you lied about where it came from."

"Pity," Marius said. "I am prepared to pay handsomely for such items." Replacing the dagger in his bag he pulled out a handful of moon pearls.

Mistress Ullmark leaned back with a laugh. "Moon pearls? I have no need for such. You'd do better with an apothecary who could grind them into potions to restore your manhood."

Santiago bristled at the insult, but Marius was above such things. "What would interest you?"

"If I were to hear of such items for trade, whoever sold them would expect gold. Measure for measure."

He'd heard the same from others. And while he had a supply of gold for trade, even star-steel was not worth its weight in gold. Though the time to haggle was after the weapons were offered and not before.

"I thank you for your time. If you do hear of such, please send word to Archon Marius at Water Gate. I will ensure that you are compensated… appropriately."

Marius took his leave. He could not force Mistress Ullmark to tell him where she acquired the dagger. Having seen her shop, he doubted very much that she had another such item in her possession. Indeed, the trader who'd sold the dagger might have lied about where he'd acquired it.

It felt like a failure, and he was not accustomed to such.

As Archon he was the Princeps' eyes and ears, empowered to both investigate and take whatever action he deemed necessary. He spied on allies and enemies alike, navigating the shifting politics of the homeworld with ease. Most assumed him a bureaucrat and even those he ultimately destroyed had no idea that he was the author of their downfall. His methods varied depending on what was needed, sometimes a few well-placed words sowing the seeds of conflict, other times forged documents showing criminal activity. And if all else failed, a knife slipped between the ribs had a way of permanently ending a problem.

He had never failed to complete a task given to him.

But after a month in Ampyrium, he had little to show for his efforts. He had inspected the account books, comparing the official totals to the inventories in the storehouses, and found that they very nearly matched. If they had matched exactly, he would have been suspicious, but as it was, the small differences—a half-full cask counted as full, a shipment of agate that was labelled as quartz, these were signs that he was seeing the true books, and not ones the envoy had crafted for his consumption.

And with each day that passed, his frustration grew. He knew that the Therans were cheating them out of their rightful share of the gate wealth, though he was no closer to proving it than on the day he'd swum through the gate.

He had spies watching every move Valeria made, but except for the unscheduled meeting with Master Ola, she'd done nothing that he could officially object to. Her days were spent supervising the workshops where foreign workers turned raw material into trade goods, and supervising the market stalls in the outer gate where goods of lesser value were sold. Twice, she had taken a sedan chair into the city to meet with their trading partners, escorted by her senior operarios. She'd invited him to accompany her, but with both Beatriz and Waltharius secretly reporting to him, he'd used those meetings as a test. A test that she'd strangely passed, as her account of those meetings matched the reports of his spies.

Her experience served her well, as merchants strove to outbid each other for the common corals she'd requested from Thera. Meanwhile the moon pearls and amethysts he'd brought to trade had garnered little interest from the merchants he'd approached—he might as well have been offering them common glass.

It was growing clear that they could not simply replace the envoy with one of their own people. None of them had the knowledge or skill to anticipate the shifting markets, nor the relationships that Valeria had spent years cultivating. She had made herself indispensable, and it would take months if not years for another to gain the knowledge needed to take her place.

Of all the Fomorians sent to the gateworld, Xanthippe had come closest to being able to take on the role of Senior Envoy. She'd served two terms in the early months of the alliance with the Therans, then assumed responsibility for managing the Fomorian's share of the tradegoods that passed through the gates. When she'd returned last year as the senior operario, it was with the understanding that she and Valeria would alternate control of the outpost, in accordance with the original treaty.

It had been a bitter blow when the gate opened after the three-month winter hiatus to find out that Xanthippe had committed suicide. Marius was one of many who had suspected foul play, but after a month spent in the confines of Ampyrium, he was no longer certain. Those on Fomor had no understanding of the pressures of living in the gateworld. True, he often went longer without transforming at home, but then it was by choice. Now it was as if he was in prison, unable to transform, not even able to glimpse the ocean that lay beyond the city's great walls. Each day was worse than the last—his temper grew uneven, his bones ached, and his very skin felt tight and stretched. It was no wonder only the strongest survived for more than a season.

As for Valeria, well she was practically a two-legs herself. Unable to transform, rumors said she'd been dragged through the gate like prey. Perhaps that was the true secret of her success—she was more an Ampyrian than a Theran these days.

* * *

Marius watched impatiently as Valeria inspected the outgoing trade goods stacked along the platform. The shipment was clearly divided, with her pitiful offerings of cloth, threads, and the like relegated to the far end, accompanied by the least experienced operarios, while the goods he'd personally selected filled the cargo nets closest to him, each line held by a Fomorian.

As promised, he'd taken charge of the trade goods he'd brought through the gate, and the cargo nets reflected what he'd been able to bargain for in return. He'd tried—and failed—to take for himself a share of what was produced in the workrooms, but the past month's output had already been committed in trades. Valeria had promised that any excess would be set aside for his use, and that she'd welcome his counsel at winter moon, when it came time to renegotiate their trade agreements.

He repressed a shudder at the thought he might still be here come winter moon.

As Valeria joined him on the gate ramp, Marius gave the order for the gate to be opened. Water rushed through the screen, bringing with it the scents of home, and he clenched his fists, fighting the urge to transform. Around him, the operarios shifted restlessly next to their good-nets, anxious to be on their way. Only the cripple Valeria seemed unfazed.

With a final glance, he confirmed that Decimus had possession of the chest intended for the Princeps, which held the handful of star-steel and near-steel items he'd been able to trade for. In his coded report, he'd assured the Princeps that his mission was progressing well, and that these were but a sampling of the goods he expected to acquire once they wrested control of the gate away from the Therans. Privately, he admitted that he was no closer to that goal than he had been on the day he arrived.

As the gate screen was raised, Decimus cast off his robe and was first into the pool, leading the way through the gate, followed by the operarios in order of seniority. Last through the gate was Fabia who bore the official copies of their reports. He had inspected both goods and bearers personally and found no undeclared goods nor hidden message scrolls. But Valeria could easily have entrusted one of the bearers with a verbal report.

Readying himself to inspect the incoming trade goods, he vowed that next time the gate opened, the nets would be filled with the goods he'd promised. He'd spent the last month exploring the public markets of Ampyrium, it was time to see what he could find in the less savory districts. And if he could somehow ensure that the envoy was blamed for any illicit trades, that would be even better.

* * *

Valeria set the glass of wine on the shelf next to the bathing pool, then reached for the belt of her robe. "Thank you, Ema, I will call when I have need of you."

Ema, a local woman of mid-years, bowed, then left the chamber.

Untying the robe and dropping it on the floor next to the pool, Valeria settled into the lukewarm bath, taking a deep breath of the perfumed waters.

She allowed herself few luxuries, but the oversized bathing chamber attached to her quarters was one of them. The pool was large enough for several two-legs to frolic, and while nothing could take the place of the true sea, over the years she'd found a combination of salts and herbs that helped ease her spirits.

Ema was almost certainly being paid by Marius to report on her mistress's activities, and thus Valeria was careful to ensure that she did nothing out of the ordinary. Her habit of bathing without any attendants was likely seen as shame over her crippled state. It was but one of the ways in which she reminded the gate staff—enemies and allies alike—of the reason she had originally been chosen as envoy.

Though the techniques she'd used to distract others were having limited success with Marius. Despite his open contempt, he continued to dig into every aspect of the gate trade, and his latest ventures into the less than legal sections of the marketplace were proving worrisome indeed. It was not out of the question that either he or his agents would stumble across one of those merchants whose trades with her never made it onto the official account books.

She sipped her wine as she contemplated what to do about the troublesome Archon. Others had been persuaded to leave when their investigations failed to bear fruit, or the pressures of life in Ampyrium grew too great for them to endure. Xanthippe's suicide had been the result of months of effort, but the Archon was made of sterner stuff. And without the excuse of the long winter shutdown to blame, no one would believe he took his own life.

In her last visit to the marketplace she'd made a point to be overheard discussing her concerns over Marius's safety, in light of his habit of carrying gold to pay for his trades, rather than having the exchange take place under the protection of Water Gate. Unfortunately for her, the thieves who'd attacked had proven no match for the Archon and his escort. The only casualty had been one of her own who'd been assigned to accompany him.

To herself she admitted that she'd put too much faith in her own cleverness. Instead of using her hidden funds to hire an assassin, she'd tried to arrange a convenient accident. All she'd done was put Marius on his guard, which would make any similar attempts harder.

They were too close to their goal for her to make another mistake. For over a decade, the Therans had swallowed their pride, allowing the Fomorians to jointly rule the gate and the sea trade. Both sides knew that the alliance would not last, it was only a matter of time before one side got the upper hand.

Even now, Marius was meeting with a smuggler who promised he could deliver star-steel swords. Such weapons would be highly prized at home, where most made do with bronze. And while the Rainha's crown was gold-inlaid star-steel, her personal guards carried iron swords. Only a handful knew of the star-steel forges, and the weapons that were being stockpiled underneath the ruined citadel, waiting for the day when they would reclaim their homeland and the gate.

Setting aside her wineglass, Valeria slipped under the waters and transformed, her fins briefly brushing the bottom of the pool as she rolled over. After a dozen breaths, she surfaced and resumed her two-legged form.

Even such a brief transformation was a risk, as it was common knowledge that she was too crippled to transform. And while that had been true when she first arrived in Amyprium, over the years she had recovered her strength.

It served her purposes, for now, to be underestimated. Just as the alliance with the Fomorians continued to serve her people's purposes. But one day soon they would both be ready to cast off such pretenses and take their rightful places.

* * *

Marius straightened his crimson-embroidered cloak, then, for the first time since coming to Ampyrium, he donned the gold chain of his office. While the Ampyrians would not understand the precise meaning of the symbols displayed, they spoke the universal language of wealth and power.

Waltharius and Santiago were waiting outside his chambers, along with the half-dozen operarios chosen to act as his escort. As instructed, all were dressed in their finest, as befit the escort of one empowered to speak in the Princeps' name. They fell into place behind him as he led the way from the residence halls into the inner courtyard.

Valeria rose from her seat as his party approached the gate that led to the outer marketplace. "I beg you to reconsider," she said. "The Magnum act for their own reasons. It is not for us to understand."

"I am no simple trader, nor servant to be brushed off. They will hear me."

"Then allow me to come with you, to translate for you. I would not wish there to be any unfortunate misunderstandings."

And let her twist his words into something else? She must think him a fool.

"I have made my own arrangements." He made eye contact with Beatriz, who nodded, then left her mistress's side.

Shock bloomed on Valeria's face at the evidence of betrayal.

"You've had years to make changes, but instead you've squandered your opportunities. Your usefulness is over, and it's time you were replaced."

With that he led the way out of the gate, toward the inner citadel, and his meeting with the Magnum.

Ironically, it had been Valeria herself who had given him this idea, as, deep into her cups one night, she'd lamented that the Magnum had chosen to merely stabilize the gate rather than return it to its original position on land. It was a seemingly careless remark that had burrowed into his brain.

It was the Magnum who had originally created the gates and placed them on the trade worlds. The Magnum who decided who was worthy to trade and who was not. Valeria knew this, yet not once had she considered entreating the Magnum to move the gate. Instead, when confronted, she bleated her fears that the Magnum would punish them for their impertinence, perhaps going so far as to permanently close the gate, as they had done with the Shattered Gate.

The Therans were cowards, unwilling to take the risks necessary to restore trade. Why should they be content with a trickle of goods that passed through the sea gate each moon? Why shouldn't the gate be returned to dry land, with wagons of goods passing back and forth freely? Surely the Magnum, who had created the gate trade, would see the advantages of restoring the gate to its original state. And if they chose to place it in Fomor, rather than Thera, well it was no less than his people deserved.

Let Valeria rub shoulders with common traders and spend her days in the workshops, grubbing after each tin sesterce. Marius was an Archon, prepared to take bold risks and to reap the rewards.

Leaving their district behind, they made their way through the common sections, heading toward the citadel. Here, in the inner ring, the wealthy and elite of Ampyrium had their homes, the closer to the citadel, the higher their presumed status. The streets might be cleaner, and the houses larger, but the stench of the walled city pervaded even here. Only the Magnum, in their citadel that towered above all, would enjoy fresh breezes.

As they neared the citadel, the orb that had followed their progress suddenly turned and began flying west, toward Black Gate, or possibly towards their own Water Gate. Marius paused, turning to watch as a dozen orbs left the citadel and rapidly headed west.

"The Wands are likely brawling again," Beatriz commented.

Marius shook off his hesitation. Whatever was happening, whether at Black Gate or their own, it was not his concern. The orbs had seen his party approaching the citadel, and even if he could not see one of their eyes upon him, that did not mean he wasn't unobserved. Hesitation would be seen as weakness, at a moment when he needed to project strength. With a sharp command, they resumed progress, following Beatriz's lead as she guided them to a narrow road that ran parallel to the citadel.

"The public entrance is on the other side, opposite Plague Gate," she reminded him.

That much he knew. The gate was guarded but open at all hours, day and night. Few passed through the gate and even fewer returned, or so the stories said. In his judgment it was equally likely that those who entered through the main gate might leave through another, less known exit, the better to keep the rumors alive. The Magnum relied as much upon their reputation as they did their powers to keep order in the city.

Santiago took the lead, followed by Marius, with Beatriz and Waltharius behind.

Soon the road narrowed into a mere alley and they were forced to single file. As they approached the archway that signaled the division between the territory of Water Gate and Market Gate, Santiago abruptly paused. "Avert!" he exclaimed.

A white robed figure appeared in the archway, their face hidden beneath a cowl. It was impossible to tell if they were male or female, old or young. He recognized the Magnum immediately, even though he'd only caught glimpses of them before.

Brushing past Santiago, he advanced, then offered a short bow. "Lord Magnum," he said. "I bring a message for your people from the rulers of my homeworld, beyond the Water Gate."

The Magnum beckoned him forward. Only dark eyes were visible in the cowl, the rest of their features covered by a veil.

What was the Magnum doing here? Was this a chance encounter? Or had they sent an escort who would bring him inside the citadel?

He wouldn't allow himself to think of failure, or the chance that this messenger had been sent to deter him from his purpose.

The Magnum uttered something, the words so low that he bent forward to catch them.

The knife that slipped between his ribs came as a complete surprise.

* * *

"Pray convey my deepest regrets to the Princeps for the death of the Archon. His devotion to duty and courage were an inspiration to us all."

Waltharius accepted the message scrolls. Marius's possessions and those goods he'd managed to acquire had already been packed into a sealed chest, ready to be taken through the gate.

Unwilling to follow the local custom of sending bodies outside the city to be buried, they'd packed Marius's remains in a barrel of brine, to preserve him until he could be returned to the waves.

"I hope the Princeps will appreciate the pair of star-steel swords that we found in his quarters. Alas, Marius did not record where they came from, and with Santiago's disappearance, we are unlikely to discover his source." Valeria sighed and shook her head, doing her best to convey her deep disappointment.

What exactly had happened during his journey to the citadel remained a mystery. Those who survived agreed that Marius had stopped to speak with one of the Magnum, then suddenly slumped to the ground. Beatriz had been first to his side, and by the time they realized he had been stabbed, both the Magnum and Santiago had disappeared.

In her official report she'd laid out the facts as she knew them. She'd added her own speculation that Santiago had stabbed Marius, then immediately been taken by the Magnum for punishment, but made it clear that this was nothing more than speculation. Searching Santiago's quarters had revealed nothing that would prove either his guilt or innocence, as she'd intended.

Let the Fomorians wonder if one of their own had turned rogue, or if the Magnum had punished Marius for his impertinence in approaching the citadel.

They'd be too busy dealing with internal politics and the maneuverings of those who sought to take Marius's place to bother with the gate trade.

While they wondered and schemed, she would continue both her public and private missions. It had taken all of her hidden funds to hire an assassin willing to pose—briefly—as one of the Magnum, while Master Ola's agents arranged for a riot to distract the orbs. And a full-measure of Beatriz's cunning to ensure that Marius took the circuitous route to the citadel, arriving under the concealing arch at the appointed hour. Beatriz had played her role well, fooling even the Archon into believing that she would betray her own people for gold.

As for the star-steel, while Marius had been making his way toward the citadel, she had helped herself to the bulk of his finds, leaving just two swords behind. And since he'd kept no records of his trades, there was none left alive who could gainsay the count.

In addition to the Archon's remains, she had the usual trade goods packed and ready, including chests of the silver embroidery threads that Marius had sneered at. The fool had been blinded by his assumptions, not realizing those chests were worth their weight in gold. Craftsmen outside the city, far from the Magnum's watchful eyes, turned star-steel into silver threads, which Master Ola then imported and sold to his most discerning customers. Some of those threads would be woven into the embroidered cloths for which Thera was famous, providing justification for the trade. The rest would make their way to the hidden forges, to be melted down and turned into weapons.

It would take her time to rebuild the hidden funds that fueled the secret trades back up, not to mention the debt she owed for Master Ola's assistance, but with patience, all things were possible. One day the gate would open, and she would swim through in triumph, as her people once again took their rightful place as rulers of the Great Basin.

Downfall

S.C. Butler

If Ampyrium has taught me anything, it's that Death is the greatest con of all.

Think about it. You've got an entire city devoted to one thing and one thing only: commerce. A world where buying and selling are at the center of everyone's mind from the minute they wake up in the morning to the moment they fall asleep. Regardless of whether they are male or female, both or neither, from one of the five great worlds on the other side of Ampyrium's currently open gates, or one of the dozen or so lesser nations and cultures that are part of those worlds, they're all seeking profit. Glorious, dependable profit. Banking or borrowing, begging or broke, that's all anyone in Ampyrium thinks about all day.

Then you throw Death into the mix. It's like adding that last pinch of owlet's wing to your bubbling cauldron. Usually buyers know what they're buying, sellers what they're selling. But when dealing with Death, no one really knows anything at all. Caution falls by the wayside. Prudence ceases to prevail. People have no idea what they're doing. Have either buyer or seller ever actually died? I doubt it. Are they really exchanging anything other than promises? No. But they think they know exactly what they're doing because their faith is great. Their belief is strong, so buyer and seller can con each other, and themselves.

I should know. I'm the superintendent at the Bureau of Death. My job is managing the entire business, from Visitations to Internments, accountants to mediums, the entire process of buying and selling access to the Afterlife.

Our offices are located in Downfall, also called the District of Demise or the Gateway to Grief. Or, if you're one of the Magnum, simply Gate 6. Tucked into the bottom of Elysium Hill, Downfall stretches from the bleak barrenness of the Sealed Gate in the southeast to the world weary cuteness of Beast Gate to the north. Elysium Hill itself rises in stately emptiness from the middle of the District to about a quarter of the height of the great wall that circles our city, protecting us from the diseased and barren world outside, and them from us. At the western end of the District lies Deadwater, also known as the Sea of Tears, a lake too bitter for even ghosts to swim in, its eastern edge lapping the bottom of Elysium Hill. Beyond the hill, Elysium Bridge arches above the Bazaar all the way to the crumbling inner wall and outer suburbs of the city proper.

Generally, my day starts with a visit from one of our two directors, and this day was no different. A white-robed apparition was already shadowing my office window when I arrived, the Magnum watching as the Bazaar began to stir across the wide plaza below. A line was already forming for the Bureau's earliest customers. Our visitation booths, though far fewer in number than those that filled the brightly-colored tents and pavilions permitted to rent retail space in the plaza, would be at least as crowded throughout the business day. Although I could not see the bridge above, I knew it was already thronged.

The week's ledger in their hand, the Magnum turned to greet me as I crossed to my desk. "Visitations continue to be slightly down, Superintendent," they commented. Though I could not see them, it felt as if the Magnum's cold eyes were flipping from the book to me. "Have you determined the reason?"

"Not specifically, Director. Though we have heard reports that the merchants are uneasy. Something's in the wind."

The Magnum's white cloak framed their arms and shoulders like a wind-taut sail as they flipped the page, making them look like a cross between a prophet and a wizard. Which was, of course, exactly what they were.

"The reports are true," they answered. "Two houses may soon take it upon themselves to decide certain issues pertaining to market share through extralegal measures."

I was not surprised. It had been almost a generation since the last merchants' war. Even the Magnum couldn't be everywhere at once.

"You expect open conflict?"

They nodded.

"And you don't intend to intervene?"

Instead of answering, the Magnum replaced the ledger on the maccawood table that ran between the paired leather couches on either side of my desk. Only the Magnum could handle physical objects when projecting. For those like myself who were taught such tricks, that particular skill was not included in the syllabus.

I nodded, appreciative of the warning. "Then you're saying our current slowdown will only be temporary? That it will soon pick up for the same reason? That is excellent news. The new gallery won't open before next year. But if two houses go to war, we'll see increases across all the other sectors of the business. Next year's gala will be icing on the cake."

"Unrest is always our most profitable time," the Magnum agreed. "However, I do not believe we should depend on the foolishness of other sectors of the economy to enhance our revenues. The antagonists may still negotiate an amicable resolution. Have you anything planned in response to the recent declines?"

"We are thinking about featuring another promotional lottery. For both Services and Visitations. With the Jewelers Guild this time. They've been clamoring for some sort of joint venture for several months. Vendors are already designing a series of cheap trinkets for the next Festival based on the old Magnum myth of the underworld. We will receive a licensing fee, of course. The lottery should stimulate an increase in order flow. Interest always picks up when there's a lottery. The free advertising, you know."

"Hmm." The Magnum seemed almost un-Magnumly thoughtful. "Festival is still several months away."

"Do you anticipate a conflict? With the coming merchants' war, that is?"

"Yes. A promotion during a period of strife would be counterproductive. Some of the more solemn faiths might call it ghoulish."

I bowed slightly again. "Perhaps we can move the date up a month or so. Then, once the fighting begins, we can get all sorts of credit for immediately ceasing our accordingly inappropriate campaign."

The Magnum shook their head. "That will not be necessary. Public relations credit is rarely worth the effort. The public is too fickle. Better to project the proper air of prudent discretion on a constant basis than try to manipulate public perception short term. Besides, we might not even have a month before the first skirmishing begins."

"I understand completely."

"You always do." The Magnum paused for a moment, their unseen eyes and face considering me before abruptly changing the subject. "I assume you are aware that a gang of Wands has occupied one of the residences on the Hill?"

"I am. I plan on evicting them today. They are too close to the location of the party the Omparri family is hosting this evening."

"Once again, you anticipate our every request. We thank you for your service."

I could almost imagine the Magnum's smile before their projection swirled away in a twist of blurring white. My view of the Bazaar, which was already busier than before, was once more uninterrupted.

The workday began. The lobby opened, and the first clients hurried in. Unlike the Bazaar, the Bureau attracted a more affluent clientele. Lessors rather than lessees. Our merchandise, being situated directly atop the Gate to the Afterworld rather than merely adjacent, was perceived to be more reputable. And more expensive.

I continued to my next appointment. Generally, after the Bureau opened for the day, I put in an appearance at the Visitation Lobby. The clients liked the opportunity to shake hands and chat for a minute or two with the Superintendent, which also allowed us to charge more for the opportunity. Wealthy matrons, who might otherwise not have woken before noon, instead rose at dawn to give themselves enough time to dress for an event that many of them thought every bit as fashionable as a District Ambassador's Ball.

Ascending the curved staircase to Reception, I saw that all of the first session's clients had already arrived. They stood in separate small groups in the grandly furnished lobby, the carpeted floor muting the space to allow for private contemplation or conversation. Of the seven appointments, five were the usual wealthy widows accompanied by children, hangers-on, or both. Three of those were regulars, whom I greeted first, as was expected of me, followed by the newcomers. The last two patrons were a pair of brothers and a lottery winner from the Church of Unlimited Resurrection accompanied by six members of her extended family, the maximum allowed in each Visitation Parlor, or Crypts as the rest of Ampyrium preferred to call them. After a few minutes' chitchat, I handed the regulars off to their attendant clerks, followed by the two newcomers, the lottery winner, and the brothers last. According to Booking, which interviewed all patrons intensively before each visitation, the brothers had inherited their grandfather's business upon his death several years ago. They were accompanied by four retainers but in two separate groups of two apiece, with one of each group appearing to be a lawyer. One brother eyed me suspiciously, the other with naive hope, while their attorneys exchanged apprehensive glances. Recognizing a difficult case when I saw one, I wished them every success in their session, and handed them off to their clerk.

The best way to avoid litigation in difficult cases is to have a trusted witness observe the clients first hand. This can be done in one of two ways. The first, and easiest, was to listen through the speaker tubes from the Observation Booths on the floor above. The second, which was available only to myself as Superintendent, and to such deputies as I occasionally delegated, was in the same manner the Magnum Director had visited me that morning: Astral Projection. Choosing the latter, I returned to my office, locked the door behind me, and retrieved from my desk a small locked box containing seven stone rings. Each ring looked exactly the same: dull, thick, and gray. But I knew which ones led to which parlor, and picked the one required. Closing my eyes,

I slipped the heavy ring onto my thumb. My body shivered in that delicate way I would never quite get used to as I sidestepped the earthly plane.

Unlike the Magnum, my projection was invisible, but I could still travel anywhere simply by thinking about where I wanted to be. Instantly I was in the parlor with the two brothers, my insensate body left behind in my office. I found them already seated in the chairs on either side of the plush divan, which remained empty, each brother's accompanying attorney and bodyguard standing behind him. Many families use the Bureau to settle civil disputes where one side, or both, believe the courts and the Magnum to have failed, so neither lawyers nor bodyguards are unusual sights at a Visitation. The fact that the Bureau is something of a court of last resort is one of the many reasons we are one of Ampyrium's more lucrative franchises.

Soft smoke filled the room, twisting the shadows in the thin light of the oiled sconces. The session had just begun. The medium, who sat behind a small round table on the other side of the divan, welcomed her customers with open arms. If one tried hard enough, which our clients usually did, one could fancy they saw faces in the swirling smoke, moaning mouths and vacant eyes, but it was of course all an illusion. The wraiths were no more real than the medium. The Afterlife provided little in the way of theater to enhance the consultation experience. Our clients supplied more than enough drama on their own.

The medium lowered her arms. The thin bracelets on her wrists jangled loudly. Unlike in Reception, here there was no need for opulent rugs. If anything, the smooth stone floor, carved directly from the Hill itself, enhanced the echo of the voices from beyond. The walls, on the other hand, were deliberately rough, the easier to hide the aural conduits that led to the listening chamber above.

The crystal around her neck glowed as the medium asked the brothers, "Whom do you seek?"

The brothers answered jointly, despite their disagreement.

"My grandfather."

"Shouldn't you know that without having to ask?"

The medium answered her more skeptical client's question with a patronizing blink. "Do you think," she continued, "your ancestors have nothing better to do than loiter around the Gate to the Afterlife waiting for your summons?"

"No." He waved a dismissive hand around the entire room. "But then I don't believe my ancestors are here at all."

"I do!" his brother excitedly exclaimed. I was almost surprised he didn't raise his hand like an oversized schoolboy.

The medium favored the more credulous brother with a smile. "Then you are the one whom I shall channel. We at the Bureau are not the charlatans of the Bazaar. Why else do you think we had you answer so many questions, and wait so long, for your session? The Afterlife is immense, and locating specific spirits takes time."

The skeptic snorted, and mumbled not quite to himself, "Then why did you have to ask?"

His brother and the medium ignored him.

Closing her eyes, the medium lifted her face to the ceiling and spread her lightly shawled arms. Her crystal glowed more brightly, and I noted that she and her prop master made a good team. A minute passed in silence, the room darkened slightly, and a voice, not particularly mystical or authoritative, the voice of an old man called away from an afternoon nap for reasons he didn't quite understand, answered.

I immediately recognized it as the voice of one of our longer term employees.

"Euncha? Is that you?"

Euncha started forward, his eyes futilely searching the room. "Yes, Grandfather."

The skeptical brother rolled his own eyes blatantly enough that it was noticeable even through the smoke, but kept his peace.

"Where am I? Why are you here?" the grandfather asked.

"We are at the Bureau of Death," Euncha said matter-of-factly.

"Where is that?"

"You know, Grandfather. It's where you were interred."

"Why would I know that?" The actor's combination of querulous and befuddled old age was perfect. Really, it was better than a play. Sadly, I was not nearly old enough to have seen this particular player in the days when he captivated the Ampyrium stage. "I wasn't there."

"You weren't?" Euncha was genuinely puzzled.

"Of course Grandfather wasn't there," scoffed his brother. "And he isn't here either. He's dead."`

"Huncha? Is that you?"

Huncha's eyes rolled again. "Who else would it be, Grandfather?" His voice echoed with all the disdain he could muster. "Were you perhaps expecting Father?"

"That miscreant? Why would I expect him? Is he even still alive?"

Euncha lowered his head sadly. "No, Grandfather."

"Good riddance."

"That's why we've come to talk to you, Grandfather," Huncha went on. "Or whoever the person playing you is."

"Why would anyone be playing me?" the actor asked mildly.

"Why does anyone do anything?" Huncha replied, promptly adding the standard Ampyrium answer. "For money."

"How would pretending to be me get someone money?"

Huncha cast a cynical glance at his brother. "Because it might get money for someone else."

I could almost hear Grandfather shake his old gray head. "I still don't understand. I'm dead. What could I possibly have that someone might pay money for?"

"If I might interject?" began Euncha's lawyer.

Huncha cut him off. "You may not. The agreement strictly specifies that only Euncha and I are allowed to speak. You are present as witnesses only. Isn't that right, Euncha?"

"Yes." Euncha did not look happy as he agreed. Though the two brothers appeared close in age, I guessed that Huncha was the elder. And likely the better logician, too.

"Good." Huncha nodded firmly. "As long as we both understand. The minute the agreement is breached, I'm out of here." Huncha paused for a moment to see if Euncha had any objection, then continued. "Would you like to explain the situation, or shall I?"

"You can do it. You're going to get your way anyway."

"If I thought that, I'd have been the one to recommend we come here."

Grandfather's thin voice slipped through the pale, curling smoke. "I remember now. Euncha, you should stand up for yourself more. And you, Huncha, should be more patient."

Huncha gritted his teeth. "I think I'm being patient right now. I'm here, aren't I?"

"Yes, you are. And you were about to tell me why."

Huncha took a deep breath. "Well then, in case you don't remember, when you passed, you left us your business. And a very fine business it is, too, processing allumens for use in the cavvying trade."

"Yes, yes. I remember now. I left it to the two of you together because I knew your father would make a mess of it. And to encourage you to work as a team, the way brothers should."

"But that's just it, Grandfather," blurted Euncha. "We can't. We can't work together at all."

"That's not my problem."

Both brothers' jaws dropped like trapdoors. Although they looked very much alike, this was the first time they actually looked related. As if they truly were brothers. Huncha especially seemed to forget he wasn't really meeting with his grandfather.

"How can that not be your problem?" he demanded. "Avidas Cavvying is your legacy."

"It's why we're here," Euncha echoed. "You always take care of everything."

"Well, maybe not always," said Huncha.

Grandfather snorted exactly like his skeptical grandson. "Not anymore," he said. "You have to do that yourselves now. I'm dead. That's why I gave you two the firm. Have you been to law?"

"Of course we've been to law."

"Huncha sued me the moment I turned down his offer."

"Was it a fair offer?" Grandfather asked.

"Yes," said Huncha.

"Yes," Euncha confirmed sulkily.

"Then why didn't you accept it?"

"I didn't want to."

"Why not?"

"It's my business, too. What am I going to do without it?"

"I don't know. What do you want to do?"

"Run the business. I'm as good at it as Huncha is. That's why I offered him more money for his share than he offered me."

"Ha. Avidas Cavvying would fail in six months if you ran it."

"That's not true. I was the one that developed the new carbonation system."

"You had the idea," Huncha sneered. "But I was the one who actually figured out how to make it work. Your head's in the clouds."

"If I hadn't had the idea, the competition would have swallowed us whole. It's not just sales, you know. You have to have a product that keeps up with the times, too."

"Grandfather supplied the product," Huncha observed. "We just have to not wreck it."

"Precisely."

The two brothers, who had been staring at each other for a while without noticing anyone else, looked back toward the medium. She hadn't spoken, but without anyone else in the room to focus on, she was the best choice when the brothers' grandfather answered one last time.

"For the life of me," he said, his voice starting to fade. "I don't understand why you called me here. I was relaxing with your grandmother by the Fountain of Eternal Joy when I was pulled away. I believe we were eating crescent cakes. With strawberry jam. You have to remember I'm dead. The business is yours now, not mine. I don't care about it anymore. At all. If you don't want to share it, sell it to someone else. Or to whichever one of you is willing to pay the higher price. I really don't care."

The light in the crystal died. The medium opened her eyes. Gathering her shawl more closely around her shoulders, she declared the brothers' grandfather had departed.

"Of course he's departed," Huncha laughed. "He just said so. If that was Grandfather I'll eat my wallet. If I had to bet, I'd say he was an actor in a room nearby connected by speaking tubes in the walls."

The medium shrugged. "If I cannot convince you…"

"I demand my money back."

"Actually, Huncha, I'm the one who paid for the consultation. If anyone deserves a refund it's me."

Having seen enough to know that neither brother had any grounds for litigation whatsoever—and were certainly not getting their money back—I imagined myself back in my office. The disappointed voices disappeared. Although a consultation at the Bureau of Death rarely solved the dilemmas that brought people to us in the first place, people still clamored for our services. I suppose speaking to the dead brought them a sense of closure. Though I doubted very much that would be the case for this particular session.

Somewhat distracted after projecting, I stood up from my chair. Chief Inspector Kain found me standing by the window when I didn't answer his knock at the door.

"Superintendent? You wanted me to remind you to go up the Hill this morning. To meet with those Wands."

Wondering how long I had been standing, I turned away from the window. "Thank you, Inspector," I said as I reached for my cloak and crook hanging on the stand beside the door. "Projecting is quite disorienting. How long were you waiting?"

"About five minutes, Superintendent. That's why I used my own key. Though I'm not exactly sure when you returned."

Five minutes sounded about right. Any longer and I might need to be concerned.

Inspector Kain stood aside to allow me to pass. "Shall I accompany you?" he asked.

"Not necessary," I replied. "I only intend to talk. If there's any trouble, I should be able to take care of it myself." I nodded toward the crook in my hand. "And one of us should remain at the Bureau."

Exiting through the lobby, I ran straight into a funeral procession on the Avenue of Angels out front. Evidently the first internment of the day had already begun. Many of Ampyrium's wealthier residents, of every District, and even a few from the outer worlds, do enjoy a last journey through our demesne. For some reason it comforts them to be buried directly into the Afterlife. Such dearly departed are, after all, the only Ampyrium citizens allowed to pass through our Gate at any time. For everyone else, at least while they are alive, such transits are strictly forbidden.

Dressed in my black cloak and grasping my crook, I could hardly fail to be noticed, which meant it would be grossly disrespectful if I continued directly on my way. Especially since the deceased was a wealthy banker from District 2, as I recalled from the day's schedule. A double row of mourners accompanied his casket, family on the left and fellow financiers on the right. His widow, wreathed in a long vermillion mourning jacket as dark as the inside of the safest vault, followed behind the ornate hearse carrying her former husband, the traditional single small coin displayed between her long, lacquered fingers. A small crowd watched from the edge of the Bazaar as the procession turned right onto a ramp lined by a platoon of guards that led into the cold stone below the Bureau's offices. The gate that guarded the entrance to our actual Gate was not the biggest in Ampyrion, but it was the most secure. The locking spells were the most powerful the Magnum possessed, and, in addition to the guards who lined the path day and night, the District's Eye watched everything from the top of the hill. At the first sign of anything out of the ordinary, the Eye would summon the Magnum, and that would be the end of that. I might be Downfall's Superintendent and Chief Reaper, but the real power was the Magnum. Mostly I just kept the books.

The financiers nodded gravely to me as they passed. I nodded solemnly in return. At the top of the path, the widow stopped. The sign was given by the lieutenant of the guard. The outer gate swung back into the tunneled stone. The widow descended, followed by her train.

Knowing what happened next, but not being in a position to actually view it, I continued on my way past the various temples and shrines that lined the bottom of Elysium Hill. As the Magnum had mentioned at our morning meeting, a wealthy family was hosting a gala in one of the more decrepit estates that evening on the hill above. Had it been one of the brothels, or a smaller family, I'd have assessed the appropriate fee and have done with it. Such events' success or failure was none of my concern. A debut for one of their many daughters, or some such, in the ironic affectation currently in vogue in Ampyrium. But the family hosting tonight's celebration was one of our most important clients. Generations of Omparris had consulted our mediums and journeyed to the Afterlife through our Gate, and I was obligated to ensure the evening passed without a hitch.

The history of Elysium Hill is simple. Real estate speculation generally is. Centuries ago the rich, believing themselves above such things, had been much more willing to live on a hill above the Gate to the Afterlife than anyone else in Ampyrium. It was, after all, second only to the central massif that shouldered the Magnum's palace among all of the city's hills. So they constructed magnificent estates, splendid villas and townhouses with marble baths and turrets of ivory and gold. For a few years they were content, and the Bureau made a nice profit off the sale of hundred year leases and building permits. But then someone died unexpectedly. At first it was laughed off as a coincidence, until a wealthy burgher was murdered by his son, not that unusual an occurrence in a city where wealth was applauded no matter the means of acquisition, and people started to talk. Worse still, people began to whisper, especially the servants, who began to give notice, in ones and twos at first, and then in groups and by entire houses. The Lushkeys were the first to leave, their house shuttered around a single caretaker. They claimed they were not trying to sell, but that subterfuge didn't last long. In a confined city like Ampyrium, gossiping about real estate is second only to rumors of parentage. A few houses were sold at losses to newcomers who didn't know any better, but within fifty years of the first construction the baths and towers were stripped of their marble and gold and Elysium was completely abandoned, except for the tales of hauntings. All completely untrue, of course. The Magnum made sure of that. But even the Magnum cannot counter rumor and superstition, and in the end even the caretakers left. The Bureau bought back the leases, at a nice profit of course, because the District was easier to administer that way. Lowball offers were made from time to time to reacquire one of the grander properties, but since they were always from the Wands or one of the other shadier organizations, the Bureau turned them down. In the meantime, the Bazaar grew until it became the most popular part of the quarter. Temples were built at the base of the Hill on either side of the Bureau, along with the occasional retreat staffed by monks or holy sisters, while various cheaper columbariums and mortuaries rose along the inner wall. Not all of Ampyrium's many denominations joined us, especially those that professed the more ascetic life, but those that did were generally awash in color, their banners brighter and cleaner than their more humble imitators in the Bazaar. Everyone, on both sides of the avenue, had something to sell, from simple blessings to the promise of eternal life. Soothsayers and crones, herbalists and numinists, astrologers and shamanesi; all had their eager customers from the other five districts jostling for position at every cathedral and tent. The booths bustled; the temples hummed. Long lines of penitents and supplicants filled the avenue, from the Shrine of the Ladies of the White Silk to the Bethel Bong; all the hundreds of sects and creeds clustered close together around the Bureau. The wealth available for soaking was too much to allow mere philosophical differences to get in the way.

Slowly I worked my way through the crowd to Night Street, between the Shrine of Wholesome Purity and the Tabernacle of Primal Divinity. The way turned steep as I ascended the Hill, and I found myself huffing a little when I reached the broader cobbling of Heaven's Path farther up. The estate the family had chosen for their macabre celebration was near the summit, past scores of falling facades and broken brick. To my left, a small gang of porters lugged several heavily-laden carts up from the direction of the bridge. Few luxuries were to be obtained in Downfall, unless stolen from one of the temples; and they had to be hauled back as well, as anything left untended in the district tended to disappear immediately.

Unlike the rest of the hill, the courtyard of the hired mansion was crowded. At least a score of servants, supervised by a man in Omparri livery, were hammering, painting, and sweeping in a not entirely unsuccessful attempt to brighten the gloomy palace. Perhaps, as this was a party for adolescents, the purposed intent was more fantastical than morbid. Bright streamers bulged from baskets along the walls; eccentric puppets were stacked beside the stage workers were assembling under the skeletal ruins of an ancient tree, the upper arms of which already sported several colored lanterns.

Noticing me immediately, the man in livery approached. "Superintendent Clark?" he inquired, nodding the absolute minimum his station required when greeting a mere bureaucrat. "I'm afraid Mistress will not be arriving until late afternoon. There is still much to be arranged."

I waved my hand. "It is no matter. I'm here only to see that you have everything you need."

"Yes, Superintendent. As you suggested, we have avoided the market entirely. There have been no difficulties at all."

At that moment the porters I had noticed arrived at the entrance to the courtyard. The majordomo glanced at his second-in-command; she nodded and redirected the arrivals into the house.

"Please let me know, if you need anything," I offered. "Anything at all. Downfall appreciates your house's patronage."

The majordomo's gaze became slightly less impressed, but I didn't mind. What he thought of me was immaterial. Money was money, and, should it ever turn out that he required the services of the Bureau itself, his obsequiousness would no doubt increase tenfold.

"I believe we have everything in hand, Superintendent," he answered coolly. "I doubt there will be anything more we require. Although the location is a little bit more, how shall I say, abandoned than we are used to, I can assure you that we have assisted in more than enough of these affairs to make sure that not even the Magnum themselves could improve the festivities in any manner."

"Excellent." I nodded to the man more generously than his own nod to me. With a last admiring glance at the preparations, I returned to the avenue outside.

My next appointment was farther up the hill. The Wands rarely bothered us and, in consequence, we rarely bothered them when they chose to go to earth in one of our abandoned villas. Respect among thieves, I suppose, as long as they didn't disrupt our business, or the Bazaar's.

I waited outside their refuge for a few minutes, sizing up the building while allowing the occupants to discover I was there. Once I believed they'd had time enough to recognize me, I stepped through the arch. If an alarm sounded, it was silent. Crossing a courtyard not too different from the one I had just left, I ascended the stairs on the other side. The door was broken, one half still hinged, the other hanging like a windblown shingle.

The hall beyond was bare, anything of any use or value stripped centuries ago. Trash checkered the floor. I proceeded carefully, the rooms I passed on left and right as dusty and deserted as the hall. Generally speaking, footpads preferred lurking in back parlors, where the egress was easy and the view hidden from the street, so I was surprised to find the first floor empty. Were they actually loitering upstairs? In the basement?

I needn't have worried. They were enjoying the pale sunshine on the back terrace. Four of them, though I had heard there were five. Two men, a woman, and a Daruvian sensitive. Another renegade Daruvian was probably standing guard on one of the upper floors.

"Superintendent." The woman greeted me with a ready smile, though we had not yet met. Like many Wands, she was petite and nearly nyaarian in her litheness. The human variant of a cat rather than vice versa. "Have you come to arrest us?"

"I have not," I answered, my tone as easy as her own. "Other than trespass, you have violated no local ordinance. Should I?"

The Daruvian snickered, as if he doubted my ability to do so. The Wands may be larger and better organized than most criminal syndicates, but their lower orders are composed of the same riffraff as their competitors. I ignored him, and focused my attention on the leader.

She stretched lazily. "We are vacationing, as you can see. A charming place, Downfall."

I wondered what section of Ampyrium she was from. Humans, like most peoples, were scattered throughout the various districts, even the ones where the main population didn't particularly like them. Her accent was of no place or class, a sign of her intelligence. The sun, generally pale in Downfall, lit her face evenly, with hardly any shadow. I could not place her.

"If you say so," I replied. "We are not known for our spas."

"Yes," she agreed. "This is a very grave place."

I coughed. "May I ask how long you plan to stay?"

"That depends on how we are treated."

"You shall be treated the same as everyone else, free to conduct your legal business in the time and place most convenient to your counterparties and yourselves. As long as we receive no inquiries from the Magnum or any other civic authorities as to your whereabouts, you will be left alone." Grasping my crook, I took a step closer to all four of them. "Bother anyone else in the slightest, and you will be asked to leave. Which brings me to the specific reason for my visiting you today. The gathering down the street, you are aware of it?"

The woman nodded, her eyes sparkling. The Daruvian snickered once again.

"How could we not?" the leader answered. "They have been quite loud. So much shouting and hammering. We were all up way too early this morning."

"Should anything disturb their evening's festivities," I warned, "the Bureau will hold you personally responsible. Whether you are involved or not."

One of the men gaped in surprise. "Are you saying you want us to guard them?"

"I'm saying nothing of the kind. Guarding them would imply intrusion, and intrusion would be disturbance, which is precisely what I am warning you against. If anything, it might be best for you to retire elsewhere for a day or two at the very least. To avoid suspicion."

"What if we don't want to leave?" asked the Daruvian.

"Then I trust there will be no disturbance."

"You give us hardly any other option," the woman replied, managing to sound both persuaded and aggrieved as she looked out over a centuries' worth of weeds and dead leaves that filled the garden. Her easy acquiescence surprised me. Most gang leaders, especially those working for an organization as established as the Wands, would have stood their ground for at least a minute or two. Backing off, even to a district superintendent, was not something they did without at least some show of truculent reluctance. The Daruvian was watching her even now, measuring her restraint for a possible future challenge. I did not think he would be successful.

Nor did I believe she was actually acquiescing.

"Thank you," I said. With a slight nod, I took my leave. Footpads were as much potential customers for the Bureau of Death as anyone. Better, even. Which was why I tried to be as civil as possible with everyone I met, no matter how annoying, or dangerous, they proved to be.

The Wand graced my departure with an easy wave. I made a note to have Inspector Kain look into her when I returned, and to double-check that afternoon whether her company had actually left.

Inspector Kain met me on the street before I was halfway back to the office.

"Superintendent. I think we need to visit the Bazaar."

My eyebrows arched. "Really? What's happened?"

"A vendor is having a dispute with a customer."

"And you think we should get involved?"

"I anticipate the dispute expanding."

I shook my head in exasperation. I hadn't even had lunch yet, and it was already the busiest day I'd had in weeks. "Tell me it's not that new Konjin stall they set up next to the Minimite retreat at the back of the plaza."

Inspector Kain's lack of reply indicated I was right. Of all the many peoples trading in Ampyrium, the Konjin were easily the most difficult. And they were so cute, too. Who knew that large rabbits that looked more like plush toys than anything else could be so stubbornly bad at retail. I glanced down the hill at the bustle of the Bazaar, but nothing seemed out of the ordinary. Then again, unless there was an actual riot somewhere, nothing ever did. Even by the standards of Ampyrium, our district's market was chaotic.

"By the way, Inspector," I said as I led the way down the street. "That Wand I just spoke with whose band is camped at the old Mweero Palace. Do you know anything about her?"

"I believe her name is Venche, Superintendent."

"Venche? What sort of name is that?"

"An Ingrizian name, Superintendent."

"Do you know where she stands within the Wands?"

"I have no idea, Superintendent. That sort of information is difficult to ascertain for Wands. The first I heard of her was when she showed up last week. May I ask what your particular interest is in her?"

"I think she plans to disrupt the party, though it's hard to see why. Perhaps they plan to steal the guests' jewelry. When I warned her of the possible consequences, she did not seem particularly dismayed. Her willingness to move along was a little too easy."

"I'll add a few more guards to the unit watching the event. My understanding is that the Omparri have already hired three Forest Giants for protection, as well as a Menedian druid."

"A Menedian Druid?" I asked, then waved off Inspector Kain's explanation when I immediately remembered the Omparri had been an old family from Menedi.

"Three of ours should be enough. That will leave us plenty for this evening's internments without any need for overtime."

Inspector Kain's pale eyebrows furrowed. "Have you forgotten tonight's extra session at the Crypts, Superintendent?"

I had. Calamunda had a celebration coming up next week that always drove up demand for visitations. A few extra sessions were scheduled that evening to handle the overflow. It would be a busy night. With overtime.

Knowing full well that a riot in the Bazaar would be far more costly than any amount of overtime, I crossed the Avenue of the Ascended as soon as we reached the bottom of the hill and plunged straight into the mob. Immediately, I was immersed in the tidal bedlam of the Bazaar. The sights, smells, and sounds gripped me as firmly as a blacksmith's tongs. Incense from the Merdini desert lured me to a fortune teller's rainbow tent; twirling fans and jigs from Chumma Island advertised an apothecary's potions desperate for my attention; the thrum of Trueskin drums and tambourine tempted me to hear the latest discount deity's divine discourse. Not to mention the swiveling hips, knowing winks, and hinted kisses of young men and women fighting for my attention from every direction.

I enjoyed the show—who would not—but I was never tempted. The Bureau had no need for such garish promotion. Our wares were unique. The merchants spread out beyond our doorstep were selling pretty much exactly what we were, at cheaper prices and without any guarantee other than their hucksters' insistence, but Inspector Kain and I sold the real thing. Even the bankers and merchants living in the shadow of the Magnum Palace weren't immune to our attractions.

We first heard the commotion when we were a little more than halfway across the plaza. As a new establishment, the Konjin pavilion was on the outer edge of the Bazaar near the less glamorous shrines and retreats lining the ruins of the inner wall. Though actually a better location for attracting customers than the stalls crowded a few dozen paces closer to Elysium, it was the least preferred site in the entire Bazaar. Proximity to the actual Gate was valued much more highly by many of the less successful merchants, even though that meant they were pretty much lost at the back of the crowd. Perhaps that was one of the many reasons they were less successful.

The mix of gloomy and gaudy sanctuaries loomed impassively above and behind the crowd as Inspector Kain and I arrived. "You promised!" someone shouted, though I could not see who. Others took up the cry. The pavilion itself was larger than most. Trust the Konjin to make a new booth too big rather than too small. I counted five of the large lapini outside, all about half the size of most of the crowd confronting them. More probably lurked within. Their tent was an extravagance of maroon and gold, with bolts of black lightning striking at the entrance, and a spiral of magicked smoke wafting above. But none of the former or potential customers were interested in the attraction. They wanted their money back or, at the very least, the excitement of tearing down the place instead.

Inspector Kain started forward, crook at the ready, but I held him back. First I wanted to see what the ruckus was about. As of yet, it wasn't out of hand, nor did it look like it would be for several minutes. The claims of broken promises continued and, though the Konjin were suitably cowed by the size of the crowd—their furry, endive-like ears flattened behind their furry heads—they hadn't yet given way. Since a true riot had not broken out, I suspected that both sides in the quarrel were hoping someone in authority would arrive to resolve the matter before anyone actually got into trouble.

"You promised!" said the loudest voice again. This time I spotted the speaker, a young girl not much taller than the tallest Konjin at the front of the crowd. "You promised I'd see my mother!"

"It's not our fault she failed to appear. That wasn't what we promised at all."

I suppressed a sigh. It was the usual quarrel. The same, in its own way, as the one I had witnessed an hour earlier—and decided not to interfere with—at the Bureau.

The young girl shoved aggressively forward in a way she never would have dared with a human her own size, and pointed a narrow finger almost into the Konjin's nervously twitching nose. "You said I'd see her!"

"We said you *might* see her. It's not the same."

"You told me I'd see her if I tried hard enough!"

"We said you *might* see her if you tried hard enough. It's right here in the contract." Somehow the Konjin managed to cower backwards while simultaneously brandishing a sheet of paper in front of the young girl's face. She knocked it away in quivering rage.

I decided I'd seen enough. No need to let things escalate. But, just as I started forward, three more Konjin bounded out of their tent shouting, "Fire! Fire! Run for your lives!"

Sure enough, a thin plume of smoke appeared above the dark red canvas at the top of the tent.

"Burn it!" shouted the young girl. "Burn it down!"

The crowd surged. Inspector Kain and I rushed forward to head them off. "Stop!" I shouted, projecting my voice above the roar of the crowd, but only the rioters directly in front of me heard. My cowl and crook inspired them to immediately melt away. I might not be an actual ghost or demon, but my badges of office signified that I was their representative, and if there is anything the underclass wants to avoid it's a repetition of their lowly status in the afterlife.

The rest of the crowd, however, was too intent on their aroused passions to notice a mere reaper. Inspector Kain laid into a few at the front, intent on clearing a path to the pavilion, but I knew it was too late for that. Two of the lapini were already down on the ground and getting stomped by their attackers. The rest had knotted tightly, thumping feet raised and ready to inflict a little last rabid damage before they were overwhelmed. A whiff of smoke drifted our way, but any flames were still hidden behind the tent.

I raised my crook. The tent was my first concern. Mobs were far too poor to affect the Bureau's profit margin, whereas a general conflagration could destroy the entire Bazaar. Uttering the words the Magnum had taught me, I swung my staff in a wide arc above the crowd's heads. A few more of the rabble noticed what I was doing and slunk away as a pale purple fog emanated from within my encircling staff and grew larger against the sky. A few more revolutions, and the compact cloud was fat enough to cover Konjin and attackers alike.

I lowered my crook. The fog followed. I stepped back, careful to keep away from the nasty stuff. As soon as it covered their heads, the crowd collapsed, thudding to the ground like apples from a windstruck tree. Even the Konjin toppled, and Inspector Kain, too, the cloud too quick for the bunnies to get away from despite their stature. I hoped the inspector's hangover wouldn't be too massive, and made a note to buy him a drink that evening.

It also meant I was probably going to have to handle the evening's staffing issues myself once we returned to the office.

Once everyone was on the ground, I waved away the leftover spell with a quick flick of my crook. The air cleared. The smoke from the fire returned. Stepping hastily around the field of undreaming bodies, I made my way to the back of the tent. The fire was still small, at least on the outside, but the lick of orange flame at the base of the canvas was quickly growing.

By this time the nearby vendors, who had been doing their best to separate themselves from the riot, sprang into action to protect their own establishments. Nothing like the threat of fire to draw a community together. Even so, they would never have been able to stop it had I not been present. There just wasn't enough water or buckets. A few quick slashes from the blade concealed in my crook and the affected bits of flaming canvas were strewn across the ground, at which point we all stomped out the flames instead of the Konjin. Fire is the greatest danger to any open-air bazaar and would have reduced the Bureau's tax revenues significantly for at least two or three months while we rebuilt. The Magnum, and their co-directors, would not have been pleased. If there was anything I wanted to avoid, even more than a fire in the Bazaar, it was the displeasure of either of the Bureau's owners.

The smoke faded. The sprawled bodies stirred. Although they woke more or less at the same time, some recovered more quickly than others. One by one the perpetrators crept guiltily away.

Inspector Kain was among the first to rise, shaking his head groggily. "My apologies, Superintendent," he coughed as he returned to my side, still blinking hard. "I should have anticipated your response."

I waved his remorse aside. "There was no harm. We were in haste because of the fire."

"Still, I should have been better prepared."

"The Magnum have shared more of their knowledge with me than they have with you, Inspector. Someday, if you become superintendent, you will have that power. For the moment, it is mine."

Looking up and over the line of shrines toward the golden palace glittering at the center of the city, I reminded myself how limited that power actually was. And how easily it could be removed. My purpose, and the Bureau's, was not to save Konjin imbeciles, or their equally greedy prey. My purpose was profit. If, in the pursuit of profit, I could occasionally prevent greater carnage, then so much the better. In the meantime I needed to keep my head down and my ledgers' black ink off my sleeves.

Back at the Bureau, I returned to my routine. Inspector Kain's headache turned out to be insufficiently severe to prevent him from continuing his normal duties, which meant I, at least, had time for lunch. Last week's reports needed to be reviewed and signed, along with the previous month's bank statements. One might argue that the Bureau of Death, possessing vaults as secure as any in the known worlds, had no need for the extra protection of banks. But we were hardly the only business in Ampyrium, and it remains good practice to have regular and frequent dealings with one's neighbors. Sharing, at least among equals, is always beneficial. It wasn't as if we had any actual competitors, either, at least not in the city. Outsiders might want to return to the worlds of their origin, but the citizens of Ampyrium itself had no delusions that their remains would ever be allowed Outside. Not to mention the growing interest among wealthy Outsiders to ship their recent ancestors directly to us rather than engaging in their more traditional local practices.

Death's future was very bright indeed.

The sun was setting by the time I was able to stop working long enough to remember my intention to invite Inspector Kain to have a drink. Already, the mundane managers, secretaries, and clerks had joined the crowd strolling across the bridge above the plaza to their homes beyond the wall. My home was there as well, though in a better neighborhood, but it would be some hours yet before I would be able to end my day. Or Inspector Kain his, for that matter. His attention to duty was almost as good as mine, which was why I was fairly certain he would someday succeed me. Though hopefully that succession would not be for some time, and when my house was in an even better section of Ampyrium than my current prosperity allowed.

I found him in the lobby. In the dimming of evening, the lofty hall felt both comfortably gloomy and bleakly welcoming, to both of us, I think. A fitting place to rest, either permanently or for a short nap only.

"Would you care for a glass of wine in my office before calling it a day?" I inquired. "As I recall, Ampyrium is your favorite."

The Inspector's eyes brightened. "It would be an honor, Superintendent."

We ascended the stairs. Our footsteps echoed broadly. Around us, the first of the night shift was already working, cleaning crews and the skeleton staff necessary for the evening's extended visitation hours. Even a mausoleum requires housekeeping and maintenance, which, like the most bustling hotel, is best performed when the clientele is asleep. The Bureau of Death was never empty. Others, however, were generally present as well. A member of the creative staff working on a new pitch; an accountant juggling a few unusually recalcitrant entries into balance.

From the credenza behind my desk, I retrieved a bottle of my best local vintage and a pair of cut crystal cups. Normally my best was reserved for my most important guests, but there were always exceptions. The wine swirled dark and red through the glass, an obvious cliché to both of us given our current situation and occupations. I took a small sip, savoring the flavor's deep, dry perfection.

"One wonders how true Ampyrium would taste," I mused, "if we were permitted to grow our grapes outside the walls."

"Even when they're grown here in the city, it's superb."

"Which is why I imagine it would be even better if it were grown outside."

"We'd have to be allowed to go outside first, before that can happen."

"A very unlikely event," I reflected, once more twirling my glass, "given Ampyrium's reluctance to any kind of trade. And, of course, the threat of disease. What was it called? The Thinning? Personally, if I were the Magnum, I'd never have closed the city off from the rest of this world in the first place. Its abundance is too bountiful to ignore, even with the threat. I'm certain a cure could have been found."

"I suppose the citizens of Ampyrium insisted upon it."

I nodded and took another sip. "That is the accepted wisdom."

Outside, the sky had darkened more than my orb-lit office. A few lights shone here and there in the Bazaar, but even those would be extinguished soon. The Bazaar's customers were generally much more fearful of Downfall after dark than the wealthier inhabitants of the city, as proved by the celebration already in progress on the hill above. We could not hear them, of course. Elysium Hill is solid stone. The sound of their revelry would waft upwards, above Ampyrium's walls toward the freedom of the sky. Our pleasure would be confined to the night view and the wine.

I was about to make another observation when an Eye suddenly appeared in the office between us. The Bureau's Eye, the one from the top of the hill, round, white, and as empty as milk. The one that watched the Bazaar, unblinking, every minute of every day. I glanced toward the window, but nothing seemed amiss. Our Eye had not seen fit to bother about the disruption that morning. What had it noticed now?

Having acquired our attention, the Eye darted out of the office and down the stairs. Grabbing our crooks and cowls, we followed as quickly as we could. The Eye whizzed on, through the lobby and through the door. If a giant eye could hover like a wingless bird, why should a mere oak and iron door be any kind of barrier? We lost sight of it for a few seconds while the porter let us out, but spotted the bright glow immediately up the avenue to the right once we were outside. The Eye zipped off again. While the porter re-secured the door, Inspector Kain and I quickly followed the glowing path that lingered in the Eye's wake. Straight up Night Street we ran, until finally the steep ascent slowed us down.

I was certain where the Eye was leading us well before we heard the sounds of the party. Those sounds, however, were not what I expected. Instead of the bright clear voices of soon-to-be adults, screams of terror and incoherent shouts of dismay pierced the evening. A surge of adrenaline quickened my pace as the glow of the party lights appeared through the thin mist of Downfall's perennial night fog.

At the mansion's gate, we found a very small Forest Giant standing guard. There was no sign of the Eye.

"What's going on?" I demanded.

"On the roof!" The giant swallowed hard and pointed an unsteady arm to where the Eye was hovering high above. Apparently standing duty in Downfall was more than even small Forest Giants could handle. "A young girl was attacked on the roof!"

"One of the guests?"

He nodded, and winced as another scream cracked the night.

"Help me! Oh, please help me!"

A young girl in fancy dress appeared on the rooftop, only to be quickly jerked back by an unseen assailant. Inspector Kain and I dashed through the gate toward the front of the house. The guests were gathered in a tight knot at the back of the courtyard behind the other two giants and the Menedian druid, where they could all clearly see both the woman on the roof and anyone who might try to attack them either from the house or the front gate. Brightly colored lamps glowed incongruously through the mist above their heads like ghostly leaves on the branches of the dead trees. In the rainbow light, a papier-mâché skeleton slowly twirled.

The servants huddled fearfully inside the house. "Master and several others have already gone up to the roof," declared the functionary I had met that morning, his manner much more respectful now that Downfall's suspected nature had been so alarmingly revealed.

"And your mistress?"

"She's outside with the guests."

Inspector Kain and I rapidly mounted the stairs. A loud crash from above increased our speed. Two long flights and one small one brought us to a small annex that led to the roof. The door lay shattered on the weathered tar and broken tiles. Three Bureau guards, and several other men dressed to the nines, darted back and forth under the light of the Eye, but I saw no one in a gown.

The sergeant-in-charge met us with a brisk salute. Quickly I paced around the outside of the annex surveying the entire roof, but, except for the crumbled scraps of ruined chimneys, there was nothing else to see.

Horrified, I turned to the sergeant. "Has she fallen?"

"Not that we can tell, sir."

A man about my own age, but of slightly more sedentary appearance, hurried over. The rest of his dapper guests followed respectfully. They all appeared quite relieved to see a pair of reapers on the scene.

I inquired if anyone had searched the back garden. The host gasped. "Do you think the poor girl has fallen?"

"She has to be somewhere. And what about her assailant?"

"There's no sign of the assailant, sir," answered the sergeant, sending his men down to search the garden with a nod. "We never saw him."

That was interesting. While the host suggested his guests assist the guards, I strode to the side of the house farthest from the street. Even from here the nearest rooftop was farther away than any human could jump. My mind reeled at the rumors that were going to spread before tomorrow's market even opened, none of them good for business unless properly spun.

"Are there any other guests present besides humans?" I asked the host.

"A few."

"Any who can jump from here to there?" I pointed across the gardens to the next house. "Or fly?"

"No. Only one Shonka and two Clyedes. All friends of my daughter's."

"Please. Tell me exactly what happened."

The host did his best, but he was likely more confused than I was. "We heard the first alarm perhaps ten minutes ago. One of the guests appeared on the roof screaming that someone was attacking her. Other than that, we have no idea what happened, who was hurting her, or even why. It was only just before you arrived that we were even able to break open the door to the roof, only there was no one here."

"Was the door to the roof locked this morning?" I asked.

"I have no idea."

I glanced at Inspector Kain. He hurried off to question the servants as I turned back to the host.

"And you saw no assailant?"

"Actually, Superintendent, I believe I did. No disrespect to your sergeant, of course. It was all so sudden and shocking that it was hard to understand what was happening. How could there be no assailant?"

The sergeant didn't say a word. He understood perfectly whom I believed to be the more competent witness.

"Are you certain the woman was a guest?" I asked mildly.

"Why would she not be a guest?" the host replied, still completely confounded. This was not the joyful night for his daughter he had anticipated. "She was certainly dressed like one. Who else would be attacked? It certainly wasn't one of the servants."

"Sergeant," I instructed, "if you would please search the roof once again. There has to be a way a woman in a dress could descend."

The host was still not following my logic. "What about her attacker?" he asked.

"You're certain you saw an attacker? Can you describe them?"

The first flicker of doubt finally brightened the man's eye.

"The most logical explanation is of course that the attacker managed to stay out of sight," I continued reassuringly. "Still, we must remain open to other possibilities."

"What other possibilities could there be?"

"The situation might have been staged. As a distraction. Perhaps if you could check to see if any of your guests are actually missing?"

The host's mouth fell open. A moment later the sergeant called out that he had found the rope, and then a shout sounded from the back yard announcing the discovery of the dress at the rope's other end. With all the available evidence in hand, we adjourned to the courtyard to take stock of what we had.

It turned out to be very little. Some guests were already trying to leave, but the presence of the Bureau's guards helped put a stop to that. Inspector Kain and I interviewed the frightened partygoers one by one, which took several hours. We also determined that all of the attendees were present, guest and servant. No one had left. Perhaps a more thorough investigation in daylight the next day would produce something new, though I doubted it. Obviously, the Wands I had spoken to that morning had not actually followed my advice, for all that no one had been able to find a trace of them in the afternoon.

"But why?" demanded the host, twisting his cravat in nervous consternation as I explained the situation to him. "Nothing was taken."

"The servants have assured me that the roof was never explored, so for all we know an entire den of thieves was already present when you arrived." I did not bother to inform him that such was, indeed, most likely the case. "When they saw their chance, they struck."

"But not a single guest is missing a single thing," he insisted.

"Yes," I agreed. "Not even a single spoon. The caterer has also completed their inventory. Have you checked the gifts?"

"Of course."

"And none of them are missing?"

"Not that I can tell."

"Perhaps we should inventory them as thoroughly as we did the spoons."

"I'm sorry, Superintendent," the host apologized. "My daughter's gifts have already been packed up and loaded into one of the wagons."

"Did every guest bring a gift?"

"I assume that was the case."

"And what of those unable to attend? Did they send gifts as well?"

"Of that, I'm not sure. My wife would know better than I. She and my daughter will be the ones writing the thank-yous."

"Of course. But am I correct in supposing that you have no way of doing a proper inventory of who has given what?"

The host drew himself up stiffly at the thought that he and his family should ever do anything so tactless as to inventory the gifts received at their daughter's debut.

I smiled. "Of course not. Which is why, unless you object, it might help the Bureau's investigation into this disturbing affair if you could supply us with a copy of the complete guest list tomorrow, or at your earliest possible convenience, that we might undertake such an accounting ourselves. Unless you object, of course."

The host nodded his acceptance of my offer, his relief plain. One less repercussion his wife and he had to worry about.

"I believe then that our job here is done," I continued. "I will, however, leave the guard to protect the house pending further examination of the scene tomorrow. Please let me express the Bureau's sincere apologies for the night's regrettable events. Luckily, despite our first impressions, it appears that no one was harmed."

The host drew himself up to his full height. "That might be your opinion, Superintendent," he huffed, his heavy cheeks pursed critically. "My family's reputation, and my daughter's especially, might well be irretrievably damaged as a result of this horrific evening. I trust I can expect a substantial reduction in our bill?"

I bowed deeply. His trust was not misplaced. "You can be assured that I will of course take the matter up with my directors." Unlike the day's previous requests, this refund was much more likely to be granted. The directors would not be pleased, but this time it was obvious the Bureau had not properly fulfilled its contracted obligations.

Bowing a second time, I retired from the scene. The only question now was how much of the payment already received would be returned. My personal belief, however, was that the host's daughter, and the rest of their family, would live off this night's adventure for years. Their friends and acquaintances would demand nothing less than to hear every macabre detail repeated again and again. In fact, if the Bureau handled the situation deftly enough, demand for such morbid partying might actually rise rather than fall, with the right publicity. What matter the loss of a gift or two compared to the thrilling celebrity gained by a few minutes of vicarious terror?

Inspector Kain and I returned to the office by a longer and less steep route. Pausing at Elysium Bridge, I suggested the Inspector head straight home. The Bazaar loomed dark and empty beyond the heavy stone span. It had been a long day, and tomorrow was likely to be similarly busy. The evening's investigation would be much more protracted with the new day, and the incident with the Konjin warranted examination also. Plus there were eight more internments scheduled, and the usual arguments at the parlors.

"It's likely to be an even longer day for you, Superintendent." Inspector Kain waved a friendly arm for me to join him on the bridge. "I expect you could also use some sleep."

I checked his familiar gesture with my hand. "Thank you, Inspector, but my day isn't quite finished."

Inspector Kain knew exactly what I meant. With a respectful bow, he swept his cape more closely about him and started across the arch. I watched him depart, a bit jealous that his day was already over, but a bit content with my lot in life as well. Not everyone could be Superintendent of the Bureau of Death. Even if that meant you were obligated to attend the occasional midnight business meeting.

Under the pale gaze of the Eye, now returned to its perch atop the hill, I also returned to my place. The porter greeted me at the door, his candle flickering in the darkened lobby. I waved him back to the comfort of his cushioned bench, which cushion I knew quite well was borrowed from the casket display in one of the shops on the second level.

My morning meeting had been in my office with the bright day greeting us above the view of the already bustling bazaar. My midnight meeting would be in the very heart of the Bureau in a very different place.

Behind a screen in my office stood a private door. I unlocked it with a large iron key from my pocket, a key I kept separate from all the other keys that opened the many other doors and crypts in the Bureau. Behind the door a spiral stair wide enough for only one person to pass at a time dipped into the darkness. Knowing the stair well, I descended to the bottom without bothering to count the steps, where I found a second door unlocked by the same key, and a short passage, also unlit, the door at the end of which was opened in the same manner as the first two. There were no runes, no mystic enchantments between me and my destination. Some secrets were sufficient unto their normal, everyday selves, requiring no supernatural enhancement.

Oil lamps lit the room beyond the last door, but I had to step around a second screen to see them, and the rest of the Gate.

The real Gate, and not the one on the level above that we used for show for the internments. That gate—though it looked just like this one, with a large gold cap over the burial chute that led to this deeper chamber and The Eight Eternal Lamps on each of its eight walls—was a mere copy. This was the real Gate, opened by the Magnum more than half a millennium before. This was the Gate where the Recently Departed were finally dispatched to their final rest. Stacked on benches around it sat the emptied caskets of the most recent arrivals, their lids casually open, their occupants already harping on the other side of this, the final Gate. With some satisfaction, I noted the two large chests nearby filled with the jewelry, coins, and gold teeth. Another profitable day, with the proceeds ready for shipment to our subsidiaries in Bank Street tomorrow. Only after the corpses had been stripped of anything of worth did we open the Gate and send them on to their final rest. The underworld had no need of riches, at least not the main part of its inhabitants. And any need the remainder had was only useful here in Ampyrium. The Afterlife itself had no need of hard currency at all.

Or so I'm told.

Although I appeared to be alone, I knew I was probably not. That part of the Bureau's workforce that was actually from the Afterlife often preferred spending their leisure hours here rather than anyplace else, for whatever reason I'm not sure. I also knew that, though the person I had come to meet was not yet present, if anyone here wished to speak to me, they would initiate any conversation themselves.

As if on cue, a voice bubbled up from close beside my shoulder. "Good evening, Superintendent," it remarked. "My apologies for not greeting you this morning, but work does take precedence. Breaking the fourth wall is never a good idea. I trust you enjoyed the rest of your day?"

I recognized the speaker immediately, even if he was no longer pretending to be someone's grandfather. Knowing why this particular spirit had chosen to say hello, I told him exactly what he wanted to hear.

"Sadly, Sir Privis, the remainder of my day was not nearly as enjoyable as the beginning. Your performance was, as always, impeccable. As was your insight into exactly what our clients needed to hear."

Though Privis remained as invisible as a Magnum's face, I could almost hear him beam. "You are too kind, Superintendent. And, though I admit my performance was superb, I will confess that the analysts did manage another splendid job. The way that hypocrite blustered!"

"Indeed. And the medium was also excellent," I acknowledged. "Though of course her abilities hold no candle to yours. The two of you are certainly among the Visitation Department's brightest stars."

"Give her time, Superintendent, give her time. I have centuries more experience. When she finally joins me in the Afterlife, hopefully many, many years from now, she will no doubt be more than qualified to join our eternal troupe."

I laughed. "She will be honored, I'm sure. Again, thank you for your help today. But if you'll excuse me, I have one last meeting to attend."

Crossing through the scattered sarcophagi, I took the handle of the winch that operated the Gate. A golden winch, just like the cover. Slowly the Gate rose, inch by inch, exposing the darkness on the other side. The air sighed softly as a small puff escaped into the room. Perhaps a few of the dead escaped as well. There was no way to determine for sure. The living were not allowed into the land of the dead, at least not until they died, but the dead have their own rules. How often they come and go through the Gate is determined entirely by them. I had heard, not from the Magnum themselves, but from others in the city, that this was the pre-condition the Afterlife had required to permit the Gate to open in the first place, and perhaps this was true. Perhaps it was also true that the dead maintained a second gate on their side. If so, I had never seen it. Either way, it did not really matter. The dead in Ampyrium caused far less trouble than the living, be they Wands, or merchants. Hauntings and transmogrification were rarely what they seemed. The ability of people, whether human, Daruvian, or Konjin, to create their own troubles never ceased to amaze me. Even the Magnum were not immune, as that morning's meeting had demonstrated. If the conflict they were allowing to smolder ever got truly out of hand, it would be magnitudes worse than any mere fire in the Downfall Bazaar.

The Gate opened fully. No light shined. I saw no objects. I stepped back and, after a few moments, the director appeared. Unlike the Magnum, his form was not complete. His shape, at least when meeting with me, was vaguely that of a human male of the upper classes. A banker, perhaps, or someone who owned bankers. Well-dressed, but not over-dressed, wavering at the edges like a reflection in a wind-wrinkled pool. His face shimmered with bemused smiles. When he spoke, however, his voice was not human at all. Instead it was the kind of voice a wall of rock might have, or windless desert sand.

I bowed, the same bow I gave the Magnum that morning, glad that this director hadn't brought his own crook and cowl. "Welcome, Director," I said.

His smiles widened at the sight of the sparkling, and nearly full, chests behind me. "Greetings, Superintendent," he intoned. His voice, like actual stone, echoed not at all. "It has been a very rewarding day."

Death really is the perfect con.

Especially when the dead are still here.

The Gift

Jason Palmatier

The breeze, warm and languid, scented with the earthy brine of Cimberwood bark, flowed over Jan Ti's smooth face, sliding inside his slim and sharply pointed nose. He inhaled deeply. The heavy vapors filled his lungs, bronzing their inner walls with spiced warmth. Jan Ti cleared his mind, reveling in the feeling of fullness that spread across his delicate chest to his thin arms and down his mid-section into his long legs. Full peace descended as his fingers and toes began to tingle and he stilled his breath. He felt his self drift away.

He began to hear the humming voices of his inner Swarm.

He translated what they said.

Towards Warm Light, through dense tangles of barbed Savatrack vines, a thicket of white Bilory weed bloomed, its millions of flowers full to the brim with nectar that would fuel Home through two and a half dark cycles. In the opposite direction, what the Swarm called Cool Shadow, a pool of crystal-clear water bubbled with Chrysium fragments that would strengthen Home's supports on which all else hung. Towards Light Hatch, at the edge of the stand of Cimberbark, flat, chalky Palso clung to the branches, its pungent surface suffused with dust that would help seal the recent breach in Home's wall. Opposite that, towards Last Glimmer, a growth of Fronsage held oils that would moisten Home's air chambers so they could better absorb and spread the all-encompassing Ether to all parts of Home.

Jan Ti sighed, imagining his Swarm as the buzzing insects that flew about the forest day and night, always busy, always searching. But he did not, in truth, know, for they were too small to see. They had inhabited his kind from time immemorial and together they lived not *in* nature, but *as* nature, taking only what was needed in such quantities that the things that gave of themselves were not harmed. In return they gave back something that Jan Ti could not explain but he knew was vital. His people called it the Gift. Without it living things on Ampyrium withered and died.

Jan Ti frowned, sensing something that he could not identify.

The hum of the Swarm returning from Light Hatch, or East as the City dwellers would say, had changed to an agitated alert that normally meant unnatural Darkness, like when the moons covered the sun during the day. Jan Ti gleaned an outline of the anomaly from the hundred or so position reports from returning individuals. He huffed out a knowing breath.

He cracked a single, lashless eyelid and peered out, feeling his connection with his Swarm fade, the specifics of their reports morphing into subtle inclinations to stay where he was or wander farther south or east. Soon he felt only an impression of the anomaly behind him about twenty paces away. He took a final, centering breath and stood from his meditative crouch.

"Good morn, Foenstan," Jan Ti called as he stepped around the base of the tree behind which he'd sat.

"Gah! You can't do that to me, Jan!" Foenstan gasped in Meld, clasping at the odd brown garment of dead plant fibers and animal hair that covered her heart.

"But it is the way of our greeting," Jan Ti stated, confused.

Foenstan stood a good head shorter than Jan Ti and smelled of charred forest and heated animal carcass. She had woven the fine black hair strands that covered her head into two thick vines that flopped about as she shook her head back and forth.

"I know, but you gotta warn somebody before you jump out at them like that," Foenstan said. She continued to clutch at her garment, but her other hand, which had flown to the handle of the weapon she wore dangling from her waist and referred to as a "sword," relaxed.

Jan Ti frowned inwardly.

Always worried, these City dwellers. Never at peace. Why do they fear what is around them?

"Anyways, how'ya doing?" Foenstan asked, wiping at moisture that oozed from the skin above her eyes.

Jan Ti cocked his head to the side, working to separate Foenstan's run-together sounds into words he knew. Luckily, in the three moon cycles since he'd discovered her chipping away at a Glimmerstone deposit at the edge of the Cimberwood forest, he'd gotten accustomed to her odd speech patterns.

"I do well. There is fullness in me and all that surrounds me," Jan Ti replied.

Foenstan nodded her head, eyebrows rising as they often did when he spoke. "Of course. Not sure why I asked. Well, anyway, are you ready to meet my friends?"

Jan Ti nodded. "Yes, though I feel unwell about it."

"Unwell? What's there to be unwell about?" Foenstan asked as she looked away and cleared her throat.

The vague unease that always occurred when he thought of the City and those who inhabited it grew.

Foenstan is not one with herself today. She is divided, as she has been since last Shademoon. There is danger here.

"What if I do not meet your friends?" Jan Ti asked.

"Whoa, whoa, whoa!" Foenstan said, holding both hands out in front of her as if to stop him from leaving. "All they want to do is talk to you. They're coming outside and everything. You won't have to go into the City at all."

Jan Ti looked past her, to the edge of the woods, where it thinned out into shorter, thorny trees before giving way to tangled underbrush. Beyond that, farther than he could see, grew tassle-topped grasses and low vining weeds that eventually gave way to the Barrens, the wide swath of bare dirt and rocks that surrounded the outer walls of the City. Nothing grew there, nor had it for centuries, ever since his kind had drawn back from those foreign walls, beyond the normal range of their Swarms. For the City contained nothing they needed and loomed like a great black abyss in their minds.

"Look," Foenstan said, the light-brown skin around her azure eyes losing some of their tension. "If you don't want to do it, that's okay. It just took a lot of work to get them all there today and I don't think I can do it again if you don't show. They just want to talk to you about what Ampyrium has to offer. If it doesn't sound good, you can just walk away."

Jan Ti looked down into Foenstan's face, sensing the tension in her, the urgent desire she had for him to follow her warring with her realization that if he just stepped backwards and disappeared there would be nothing she could do to stop him. She understood that their meetings were never chance encounters and that he could avoid her indefinitely in the confines of his home woods. For some reason she feared that this day. And despite his misgivings he knew that he must find out why. With a grudging nod he gestured for her to lead the way.

Foenstan's face brightened with a triumphant smile and she spun around quickly, her rough traveling garment billowing out around her. She began shoving her way through the underbrush.

A wave of sadness washed over Jan Ti at the sap oozing from broken limbs in the wake of Foenstan's passage but he followed nonetheless. He was comforted slightly as he felt his Swarm leap out to collect the resources before they were lost to decay.

A used resource is not wasted.

To keep from seeing Foenstan's path of destruction Jan Ti looked skyward, past the towering, thin gray trunks of the Cymberbarks into their flat, multi-branched canopies that spread like mushroom tops against the aquamarine sky. There flitted the iridescent flocks of Cah-ti-bahna, the bright purples and greens of their feathers flashing as they called to one another, *cah-ti-bahna-cah-ti-bahna*. Around them hung the star-shaped, thick-skinned, blue Cymberfruit, its aroma spicing the air. Yellow Illicum vines hung past both fruit and birds, reaching halfway to the ground and oozing the water they had absorbed in the last downpour. The cah-ti-bahna licked at them with their flat tongues, clinging to their sides with their prehensile tails.

Jan Ti stepped to the side without looking down, avoiding Foenstan as she doubled back to find her original path, which Jan Ti could easily sense from the damage she had wrought. The City dweller muttered to herself, Jan Ti catching a few words like "cursed jungle" and "worse than the slums." He ignored her, dropping his gaze only when the Cymberbarks gave way to the short, thorn-encrusted shrubbery that marked the edge of the forest and presaged the grassy belt beyond.

He seldom ventured this far, knowing that if he were not careful he could accidentally catch a glimpse of the City through the tangled underbrush, a dark stain on the horizon. Now he felt the tug of his Swarm, as he always did, calling him back towards the center of his home woods, away from the Barrens that lay just beyond and offered no resources with which to maintain him. Jan Ti set his delicate jaw and trudged forward, ducking and sliding between the brambles as Foenstan hacked at them with her sword.

As they walked, a deeply seated anger buzzed within him, building with each step. He opened his mouth to speak to Foenstan about her wanton destruction just as they stepped out into the waist-high grass at the edge of the woods.

The sight of the City stopped him.

Massive and foreboding, the City's dark gray walls rose an almost unimaginable height from the desolate flatness of the rocky Barrens, eclipsing the sky with sharp, angled lines that cut at Jan Ti's eyes. Crenelations along the top and the towers at the corners of each of its eight walls gave it the visage of a great worm-beast erupting from the earth to devour the sun and moons before falling back to ravage the world that had birthed it. The sea beyond the peninsula upon which it sat, and which it filled from cliff to cliff to cliff, boomed with high rolling waves churned up from a storm that could not be seen because of the City's mass. Jan Ti smelled the salty brine but quickly exhaled through his nose at the pungent odors of flame and sweat and excrement that accompanied it. A hundred other foreign scents assaulted him, too.

"There they are!" Foenstan exclaimed with relief.

Jan Ti blinked and looked to his feet, letting the soothing greens and blues of the grasses swishing past his legs center him. The stalks turned shorter and patchier with each step and finally gave out altogether to the hard-packed red-brown soil and rocks of the Barrens. Reluctantly, he looked up, spying the group assembled exactly halfway between the walls of the city and the last tuft of grass, framed by the Great Gate. That gate stood as tall as two Cimberbark trees and half as wide, imposing even at this distance. Jan Ti huffed out a disconcerted breath.

"Now, now, Jan, don't be too quick to judge, they're a respectable lot, I assure you," Foenstan declared, misinterpreting his huff for derision. They walked the distance to the group, who fidgeted under Jan Ti's silent gaze and stopped within five strides of them.

Foenstan began the introductions.

"This here is Tentoran Hibershan, leader of Overwall Adventures, who hales from Calamunda," Foenstan said, gesturing to a round man wrapped in red and yellow sheets of fabric that shimmered when he moved. Long hairs beneath the man's nose had been twisted together to extend past his puffy, red cheeks and a strange, rounded covering encased his head above his twinkling green eyes.

"Tentoran's the one that came up with this wild idea and sent me out to see what there was to see," Foenstan finished.

Tentoran bowed as deeply as his belly would allow, turning slightly redder as he did so.

"Next we have Ocqounus Silveray, company comptroller and weaver of the mystic arts from the Water Gate," Foenstan said, nodding towards a woman draped in thin gray strips of fabric with ruffled edges that reminded Jan Ti of the plants that grew in the lapping waters of the wide salt lake. Ocqounus puckered her lips at Foenstan's mystic arts comment but inclined her head and fluttered her arms down by her sides in greeting.

"Then we got Hilvestri Rorson, quartermaster and supply guru, from Samiluna," Foenstan continued, pointing at a beast that looked like the fearsome cats that hunted on the Golden Plains. Only this cat stood on two legs and wore an outfit of tight-fitting, green cloth detailed with gold braids of something as thin as a single Akta fur. The beast bared its teeth and bowed its head, but its eyes never left Jan Ti's.

"And finally, but not finest," Foenstan said, a smile tugging at one corner of her mouth, "we have Grable Forsten, from Daruvia, who handles security and, uh, other matters." The man to whom Foenstan gestured with an elaborate bow merely smirked back at her, then inclined his head towards Jan Ti, his gray eyes glittering like a hunting Nightstriker. He wore dark gray clothing of the same rough fabric as Foenstan's but he stood a head taller than her. The skin of his face was heavily tattooed in elaborate red mazes that stood out against his long, blond hair. A flowing cape about his neck only partially concealed the handles of some curiously small swords he wore strapped to his sides.

"And that's it, that's the whole company for now," Foenstan finished, stepping back slightly with a nod to Tentoran. "Everyone, this is Jan Ti."

Jan Ti nodded and said simply, "Good morn."

Tentoran waited as if expecting more, then stepped forward at a slight push from the cat, Hilvestri. "Oh, uh, Honored Jan Ti, we wished to meet with you in order to discuss a possible partnership in trading the resources of this world with the residents of Ampyrium and beyond. We, uh, understand from our dear Madame Foenstan that you are the caretaker of the lands which stand outside the City and we would like to ask your permission to survey them for possible minerals or plants or other things that could be of value. You would, of course, be allotted a share of any profits we gain from our adventures therein, pursuant to a contract signed by all constituents and notarized by the Trade Guild prior to any expeditions taking place."

The other members of the group shifted uncomfortably at the mention of "expeditions," and a brief, angry scowl flashed on the face of the one called Grable when he glanced at the forest. Jan Ti narrowed his eyes. He had only understood a few of the words spoken so far, but had felt his Swarm buzz as he thought of resources and minerals and plants. He vaguely sensed that the newcomers wanted to venture into his home forest and look for things that they might use, which seemed a nightmare given the amount of destruction Foenstan wrought just making her own way in and out. But one word completely perplexed him.

"What is 'profit'?" Jan Ti asked, the word thick on his tongue.

The tension in the assembled group broke as they all uttered amused chuckles or barks of outright laughter. They exchanged looks and mouthed the word until they noticed that Jan Ti had actually meant what he asked.

"Oh, uh, profit, sir?" Tentoran looked to Foenstan, who flared her eyes at him and gestured to Jan Ti with her head, hair vines flopping. "Well, profit is the money you make after paying all of the expenses of the endeavor."

Jan Ti nodded his head, deciphering the words, but only understanding money. Foenstan had shown him "money" once and explained how you could trade the odd bits of metal for services or clothing or food. But it made no sense to him aside from the food, which City dwellers apparently consumed with their mouths as if they were common forest animals. Why would you hand money to someone for food when you could just walk into the forest and let your Swarm harvest it, or, if you functioned so low, pick it or catch it yourself? But he knew that the City dwellers coveted it, had somehow built their entire society on it, and he knew that terrible things had been done— were being done—in the quest to get it. And now they wanted to bring that quest beyond their walls into his world. The idea resonated deeply inside him, roiling a darkness there that threatened to unbalance him. He felt the need to seek inner peace.

"I must speak with my people about this," Jan Ti said. "They will want to know many things. Do you have this 'con-tract' of which you spoke?"

Tentoran stood straight in surprise, while the assembly behind him let out gasps of "oh" and "I say." Foenstan's head whipped around, her eyes wide with shock.

"Well, I—yes, yes, we do have the contract right here." Tentoran gestured towards Ocqounus, who hastily rummaged in a sack of stitched-together animal hide and produced a rolled parchment. Tentoran took it and handed it to Jan Ti. "That is just a copy, the original is at the Trade Guild office registered under Overwall Adventures Trading Company. You would have to come inside and sign either of those under the Notary's visage, along with all of us, to make it official."

Jan Ti nodded, taking the parchment but keeping it rolled.

"I will bring this before my people and they will decide," Jan Ti said. "Send Foenstan in a half moon's time and I will have your answer."

* * *

Foenstan walked purposely down the middle of the wide main avenue that lead to the inner gate, careful to keep her face neutral as the two imposing Magnum who stood guard here closed the small man-door in the main gate behind her. She fought down a powerful urge to squirm at the gaze she knew the white-robed figures were casting at her back and instead concentrated on maintaining a non-hysterical pace through her eerie surroundings.

Unlike the rest of the City, the space around her was not jammed wall to wall with gleaming palaces, tottering shanties, timbered ale houses and cobbled district squares. Instead it stood ominously empty, a sight so shocking that few City dwellers dared peek at it from the safety of the inner gate that lead here, let alone pass through it to step out the main gate behind her into the Barrens beyond. In fact, as far as Foenstan knew, she—and now the four other dumbfounded merchants of the newly-formed Overwall Adventures Trading Company—were the first to step outside in over six hundred years.

After a couple hundred paces, she dodged behind a crumbling warehouse, pulling the other members of the trading company with her.

"I can't believe that just happened," she said, grabbing the base of her twin hair braids in disbelief.

The other trading members looked at each other in shock as well.

"Did we just begin trade negotiations with a native Ampyri?" Hilvestri asked. His magnificent orange fur ruffled slightly in the breeze that found its way off the top of the wall and over the entire city from the storm out at sea.

"I believe we did," Tantoran replied, removing the tightly woven turban from his head and mopping the perspiration that had formed on his brow.

"Bee yow!" Foenstan shouted, throwing both her fists into the air with a minimal loss of hair. Her feet began patting the ground faster and faster, running in place until she finally stomped both boots flat, threw her hands out to the side and screamed, "You're welcome! Now, where's my money?"

Tantoran rolled his eyes, the folds of his neck creasing as he shook his head. "You make first contact with a native Ampyri, befriend him and get him to agree to an historic meeting to discuss the first ever native trade contract, and your first thought is money?"

Foenstan didn't even blink. "You stiffs are all broke. There's about a two percent chance this crazy adventure will pay out more than half an Amp to anyone and I need way more than that to sail out of here. So, cough it up."

Tentoran smirked but motioned to Ocqounus, who slid her suckered fingers across the clam shell satchel that hung at her waist, enticing it to open and reveal the company's meager petty cash. She plucked out two small coins and held them out to Foenstan, who snatched them with a cackle.

"This almost gets me there. One more meetup with Jan and I'm cruising the Teliune river delta on a dinghy with a HerAle in one hand and a fishing pole in the other."

"Have you ever actually gone fishing?" Ocqounus asked, shuddering slightly at the thought.

"Nope!" Foenstan replied with a wide smile.

"Then how do you know you're going to like doing it for the rest of time?" Ocqounus continued logically.

"Gotta be better than this place!" Foenstan said, shoving the coins in a pouch she pulled from under her shirt where "the girls kept it safe."

Grable unbuttoned the top button of his collar and said, "You know, Foenstan, for someone who wants a quiet life away from the city you sure like taking risks."

Foenstan's smile faltered just a bit as she flashed a look at Grable. "Yeah, well. Risk gets riskier the more you risk."

"That literally makes no sense," Ocqounus said.

Foenstan waved her away. "It's gonna be great, don't worry. Anyway, shouldn't we get out of here before anyone other than those two spooks notice we're here?" Foenstan hooked a thumb over her shoulder at the two out-of-sight Magnum that stood perpetual guard by the forbidden outer gate. Not that they had much to guard. Nobody, not even the most debased, down-on-their-luck, lowest-of-the-low gutter scum even considered passing through those doors into the world beyond, thanks to the legends of what happened to those that did right after the City's founding.

Tentoran raised a single thick eyebrow. "If you don't think everyone and their dead Downfall uncle are talking about this then you are more than a few Amps short of a loan payment, Foenstan. The Trade Guild is a sieve punched full of holes for those without enough riches to plug them. Rumors have been flying ever since we scraped the money together for our charter."

"True," Foenstan said, remembering the feeling of foreboding that had pressed down on her as the Magnum had turned the ancient key in the man-door's lock and pulled it open with a tortured screech. Foenstan had stood staring past a mound of accumulated debris, out beyond the flat, parched expanse of the Barrens, to the terrifying clash of greens and purples of the distant forest.

"Even so, I think Foenstan has a wise idea," Hilvestri said. "Let us retire back to the city proper."

They tumbled back out onto the avenue, keeping their eyes on the buildings that had sprung up here shortly after the City's founding to avoid glancing back at the Magnum still guarding the main gate. This area was to serve as the indigenous population of Ampyria's access point into the City proper and all the wonders it had to offer. But the indigenous population had never come. And so, after the other space in the city had been filled, the citizens of Ampyrium petitioned to move in, to build, to venture out and explore.

And the Magnum had obliged.

Within weeks, warehouses sprang up, built to house the resources culled from this new world by the industrious new citizens who had never ventured outside, but meant to soon, and wanted to be ready for the riches that awaited. And when the first few expeditions that had sallied forth amidst cheers began bringing back their spoils, it seemed as if all of the planning had been worth it. Fortunes were made in months off the exotic wonders discovered outside the walls, drawing more people to the octet. Soon it was filled to the brim, bustling with the raucous shouts and rumbling cart wheels of trade.

Then the Thinning had come.

Few took notice, at first, the rumors of people wasting away filtering through the octet like flour sifting through the miller's floorboards: those that died were not missed. But slowly the deaths began to mount, taking more and more of those who had ventured beyond the walls, leaving behind relatives who described their loved ones fading to skeletons wrapped in sagging skin before dying. No magic, no medicine, not even the wisdom of the Magnum, could save them.

And when the sickness spread to those who had never set foot outside the city, the octet had been quarantined, the inner gate that lead to the City proper sealed. Those trapped inside were forced to venture through the outer gate into the wilderness beyond or perish. And now, six hundred years later, the area between the outer and inner gate was still taboo. No one wanted to live there.

"What is this?" Hilvestri growled, swishing his great coat to one side to clasp the handle of his serrated longsword, *Saberclaw*.

A figure in a ragged, brown cloak leaned casually against the frame of the inner gate's man-door, arms crossed. Two luminous, orange eyes stared out from the shrouded depths of the stranger's hood, framed by stringy gray hair that stuck out around the hood's edges. A long piece of straw traced slow circles before the figure's face, animated by languid chewing.

Foenstan's heart stuttered and her hand slapped down to her sword's pommel, even though, deep down, she knew she would not draw it. You did not bare steel against one of the assassins of Yaasur unless you wished to die.

"Well, well, well," the figure said in a voice dripping with poison. "You did go beyond the walls. I thought it was just hysteria and greedy talking. What did you find? Death?"

Tentoran, face pale as fresh snow and sweating profusely, held up a shaking hand and stuttered, "W-we are just simple merchants, looking into business prospects. We have no quarrel with anyone."

"Ah, but you do," the Yaasur said. "The city is set for a trade war and you know it. Your adventure outside the walls will cut the strings pulled by those that fueled the war's fire. New resources, new goods, new prospects? Why those just might launch an age of prosperity, and prosperity doesn't feed a war…it kills it."

The Yaasur's orange eyes flashed on the word "kills," sending an icy stab of fear into Foenstan's heart. All it took was a single brush from a Yaasur's weapon to bring excruciating death by incurable poison. Only the Yaasur themselves could withstand it, and only then by ingesting a counter poison daily that gave them their luminous orange eyes.

Tentoran swallowed heavily, breaths coming in increasingly frequent gasps. He looked as if he had only moments before he passed out.

Ocqounus had frozen in an odd pose, the faint shimmer of a shielding spell encasing her.

Hilvestri growled menacingly, but his ears lay flat against his head in fear.

Foenstan felt her hand slowly sliding over her sword's pommel so that it gripped the handle, despite every fiber of her being screaming for it to stay still. But before she could do anything colossally stupid Grable stepped forward.

"Prosperity can be shared, assassin."

The Yaasur's eyes flicked to Grable, narrowing almost imperceptibly.

"We know the cost of business in this city," Grable said. "Tell your employer they'll get their share if anything comes of this."

"And if ruin comes of it? Death?" the Yaasur hissed.

Fear eclipsed the orange of the Yaasur's eyes and Foenstan realized the Yaasur had spoken words of its own, not of its employer. Grable's face contorted in the same angry flash that had passed over it at the sight of the forest, but quickly fell into its usual hard glare.

"Your employers would profit from that, too."

"Not if they're dead!" The Yaasur whipped a razor-thin blade from the folds of its cloak and pointed it with quivering malice, rage twisting its face. "You play with the lives of us all, merchants. What you bring back from the foul lands beyond the walls will doom us. Only this illusory form and the binds of my contract keep me from killing you now."

With a sharp snap, the Yaasur stowed its blade and faded to nothingness, the orange of its hateful eyes the last to disappear.

Foenstan sagged back and let out her held breath, the relief she felt at the Yaasur only being a projection tempered by the knowledge that Yaasur could only project over short distances. The assassin likely stood within a hundred feet of them, almost assuredly on the other side of the octet's inner wall.

"How about that?" Hilvestri said, ears twitching back up to their normal alertness. "Not even a Yaasur would set foot in here. It seems we know where we can hide out, if we need to."

Tentoran held himself upright against a crumbling half-wall and mopped at his fevered brow. "I think we need to right now, with assassins taking an interest in our company."

"No," Grable said, stowing a blade Foenstan had not seen him draw. "We'd be dead if the assassin's sender wanted us to be, and we all know who that sender was."

"The Wands?" Ocqounus asked.

"Who else?" Grable said. "But we've received their message and that's all that will come of it."

"For now," Tentoran shot back.

Grable shrugged. "Everything in this life is 'for now.' Only death is forever."

Foenstan watched Grable's eyes flick to the outer gate before he placed a hand on the inner gate's man-door and push it open. She glanced back herself as she followed him through, expecting to see something burst it to pieces and ravage the derelict buildings in a blind fury. But they remained closed and barred, as they had for centuries.

Unease crawled from the depths of her, prickling her scalp.

Should we really be going out there?

* * *

Jan Ti jogged through the undergrowth of Hwa Rang's mountain jungle range, brushing aside green leaves twice his size inlaid with violet veins that pulsed as he touched them. He ducked under purple hanging vines that trailed fine gray mushroom tendrils, sprang from pockmarked igneous rocks whose many holes housed colonies of miniature swimming fish and slid down inclines upon the smooth, shed bark of the towering Samilack trees.

The Samilack's branches grew straight out at intervals of eighty feet above him, making seven distinct levels above the jungle floor that all teamed with life. Jan Ti could feel it around him: the buzz of ten-legged insects in the intense humidity, the squawks of amphibious snake birds in the trees and ponds, the hooting call of marsupial cats as they licked their fur and alerted one another to prey. All of it sounded foreign from his forest, yet still natural and right, forming a part of the oneness that made all things whole.

Unlike the wilting, rancid parchment he clutched in his hand.

He wrinkled his nose at its foreign smell, almost gagging at the thought of what he would have to do with it in just a few moments. But that time needed to come, for he already felt weakness taking hold of him due to his dormant Swarm. He had called them in so as not to lose any on the journey and now they buzzed impatiently within him, rife with alerts about the resources Home was short on and eager to go forth and collect them. He felt all of this as a vague queasiness.

Soon, he thought. He had but one small obstacle to overcome first.

He spotted what he need ahead, bobbing in his vision as he leaped from log to log across a steaming stream, ignoring the gnashing teeth that churned the water at his passage. With a quick twist he snapped a Sorain sapling from its host tree on the shoreline and shoved the parchment between his teeth with a grimace. He flipped the sapling over his shoulder, stuffed his hands into the pockets of its two primary leaves and grasped the inner cord that ran through it tightly. Three steps later he burst through the foliage into thin air, arms snapping out to the side to catch the upward rushing wind, while his feet kicked backwards to hook over the stems of the two smaller leaves that jutted from the base of the sapling.

The sheer red rock cliff face of the plateau rushed past a body length from his feet until the primary leaves snapped taut, yanking his arms upwards and dragging the rest of his body with it. Jan Ti grunted around the parchment in his mouth, straining to level out his glide so that he could steer with slight pressure on the leaves at his feet. The cliff face drew away as he stabilized his descent, angling towards his intended destination near the center of the broad valley below. He took a moment to survey the majesty of his surroundings.

Beneath him the low mosses and short ferns at the base of Hwa Rang's plateau gave way to a wide river that wound around the southern edges of the valley before disappearing into the jagged, rocky peaks of Te Nua's mountain home, where short trees and grassy meadows hid in the peaceful vales tucked within. The northern edge of those mountains touched Qui Path's expansive golden tundra, which could be glimpsed through a broad pass to the northeast bordered on the west by Shi Nol's gentle, rolling hills with its dotting of wispy white Confalia trees and herds of grazing ungulates. To the west of those stood Hri Towga's sparse desert land, the ever shifting patterns of its brown and yellow sands punctuated by bright oases that flourished around its many artesian wells. And in the broad valley around which all of these lands stood, sat Fri Te's small domain, surrounded by a ring of barren rock and dirt.

Jan Ti adjusted his flight path slightly with a push of his shin, hearing the flap of the leaf edges change pitch as they swished through the air. The sparse blue grasses and withered orange trees of Fri Te's domain slid to the right, stopping their sideways movement when Jan Ti let off his shin pressure and staying in relatively the same position, though growing slowly larger. Jan Ti settled in for the rest of the glide, breathing deeply through his nose.

A few moments later a pair of soaring Hoosek monkeys angled towards him, cocking their crested heads with quizzical looks as they hooted out a greeting. Jan Ti hooted back, careful to keep from dropping the parchment in his mouth as he turned his head to each in turn. Satisfied, the Hooseks barked a final note and dove back towards the sparkling river, wings held tight to their sides. Jan Ti craned his neck to watch them skim along the surface of the water, kicking up plumes with their astonishing speed before they snatched an unsuspecting eel from the current with their tales and rocketed skyward once again.

Jan Ti smiled and turned back, finding his landing spot had drifted upwards in his line of sight. He chided himself and stretched his front leaves forward, working to get as much distance as he could even though he knew he couldn't make it. He selected a fairly clear section of ground about a hundred steps short of his first spot and angled towards it, slowly pulling back on his front leaves to bleed off speed before dropping his feet from the back stems. He yanked back on the front leaves to cause them to flair into a sharp upward jaunt, which dropped him onto the ground from a height of three feet.

Jan Ti staggered forward, tripped on a dead log and fell to his hands and knees. With a groan he shouldered the Sorain sapling to the side, spit out the parchment and rolled to sit on his butt. The palms of his hands and fronts of his knees burned where they had been abraded and he felt the slight tug on his skin from his Swarm as it burst forth to collect resources and effect repairs. Already he was lightheaded from lack of foraged sustenance and it was with some effort that he climbed to his feet and dusted himself off.

Instinctively he picked up the Sorain sapling to plant it, knowing it would sprout roots from the broken end of the stem and take hold, but the barrenness of the land stopped him. Dry, brittle brush and snags of old trees rustled in the slight daytime breeze, stark reminders of the bounty that had once grown here. But over the years the cacophony of life had slowly stopped reproducing, the older plants dying with nothing new to take their place. Inexorably the decay had eaten away, always at the edges, edges that shrank back towards the center, towards Fri Te.

And Jan Ti knew why.

Fri Te was dying.

Jan Ti stooped to pick up the City parchment and stepped forward, over the dead logs and crackling branches, carrying the Sorain sapling with him towards the faltering greenery ahead. He crossed the meager tufts of grass at its outskirts and carefully stepped around the drooping ferns that followed before picking up a flat stone and digging a hole to place the Sorain sapling in. When he had patted the dirt back in place around its stem he dropped the stone and strode past the short, struggling trees into the clearing where Fri Te lived.

A softly burbling stream flowed in an arc between stacked, rounded rocks whose edges were tinged with lime green mosses that spread across the ground around them. A Calcal tree, the fine blue hairs that trailed from its drooping branches floating lazily on the breeze, stood sentinel in the center of the arc. Beneath the tree sat Fri Te, cross-legged, bent from his many years, skin gray and flaking except for a dark crescent next to his left eye, hair mass a faded shade of its original brilliant blue. His eyes, lately wandering and vague but sharp now as he looked about the clearing at the others already gathered there, snapped to Jan Ti's face immediately.

"Jan Ti," the old man said, "You have finally come. Let us see the portend."

Jan Ti dipped his head and strode forward, stepping around the half dozen others who sat cross-legged at Fri Te's feet. All of them looked similar to Jan Ti in most respects, though heights and weights varied, as did the colors of their skin and hair masses. Normally Jan Ti would have exchanged formal greetings with each, clasping forearms and touching foreheads as their Swarms co-mingled, learning of resources from one another, but the business of the day made that impractical. Instead, he handed the parchment to their chief elder and sat in the cool moss to Fri Te's right, facing the others.

Fri Te unrolled the parchment and inspected the writing upon it.

"Hmm," Fri Te murmured, the deep wrinkles at the corners of his red-rimmed eyes multiplying as he squinted. "It is as the stories foretold. Jan Ti, fetch my charge, please."

Jan Ti dipped his head again, expecting nothing less given all that had happened. He rose and walked to a pile of rocks at the opposite end of the clearing, far from the water, and knelt once again. With a heave and a grunt he rolled a large stone from the front of the pile, revealing a small chamber within, from which he dragged an unnaturally shaped box he knew the City people called a "chest." He hefted the chest up and walked back to Fri Te, setting it at the elder's feet.

Fri Te nodded his thanks and slid the bolts that held the chest closed to one side. He lifted the lid, peered inside and pulled forth another parchment. A ripple of unease passed through those assembled, the presence of so many foreign objects disturbing the oneness they felt around them. Fri Te held the two parchments side by side and nodded to himself.

"Those before us knew much, for they predicted this day would come and warned us of the danger. The City dwellers want to come into our world and take things from it. They will share any 'profits' that they make with us."

"Prah-fitz?"

Jan Ti spoke quickly, "Extra resources that they do not need."

"Why would they take more than they need?"

A disquieted murmur ran through those assembled.

Fri Te held up a hand.

"I know this is disturbing, but if we are to deal with the people of the City we must be shrewd and thoughtful, for what we do will affect not only us, but all of Ampyrium. What Jan Ti has brought is but the first of many and to ignore this one is to hand our fate over to the City. So I call on you, speak your mind now, so that we may meditate on the matter and reach a decision."

Qui Path stood, the early afternoon sun shimmering in her orange hair and glowing off her golden skin. The lithe muscles that propelled her to great speeds across the flat expanses of her tundra range flowed like water as she spoke her peace.

"My range is far from these City dwellers and their blight. I have no need for their things—" Qui Path gestured with disgust at the chest and parchments. "—and do not welcome the destruction the ancestors tell us they would bring. Let them decay where they are and not bother us." She jerked her chin up in derision and sat down, the peace within her disrupted.

Fri Te nodded and looked about for the next speaker.

Hwa Rang pushed his small, compact body up slowly, the red stripes on his lime green skin flashing in distress, highlighting the purple hair he brushed from his eyes. His normally agile limbs moved stiffly in agitation as he spoke.

"What Qui Path says is true. We have no need for the things of the City. But my range is not so far from it as hers. Only Jan Ti's forest is between my plateau and its dark walls. On clear days, from the Akthang's Rook, I can see it." Hwa Rang shuddered, the inner peace he had tried so hard to hold on to collapsing. He looked up at each face, stricken. "If the City dwellers have decided to come out and they find something they can use, they won't stop. I have had visions of it, of Jan Ti's forest burning while I look down upon it, of small blights spreading beyond the City's walls, the areas around them hacked down to a few plants sown in torn earth. It will be the end of much, unless we control it."

Hwa Rang sat abruptly, avoiding the eyes of those around him.

Fri Te inclined his head in respect and looked for another.

Te Nua rose with a grace inconsistent with his muscled size and looked to each of those gathered with a solemn inner peace that matched the even gray coloring of his skin. His eyes flashed to match his silver hair when his long, drawn out jaw finally moved to deliver his mountain wisdom.

"We all know that what we are now is not what we once were," Te Nua said. Sharp looks were exchanged. Te Nua continued.

"Before the City, before the First Dwellers emerged, we were very different. We functioned the same, living in nature, spreading the Gift, but we looked nothing like what we do today." Te Nua paused, looking to everyone as he continued. "And we all know why. It is written there in the relics, those things that remain from the First Dwellers. They found us, studied us, began to understand us. But by that time it was already too late. The things that they did not understand had taken hold and there was nothing they, or we, could do to turn it back. And so we, and much of what was around us, Changed. Contacting them again, working with them, will bring new change…" Te Nua glanced at Fri Te's frail form. "…but perhaps change is what we need."

Fri Te cast his eyes to the ground and pressed his lips together, nodding.

Hri Towga's tall, thin frame rose, the sandy hue of her skin complimenting the coppery hair that hung stiffly about her long, drawn out face. She placed her wide, flat feet carefully in the wet moss and pointed to Fri Te. "One of our number is dying. His swarm has dwindled, his range suffers. Soon he, and all that depends on him, will pass away." She ran her gaze over the other faces there. "You all know that the sand gives and the sand takes. This messenger from the City, the sand has given us. We must take what it offers and use it. You know in what way."

A shock of fear raced from Jan Ti's spine to the tips of his fingers and toes at Hri Towga's words. *She cannot be speaking of…*

Jan Ti looked to those assembled around him, noting Qui Path's contemplative look, Hwa Rang's stricken expression and Te Nua's slow, considering nod. As Hri Towga sat, Jan Ti almost leapt to his feet, feeling the blackness of the City pressing in towards him, its walls stretching, threatening to burst their foul contents across his lands.

But Shi Nol stood slowly and brushed the moss that matched the color of his hair from his tan skin. His round face split in a strained smile of understanding as he looked at each person in turn. He puffed up his barrel chest, and held his hands out to the side as he spoke.

"What Hri Towga has said has shattered the peace within you, I know. For I feel the same when speaking of such matters. But the time for change is upon us. Many lands beyond ours have died, their verdant life withering along with their caretakers who did not change, and whose old forms could not survive in this new world." Shi Nol inclined his head towards Hri Towga, who's lands bordered those beyond their own. Hri Towga nodded in affirmation. "To revive them we will need a flock. I believe what Hri Towga says, that the sands have given us a gift at the very time that we need one. We should use it."

Shi Nol inclined his head in a short bow and sat.

Silence settled in the clearing.

Jan Ti jumped up, hands gesturing sharply as he spoke. "We have avoided everything from the City since the First Dwellers came. We have kept our Swarms from them, kept our lands away. What will happen if they are again among us? What will they change? What will we change in them? They will hack down our forests for their ever-burning fires, they will slaughter our creatures for eating, they will dig up our soil for the rocks within them and put their own plants down when they are through. The ancestors told us this! If we are to honor them, we should listen."

Jan Ti sat down abruptly, only the smallest sliver of inner peace remaining within him. His heart pounded in his chest and the sights and sounds of the plants and insects around him were sharp. Somewhere, just beyond them, the darkness loomed, threatening to burst through, to drown him. He swallowed hard and looked to Fri Te.

The elder kept his eyes on the ground, nodding. Slowly he raised himself up, staff wobbling as he used it for support. When he reached his full, bent height, he looked to each in turn before leveling his gaze at Jan Ti.

"What Jan Ti speaks is truth. All those things will come to pass if we do not deal with this correctly. But what is our fate, what is the fate of this world, if we do not take this gift that has been given to us? No City dweller has come from that gate since the time of the First Dwellers. Yet, here, now, just as I am passing from this world, one does. If that is not Fate then I do not know what is. And we all know that we are not powerless beings."

Fri Te cast a knowing look at all assembled. They shifted uncomfortably, keeping their eyes down.

"The harmony in which we live was not always thus. It settled in from the time of the Great Change, and it took every gift we had—*every gift*—to make it so. We can use those gifts again if called upon."

Fri Te allowed the weight of his words to sink in before lowering himself to the ground.

Jan Ti watched as the others closed their eyes one by one, sinking into meditative states to contemplate what was said and find peace with it before reaching a decision. But when his own eyes closed he felt only the press of the great void that lurked at the edge of his range, that darkness that he would not let his Swarm approach. What would become of them if they opened themselves up to that darkness, let it flow out of its prison into all that they had?

And what would his people have him do with the City dwellers? For surely he was the one who would be tasked with implementing their plan…

* * *

Foenstan walked with steady purpose, eyes casting about at the silent crowd who parted before the heavily-armed cadre of Council Guardsmen that surrounded her and her stoic guest, Jan Ti. Regular city folks craned their necks to catch a glimpse of an Ampyria native here, in their own domain, curiosity but also concern etched on their faces. They hung from windows, clung to crier's towers, stood on tiptoes at the top of steps, to see this creature that should not exist. For not even the legends of the time before the Thinning had recounted one such as this.

Whispers rippled through the crowd at their passing, hushed tones laced with phrases like "not so different" and "not a scrap of clothes" and "devil." Foenstan forced the hand resting on the pommel of her short sword to relax, glancing over at Jan Ti to see if he had picked up any of what was said. But the odd native stared straight ahead, back uncharacteristically stiff, just as he had done during their meeting at the edge of his woods two hours earlier. He held in his hands two rolled parchments, the contract from Overwall Adventures he had left with two weeks ago and a second one that appeared shrunken and stained. The shock of seeing the second scroll in his hand had faded from rabid curiosity into something akin to dread in Foenstan's chest.

Where the heck did he get that old animal skin?

Foenstan pulled up short as the guards in front of them clomped to a halt at a call from their commander. With a second barked order, the guard's formation split at the front, leaving a pathway up the broad steps of the Trade Guild office to the gold-filigreed front door.

Foenstan looked over to Jan Ti as he stared at the paneled motifs that depicted trade milestones in the history of the city.

"Pretty impressive, huh?" Foenstan said. "That door costs more than most districts in this place."

But Jan Ti did not respond. He had drawn in a sharp breath and now slowly approached a panel from the early years of the City, hand reaching up until his fingers hovered just above the face of a man depicted there.

A spike of fear shot through Foenstan and she opened her mouth to call out, knowing, as everyone in the City did, that touching the gold of the door was a capital offense. But just as the hands of the guardsmen around Jan Ti tensed on the shafts of their pole arms, the Trade Guild doors swung inward, revealing the Master of the Trade Guild wrapped in opulent robes of purple and blue, a grandiose smile plastered on her alabaster face. The smile faltered as she spied Jan Ti.

For an instant Foenstan saw fear in the Guild Master's eyes, though whether it was fear of the foreignness of Jan Ti himself or fear of the possible implications of Jan Ti's upraised hand and proximity to the door, she could not tell.

The Guild Master quickly looked to the guard commander who stated simply, "He did not touch it, Honored One."

The small amount of color that tinted the Guild Master's face returned. She turned back to Jan Ti and said, "Honored Guest, Jan Ti, it is with great pride that I welcome you to the Trade Guild of the City of Ampyrium and extend to you our most lavish hospitality. Would you please join us so that we may discuss these historic matters?"

The Guild Master stepped aside and swept an arm towards the dim interior where Tentoran, Ocqounus, Hilvestri, and Grable stood in their finest clothes.

Foenstan swept up the stairs, unbuckling her short sword as she did so, so the guard would not skewer her for entering the hall armed. She stopped by the still-stunned Jan Ti, who had yet to turn around and acknowledge the Guild Master, and whispered, "Hey, Jan Ti, they're ready to see you. You still, uh…good?"

Jan Ti's eyes slowly regained focus. His arm drifted down to hang by his side. With a slow blink he turned to Foenstan and whispered, "Yes."

Foenstan frowned, uncertain, but still thrilled that he was speaking and not slapping forbidden gold with abandon. She jerked her head towards the other members of Overwall Adventures and said, "Then come on, the others are waiting."

Jan Ti responded to the gentle tug Foenstan gave to his elbow with a dazed walk across the gleaming purple of the marble threshold. Foenstan glanced at the panel that had affected her native friend so, frowning at the figure depicted there, unremarkable save for a marred spot near the man's eye. She shook her head and decided it didn't matter, she'd met with Jan Ti one more time to get him here and that was enough to get her out of the City and onto a fishing boat. Everything else could go hang.

The opulence of the Trade Guild stunned her, even on this, her second entry into it. Marbled pillars, etched with silver, held aloft arched ceilings that twinkled with a thousand gemstones arranged in murals that changed with the passage of the day. Their beauty was reflected in the floor that shone like water shot through with swirls of orange and red, purple and blue, black and gold; all granite stones from the various worlds that populated the City. Paintings in stunning hues covered the walls, their worth incalculable, flanked by sculptures of such fine quality that Foenstan felt they were alive, watching her, judging her, especially the armless mer-elf from the Water Gate. Every square inch of the place bore some embellishment, from the platinum vines that climbed the corners to the precious stone flowers that bloomed along the base of the second floor rotunda.

But Foenstan had no time to enjoy it. The other Overwall Adventure members beckoned her and Jan Ti to a meeting room directly between the two curving staircases that lead up to the rotunda, which was packed with respectfully curious onlookers.

The rich scent of polished hardwood greeted them as they sat behind a dark cherry, triangular table with a large circle inscribe in it, in high-backed chairs whose centers were upholstered in plumped up cerulean velvet. Foenstan's eyes rolled back in her head at the unheard of softness of her seat as she settle into it. They far outshone the stiff wooden chairs of the common charter court that they had been roughly ushered into on their first visit to the hall. She sighed inwardly in bliss and fought her way back to consciousness to take in the scene around her.

On one side of the table sat the trade guild officials: the Notary, the Recorder of Contracts and, due to the momentousness of the occasion, the Guild Master herself. On another side sat Tentoran, Ocqounus, Hilvestri, and Grable, looking hopeful but haggard, the intense scrutiny of their every move plainly wearing on them. Even Grable looked uncharacteristically tense, as if expecting mayhem to break loose at any moment.

Foenstan herself sat on the remaining side of the table, next to Jan Ti, who had perched himself awkwardly on the front edge of his chair, back rigid.

"You should slide back in your seat, Jan Ti, you're really missing out," Foenstan said, grinding her shoulders into the cushioned back with half-lidded eyes.

The Guild Master cleared her throat.

"If we may get started?" she asked, sharp eyes lingering for a moment on Foenstan before fixing on Jan Ti and brightening. "It is our understanding, Honored Jan Ti, that you bring with you the contract from the company known as the Overwall Adventures Trading Company and wish to sign it in the presence of Guild officials to make it legally binding?"

Foenstan watched for Jan Ti's familiar pause as he processed the Master's words but instead he nodded quickly and whispering, "Yes."

"Excellent. May we see the contract?" the Guild Master asked, gesturing towards the table.

Jan Ti laid the familiar parchment on the table in front of him but then glanced over at Foenstan.

Foenstan raised an eyebrow in question, not sure why Jan Ti was looking at her until she noticed he was holding the second parchment up just below the edge of the table in her general direction.

"Oh, uh," Foenstan said, not sure herself of the proper protocol at the moment. "Jan Ti has another, um, document he would like you to look at…" she let the last trail off as she gave a questioning look to Jan Ti.

Jan Ti nodded.

The Guild Master hid a slight frown with a quick smile and incline of her head that silenced the affronted objections of the Notary and Recorder.

"By all means. You may place it on the table with the other," the Guild Master said.

The shriveled edges of the mysterious parchment partially unrolled as Jan Ti placed it next to the Overwall Adventures contract. Foenstan glimpsed writing in an embellished script with some familiar characters. She restrained herself from looking further as the documents spun away, carried on the outer edge of the inscribed circle to the left, where they stopped in front of the other members of Overwall Adventures.

"Entrant Tentoran, would you and your company please inspect *your* document for fidelity and sign it before passing it back to Entrant Jan Ti?" the Guild Master asked.

Tentoran nodded and picked up the parchment, pulling his fingers away at a smear of something brown on one edge, but quickly grabbing it again and smoothing it out on the table so that those around him could read it, too. After a few moments of careful consideration, he looked to Ocqounus, Hilvestri, and Grable, who all nodded. Tentoran nodded back and declared, "The document is unchanged from that registered, Guild Master, save for a clause giving veto power to the currently designated native representative over any proposed exploration or resource taking."

The Guild Master raised a single eyebrow as the Notary and Recorder exchanged surprised glances. "That is a very significant clause," the Guild Master said. "Do you accept it?"

Tentoran looked again to the other members of Overwall Adventures, including Foenstan herself, who all nodded to reconfirm. "Yes, Guild Master, it is what we expected."

"Very well," the Guild Master said, "you may sign it and pass it back to Entrant Jan Ti for his consideration.

Jan Ti looked to Foenstan as the other members of Overwall Adventures signed the contract. "Foenstan, the guild master must look at the other writing first," Jan Ti said, a tremor in his voice.

Foenstan held out a reassuring hand.

"Um, Guild Master?" Foenstan interrupted, voice breaking the revered silence.

All of the guild members fixed her with a withering stare.

"Yes?" the Guild Master asked in an icy monotone.

"Jan Ti says you need to look at the other document first. I think he means before he signs our contract."

The Notary and Recorder looked around, scandalized, but the Guild Master merely inclined her head towards Jan Ti and motioned for the documents to rotate to her next.

The hairs on the back of Foenstan's neck rose as the documents glided silently to a halt and the Guild Master delicately smoothed the aged parchment onto the table using only the tips of her fingers. She, the Notary, and the Recorder, leaned forward to peer down at the text written there.

After a moment, the Recorder drew in a sharp breath, head snapping first to the Guild Master's face, then to Jan Ti's. A second later the Notary gave a start, hand gripping the arm of his chair tightly as if he were forcing himself to remain seated. The Guild Master's eyes simply grew wider by degrees until they fixated on the bottom of the page, where signatures resided.

The Overwall Adventures members shifted uncom-fortably in their seats.

"This is an Article of Incorporation for a company located within the native district signed by Lord Frian Teagood himself, dated over six hundred years ago," the Guild Master declared. She looked up at those around the table. "However, it establishes the company in the name of the native inhabitants and holds that the head of the company and sole required signatory is Janeck Tibenry, quartermaster of Teagood Expeditions and the first…" the Guild Master's voice failed her. She cleared her throat and looked up at Jan Ti. "… the first to fall ill."

Everyone turned to Jan Ti, dawning looks of horror on their faces.

Jan Ti blinked slowly, head turning as if caught in a Magnum Time Slow spell. He opened his mouth to speak.

* * *

The memories had crashed through Jan Ti's inner peace like a torrent in the deep gullies of Hwa Rang's plateau after the summer rains, touched off by the face of Fri Te etched in the Trade Guild's outer door. All of the years of careful meditation and focus on the harmonies of nature that had allowed him and all of the others to keep the remembering at bay had collapsed completely, leaving him awash in the past.

Cow bells clanged as oxen struggled to haul wagons over the rocks and debris piled upon the flat flood plain of the river. Company members grunted and cursed, smelling rank as they shoved on solid wagon wheels to help them surmount fallen logs. Dogs barked, racing to and fro, flushing out scaly birds who burst into the air with annoyed croaks. Sheep blatted, the bells about their necks clanging. Hunting birds screeched as their druidic handlers let them loose, their eyes closed to see what their charges saw, scouting the terrain ahead. The heat of the lower valley that cut past the formidable plateau on their left and the high, rocky mountains on their right clung to everything.

Janeck Tibenry mopped his brow and mumbled an oath at having signed up for such an asinine adventure.

They had been pushing hard for two weeks and were almost through the temperate woods outside the City to the flat basin their scouts had discovered beyond. There, in the center of it, they would establish their base camp and launch expeditions into the diverse surrounding lands, looking for resources they could exploit for profit, or so the official charter said.

"Janeck! Janeck! Come look at this!" Frian Teagood shouted, fifty-year-old fingers beckoning in spasms of excitement.

Janeck sighed and stepped around a yeoman who had gone sprawling after slipping on a rounded stone to see what his boss wanted.

"Over here, in the woods, it's another one!" Teagood said, eyes alight.

It had only taken two days outside the walls for Janeck to realize that this entire enterprise had really been organized to satisfy Lord Frian Teagood's childlike fascination with discovery and adventure. Never had Janeck seen another being become so enraptured with the lilt of a flower or the snap of a lizard's tongue as it snagged its prey. Even the most mundane leaf shape fascinated the man who would spend hours sketching it and documenting how it funneled water to or from the plant's base depending upon the humidity that day. Janeck was almost certain the man had spent all of his considerable fortune to fund this farce and that they would recoup none of it by the time all was said and done.

"I've been watching it," Teagood continued as he led Janeck into the relative cool of the forest edge, past tall ferns and thick vines that clung to robust tree trunks, "and I think it is much more than just an ambulatory mushroom."

Janeck rolled his eyes and blocked a branch that flopped back at him from his boss's passage. They broke out of the dense underbrush into a small clearing and beheld a three foot tall, silky-smooth mushroom with a cap that descended all the way to the ground, standing near a tumbling stream. Bright blue leaves, soft lime mosses, and a multitude of small, blooming plants surrounded the mushroom, all glowing in a shaft of midday sun that cut through the high forest canopy. Janeck gazed at the idyllic setting in wonder, the heat and toil forgotten, his hardened City soul softened by the tranquil beauty.

Here was something existing right where it should be, not fighting every day just to survive, to get ahead. It was simply being, a part of the whole that surrounded it. This entire world seemed to function that way, plants and animals coexisting without conflict, each complementing the other in some way that helped both survive.

Teagood's running monologue cut through Janeck's reverie.

"So, you see, it's as if the thing gives something to the things around it, a sort of gift. Yes, I'll call it the Gift. And anything that is close to it, in a certain radius say, benefits from this Gift. The plants are stronger, healthier, they display some differences from similar plants that are farther away…but how does it give this Gift? Does it deposit droppings?"

Janeck shuddered at a tingling sensation that spread across his skin as Teagood began inspecting the ground around the mushroom with his ever-present magnifying glass, muttering about beneficial scat and the importance of good soil nutrition. The mushroom itself continued its slow crawl on some predetermined course, completely ignoring the two foreigners who had crashed in on its personal nirvana.

The squeals of pigs shattered Janick's peace and he hastily cleared his throat, anxious once again about the state of their supplies and whether all of them would make it to their final destination. "Lord Teagood, sir, shouldn't we get back to the supply train and oversee this last difficult bit of passage?"

"What?" Teagood popped up from his bent position, immediately grabbing his back and grimacing.

"The wagons, sir. Shouldn't we see to it that they make it past the river bend?"

"Oh. Yes, I guess we should." Teagood stretched his back slowly and motioned for Janeck to lead the way. Janeck cast a final glance at the glen, barely seeing it as the worries of the day consumed him. They both shoved their way out of the woods and into the open to behold the debacle of stuck wagons, barking dogs, squealing pigs, and grass-munching goats.

"Such a bother, all this," Teagood harrumphed. "Gets in the way. I'm going to keep investigating those things when we're all settled. Everywhere they are you see life, Tibenry, thick and thriving. There has to be a reason."

Janeck merely nodded, distracted by the sight of a wagon wheel main pin splintering as its load overbalanced to one side and crashed to the ground.

Over the weeks that followed, Janeck accompanied Teagood on many expeditions, while the curved wall of the stacked stone mill at the bend in the stream was constructed and the brush cut back and the first crops planted. They spent hours in the thick forests around the many Givers, as Teagood took to calling the mushroom beings, watching them carefully, noting how they seemed to thrive despite no overt signs that they were taking in nutrients of any kind. Teagood sampled their faint slime trail, looking for minerals they may have dissolved and possibly sucked up through their single, slug-like foot. But no evidence could be found of such action.

All the while Janeck helped Teagood take notes, cataloging all they saw, identifying the interdependence of everything on everything else. They focused especially on the way things seemed to change almost overnight, taking on characteristics of things close to them while losing features that no longer seemed mutually beneficial. And while they did, their own bodies began to change, though in ways they wrote off as simple byproducts of their exploration of strange new lands.

Rashes developed on arms then sloughed off to reveal unnaturally smooth skin tinted with the greens and blues and grays of the forest. Some, like the horse wrangler, Hwalen Ranglos, began to lose hair that regrew thicker and fuller and seemed to absorb and retain water. A few grew alarmed and reneged on their contracts, leaving for the safety of the City. But some returned, saying they felt restless within the walls. It was during this time that they began to see the first oddities in the native life, too, mostly in places near their rapidly expanding settlement.

"Now, look here, Tibenry," Teagood said one day, at the edge of one of the closest Giver domains. "Does this furred lizard not move like a hunting dog?"

Janeck barely glanced up from the notes he was taking on the increasing aggressiveness of the ordinarily docile flying macaques that inhabited the forest edge. He stretched the sore muscles in his writing hand, ignoring the shake of his fingers that he could not control as of late. "Yes, we noted that a week ago, along with the growth of thorns on the sweet vine near our new raspberry patches," he replied

Teagood frowned, forgotten finger still pointing at the arm-length lizard. "But they are herbivores who dine on flowers, why would they need to stalk up on—ouch!" Teagood yanked his hand back from the clumsy, toothless jaws the lizard had clamped down on his finger. "By the gods! It bit me!"

Janeck looked up wearily, witnessing the orange and black furred lizard leap a second time for Teagood's hand.

"Good gracious!" Teagood shouted, shuffling backwards and grasping his walking cane before him defensively.

Arooo-awk!

Janeck's and Teagood's heads snapped towards the strange call simultaneously. It sounded like a common Wyfern, one of the odd plant and animal hybrids with the body of a crane, a head like a snapping turtle and wings composed of fronds that closely resembled ferns. But this call assaulted the ears with unnatural volume.

Janeck rose from the rock upon which he had rested and closed his notebook, forgetting to let the ink dry.

"That was near the Giver's glen," Teagood whispered. The lizard leaped for Teagood's hand again, but the old man barely noticed. "Quickly, my boy, we must see what has transpired!"

Teagood plunged into the underbrush.

Janeck sprung after him.

They burst into the nearby grove and skidded to a halt, soft traveling boots digging furrows in the delicate blue and green mosses, mouths dropping open in shock.

The Giver stood ragged and torn in the middle of its paradise. A flock of wyferns circled above it, squawking and swooping, soft, fleshy bits falling from the beaks they usually used to scrape mushrooms from the backs of trundling, cow-sized Og Beetles upon the nearby plateau. But as Janeck watched with rising alarm, a wyfern broke from the formation and dove down to sink its beak into the already pitted cap of the Giver. With a savage tug it pulled forth a soft mass and gulped it down. Its new, vicious talons, like those of the settlement's hunting falcons, gouged deep furrows in the mutilated Giver's top as it leaped back into the air.

The force of the wyfern's departure toppled the Giver onto its side.

"No!" Teagood cried, rushing forward with his walking cane raised. Janeck leapt after him, waving his arms and shouting, but the next wyfern dove at them, beak snapping, dropping them to the ground. It swooped around and landed upon the Giver, tearing at the tough, exposed foot.

Teagood crawled towards it and swung.

Janick grabbed a rock and threw it.

The wyfern cried out and took to the air with an angry squawk that turned into a cacophony as the other wyferns joined in. Janeck plucked another rock from the ground but dropped it and dove as a dozen of the flying beasts swooped down at him. A wyfern knocked Teagood away from the Giver, sending him sprawling to the edge of the glen, then joined in the assault on Janeck.

Janeck covered his head with his arms and rolled towards the Giver, stopping only when he bumped against its soft flesh. He flopped onto his back and kicked upwards, eliciting a furious squawk as his foot connected with the flexible, fibrous ribcage of a wyfern. He snatched the knife he used to eat from his waist pouch and swung blindly, covering his eyes with the crook of his other arm. A high-pitched screech mere inches from his ear staggered him as his blade found feathered flesh, but a blast of wing beats and angry caws followed. Silence descended as the wyferns retreated, seeking refuge beyond the tree canopy high above.

Janeck dropped his arm from over his eyes and beheld Teagood panting at the edge of the grove, cut and bleeding. He looked down at his own arms, covered in scratches, felt the burn of lacerations on his face and neck and… something else.

A strange prickling sensation, like the one he felt every time he was in the presence of the Giver, but this time stronger, more forceful, more intense. As he staggered backwards to sit roughly on a stone by the tattered Giver's side, he felt a growing fullness, not in his stomach or chest, but throughout his whole body, every single part of him, as if something were taking up the spaces in between what made him up. His head drooped and he noticed for the first time that the Giver's foot, which had always been a solid mass upon which it stood, had at some time in the past split in two, becoming long stalks that could only be described as legs.

Janeck looked to Teagood, who sat staring back at him in a world that was rapidly skewing sideways. Amidst the pain and the heat and the calling sounds of the forest, he swore. Just before he lost consciousness, he felt a buzzing… from within his own body.

* * *

Jan Ti snapped back to the present, the past receding away at the urgent shake of a hand on his shoulder. The inner peace that those who had survived the Gift given to them strove to achieve every day, did not return. But the smell of the now familiar wood, the echo of voices in the sharp-edged room, and the feel of the chair's edge cutting into his flesh did.

"Jan Ti, what's wrong?" Foenstan asked, worry creasing her face.

The guild officials had risen halfway from their seats, save for the Guild Master who stood fully and backed away, hand rising to cover her mouth.

"Jan Ti?" Foenstan asked again.

"My people have decided on a course of action…" Jan Ti intoned, feeling the urgent buzzing of his Swarm at being trapped inside him for so long. "…that I do not agree with."

"For the City, for the Wands!" Grable suddenly shouted, bursting from his seat and hurling a finely embroidered tobacco snuff sack towards Jan Ti's edge of the table.

"Watch out!" Foenstan yelled.

Jan Ti's world skewed skyward as Foenstan flung herself across him.

A deafening roar, like the tempest's thunder during the monsoons, shook the paneled ceiling. Heat and pressure washed to the sides of Jan Ti, singeing his arms, shriveling his hair mass. He landed upon the hard jade floor, head ringing off of it, the weight of Foenstan crushing down on him. He struggled to pull in a breath, the frightful, foreign smell of acidic smoke choking him, causing him to retch when he managed a lungful. His world shrunk to a thornprick, wavered and began to snuff out, when through the smoke burst Grable, eyes alight with righteousness and face twisted with hate.

Foenstan's weight lifted from him as Grable flung her body to the side and then the red-faced man's hands clamped about Jan Ti's neck with ferocious force.

Jan Ti's eyes bulged, the comforting blackness retreating as blood surged into his head. Silence descended, broken only by the raging buzz of his Swarm that wanted to burst forth and defend Home as they had done so often in the past. But Jan Ti knew that any contact his Swarm made with the world around him would also bring with it the Gift, and the Gift had not touched any part of the City for six hundred years.

"Die, you filthy Outwaller!" Grable screamed, hands clenching so tightly that Jan Ti felt a pop at the back of his neck and a numbness in his legs.

Jan Ti looked into Grable's eyes, so full of hate, of fear, and saw the future: the burning of the forest, the leveling of the earth, the parties of hunters wandering into the desolation for the heads of Hwa Rang and Fri Te and the others. There would be no one to stop them.

Unless someone controlled access to the gate. Someone like him.

Jan Ti blinked slowly, forcing his eyes to focus on the apoplectic face of Grable, inches from his own.

He summoned the last of his inner strength and thought a single, deadly word.

Kill.

* * *

Foenstan felt the scorching pain, the splitting of her skin, and the sharp blackness that snapped in then bowed out a moment later, revealing the horror that would not leave her.

Grable, red face shading to purple with the effort of crushing Jan Ti's windpipe, straddled the body of her native friend amidst a cloud of dissipating fire-powder smoke. The tendons in his strong hands stood out, the muscles of his arms bulged against his fitted fineshirt and through the shouts of confusion and ringing of her ears she heard the telltale popping of bone joints.

I gotta help Jan…

But her arms would not move, nor her legs, and the coldness of the room seeped insidiously into her body.

She glanced down at a persistent ache in her side and beheld a splinter of wood as big around as her arm sticking out of her singed travel shirt, surrounded by red.

Ah…

A flash of bright white and loud boom signaled the arrival of a Magnum and she slowly turned her head to behold one of the white-robed overseers lifting an arm to point at Grable, a wisp of magical energy building about its thin hand. But before it could unleash its magical force, Grable's head jerked one way, then the other, in a motion that Foenstan had only seen once before in a dog in the throes of water madness.

Grable blinked and snorted and smooshed his lips around and stretched his neck oddly. Bloody spots appeared in the whites of his eyes, oozing down to pool on his lower eyelids. A scream from deep within him built slowly as he let loose his grip on Jan Ti's throat and clamped his palms over his eyes. He lunged to his feet and staggered backwards, blood oozing around his palms and trickling from his ears. A mangled chair tangled his legs and he fell to his knees, his scream turning into a deep gurgle.

The Magnum's hand lowered in a gesture with all the hallmarks of dumbfounded shock.

Frantically Grable tore at his clothes, the skin of his hands sloughing off with each mad pawing, the tissues of his face collapsing to reveal the outline of his skull. Then, with a sound like fish falling into a bucket, the disjointed parts of his body fell backwards into a heap of fine, bloody clothing.

The Magnum stared at the pile, arms by its side, motionless.

Foenstan swallowed hard, knowing that the horror that she had just witnessed was not going to fade, and knowing, at some level, that her funny native friend, Jan Ti, was somehow responsible. Yet she was not afraid, not really. She was more intrigued and a little sad that she would not be around to see how this newfound knowledge would play out. Because a splinter that big wasn't something one shook off and got back to living from. No, a splinter that big only ended one way…

But the familiar darkness did not come. The childhood memories did not flood back. The hard years on the streets did not spin by with their mocking laughter and cynical looks. And the fishing boat did not appear and sail *this close* before swinging away across the broad waters of the Teliune River, buoyant and happy without her. No, none of those things that had repeated over and over for her for what seemed like eternity occurred this time.

Instead, Foenstan felt her eyes opening, groggy and heavy. She had no expectation of seeing the gate in Downfall that led to the underworld before her, but vaguely hoped that something better than Ampyrium City awaited her in the afterlife. Unfortunately, what she saw left her underwhelmed.

"Oh, Amp me! I throw myself on top of you to save you from that Wand turncoat and you end up dying anyway? What a waste of fishing time."

Jan Ti scowled down at her and said, "I am not dead, Foenstan."

Foenstan scowled back and looked down at the splinter in her side that had nearly cut her in half. It wasn't there.

"So, what, I'm a Wraith Walker now?"

Jan Ti blinked once, obviously clueless as to what a Wraith Walker was.

"No," he answered.

Foenstan finally noticed the off-white robes that covered her prone body and took in the three other faces that surrounded her.

"Tentoran, you're alive!" Foenstan cried, slightly disconcerted at how happy seeing her nominative boss made her feel.

"Yes, though I fear my turban is now a required part of my wardrobe," Tentoran said with a slight slur as he removed his head dressing to reveal a wicked scar cutting front to back across his bald pate.

Foenstan cringed a bit but turned to Hilvestri as he clapped a rough paw with a few fur patches missing on her shoulder and helped her to sit up. "You had us worried, Foenstan, bleeding out on the floor and all. But you saved Jan Ti and then he saved you, though it took many months and much meditation. So, it all worked out in the end." Hilvestri smiled his happy, but still somewhat terrifying, smile.

"You saved me?" Foenstan asked, turning to a solemn Jan Ti. "How? I was like a lake trout speared with a whale harpoon."

Jan Ti bowed a head, looking around furtively at the others. "I gave to you a gift."

"A gift?" Foenstan asked, suspiciously. "What kind of gift?"

Jan Ti cleared his throat. "A part of what nourishes and heals me. What keeps me young."

"Young?" Foenstan asked.

"Jan Ti is over six hundred years old, Foenstan," Ocqounus said, fire-scarred, suckered hands clasped before her, her eyes on Jan Ti's reddening face. "He was one of the original explorers who disappeared into the wilderness.

The world outside exists as it does largely because of him. He used a part of himself that the forest gave him, what he calls his Swarm, to heal you, and now some of it resides in you. It has made you its Home."

Foenstan stared for a countable number of seconds, one eyebrow cocked high. "Is this Swarm the same thing that picked apart Grable until he was nothing but a pile of goo bones?"

Jan Ti turned bright red and looked down in shame. "Yes. A Swarm can do many things. It is how we survived the Great Change that occurred after we tainted the world around us with our presence."

Foenstan nodded. "Welp, I'm sure glad it did, 'cause he was about to squeeze your head off."

Jan Ti looked up in shock.

"And yer gonna have to teach me how to work that Swarm magic, now that we got Wand agents trying to off us."

"What?" Tentoran exclaimed. "You knew Grable was a Wand?"

"No," Foenstan said, "but I saw the way he looked at the woods when were outside, and he gave a subtle knife sign to that Yaasur they sent to spook us. I think he told him to back off, 'cause he thought he had it handled. And he almost did, didn't he? Except for Jan's swarmy thing."

"Hmpf. Well, he ultimately failed," Tentoran declared. "Jan Ti signed the deal after he recovered. Overwall Adventures Trading Company is now officially in business."

"Speaking of which," Hilvestri interrupted. "We should see to the first expedition's supplies. They leave for the Glimmerstone fields tomorrow."

"Right, off we go then," Tentoran said smartly. "Join us when you feel up to it, Foenstan."

The company departed with hearty handshakes and pats on the back. Foenstan watched them disappear out a small side door of what appear to be a market stall and for the first time she looked around at her surroundings. "Whoa, what'd you do to this place?" she cried, barely recognizing the warehouse ruins of the native gate's inner courtyard.

Native Ampyri plants grew in the cracks and crevices of the rubble, sprouting in purples and greens, yellows and blues, climbing the half-collapsed sides of buildings and flowing across the debris-strewn streets. Animals hopped and flittered, flowers bloomed, insects buzzed and old fountains poured forth water that ran in burbling streams down alleys covered in moss and through twisted doorways draped with vines. Just looking at the abundance made Foenstan feel satisfied in a way she had never felt before. "So, is this where my Swarm is getting the goods for me?" she asked as she stood carefully.

Jan Ti clasped his hands to his forearms and nodded. "Yes, very insightful, Foenstan. It takes from what is all around you. If it lacks something it will tell you through urges to travel to places it knows have what you need."

"Do I need fish?" Foenstan asked, raising a single eyebrow.

Jan Ti smiled.

"That's the first time I've seen you do that!" Foenstan exclaimed.

Jan Ti chuckled. "No, you do not need fish. But there is a very pleasing Tooklat bush near a slowing of the river that your Swarm will want to visit and collect from for a long time. You could fish while they work, though you won't want to eat it."

"Fine by me. Fish taste nasty. I just want to hang out outside and enjoy the weather."

Jan Ti raised both his eyebrows in surprise. "Then you are the perfect Giver."

"'Bout time I was perfect at something," Foenstan said.

Jan Ti's good humor darkened slightly. "But you must learn to control your Swarm. It will defend you zealously without proper control. It is why we stayed away from the city for so long. We had to learn to connect to it, to commune with it, so that we could influence it. Only when you have achieved inner peace with it will it be safe for you to interact with those that do not have it."

Foenstan felt a sudden inspiration. "Is that what caused the Thinning? Rampant swarms?"

A sudden sadness passed over Jan Ti's face. "No. The Thinning was of our own making. You see, a Swarm will move to a new host if the one it resides in dies. And when Fri Te, that is Frian Teagood, saw that the Givers as they existed were no match for the new, violent creature forms that were appearing, he gathered them up to save them. But the world got to them anyway and their swarms burst from their dying bodies and found new homes in the things closest to them…the other members of the Teagood Expedition who were trying to protect them. When those members returned to the City, they began to starve—their swarms had nothing to eat. Some died and their swarms found new hosts within the City. But those hosts also starved. Soon the swarms began dividing, inhabiting multiple new hosts in a vain attempt to survive the famine all around them. Their spread doomed the octet. Everyone died, except those that fled back beyond the walls."

Foenstan swallowed hard, feeling a strange double sadness within her: one for the clueless people and one for the lost Swarms.

A furtive movement near the inner gate of the octet interrupted the tense mood. Jan Ti stood straighter, instantly becoming stiff and alert.

"Yo! You there, at the gate, are you looking for something?" Foenstan asked, shaking off her malaise quickly and walking out the side door of the booth. She stretched against the tightness in her side, where her Swarm had repaired the gaping hole in her body.

A thin, dirty face, topped with stringy brown hair, peered around the cracked-open inner gate. The eyes widened at the sight of all the native plants and the head started backing out of sight.

"Whoa, wait up! Nothing here is going to hurt you!" Foenstan shouted. Out of the corner of her mouth she asked, "Right, Jan Ti?"

Jan Ti nodded and said with a slightly raised voice, "Foenstan is correct. We are here to help."

The head halted and a timid voice asked, "Are you *the* Foenstan, the Wall Breacher?"

Foenstan stood up a little straighter in surprise. "Um, probably…" She looked to Jan Ti who simply nodded. "Yep. I am *the* Foenstan, Wall Breacher."

The furtive eyes ran up and down Foenstan's simple bed robes, settling on her face.

"You were dead, but then you received it…" the visitor said, voice trailing off.

Foenstan sensed a lot of loaded meaning in the visitor's use of "it."

Slowly the visitor stepped around the door frame, revealing an emaciated frame hung with rags clutching a baby wrapped in a discarded tobacco sack. Foenstan guessed the girl's age at no more than sixteen, though with chronic malnutrition she could have been thirty and that size. Foenstan's gut twisted even though she'd seen a thousand gutter rats in a similar state during her years in Ampyrium. Usually she avoided looking at them and kept on keeping on. There was nothing else to do.

"I'm Natalia and this is Lukan," the girl said. "We want to accept the *Gift*."

Foenstan raised her eyebrows and looked to Jan Ti.

Jan Ti's eyes widened and he bowed deeply. "We would be honored to have you, Natalia and Lukan. All are welcome to partake of the Gift. But, you understand, once taken, the Gift cannot be returned, and you will have to leave your home and live in the wilderness of this world, only visiting the City for short periods of time. For the Gift given to you must be shared with the world to help it grow."

Natalia's baby began to squirm in her arms, head moving in hunger. Natalia clutched him tightly to her and said, "Yes, I understand."

Jan Ti smiled and held out a hand. "Then come, acolyte, Ampyria has much to offer those who are willing to help it."

Natalia took Jan Ti's hand, a shy smile brushing her lips. Her eyes flicked to Foenstan, full of hesitant wonder and something Foenstan saw little of in someone in her state in the City: hope.

"Welp, looks like I'm a cult leader now," Foenstan said, shaking her head and following Jan Ti into the growing lushness.

And as they disappeared into the buzzing native garden transplanted within the City walls, a white Eye upon the towering citadel of the Magnum watched from afar…and wondered.

About the Authors

PATRICIA BRAY is the author of a dozen novels, including Devlin's Luck which won the Compton Crook award for best first novel in the field of science fiction and fantasy. Her storytelling skills and imagination also come in handy in her day job as a business intelligence analyst. Patricia lives in New Hampshire, where she balances her time at a keyboard with cycling, hiking and curling. Find her on the web at www.patriciabray.com.

S.C. BUTLER lives in New Hampshire with his wife and son. He is the author of the Stoneways trilogy: *Reiffen's Choice*, *Queen Ferris*, and *The Magician's Daughter*, originally published by Tor Books; the novel *The Risen*; and a contributor of short stories to several anthologies and magazines. All of his novels are available as ebooks at his very primitive website, mutablebooks.com, and several of his stories are posted there for free. He also posts regularly on Facebook as S.C Butler.

DAVID B. COE is the author of thirty novels and as many short stories. He has written epic fantasy – including the Crawford Award-winning LonTobyn Chronicle – contemporary urban fantasy, and media tie-ins. He has also co-edited five anthologies for Zombies Need Brains. As D.B. Jackson, he writes the Thieftaker Chronicles, a historical urban fantasy set in pre-Revolutionary Boston, as well as the Islevale Cycle, a time travel/epic fantasy trilogy. David has a Ph.D. in U.S. history from

Stanford University. His books have been translated into a dozen languages. http://www.DavidBCoe.com; http://www.dbjackson-author.com; http://twitter.com/davidbcoe; http://twitter.com/dbjacksonauthor

Nebula Award winner **ESTHER FRIESNER** is the author of over forty novels and more than two hundred short stories. She received an M.A. and Ph.D. in Spanish from Yale University and a B.A. in Spanish and Drama from Vassar She is a poet, a professionally produced playwright, and the editor of eleven anthologies. The best known of these is the **Chicks in Chainmail** series that she created and edits for Baen Books. In addition to sf, fantasy, and a bit of horror, she is the author of the **Princesses of Myth** series of Young Adult novels from Random House.

JULIET E. McKENNA is a British fantasy author living in the Cotswolds, UK. Loving history, myth and other worlds since she learned to read, she has written fifteen epic fantasy novels. The Thief's Gamble, began The Tales of Einarinn in 1999, followed by The Aldabreshin Compass, The Chronicles of the Lescari Revolution, and The Hadrumal Crisis trilogy. The Green Man's Heir was her first modern fantasy rooted in British folklore, followed by The Green Man's Foe and The Green Man's Silence. She writes diverse shorter stories enjoying forays into dark fantasy, steampunk and SF. Visit julietemckenna.com or @JulietEMcKenna on Twitter.

JASON PALMATIER is a speculative fiction author and stay at home dad who has written for screenplay projects (the short film "Hunter"), independent comics (*Lords of the Cosmos*, Ugli Studios), graphic novels (*Plague*, Markosia Enterprises Ltd.), and short story anthologies (Zombies Need Brains, LLC.). His award-winning story "Under My Cypresses" placed second in the L. Ron Hubbard Writers of the Future Contest for the 4th quarter of the 2023 contest year, and appears in volume 39 of the anthology. See details of his various projects at http://www.jasonpalmatier.com.

JOSHUA PALMATIER is a fantasy author with a PhD in mathematics. He currently teaches at SUNY Oneonta in upstate New York while writing in his "spare" time, editing anthologies, and running the anthology-producing small press Zombies Need Brains LLC. His most recent fantasy series, releasing Spring/Summer 2024 is called the "Crystal Cities" and includes *Crystal Lattice*, *Crystal Rebel*, and *Crystal War*. You can also find his "Throne of Amenkor" series, the "Well of Sorrows" series, and the "Ley" series still on the shelves. He is currently hard at work writing his next fantasy and designing the Kickstarter for the next Zombies Need Brains anthology projects. You can find out more at www.joshuapalmatier.com or at the small press' site www.

zombiesneedbrains.com. Or follow him on Blue Sky at joshuapalmatier.bsky. social or on X as @bentateauthor or @ZNBLLC. And check out the Zombies Need Brains Patreon at www.patreon.com/zombiesneedbrains.

About the Editor

JOSHUA PALMATIER is a fantasy author with a PhD in mathematics. He currently teaches at SUNY Oneonta in upstate New York while writing in his "spare" time, editing anthologies, and running the anthology-producing small press Zombies Need Brains LLC. His most recent fantasy series, releasing Spring/Summer 2024 is called the "Crystal Cities" and includes *Crystal Lattice*, *Crystal Rebel*, and *Crystal War*. You can also find his "Throne of Amenkor" series, the "Well of Sorrows" series, and the "Ley" series still on the shelves. He is currently hard at work writing his next fantasy and designing the Kickstarter for the next Zombies Need Brains anthology projects. You can find out more at www.joshuapalmatier.com or at the small press' site www.zombiesneedbrains.com. Or follow him on Blue Sky at joshuapalmatier.bsky.social or on X as @bentateauthor or @ZNBLLC. And check out the Zombies Need Brains Patreon at www.patreon.com/zombiesneedbrains.

Acknowledgments

This anthology would not have been possible without the tremendous support of those who pledged during the Kickstarter. Everyone who contributed not only helped create this anthology, they also helped support the small press Zombies Need Brains LLC, which I hope will be bringing SF&F themed anthologies to the reading public for years to come. I want to thank each and every one of them for helping to bring this small dream into reality. Thank you, my zombie horde.

The Zombie Horde: Cory Williams, Axisor and Firestar, Lisa Kruse, Chris Matosky, Ian Chung, Kathryn Smith, Karen M, Sheryl, John Markley, Jaq Greenspon, Raymond Lowell, Beth Coll, Jamieson Cobleigh, Sarah Cornell, Kerri Regan, Henry W. Schubert, Anne Burner, Kris W, Robyn DeRocchis, Richard O'Shea, Jeremy Audet, Rowan Stone, Andrew Hatchell, Nicholas Stephenson, Ian Harvey, Becky Boyer, Stephen Ballentine, Phillip Spencer, Cindy Cripps-Prawak, Andrija Popovic, Millie Calistri-Yeh, Eva Jayet Alaminos, LetoTheTooth, Miranda Floyd, Wulf Moon Enterprises, Michael Axe, Lindsay Knight, Claire Sims, Taia Hartman, Cathy Green, Wolf SilverOak, Beth LaClair, Duncan and Andrea Rittschof, Patricia Bray, Megan Beauchemin, Stephanie Lucas, Mark A Kiraly, Rich 'Razmus' Weissler, Michael Kohne, Beth Lobdell, David Rowe, David Lahner, Michael Hanscom, Edward Ellis, Mary Jo Rabe, J.R. Murdock, Arej N Howlett, David Hankins, R.J.H., Niall Gordon, Michael D'Auben, Jakub Narębski, Ezra Lee, Juanita J Nesbitt, Piet Wenings,

R. Hunter, Dina S Willner, Jenny Barber, Todd V. Ehrenfels, E.M. Middel, Sasha, Tania, L.C., Rory King, Joe Hauser, Dino Hicks, Charles E Norton, Stephannie Tallent, Mustela, Jennifer Berk, Michele Hall, Owen Blacker, Jeff Eppenbach, Kit Rodgers, Jason Swensen, Leah Webber, Random Yarning, Jörg Tremmel, Carol J. Guess, Kerry aka Trouble, Jen1701D, Shayne Easson, Hoose Family, Richard Leis, Jenn Whitworth, Jackie Coleman, Curtis Frye, Helen Ellison, Jacen Leonard, Angie Hogencamp, Joanne B Burrows, Jessica A. Enfante, Colette Reap, Maggie Laigaie, Vulpecula, Colleen Feeney, T Lynn P, Kat Feete, Vana Smith, Sandy Bryant, Ruth Ann Orlansky, Samantha Sendele, Craig "Stevo" Stephenson, Margaret Killeen, Ron Currens, Alicia henness, A. Kristina Casasent, Kelly Snyder, Jo Beere, Cherie Livingston, Chad Bowden, Keith E. Hartman, Kate Stuppy, A.H. Gillett, Brenda Rezk, Ryan C, Rebecca Buchanan, Darren Lipman, Lorri-Lynne Brown, Andy F, Margot Harris, Rebecca M, Lace, Christopher Wheeling, Susan Simko, Bonnie Warford, Heidi Lambert, Tina M Noe Good, S Horvat, Brynn, Sheryl R. Hayes, Robert B Tharp, Annette Agostini, Charlie Russel, MykeTea, Debbie Matsuura, Trisha J. Wooldridge, Anthony R. Cardno, Svend Andersen, John 'Doc' Strange, Howard J. Bampton, Robin Hill, John H. Bookwalter Jr., rissatoo, Ilene Tsuruoka, Tris Lawrence, Jim Gotaas, Cyn Armistead, Margaret Bumby, Keith West, Future Potentate of the Solar System, Sonya R.Lawson, Katy Manck - BooksYALove, Brita Hill, Elaine McMillan, Ane-Marte Mortensen, Chris McLaren, Crysella, Randall Brent Martin II, G. M. Persbacker, Simon Dick, Ashley Clouser Leonard, Sidney Whitaker, Elyse M Grasso, Senhina, Mary Alice Wuerz, Chantelle Wilson, Jerrie the filkferengi, Elektra Hammond, Patrick Osbaldeston, Lou/justloux2, Niall Spain, Mark Carter, Bess Turner, Stephanie Cranford, Ryan Hunter and Cameron Alexander, R.G. Roberts, Bona Books, Adam Goldstein, Jesse N. Klein, Scott Raun, Brad L. Kicklighter, Penny Ramirez, Lynn R, Joshua McGinnis, Ian F Bell, Craig Hackl, Konstanze Tants, Eric B, Michael Fedrowitz, Terry Williams, Eric, Brendan Lonehawk, Anonymous Reader, Ronald H. Miller, Steve Arensberg, Steve & Beckey Sanchez, Patrick Dugan, K. Hodghead, Caroline Westra, Chris Huning, Sharan Volin, Kari Blackmoore, Robert Claney, Jonathan Brown, Krystal Bohannan, Cliff Winnig, John Senn, Kat Haines, Jim Landis, Jamie M. Boyd, Nathan Turner, Helen Cameron, Jeanne Talbourdet, KennyBoy, Robert Bull, RJ Hopkinson, Heidegger Dart, JMC, Janet Piele, Sue Phillips, GMarkC, Vicki Greer, Leane Verhulst, Dana Carson, Chris Munroe, Jenni P., L.C. Parfomak, Kate Malloy, Tanya K., Joshua Hair, Brooks Moses, Melissa Tabon, Lisa Dees, Mark Newman, Nightwing Whitehead, Tommy Acuff, Pamela Lunsford, Richard Hailey, Steve Blount, Gail Z. Martin, Craig Maylor, Kenyon Wensing, BOBBY ZAMARRON, Brent J, Olivia Montoya, PunkARTchick "Ruthenia", Brian, Kay, and Joshua Williams, Misha Dainiak, Yankton Robins, Bethany Jezerey, Tina Connell, Patti Montgomery, Jennifer Flora Black, Deborah

Nossaman, Kevin, Yosen Lin, Dagmar Baumann, Clarissa C. S. Ryan, Jessica Meade, Robert K. Barbour, Abi Scott, Mallory A. Haws, The Other Yvonne, Paul & Laura Trinies, Tara Paine, J.L. Gerrard, Shirley, Amanda Saville, Aysha Rehm, Daniel Hopersberger, Alice "Huskyteer" Dryden, Katie Mergener, Mike Rimar, Ryan Power, Bobbi Boyd, Taylor Munsell, Jackie Duckworth, Tasha Turner, Susanne Schörner, Joseph Jerome Connell, Shay Dinur, Steven Halter, Alice Bentley, Elaine Tindill-Rohr, Jonathan Olsson, Elise Power, Julia Hart, Risa Scranton, David Myers, Michelle P., Regis M. Donovan, Robert D. Stewart, Herbert Eder, John T. Sapienza, Jr., Thomas Booker, Rolf Laun, Max Kaehn, Lorraine J. Anderson, Donna Royston, Mervi Hamalainen, FOS Grace, Andrea Tatjana, Kristin EvensonHirst, In memory of Tammy Greco, Rob In AU, CL McCollum, BT McMenomy, Hayden Trenholm, Francesco Tehrani, Katherine, Barb Moermond, Tibs, Ian, Brenda Carre, Venessa Giunta, Andrew Foxx, Miriah Hetherington, jjmcgaffey, Emy Peters, Jacob H Joseph, Holly Elliott, Keith A. Kline, Joachim Verhagen, Paul Alex Gray, Sandy Komoroff, Michael M. Jones, Gail Morse, Fantastic Books, Edward K. Beale, V Hartman DiSanto, Yosef Kuperman, Meyari McFarland, Gary Ehrlich, M Glasser, Stephen Buchanan, Deborah A. Flores, J Millwood, Alison Scott, Sarah T, Cyn Wise, Karen Dubois, Pat Knuth, Dale Cozort, Blade McMicking, D.I., Jennifer Crow, Brad Roberts, K.tee Magrowski, kayliealien, Tim Jordan, Julie Pitzel, Lee Dalzell, Bob D. M, Adam Nemo, Anne Walker, Sheila Huijbregts, Abra Staffin-Wiebe, Matthew Egerton, Merav Hoffman, Mervi Mustonen, Arin Komins, Louisa Swann, Sylvia Greenwich, J.P. Goodwin, Michael Abbott, A. L. Kaplan, Arinn Dembo, Julie Halperson, Kathy Brady, RickyD, Tracy Popey, Darrell Z. Grizzle, Wingnut, R Kirkpatrick, Agnes Kormendi, Ellery Rhodes, Robin Schwarz, Alan Smale, Fred and Mimi Bailey, Mary Ann Shuman, James Enge, Caryn Cameron, Sarah L., Karen Fonville, Gavran, Tal S, Cat Ellison, Amelia Smith, Coleman bland, Winter Hart, Jason Palmatier, Will Gunderson, Geoffrey Willmoth, Cynthia Porter, Stuart Hall (aka Celt), Alexander Gent, Jeff G, David Keener, VikingSnail, Carol Mammano, Linnéa G, Lavinia Ceccarelli, David Futterrer, Bob Thibodeau, Alphonzs, Katelyn Cserjes, Carver Rapp, Mandy Stein, Connor Bliss, John Jason Lau, Tania Clucas, Holly J, AM Scott, Author, Robby Thrasher, CGJulian, Tracy 'Rayhne' Fretwell, Leah Smith, Stephen Kotowych, Gary Phillips, Lotta Fjelkegård, Katrina Knight, Kat D'Andrea, Powell Zucks, Michèle Laframboise, James Olsen, Jon Nepsha, Nick Mandujano III, Chris Vincent, Mike Smith, Jakiette, Acer R., Zalyn Schwartz, Fren & Edna, R. McKean

.